W9-DBZ-827

Advance Praise
for
Beatriz Rivera's

PLAYING WITH LIGHT

"Havana-born Rivera—author of the well-received *Midnight Sandwiches at the Mariposa Express*—reaffirms her reputation with this innovative allegory on the pitfalls of human vice and the redemptive power of literature . . . **Leaves the reader dazzled** by the implications . . . An **inventive, provocative** oddity, this is a tantalizing work that draws readers into an engrossing twilight world."

—Publishers Weekly

"A novel worth reading twice, at least. It's **humorous and serious,** and the multiple plots move it along, but it's Rivera's additional talent to present memorable characters and their characterization that **keeps one turning page after page.**"

—Rolando Hinojosa,
author of *Becky and Her Friends*

"A well-to-do woman decides to revive the old Latin American tradition of the literary *tertulias* with her amigas—with **dizzyingly comic** results."

—Latina

"Fans of the Cuban-born Rivera's *Midnight Sandwiches at the Mariposa Express* will be **delighted** with her latest novel. Set alternately in contemporary Miami and Havana a century ago, the story interweaves the lives and fates of several generations of women . . . **Recommended** for fiction collections of **all** libraries."

—Library Journal

"What at first seems a straightforward story of Cuban-American women in contemporary Miami becomes a fanciful blurring of life, art, and time . . . Prose that is **often playful and lusty** . . . **Increasingly rewarding** with further reading and reflection."

—Booklist

(please turn the page for more acclaim for Beatriz Rivera)

Critical Praise
for
Beatriz Rivera's

AFRICAN PASSIONS
AND OTHER STORIES

"This is **a fine collection** of eight stories, most of them connected by recurring characters and themes . . . Dreams and illusions, goals and ambitions, love and loss are portrayed with both humor and understanding. **Recommended.**"

—*Choice*

"Humor, irony, affection, and zest . . . . All of Rivera's stories strike an empathetic chord in the reader. We are reminded that, even in tragedy, there is often comic absurdity. This delightful anthology is **highly recommended.**"

—*The Denver Post*

Critical Praise
for
Beatriz Rivera's

MIDNIGHT SANDWICHES
AT THE MARIPOSA EXPRESS

"The **engaging** voice of Cuban immigrant Trish Izquierdo suffuses this first novel with a high-spirited intensity . . . Despite serious underpinnings, the novel grows **expansively funny, even quite daft** . . . A large cast of endearingly self-absorbed characters struggles along in Rivera's **sure-handed comedy** as private fantasy, public aspiration, and reality repeatedly collide."
—*Publishers Weekly*

"The chapters of this first novel whirl and flash around [the heroine] Trish, capturing her **energy and on-the-edge style.** Sharing the intensity established in Rivera's book *African Passions and Other Stories,* this novel is **recommended.**" —*Library Journal*

Playing with Light

A Novel

by

Beatriz Rivera

Arte Público Press
Houston, Texas

This volume is made possible through grants from the City of Houston through The Cultural Arts Council of Houston, Harris County.

Recovering the past, creating the future

Arte Público Press
University of Houston
Houston, Texas 77204-2174

Cover design by James F. Brisson

Rivera, Beatriz, 1957-
    Playing with light / by Beatriz Rivera.
        p.   cm.
    ISBN 1-55885-310-3 (pbk. : alk. paper)
    1. Cuban American women — Fiction. 2. Women—Books
and reading — Fiction. 3. Fiction—Appreciation — Fiction.
4. Female friendship — Fiction. 5. Books and reading — Fiction.
6. Miami (Fla.) — Fiction. 7. Book clubs — Fiction. 8. Cuba —
Fiction. I. Title.
PS3568.I8287 P58 2000
813'.54—dc21
                                                    00-042005
                                                    CIP

0 1 2 3 4 5 6 7 8 9   10 9 8 7 6 5 4 3 2 1

For Casey Barnes, whom I met in Miami.

I'm thinking about Marina Tristán and Virgil Suarez.
We seem to go back a long way now, and here's another
one of our projects. Here's to more. I'm also thinking about
Clifford Crouch, who knows who I really am. Gracias y cariño.

"I didn't know then that the art of reading out loud had a long and itinerant history, and that over a century ago, in Spanish Cuba, it had established itself as an institution within the earth-bound strictures of the Cuban economy."

Alberto Manguel, *A History of Reading*

THE SUN, COMING THROUGH the rosewood louvers, cast distorted geometric patterns of light and dark over the roundness of her thigh. Dust motes drifted, suspended in the rays of midmorning light. Rebecca in the rocking chair, her hand in the sun, her knee in the shade, the book on her lap between the broken lines, and her bare foot moving from the shade to the light and back to the dark. She rocked gently, all the motion coming from her right foot, on the cool floor, up and down went her heel; the other foot was on her knee, she was moving her lips, she was thinking in bits and pieces, voices, letters, while she made circles with the foot that was on her knee.

Rebecca didn't go bicycling on the causeway this morning, over by the Seaquarium. She's even questioning the benefits of daily exercise these days. After she dropped Nell off at school she just kept on going instead of making that turn, and drove straight to her parents'.

As she pulled into the cracked and grassy driveway she immediately caught sight of her father, sitting out on the porch, on his wheelchair, reading *The Miami Herald* to the cat.

Rebecca still feels this trickle of cold in her stomach each time she sees him. She keeps reminding herself that it has only been six months. Six months is nothing. Eventually she'll get used to this new situation, to her father in a wheelchair, incapable of doing anything for himself. What's more, people recover from strokes, *don't they?*

His body is a wiry, lightweight, lopsided cage, and his eyes make her think of two little finches inside it. He can talk, and he has limited use of his hands, so he is not in a bell jar, he can reach out through those thin, rusty bars, but never again can he come out, it seems like his life sentence.

1

He is happy though, he boasts that it has taken him eighty years of being a bad man—and a nasty stroke—to make him discover what he loves the most, reading out loud. Not only that but he is looking forward to doing it for the rest of his life.

"It's okay, Becky," he says all the time.

As to the stray black cat in the shrubs, he is a gift from God, he is the audience.

A loving and enthusiastic, "Becky!" was Papi's greeting.

Right away the cat leaped up and disappeared into the croton shrubbery nearby. Papi didn't even notice. He simply reminded Becky that she hadn't come to visit for two days. Where had she been? "You keep on abandoning me with your mother," he whispered and pointed to the screen door, made a gesture with his tangled hand, shaking it at the wrist, up and down, twice each time, fast.

It meant trouble. Trouble as usual. Each morning Mami blamed the world for last night's dishes. Why her? And didn't she deserve better? Her days are downward spirals, and as the day progresses, so do the illogical premises, the paranoid conclusions, it's everyone's fault, she's a victim, they want her to suffer, it's a conspiracy. That's why she often says that she feels alive when she's angry.

"Your mother's a good woman though," Papi said. "Don't ever forget it."

"How could I forget?"

"How's Nell?" Papi asked.

"She's still scared of getting shampoo in her ears and going deaf."

"And your husband?"

"Tommy's working all the time. I never get to see him," Rebecca said, then pointed to the door and added, "I'd better go in before she thinks we're gossiping about her. We'll talk later."

Rebecca braced herself, as she opened the screen door, walked into the house and let the door slam, she rehearsed. A cheery greeting, pay no attention to the bitter mood, pretend you don't notice, ask Mami how she is, then quickly change the subject and ask her where they are, the old Academy of the Assumption yearbooks.

But Rebecca couldn't find the Spanish word for *yearbook,* so after having walked around the broken glass and spilled milk of her mom's demons, she had to explain it awkwardly, the books with the pictures of all her classmates at The Academy of the Assumption, grade by grade, year after year, from second grade until 1973, the year she graduated. Come to think of it, she didn't want all of them, just the last one.

"Who are you looking for?" Mami's question sounded like a mouthful of thorns.

She is a furious little woman in her early sixties with puffy eyes and skin that can't absorb any more tears. She reigns like Bloody Mary over this crumbling mansion and her fifteen-year-old Cadillac (with only forty thousand miles).

The truth is that both Rebecca's parents jettisoned their lives many years ago with their nightly, messy, quarrels, so they have to pay the price for squandering, in installments that strangely resemble a buzzing myriad of minimum payments to chrome green, silver, and gold Visas and Mastercards.

Often Mami complains because *el jardinero* wants to charge her too much to mow the lawn. "Who does he think I am? Does he think I'm rich like the Jewish people?" is her cry of lament.

They have had this conversation over and over again.

"He thinks you're just another rich Miami Beach Jewish woman," is Rebecca's reply.

"Do you really think so?" she asks, and on those occasions she sounds flattered. She never did want to be who she was.

But they were rare, those times when her mom was pleased or flattered. Rebecca couldn't visualize her smiling, much less laughing. If everyone has a superlative, an "-est" that's all theirs, Rebecca's mother was probably the unhappiest. Or was it the angriest?

Today it is slowly approaching as bad as it gets. Rebecca knows this particular mood of her mother's well.

"Could it be that you're looking for yourself in those yearbooks?" Mami then asked, dying to be galvanizing.

"Maybe," said Rebecca in her slippery way. "Me before Tommy lost his business and Papi had his stroke. Before I had to get my priorities straight." She glanced at her mother's nails. "I like that red," she said.

Mami, who was drying her hands with a piece of paper towel, stopped to inspect the flattered red on her nails. "Brr, my hands have gotten so old and ugly and if I had known that this was my lot in life I would have gladly killed myself."

"So do you have any idea where the yearbooks are?"

"Remember how nice your hair was?" was Mami's reply. "I just remembered because you mentioned the yearbooks."

"Huh?" was Rebecca's reaction while she ran two fingers through her hair, just to make sure it was still there. If she had to name that red, the red of her mom's nail polish, what would she say? And what about her jet-black hair dye? What name would she give it if she were finally angry? Never mind the hair dye, what about the red on her lips? Mami always put on lipstick, even to do the dishes, and she always managed to get some of that blood red on her teeth.

"It was before that man you married taught you to disdain and mistreat your own mother . . ." Mami momentarily stopped to think, and sighed. "When I think of all the sacrifices I made to send you to that school . . . so that you could mingle with the best people in Miami . . . and go to the best university . . . have a career . . ."

Before she finished saying all that Rebecca was already upstairs.

The yearbooks sat in a bookshelf, at the end of a dusty corridor, upstairs, in a part of the house her parents didn't use any more. They'd moved downstairs for good when Rebecca left, twenty years ago. So the slats of the jalousie windows refused to close, the rain came in, the heat came in, the sun came in, faded all the colors, warped the wood paneling, finished turning everything into junk. A pair of canvas Keds with holes at the big toes, a torn bathing cap with frills, a pile of old LPs, a bikini bottom with no elastic, plasticized wooden plaques congratulating her dad for having sold millions of dollars worth of insurance policies, a tainted trophy, and a faded family photograph under an oxidized can of roach poison only added to the mustiness.

Too much light up there, and no curtains, Rebecca squinted. She sat down on the red tile floor. It was grainy and dusty. There was one of Mami's brittle yellow and hardly used "*Aprenda Inglés*/Learn English" or-your-money-back-fifteen-minute-a-day-miracle-language-learning-method, the ninety-minute cassette, the workbook; all reminiscent of those mornings when her mom would wake up and say, "That's it! I'm going to learn English." There was a yoga book, there was a Nancy Drew Mystery, the A-B volume of the encyclopedia, a heavy one, *Second Year Latin, The World's Most Beautiful Poems,* and there were novels from the time when all Rebecca ever did was "read, and never listen."

When she took out the 1973 yearbook several empty roach eggs fell to the red tile floor near her toes. She could hear her parents quarreling downstairs, and her mother shouting, "I'm tired of life! I want to die! Your daughter treats me like dirt! She's an ungrateful shit! My biggest failure!"

Sooty dust had accumulated on the top edge of the yearbook. The corners had been chewed by rodents. The cover looked as if it had been drenched by several Miami rainstorms and then left out in the sun to bake.

She coughed, stood up, shook the dust off the back of her thighs and her shorts. "Whatever happened?" she wondered. What happened to the girlfriends she threw out with the old address books?

Well, she still has her girlfriend Conchita, who lives near here in North Bay Road and whom she sees just about every day. They take turns picking their daughters up at school. Conchita's picture is in here.

And Helen and Daisy, her two sisters-in-law, are also in the yearbook.

Those three are in Rebecca's life for good, or so it seems.

Sometimes she even wishes she could lose Daisy. But that's when she's being chummy with Helen.

On the other hand when's she's being chummy with Daisy she finds Helen too obnoxious and opinionated.

And there are times when Daisy and Helen are being chummy with each other. That's when Rebecca gossips the most with Conchita.

But those are the moody musical chairs of the present. Never mind the present. This yearbook here is ancient history, and the question is, Quick! right now, what's the first thing that comes to mind? What can she remember about those times, so far away now? Those sad times that seem so appealing now. Because it's time to set those priorities straight now . . .

Selene Machado always drew a happy face in the "o" of Machado.

Rebecca didn't admit it to herself right away. She tried to come up with something better.

Something better . . .

So was that it? Did it all come down to that? Ten or twelve years of her life that can be resumed with a happy face in the "o" of Machado. In peacock-blue ink.

Can't be. There has to be more, Rebecca was thinking as she pulled out of her parents' driveway onto the charming coconut-tree-lined Flamingo Drive.

U MBERTICO BARRIOS STOPPED READING MOMENTARILY and took the glass of ice water to his lips. María Fernanda looked at him and stuck her tongue out. He noticed. He always did. And her scorn embarrassed him.

This is how María Fernanda spent her childhood. In the dress factory, on the floor, playing with the light, listening to the *lector,* the Reader. Who are those people? she wondered. And does that book talk to me? The Reader is supposed to make it talk. Fine. With the books of the past it just takes a little philology, or so it seems. That's what the Reader said last week. He's always saying things like that because words are his life. But these women are *one hundred years* from now. Why this contrast? Do they talk to me? Or do they simply remind me of my aunt and of my mother?

In the morning there were perfect diamond shapes of on the worn terra cotta floor. It had something to do with the way the light came in, the divided light. At one given moment the shapes were perfect. Then each hot long hour that passed pulled and pulled on the shapes, until they couldn't take it, turned into lines and seeped into the cracks. Those were María Fernanda's toys. The most permanent and fleeting toys there ever were.

The Reader cleared his throat. The factory workers stopped murmuring and started cutting. They wondered, Will they name the next gown after one of these women? Rebecca, Daisy, Helen, Conchita, The Mad Mother. After all, cigars had been named after Romeo and Juliet and the Count of Monte Cristo. Couldn't they do the same thing? Hush! Umbertico Barrios has sipped enough ice water. He is ready to resume his reading.

THE MINUTE SHE GOT HOME Rebecca put on the Balinese music, then dragged one of the wicker-bottom rocking chairs out to the back terrace and sat down. She was dying to open the book on her lap, but at the same time she enjoyed extending the thought of it, the pleasure. Gently she rocked, her distorted shadow jumping from wall to wall. One minute it was in the bookshelf, then it was hanging on to a painting, then it was in the wineglasses, then back to where it began. "Who are you looking for? Yourself?" her mother asked.

"That's right, myself," Rebecca whispered. Before Papi had his stroke. Before Tommy lost his business and his freedom and left her all alone here all day, with no purpose, just a bunch of old raggedy ridiculous priorities. Take Nell to school, go for a bicycle ride . . . Looking for herself, along with everybody else. "Whatever happened to your hair? The sacrifices I made to send you to that school. Your father drank all the money he made . . . It was before that man you married . . . When all you did was read. I have nothing to live for, I want to die." Oh! Oh no! Don't bring me down! "Becky, is your hair falling out? And who are you looking for in there? Yourself?" Before . . . When . . . "When you had such nice hair."

Rebecca suddenly remembered that while searching through her father's things after he had his stroke—trying to determine what bills to pay (keeping in mind that he said, "Never mind Visa and MasterCard, just pay the Platinum AmEx")—she found an old black-and-white photograph of an interior in Havana.

IMMEDIATELY SHE WAS TAKEN by the photograph. The light was shining in through curly iron bars, into a room, creating odd shapes on the floor. The pattern was broken by the empty wicker rocking chairs that had been placed in a circle.

That afternoon at the hospital Rebecca showed the photo to her father and asked him about it. He glanced at it and smiled. "I never knew those people," he said before closing his eyes.

He still had that smile.

He was in intensive care, and after her father fell asleep Rebecca looked around.

The room had a wall of windows that gave out to the water, the causeway, the Miami skyline. Actually it got so bright at times that the shutters had to be pulled down. She pulled them up now that it was sunset, but then she realized what she was doing and pulled one shutter down halfway, just so the room wouldn't look like everyone else's and she wouldn't have any trouble recognizing it once she was downstairs, in the parking lot. She could then look up and know which room it was. She wanted to do that.

"There aren't any people in the picture," she said, believing he was sound asleep.

"Yes there are. They're in the shadows."

Usually there are more chairs, so that the guests can converse, drink ice water, eat finger sandwiches made with soft bread.

His speech was slurred.

The next day Rebecca returned to the hospital and asked him about the photograph again. He seemed more alert.

"*Tertulias* they're called," he replied.

Not a dance, not at all. You sit, you talk, you rock. That light? Where did that Cuban light go? Is it gone? Should we blame Fidel?

Maybe, because one of these days they're going to have to tear all those old houses down, and without architecture, is there light?

"That's what Cuba is about, light and . . . sugar . . . *azúcar*," he said. "Sugar. *La niña linda de Cuba.* Cuba's pretty little girl."

"I still don't see any people in the photograph."

When she got home from the hospital Rebecca immediately dialed her sister-in-law's number at work.

"Listen to this, Daisy," she said.

Rebecca and Daisy talked so often that they always skipped polite beginnings such as "Hello, how are you?"

"I'm going to try to contact as many girlfriends as possible and invite them to a weekly Friday afternoon *tertulia.* Not only that but I'm even going to buy a white wicker rocking chair with a pretty cushion for each guest. Isn't that a great idea?"

Rebecca was leaning against the kitchen counter scratching her ankle with her toes.

"Don't do it without me," Daisy said.

"Of course you're invited!"

Rebecca was all excited, she glanced at the old black-and-white photograph that she still had in her hand.

"No, I mean don't go buying those *rocking* chairs without me. Those wicker ones you have are too short in the front and if you rock too hard you can fall flat on your face. I know a place in Hialeah where you can get wonderful wicker ones . . ."

"But what do you think about the *tertulia?*" Rebecca interrupted.

Now that she was through scratching herself with that free foot, she kept on slipping it in and out of the wrong shoe.

"Oh, it won't work," Daisy replied matter-of-factly. "Nobody in their right mind is going to drive to Miami Beach every Friday afternoon without a reason. Are you kidding? With the traffic on I-95 these days? I swear, it's never been this bad. Just the other day it took me . . ."

"Daisy! I'm being serious."

Rebecca had walked out of the kitchen and was already in the Florida room inspecting one of her wicker rocking chairs to see if Daisy was right.

"I know you're being serious, *corazón,*" said Daisy, "and it's my mission to keep you from becoming too serious. You know how you tend to get too excited about things and then you feel let down. By the way how's your dad?"

Rebecca was rocking slowly.

"Now he's down to a hundred and five pounds. First Tommy loses his business, then this happens to my dad."

With the tip of her index finger she counted each one of the chairs on the photograph.

"Things will never be the same again," she said finally.

She wants to be Alice, and step right into that photograph.

THEY DON'T KNOW ABOUT THE FUTURE. María Fernanda chuckled and stuck her tongue out at the Reader. It made him clear his throat. Read on! she shouted. My family pays you, *carajo!* If you stop reading I'll have you fired! You'll starve! You'll eat *tasajo* for the rest of your life! Read on! That's all you're good for! *¡No sirves para más nada!* You don't have a future! Idiot!

Poor Umbertico didn't even bother to take a sip of ice water and just kept on reading. He hated *tasajo!* And he was waiting for the future to become wonderful and bright. Why was she saying things like that?

You could also hear those scissors going at full speed. María Fernanda scared everyone in the factory. They were convinced she was bad to the bone. So they were cutting cutting cutting and hoping the little girl wouldn't take notice of them.

While they were cutting the fabric you could see all that lint suspended in the light. They were working with Jamaican cotton, so they had to work fast. There was an embargo, and Jamaican cotton was strictly forbidden on the island.

All María Fernanda wanted was to hear more. She had no idea she frightened all these people so much. And she always felt bad after she said bad words, but she couldn't help it. Truly, this little girl never meant half the nasty things that came out of her filthy mouth and she would have been surprised and perhaps even hurt to hear that no one even suspected that she was a highly sensitive person who suffered intensely. She would have sworn that her rawness was obvious, she even thought she smelled of raw burnt flesh. Didn't they know anything about her?

What it all came down to was that she didn't want the Reader to stop. It always broke her heart. Sometimes the pain was so bad that she'd roll on the floor and holler and curse the Reader for stopping. "I'm going to turn you into a finch!" she yelled. "And put you in a wiry, rusty, banged-up cage for the rest of your life! That'll teach you to stop reading, old man!" The factory workers thought that she was simply having another one of her tantrums.

EVERY EVENING UMBERTICO BARRIOS STOPPED READING at six. This was Hell for María Fernanda. At six the Reader's voice stopped, the final little cough, and he stepped down from the podium, and the diamond shapes were pulled into nothingness, swallowed by the floor, the light flew away, the colors cracked and fell off, catapulting you into the black-and-white page of existence, the interruption, all happiness and interest oozed into the cracks, there was this sucking sound and it was all over.

FROM THE CORNER OF HER EYE Rebecca could see the outline of her head and her hair, way over there, against the yellow stucco wall of the dining room. She rocked gently and finally opened the book. She leafed through the last pages, the ones purposely left blank for autographs. Peacock blue was the favorite color ink in those times. And they still used fountain pens. On the verge of felt tips, but not quite there yet.

"Have a great summer and a great life if I don't see you again. *Tu amiga,* Selene Machado." There it is, the eternal happy face in the "o" of Machado. Rebecca had never seen Selene again.

"Who are you looking for in there? Yourself? And what happened to your hair? Always reading, never listening. The *sacrifices* I made to send you to The Assumption Academy!" Mami's voice was in her head.

Rebecca felt like seeing her own picture first. Again, she could hear her mother, You used to have such nice hair! Are you taking the right vitamins? It was before that man you married . . . Becky, with the education I gave you, I never thought you'd end up being a traditional wife!

And you never used to criticize your own mother. It's because you married an *americano,* and *americanos* have no sense of how close mothers are to their daughters.

By the way, your cousin Alma's breaking up with that *americano* she married. *Cubanas* shouldn't marry *americanos.*

Becky, I really wonder what happened to your hair! Are you sure you're as happy in your marriage as you say? Ever since Tommy lost his company and started working like normal men do, you just haven't been yourself.

There's also Papi's stroke, she tried telling her mom.

Oh, really? Does that affect you? her mom asked in her usual, insulting way.

There she was, before she suspected that men lost their businesses and perfectly so-so fathers had strokes. It was one of those *chiaroscuro* photographs with half her face in the sunlight and the other half in the shade, with too much contrast between the two in order to give the teen-age mysterious effect. Definitely too dark in the shade, almost in the dark, and too bright in the sunlight, one eye almost shut. To think that this used to be her idea of "looking great." It was exactly the image she'd wanted to give of herself. Reflective, turned inwards . . . and all the desired effects seemed so obvious now . . . looking at the photograph ended up being quite embarrassing. But look at that head full of hair. It seemed so strong and shiny.

Rebecca Barrios before she became Becky Atkins. Would have done anything to have straight stringy hair with absolutely no body. What a head of dark brown hair! French Club, Spanish Club, Literature Club, Poetry Club, Etiquette Club (she couldn't remember belonging to any Etiquette Club), Tennis (that backhand!), Vice President, a fan of Chris Evert, and in the fun part it said that she was the ultimate reader, *lectora,* lonely-ísima, serious-isísima, shy-ísima . . . Are my legs long enough? *¡Esa Mente!* . . . Do I really look like Cher? . . . perpetual hunger . . . deep, deep, deep . . . Maybelline lashes, frosted lipstick, Cover Girl, Honey Glow. Loves to listen to Eric Burdon and the Animals while rocking on a rocking chair. Fast! Destined to marry a rich man and spend her days reading after getting a Ph.D. in Comp Lit.

Rebecca scratched her head. Who did she want to see now? Daisy, yes. C-D-E-F . . .

Ana Daisy Santiago before she turned into Daisy Atkins. Rebecca smiled when she saw Daisita's picture. Drama Club, Glee Club, Volleyball, Varsity, blonde and cute, tanned, those glutes! that back talk! those hamstrings! . . . Is definitely capable of being mean. Aggressivisísima! Can't wait to get married! Enthusiastic-ísimost of them all. Destined to an Ivy League business school in which she'll achieve her typing goal.

The once-hated sister-in-law!

What about Helen? R-Q-P-O . . .

Elena Medina, who still had a long way to go before she became Helen Atkins at two hundred and twenty pounds. Here she weighed eighty and they already called her Helen. Always on a diet. Nervous wreck, that laugh! Neatness personified. A collector of all things. It's either feast or famine! Hungry-simaaa! Starvation diet on Monday! Oh the munchies! One dozen jelly donuts! We have total control of our bodies. This girl's gonna make lot's of money! Destined for great success.

La otra sister-in-law.

So far that's three rocking chairs including her, but she has four rocking chairs here already.

The yearbook fell and when Rebecca picked it back up it was on the class of 1975. Almita! *¡La prima! ¡La cousin!*

Alma Cuevas wasn't a senior then. She was still in tenth grade. That was the year she fell in love with the first Frank and dropped out of The Assumption Academy in the middle of the year to go to Beach High. She was hoping to take summer classes and do silly things for credit like hospital volunteer work, driver's ed, working at the cash register at Publix Market to learn what real life is about. All this because she wanted to graduate earlier and get married. Had she been a senior, the year book staff would have chosen a word like upbeat-isísima. They would have said that she was destined for a fairy tale wedding on a perfect Saturday in March at Vizcaya, and a great marriage.

All wrong of course.

Rebecca decided that from now on she'd see Alma more often.

Alma will get rocking chair number four, and Rebecca has to start buying rocking chairs from now on.

Oh, look at Conchita!

Conchita Pérez was the trig whiz, the math genius, destined to beat Einstein's I.Q. This was way before she married Dr. Stanley Fish the dentist and became Mrs. Stanley Fish. Tiny! *¡Tan flaquita!* The Twiggy look but shorter. Never have to worry about gaining weight. Smartísima.

Still *la closest girlfriend.* It also helps when *una girlfriend* lives in Miami Beach. If they move to South Miami, the Gables, or the Grove, seeing the amiga often gets more difficult.

So far that's five people that she can invite to the *tertulia,* but no long-lost friends yet.

Here's one.

Here's another one.

And here's . . . Oh, no, not Prisicilla Drake. No *way.*

She dated Tommy, and Rebecca hates anyone who dated Tommy.

Priscilla Drake, *¡la Cubanísima!* One side of her bob curls in, the other curls out. *¡Mujer linda!* The poet of the class. When she thinks, it rhymes. Can't wait to graduate! Failed driver's ed three times. *Poetísima.*

E-F-G . . . who else? M-L-K . . . Who else? What about her?

And her.

By the time Rebecca got to long-lost girlfriend number nineteen she decided it was time to cut back a little, that's too many rocking chairs to buy and too many people for a *tertulia.*

After all, a *tertulia* is supposed to be intimate.

Her shadow was nowhere to be seen now.

She stood up, left the yearbook on the rocking chair. For a while it rocked by itself.

The kitchen smelled of vitamins, of celery, of fresh fruit.

While Rebecca ate she kept on counting, trying to decide how many they should be. Fifteen? Too many. Ten? Maybe. Which ten?

After Rebecca finished lunch she got in her car and drove to her old neighborhood.

The entrance to the school was on Brickell Avenue. Today, on these grounds stands a thirty-story multi-colored building with an architecturally arrogant hole in the middle. There's a guard in an air-conditioned booth where there used to be huge iron gates that were always left open. They bulldozed the two enormous banyans that made an arch of mysterious greenery above the gate. They bulldozed every single Royal Palm that lined the figure-eight-shaped driveway. The church still stands, to the left, but the convent and the dormitories adjacent to it are gone, and so is the main building, a splendid old southern mansion, so is the banyan in the middle of the top loop of the figure eight, so is the white stucco building that used to house the classrooms, and so are all the airy open-sided pink granite-floored terraces that used to face the back lawn and the bay. A long stretch of green green lawn rolled gently down to the waters of Biscayne Bay.

There was always a smooth breeze and something salty about the place and something spooky and sad that had nothing to do with those white statues of the Virgin Mary with outstretched arms perpetually ready to bless and to blame.

For a minute Rebecca felt as if she were snooking the memories, from this far, present time, now that . . . now that . . . what? . . . that Tommy had lost his business and her father was paralyzed?

This was about as bad as the funny face in the "o" of Machado.

In fact, there was nothing left, it was even difficult to remember how it used to be, standing there, looking at the bay, even the water seemed new, newly poured, had Biscayne Bay been emptied and refilled with new water? Had they really lived in that house across the street? She couldn't even hear her parents shouting. The real word here is *gritando*. They'd take Valium and alcohol and before you know it they were tearing the world apart.

Now it seemed as if the spirit of the place had erased her. For a few minutes she imagined how much better it would have been to have spent her childhood somewhere else, far, making it more difficult to return to the actual place of this morning's musings and memories.

When there was stormy weather, *la tormenta,* the waves would slam against the debris on the shoreline which was south Florida's version of the Seven Cities of Cibola. The rubble of one house after the other had been left there for the barnacles after the swift passage of hurricanes that, way back when, only had women's names. This is where the girls would walk. Their regulation saddle shoes had to be polished daily. They'd try to avoid a salty wave, a spiky barnacle, a crab, an ugly critter that could bite. The most slippery was the seaweed-green chunk of wall that once belonged to a splendid house. It stuck out of the ocean at a forty-five degree angle.

Las girlfriends joked about having purple nuns teaching them. In a world that took LSD without them was that psychedelic enough? But imagine what it's like to spend all year knowing you're the last graduating class and that after you leave the whole place will be torn down. School's out forever! Imagine!

The decade was young, but most of *las girlfriends* had already experienced revolution and had heard the sounds of conflict, artillery being fired, shattered glass, and they also knew what it felt like to leave everything you own behind. One thousand dolls and a Cuban princess bedroom. Vaguely, they could remember what not speaking English was like, but this memory was fading rapidly, it seemed to belong to someone else, the very beginning, how hard it was to learn the days of the week, mixing up Tuesday and Thursday, kitchen and chicken. Between *you* and *I,* or *you* and *me?* Angry *at* or *with?* Different *from* or *than?* Is our school "on" or "in" Brickell Avenue? Those prepositions! Yellow house or house yellow? Shake, shook, shaken. Do "together with" and "as well as" affect the number of the verb? For some, two negatives never made a positive and the trials and errors of learning a new language were nothing compared to being separated from their mom or their dad, or never getting to know their grandparents . . .

By the time this "*grupito de Cubanas en el Exilio,*" as they called themselves, graduated from The Assumption Academy, even the departure from Cuba and the arrival in El Exilio seemed so distant that it no longer concerned them. El Exilio was their parents' nickname for Miami, but Miami was home for them, and, in secret, it was becoming home even for their parents.

On the weekends they wore bell bottoms, hip huggers, tight tight tie-dye T-shirts, leather sandals, and tried to look as "mod" and as "hippyish" as their old-fashioned moms allowed them. (Perhaps not Nancy Corcuera. And Alma Cuevas always wanted to look like Audrey Hepburn.)

The Assumption Academy was a "normal" school for *americanitas* up until 1960. Then Fidel took over Cuba and a privileged number of families arriving in El Exilio decided that The Assumption (aka La Asuncion) was the only place for their daughters to get the best education. Little by little the *americanitas* who had been studying there got overwhelmed by the mores and the bilingualism and left for other schools where none of the kids had been uprooted and lost their house and their language and their past, where they spoke only English and not some kind of "*Ay, m'ija!*" mixture. And where they didn't have that snobbery; what's your name, who's your Daddy (who's your Daddy), is he rich (is he rich) like me?

Every Friday they had to go to confession. Do you dare tell a priest that the nuns smell strange, as if they had been put away for years in a mildewy chest? Wondering about their hair. Bald underneath the veils? What do they look like naked? Will I grow up to be ugly like that? Am I white? Do thoughts count? Sometimes I get so angry. Thou shalt not kill, got that, but what if you want someone to die? Is it a sin if you don't tell? It's so embarrassing. Did the Jews really kill Jesus? Bless me father for I have sinned, parents quarreling again, wanted to die. All I can think about is being in a man's arms, Father. Do thoughts count? Is it a sin if you don't tell? Am I white enough? Hate this place. Not rich and Mrs. T. clings to the rich kids. Mother B. said I should kill myself cause I'm left-handed. She said, Left-handers never make good secretaries. Not only that but she said I didn't even have a name. Don't want to make any efforts, don't want to learn, don't want to do homework, want to be with Lucy in the Sky all day, in the Court of the Crimson King, Bye bye Miss American Pie, you're giving me penance and I'm wondering how old I'll be in the year 2000, Anticipation. Why do I have to be a kid? Leave me alone with my silly book, I want a *novio,* I want to play, I want a pretty dress, bless me Father I touched myself, it's been a week, I want makeup, I want to be Audrey Hepburn, I want to sing! I want an audience, me! the center of things, I want a man with long hair who lies down on top of me, it gets all swollen when I think, can we go through that penance again? I lied, I lie, I'm lying now, making up sins, and hiding the real ones.

After confession the priest silently emerged from his tiny cubicle, tried to slip by unnoticed, he looked worn out.

Rebecca walked back to her car. On her way to school she stopped at Dunkin Donuts and bought a dozen jelly donuts. It was her turn to pick up Conchita's daughters, and the girls were usually starving after school.

Sitting in the car, taking gulps of mineral water from the big bottle, dying to eat a donut, but won't, waiting for the bell to ring, and for Nell and Conchita's daughters to walk toward the car, complaining about how heavy their books are, how hungry they are, Nell whining as usual, "Ma! Do I have to go to ballet today? I've got tons of homework and I'm tired!" Ready to say, "Jelly donuts! Surprise!", Rebecca wrote an invitation.

"Every Friday at five in the afternoon, you're invited to a *tertulia* (a get-together) at Rebecca's house (Rebecca Barrios, The Assumption, class of '73), 12 Hibiscus Drive, Sunset Island, Miami Beach. The entrance to the island is near the Alton Road Animal Hospital. Tell the guard you're going to the Atkins house. Food and refreshments will be served. Cuban *hors d'oeuvres: bocaditos, croqueticas, cangrejitos, pastelitos de carne.* YuCA (Young and upcoming Cuban-American) entrees: salmon, stone crabs, fancy rice, mesclun salad with dandelions. All you can eat for dessert: Key Lime pie, Cuban pastries, *mamey, cherimoyas,* chocolate pudding. Wine, beer, alcohol, Materva, Ironbeer, and mineral water. Men and children are welcome. Limited number of rocking chairs."

THAT SAME EVENING, REBECCA was helping Nell with the homework and at the same time talking with her sister-in-law Daisy on the phone.

"But why every Friday night?" Daisy asked.

Nell interrupted, "Ma! Will you please help me with my math?"

"Nell, honey, wait a minute, drink your milk. Are you still there, Daisy? Sorry about that. Like I said, it'll be a get-together, a *tertulia.* To talk and to rock! Just like they used to, in old Cuba!"

"Ay, Becky, *chica,* I'm all for it but I really think we need a reason. Miami's too big. *Las old girlfriends* aren't going to drive all the way to Miami Beach just to talk and to rock. We need a reason."

"No. I'm sure they'll all come. We just have to get a hold of them. My problem is, how many rocking chairs should I buy? Ten? Or fifteen? How many should we be?"

"In 1865, Saturnino Martínez, cigar-maker and poet, conceived the idea of publishing a newspaper for the workers . . ."

Alberto Manguel, *A History of Reading*

HE COUGHED. He closed the book and took the glass of water from the lectern to his lips. That's it for today. He smiled. He was shy. María Fernanda had convinced him that reading was what he was all about and when he wasn't reading, he was embarrassed about being a little lopsided and worried about losing his job.

It had been raining all afternoon and the light was dim. All day they'd been working on pale green and blue cotton dresses. Hardly any light was coming in through the stained glass windows. The seamstresses put their scissors away. Outside, the city was noisy and wet.

Who's your favorite character?

Too early to tell. There's too many of them, that's a mistake. But I do like Miami. Love Miami. And the music. Bye bye Miss American Pie.

How many rocking chairs do you think she's going to buy?

Is *that* what the plot is about?

I love the music she listens to while she rocks. *¡Fiesta fatal!* Balinese.

Why won't she eat?

I love Miami. I even love to repeat the word. Miami Miami Miami. Where are my scissors? *¡Se me olvidaron las tijeras carajo!*

They had so much freedom. And good food. And vitamins.

They will have. Don't forget it's taking place in the future.

Do you mean that when they are, we're not?

When they will be, we shall no longer be.

Why will they leave Cuba?

And who is that *Fidel* who will ruin the architecture and make the light go away?

Probably another Generalísimo Anacleto Menosmal, like we have now.

Do you suppose they knew about us? I mean, "will know?" What do you suppose?

"How does one read? Contrary to what many people assume, our eyes do not flow smoothly across the page as we are reading. Instead, our eyes move in a series of jumps and pauses. These are called *saccades* and *fixations*. We only read during the fixations—not when the eyes are moving."

Anne Marshall Huston

IT IS EASY TO MISS the bridge to her island. You can drive around in circles all the way to North Bay Road and La Gorce Country Club looking for the entrance, which is tucked into the coconut palms, the hibiscus, the giant crotons. This old white stucco bridge resembles a daintily arched foot reaching across a narrow waterway to avoid getting wet. The Alton Road Animal Hospital and the Publix Market are the closest landmarks, so is that giant ponytail palm, but you can't make a left turn when you're coming from Dade Boulevard.

There is a guard in an air-conditioned booth at the entrance to Sunset Island. He can give directions to the Atkins house. It has a red clay tile roof, stucco walls with antique brick arches, and divided light windows made of rosewood. Go straight to the end of the island and then make a left. The house is on the water. You will see a yellow stone wall under a throw blanket of red bougainvillea. It is difficult to see the hand painted blue, white, and yellow Mexican tiles that read: 12 Hibiscus Drive, because of all the flowers.

The two wide iron gates are always locked, but they do have a video intercom entry system. Once you're inside the walls, don't mind the dogs, they're friendly. There is an open carport to the left, and a coral walkway that leads to the front door, which is another iron gate into a courtyard.

Orange bougainvillea hangs from one side of the carport. Flowers of all sizes, shades, and moods lead you to the house; tiny pink roses, delicate cream colored hibiscus, brazen sprays of orchids, ballerina pink hibiscus, and others the color of painted lips, splendid yellow roses, red red I love you roses. Before all these bad things happened Rebecca swore that they would always live surrounded by beautiful things. So far she's kept that promise. Tommy is always working on the house, detailing, examining it over and over again, fine-tuning. Every weekend he has some kind of project. They both love antiques, as well as kitsch, old brick, *faux* finishes, gold leaf, precious wood, smooth cobblestones, erotica, and they are always searching for new ways to play with the light, both inside and out.

Whoever comes to visit always has the same reaction, "Wow! Some kind of place you got here! Will you take a look at this! It's absolutely breathtaking! Wow! And take a look at this!" You hardly know where to look, you hardly know what to touch, what not to touch, there are even textures, colors and details that you want to take to your lips and taste with your tongue.

Their reaction used to make Rebecca so proud. She even said so herself—that she was the ultimate Miami Beach housewife. Everyting was absolutely perfect in her house.

In the morning there are diamond-like splashes of light on the lawn, cast by the trees. The light moves with the breeze. One of the flame trees canopies the two-story house. The ceiba looks like a man's wet body, some gladiator getting ready to throw a disc, it is pure movement. There is yet another canopy tree close to the sidewalk that Nell and Rebecca call the rice tree. When mother and daughter were feeding rice to Barbie, to the Cabbage Patch Kid, to Polly Pocket, to Ken, to Skipper, and to the long curly-maned little purple pony with glitter, they used the tiny rice-shaped leaves from this tree.

Isn't this paradise?

And whenever the dolls got tired of rice, no problem at all! Not only was there plenty of dirt with which to make hot chocolate, but nearby, separating 12 Hisbiscus Drive from 14 next door, is a big croton, not the kind with the big green shiny leaves, but the curly dark mauve type that really looks like bacon. Ken liked it crunchy, so did Skipper. The Cabbage Patch Kid was drinking formula from a bottle. The formula disappeared when the bottle was tilted. Polly Pocket was too little. Barbie was riding the pony. She was on a diet. She liked to exercise and for lunch she just wanted a salad. And the pony liked to eat grass.

Of course there was some trouble in paradise.

Nell is ten years old, ten years old going on ten and a half, not sixteen or eighteen, for she is still quite the chubby little girl who has too much trouble with homework, who whines, who giggles, who eats too much, and who has problems learning. At the beginning of the school year, after the new teachers have met Mr. and Mrs. Atkins, they turn to the old teachers and say, "Nell Atkins sure has good-looking parents."

To this at least five old teachers react at the same time, "Her mom shouldn't force her to stay in this school. That child belongs on the slow track!

She'll never make it! Her mom does all her homework for her! Listen to this, Mrs. Atkins writes these three-page essays on T. S. Eliot and wants us to believe they're Nell's! When Nell can barely spell her own name! What does she want us to believe, that she's a genius at home and retarded at school? That child is totally dyslexic and her parents won't accept it. And she's lousy in math. They're wasting their money! It doesn't matter, they're loaded. That little girl belongs in a remedial school but her mom wants her in prep school with her smart cousins. You'll see, she needs to be spoon fed! She can barely copy something from the blackboard! It takes her an hour. She says the numbers and the letters fly away like a flock of birds!

"Don't they have plenty of schools for children with learning disabilities? Why do we have to babysit? Go tell Mrs. Atkins! Isn't she overfeeding that child? Have you seen everything she puts in Nell's lunchbox?"

Practically in the beginning of the school year the principal did tell Rebecca that Nell was definitely smart, no doubt about that, but that she was having problems keeping up and that they should probably look for another school, a school where she could perhaps feel a bit more comfortable with smart children like her who simply need a little more attention. That day, while she drove back home with Nell in the back seat, Rebecca could barely see. At first she was trying to keep from crying so Nell wouldn't notice and ask her what she was crying about, but she couldn't hold it back, so she kept sobbing in silence and drying the tears. The worst part about it was that not all her feelings were noble ones and she felt ashamed, they wouldn't go away, they were there, so embarrassing, she wished she could start all over again, get it right this time, she envied Daisy and Conchita for the smart children they had. Why Nell? Was it because she was still smoking a pack of Marlboro Lights a day when she was pregnant? And Nell hardly ate when she was a baby, perhaps she was undernourished like those children in Africa.

That same evening Rebecca did all of Nell's homework. She read *White Fang* out loud to her and then worked on the book report until two AM. In truth, this has already been going on for so long that Rebecca can fake her daughter's handwriting.

There used to be so many problems! They were overwhelming! They'd make her cry! And Nell wasn't the only problem she had.

Rebecca even remembered crying because she couldn't believe how old she was. "Forty's too old!" she sobbed. Suddenly she didn't feel as safe. Forty seemed all right for Tommy, but not for her, it seemed too old for her. Did Tommy deserve a forty-year-old woman in his bed? Forty, and then what? An avalanche of bad thoughts. How could she have ever felt safe in her entire life? Tommy!

The memory embarrassed her.

They dropped Nell off at Conchita's, they had a few drinks, ate over a dozen conch fritters, a few slices of Key Lime pie, and they quarreled, instead of making love in the back yard. The truth is that before all this happened they were quarreling all the time.

Oh, it used to be that all day, every day, Rebecca would deprive herself of food. She was picky, annoying, manic about low fat, a tiny portion, healthy, lite, and if she resisted temptation after temptation, it was for a reason.

At the Burger King, at Carvel's or at the Dunkin Donuts with Nell and her cousins Rebecca wouldn't touch a thing, even if she was dying for something, a taste of hot fudge, a bite of that donut, a cheeseburger! When she did lunch with a girlfriends she'd pick on a salad, and when she realized the girlfriend's annoyed (not Conchita, never Conchita who's anorexic) she'd say, "Oh let's pig out! Let's order dessert!" So the girlfriend immediately orders strawberry cheesecake, and what is Rebecca going to have? Lime sorbet. Without the cookie.

And when Rebecca got the munchies at four o'clock, did she run for the Milano Cookies? Definitely not. Her life was so shallow that she chewed on a plastic straw.

But it's not all that shallow, if she was always depriving herself like this it was because she was hoping for a feast with Tommy. Little did it matter if she was often let down, she still looked forward to Tommy, as if he were a treat or an event. They could either stay at home or go to one of the finest restaurants in Miami, they could go to a taco joint, to a steak house, to TGI Friday's, they could go eat Cuban food at La Carreta, at El Versailles, or at La Esquina de Tejas, they could eat standing up, perched on a stool, facing the Miami skyline, a parking lot, or the ocean, if Tommy was around in the evening (only in the evening) and paying attention to her, she would not deprive herself.

There was a time when it couldn't be said, when it was too maudlin, but it's over now.

Things will never be the same, so just about anything can be said.

Let's not forget the drinking.

Being the daughter of an alcoholic, drinking during the day meant drinking fruit and vegetable juices, carrot juice, celery juice, beet juice, wheat grass juice, apple juice, orange juice, and at least two big bottles of mineral water. But things changed in the evening and she did look forward to it.

In the evening, if Tommy didn't come home too late, she'd drink. She'd drink a whole bottle of wine once she got going and little did she care if she was the daughter of an alcoholic. Sometimes it is hard to believe that she is the same woman who is always lugging the big bottle of Volvic or Evian.

Tommy prefers single malt Scotch. They can either talk, argue or play with each other for hours while he drinks Glenlivet and she drinks Cabernet Sauvignon. Tommy can drink quite a bit. And it barely shows. Nobody has ever seen him drunk. But ever since he lost his business he does seem to drink even more, and he's so self-absorbed!

Rebecca used to have this fantasy about it being Thursday, because Thursday is still the day that Nell spends the afternoon at Conchita's. Anyway, she used to daydream it was Thursday afternoon and all of a sudden Tommy came home in the middle of the day and they had sex all afternoon.

Last Saturday afternoon, while she was in the yard having this recurring fantasy, Tommy momentarily and miraculously stopped working on the house and came and sat down next to her. That's when Rebecca wiped her mind clean of that fantasy as quickly as if it were some nasty spill that needed lots of paper towels, and said bitterly, "You quit working on the house to come here and sit next to me? What a miracle!"

"You're always angry at me lately," Tommy said. "And you've become really nasty."

"Imagine that! Well I happen to be angry because I don't get to see you enough. So I spend my days angry at your absence. Then I hate you by the time I get to see you. It's a vicious circle."

"We seem to be doing great," he said.

"Well I need more than this. We just can't go on in our fancy house, pretending."

"Pretending? What is it that you're pretending? Are you pretending to be nasty, perhaps?"

"Perhaps."

If only Daisy could overhear their conversations! Because Daisy is always saying with a tinge of envy in her voice, "I bet you get it all the time," and whenever Rebecca hears this she smiles and acts coy, not agreeing, not disagreeing, just loving it and going as far as trying to make Daisy say a little more. "So you're convinced I have a really exciting sex life," Rebecca eggs her on. "What do you mean?"

"You know exactly what I mean," says Daisy. "And, yes, I'm convinced."

That Daisy is right, there is no certainty. Rebecca's sister-in-law is not happy with her own husband (who happens to be Tommy's brother) and therefore believes that everyone has it better. More love, more sex . . . She's wrong, of course. It's been quite a while. Rebecca and Tommy don't make love all that much.

"Oh, Daisy, if you only knew the truth!" Rebecca thinks. "I wouldn't tell her the truth for anything! Oh, just a hint . . ." Rebecca is still thinking. And now she's saying, "We have such little time, you know . . . It's impossible in the morning since Tommy leaves and six AM, and it's impossible on weekend mornings since Tommy gets up at the crack of dawn and immediately starts to work on the house. It's also impossible in the evenings because by the time we're in bed, either I've had too much to drink and I'm on the verge of getting aggressive, or I've spent too much time with Nell's homework, or Tommy has worked too hard, drunk too hard, played too hard. But, yes, definitely, that does leave other times . . . But you know, Daisy, ever since Tommy lost his business and my dad had his stroke I've been lonely, and things have been quite different."

"He's the one who chose to go and work in Palm Beach. He could've stayed here. He had the choice," Daisy argued.

"Well, I've gone back to reading the way I used to," Rebecca said, almost to herself. "Remember how much I used to read?"

When Tommy's at work, or working on the house, or out on the boat, fishing, when Nell is at school, or at Daisy's or at Conchita's, when Rebecca is all by herself, and she's on the stationary bike, while she's lifting weights, drinking vegetable juices, swallowing vitamins, hosing the courtyard, and even while she's doing housework, Rebecca reads. Rebecca reads all day. The minute she wakes up she reaches for her book on the night table and takes it with her to the bathroom. She reads while she makes breakfast for Nell, while she scrambles the eggs, butters the toast, warms the waffles in the microwave. She reads while she prepares lunch for Nell to take to school, while she spoons cream cheese on the bagel. She reads while she wraps the cookies in foil and pours the chocolate milk in a thermos. And ever since Tommy lost his business, Rebecca even reads while she's waiting at a red light.

R EBECCA WENT TO THE UNIVERSITY in the seventies. She never felt she had to stand for her rights or to fight for freedom, she was never a victim, she never met the wrong man. She applied to one of the top universities in the nation and got accepted. Nobody expected her to become a nice wife, or to give up her career for a man. On the contrary, she was supposed to be independent, self-sufficient, career-minded. And Rebecca went to the university with this in mind. She liked literature, she liked to read, so she'd get a Master's in Comparative Literature, go to New York and get a job in a publishing house. Working in publishing probably meant reading all day and that sounded wonderful to her. It was either that or becoming a literary agent, which also sounded wonderful to her. She looked forward to this exciting career life that awaited her.

But things didn't go as planned. She did earn her master's degree, but her parents weren't doing very well financially by then, they were sorry but they really couldn't help her get settled in New York, she'd have to come back to Miami, make a little money waitressing, and then move to New York.

One week after she was back in Miami she bumped into her old classmate from the Assumption, Ana Daisy. They chatted, it turned out that Ana Daisy was working in advertising and married to a wonderful guy named George. "*¡Me casé señorita!*" Ana Daisy added (*Señorita* is one of the elusive words for *virgin* in Spanish). She made it through all those free love years, kept her legs crossed tightly and made it to the altar, *virgo intacta*. What was Rebecca up to? Did she have any plans for the fourth of July? She didn't have any friends, much less plans. Great! They were having a barbecue at Daisy's house on Rivo Alto Island, and then they were going out on Tommy's boat.

Tommy was Daisy's brother-in-law, George's brother. "A bad boy, but in a good way," Daisy said. "Going out with this dumb arrogant selfish bitch. *Una cualquiera*," she added in a whisper. "And I'm really possessive with all the Atkins brothers. I have the impression they're all mine! *Ven y levántaselo,*

and you can have a summer fling. Priscilita Drake went out with him ages ago, it was through her that I met George. Join us! *El Tommy está buenísimo.*"
Rebecca accepted.

That Tommy Atkins does not speak Spanish, there is no certainty. With a name like Tommy Atkins she never expected him to speak Spanish. But when Daisy introduced her to him he said, just like a Cuban, *"Rebecca Barrios. ¿Cubana? Mucho gusto. Daisy me dice que lees mucho . . ."* He said that just like a Cuban.

Of course Rebecca brought a book along for this barbecue. She carried a chair, an umbrella, her book, her lemonade, and her hamburger to the floating deck and sat there to read. Tommy followed her. "How come you speak such good Spanish?" she asked.

"My mother is Cuban, but I'll tell you more if you have dinner with me."

"What's your girlfriend's name?"

"Jess."

Jess was quite a good-looking brunette with an aerobic teacher's figure and a British accent and not at all the bitch Daisy had painted her out to be. Rebecca looked at her, standing over by the barbecue, talking to George, Daisy's husband, who was staring at her and squeezing the bottle of ketchup over her food.

Tommy gave Rebecca that smile of his, and shrugged. "Take it or leave it."

"I'll take it," she said and gave him her phone number. He said he didn't need a pencil, he'd remember it. *"¿Cómo se me a olvidar el número de una cubana tan linda?"*

The next evening they went to The Rusty Pelican, a restaurant off the Rickenbacker Causeway and got a table right on the ocean. He told her about his great grandfather, Joseph Atkins, who went to Cuba in the nineteenth century and bought a sugar mill right outside Cienfuegos. As a matter of fact he wrote a book about life in Cuba. Perhaps Rebecca would be interested in reading it, since she liked to read. Tommy confessed that he himself had not read it.

The waiter came and said, "Hi, I'm Jeff, and I'm gonna be your waiter tonight. Can I bring you guys something to drink?"

The lady will have wine. What kind of Scotch do you have?

After they ordered, Jeff said, "You've got it! I'll be right back with your drinks."

Anyway, this great grandfather married a Cuban woman and had five sons who all went back to the States and married New England women. Two of the sons went back to Cienfuegos with their wives. "My grandfather was one of them," Tommy said.

"Are you guys ready to order dinner?"

No.

Jeff said, "I'll give you guys a minute. In the meantime you guys can help yourselves to the salad bar if you want. It's either that or the Caesar salad."

But instead of looking at the menu Tommy just kept on talking. Where was he? Oh, yes . . . "My grandfather left the island for good in the early twenties but he did keep some business interests there and traveled back and forth often. Then my father went in the forties to work on a hotel development project in Varadero and on the construction of one of those wedding-cake hotels in Havana. That's when me met my mom, who's Cuban."

"How many siblings are you?"

"We used to be four but one of my brothers died in Vietnam."

"And I met George at the barbecue," Rebecca said.

But she didn't meet Harvey. No, he wasn't at the barbecue. Next year, hopefully, *si Dios quiere* as they say, there'll be a big Fourth of July barbecue with the whole family. So that makes Harvey thirty-four years old now. Pretty old huh? He was an attorney. One of those Miami attorneys with a boat and an airplane. Got into some trouble. Hopefully he'll be out next year. Yes, he was disbarred, but he says that once he's out he's going to get it all back. He's in good spirits.

As to George, Daisita's husband, who was at the barbecue flirting with Jess, Tommy's girlfriend, he does have one weakness that we won't delve into right now, but he is definitely the good boy in the family. George did everything the way he was supposed to. He went to Harvard, got an MBA, he didn't take drugs, he didn't get anyone pregnant (Harvey did), and he married a virgin.

"*Yo te lo digo,*" Tommy said. "I'm telling you this because they are both really proud of Daisita's virginity. Sometimes I wonder why they didn't keep the bedsheet."

"Are you guys ready to order?" Jeff asked.

"We guys sure are!" said Tommy.

To get back to George, he's twenty-nine now and he's the one who'll take over the family construction company someday soon. He's a great business man.

"What about you?" Rebecca asked.

"I own a nightclub on the Beach, South Beach, Washington Avenue, a little bit past Española Way. I never went to college or did any of that stuff. I like to play, to sail, to go fishing, to wine and dine beautiful women, and you, Rebecca?" he asked and said Rebecca in Spanish.

"I like to read. As a matter of fact I was offered this great part-time job reading out loud in an old people's home."

He took her hand and held it against his cheek.

When he dropped her off that night he took her hand, kissed it, and then said, *"Nos vemos pronto, Rebecca linda."* From then on he always said her name in Spanish. Not Becky, not Becca, in Spanish, *Rre-be-cca.*

The following week he took her to his club.

In the days that followed they went to a French restaurant, to an Italian restaurant, a Chinese restaurant, they went to a top floor bar with a panoramic view of Miami, they never went to lunch, they went to Latin clubs where they could dance slow to the music of Trío Los Panchos. Then they went to a very fancy restaurant in Coral Gables, no Jeffs for waiters and this time she was Madam. It was so hot outside, but in the restaurant they had the air conditioning all the way up. Rebecca kept wanting to wrap herself up in one of the tablecloths. She took one of Tommy's hands and pressed it against her lips for a long time.

She was shivering and he asked her what was wrong. Just when he was about to take his jacket off the *maitre d'* rushed over and told him that it was out of the question. Under no circumstances could a man take his jacket off. They argued a little. Finally she ended up with one of those white starched tablecloths wrapped around her shoulders.

Tommy had to return to to the club later that night. He led her to the bar and said he'd be right back. Rebecca wondered if the humidity had made her hair too flat, so she tried to catch a glimpse of herself in the bar mirror, but it was so smoky and the different light spectra were so confusing in there, that she could barely recognize herself.

Whenever Tommy returned their conversation was often interrupted, someone would come with a whispering question, he'd whisper back, or his presence was needed somewhere else, he kept coming and going; it was all right. Every hour or so, when security was clearing the cash registers and taking the money to the counting room he seemed a bit uptight, but his attention was focused on her most of the time.

"There can't be that much cash," she said. "Don't they pay with credit cards?" He laughed when she said that.

He was never gone for too long. The music and the darkness were just right while she waited. That summer they were playing the hits of 1979.

Rebecca could tell the bartender was used to this kind of arrangement, Tommy busy, and his girlfriend waiting. Tommy didn't seem to want to be gone though, and that felt good. She could feel it all over her skin. On one of his brief returns to her side he put his arm around her shoulders and kissed her neck, and then he disappeared again. When he returned he put his arms around her waist and pulled her to him. She tilted her head, closed her eyes, and took a deep breath. She ran her fingers through his hair. She felt him against her. Oh Tommy.

Ana Daisy called the next day. "So are you having a summer fling *con mi hermanito?*"

"Kind of."

"Don't let him take you to bed too soon or he'll lose interest and you won't get through the summer. I know him, that's the way he is! Well, all guys are like that, right after they take you to bed they're no longer interested."

"Is that what your *abuelita,* your mother, and your solfeggio teacher told you?"

"Hey! we did have the same solfeggio teacher, didn't we?" Daisy suddenly remembered.

"We sure did! And while the chronometer was going tic tac tic tac she'd explain that once you let a man fool around with you, and that didn't necessarily mean fucking, *m'ija* you can say good-bye to being the mother of his child, or or anybody else's child, *ni con el guajiro de la esquina,* from that day on *ya eres una puta cualquiera entregada.*"

"So have you two . . ." Daisy started to ask.

"He hasn't taken me to bed yet. I don't even know where he lives! Besides, he has a girlfriend."

"Who? Jess? Are you kidding? That fortune hunter? He fucked her a couple of times and she's history now!"

For the rest of the day all Rebecca could hear in her brain was Daisy's voice, "he fucked her a couple of times," and she could barely read, she was all swollen and her juices were flowing, she had her eyes half open.

Labor Day weekend was approaching. Rebecca bought her plane ticket to New York. Nancy Corcuera had told her that Helen Medina, another one of *las girlfriends,* happened to be living there and had a great job in an investment bank, maybe they could be roommates. So Rebecca contacted Helen and asked shyly. As it turned out Helen said she'd be glad to have her.

Tommy and Rebecca were driving north on Collins Avenue in the evening when she told him about her plans to leave for New York. He made a fast right turn on Twenty First Street, and then a left when he reached the stone wall before the beach, and he kept on going, on the sidewalk, past the stone wall, through a narrow entrance for the City of Miami Beach vehicles, and he drove right onto the sand. Rebecca was screaming and laughing. "Tommy! You're not supposed to drive on the beach! We'll get arrested! What you're doing is illegal!" He left the motor running because it was ninety-six degrees outside at ten in the evening and they needed the air-conditioning, he pulled her to him and they kissed, she moaned it was almost too much pleasure to bear, his hands were on her breasts his hands were on her thighs his hands were between her legs she felt like *la puta cualquiera entregada* they had warned her about and she loved every beloved second of it she reached for his fly and felt his hard-on she undid his fly and took him in her mouth. Even today as they drive past there Tommy always points to the beach and says, "Remember over there? When you took me in your mouth and drove me slowly out of my mind?"

She never did get a job in publishing, she never became a literary agent, she never even made it to New York. Six months later he bought her a diamond. A rock! A year later, Tommy had somewhat changed his lifestyle, and they were engaged to be married. They both managed the club. She got the hang of it right away, she quit being naïve, she realized what went on, and when, there were split seconds when everyone was right on the edge, who's carrying? and when they relaxed, and all those times she stood up and threw a drink in some woman's face, and the wee hours of the morning, salt in the air, it smelled like the beach and like breakfast, when the Brinks truck came, the light was brand new and they hadn't gone to bed yet.

Boy, was Ana Daisy pissed! Boy, oh boy! She said things like, "Congratulations! You came to Miami and won the lottery!" It was great while she was in control, but she couldn't take it once she realized that Tommy and Rebecca were seeing each other all the time not even bothering to tell her. She even accused Rebecca of being a fortune hunter. And she said mean things like, "I had something better in mind for Tommy!" Finally Rebecca said, "Don't you dare call me again, *cabrona!*"

"*¡Chusma!* That's what you are!" Ana Daisy yelled. "You're a vulgar slut!"

At times Rebecca felt so much hatred for Daisy that it hurt her chest.

"You two have nothing in common!" was Daisy's last feeble attempt at separating them. She threw her hands up in the air. "Do you like boating? Do you like fishing? Antiquing? *Faux* finishes? Gardening? He owns a club as you know by now. One of these days you're going to have a baby and he'll be out all night with women who are all over him while you're at home with the newborn, your episiotomy, and your hemorrhoids. Women love to fuck the owner. They'll give him a blow job right there in the dark . . . Hasn't he told you the stories? And he didn't go to college. He doesn't even like to read! So tell me, what will you do while he's out on his sailboat or screwing some other woman?"

"I guess I'll read. I'll talk to you later, Daisy. Damn! I just spilled water, I gotta go!"

REBECCA READS. She reads at the ballet studio while Nell's in class. Once in a while she looks up and wonders if Nell's too fat and uncoordinated. Daisy's daughter, Sylvia, is just gorgeous. Such grace! Such a flat stomach! Such good grades! Sylvia's twelve and asking for a belly button ring. Her dad would go bonkers! And she's already on toe shoes, God she's so graceful, and she's sharp, she'll learn something in a split second. Will Nell be like that in two years? Rebecca went back to her reading.

Later that evening she read while she sat next to Nell trying to coax her to do some of her homework by herself. Just a little effort? The phone rang. It was her Mom who said, "Becky, what was it you told me that Nelly's illness was?"

"Dyslexia," Rebecca whispered.

"I'm going to ask Pedrito about it, his father's a pharmacist. Maybe if she took some vitamins or enriched protein shakes . . . Are you sure she's getting enough protein? By the way Ofelia gave me the name of this doctor who's supposed to be great with the spider veins. Becky, you should really do something about your spider veins. It's a shame to have such nice legs and to have spider veins!"

Immediately after she hung up the phone rang again.

"I don't know if this is the right number, but is this where Tommy Atkins lives?"

Rebecca replied "Yes, why?"

"Is he there?" the woman asked.

"No, who's calling?"

"Do you know when he'll be home?" she asked.

"Yes, who's calling?"

"I heard he owns a club and a friend of his told me he might need a book-keeper. Can you take my name and number down?"

"What friend was this?"

"Dr. Cohen from the animal hospital where I do some bookkeeping."

"Well he doesn't really own a club any more, he just rents it out. But he is planning to go back into business for himself, so I'll be glad to take your name and number down."

"Selene Machado . . . "

Right away Rebecca asked, "From the Assumption Academy?"

They were thrilled, what a coincidence! Rebecca said, "You always used to draw a happy face in the 'o' of Machado!"

"I still do!"

They chatted for a while. Nell whined. She needed help. She couldn't do it by herself! They promised to see each other soon, very soon, Rebecca shot a dirty look at Nell while she said to Selene, "Let's not be strangers, okay? It was great talking to you!"

"Nell, sweetheart, you've got to try!" Rebecca almost shouted.

Nell shouted back, "I can't do it!"

"Are you really this stupid or are you trying hard to be this stupid? Give me that goddamn homework! *¡Carajo!*"

Nell started to cry. "I'm going to call Abuelita and tell her you're being mean! I'm hungry!"

"You can call the fire department for all I care, *carajo!*" Rebecca shouted. Then after she was silent for a minute she asked, "Are you really hungry, sweetheart?"

"Ooops!"

"Damn it, Nell! Do you always have to spill everything? *¡Carajo!*"

A HEM!

FROM THE WATERS OF BISCAYNE BAY you can see the back of the house. There was a soft glow coming from Nell's room. Rebecca told her she was sorry for calling her stupid, kissed her good-night, turned the light out.

Then she went downstairs to join Tommy.

He poured the drinks and they decided to sit outside, in the dark, by the water. He asked her about her day and what she'd done and what she'd read. She put her head on his shoulder and while she talked she stared at an outdoor lamp shining on one of the flame trees, bugs were swarming around the light, madly attracted to it.

> "[Saturnino Martínez] hit on the idea of a public reader. He approached the director of the Guanabacoa High School and suggested that the board assist readings in the working-place."
>
> Alberto Manguel, *A History of Reading*

HURRY! IT'S RAINING, HURRY, don't get wet! Can't stand the rain, *maldito aguacero.* Everyone's standing under the eaves, even the lottery vendor, and Paco who wants to sell his pig, look! even the pig hates rain. If you're from Havana you don't want raindrops falling on your head. You run! You run when it's raining. Even when they're at the beach, Habaneros and Habaneras, the minute it starts to rain, they run out of the water and stand under an umbrella.

Do you think he makes it up as he goes? For a while I thought today's reading would end with the word *carajo.* Remember when the mother shouted "*carajo*" at her daughter and Umbertico lost his voice? And he kept spilling glasses of water on the seamstresses in the first row. I thought it would end there. He's so clumsy.

Then Umbertico Barrios said he was going to get a job reading in another dress factory. He won't get anywhere thinking *coño* and saying *carajo* and spilling ice water. Look at those black clouds! How can you see black clouds in the night? I can! What are you thinking about? Making love with Tommy Atkins. Oh Tommy! *¡Loca!* What wouldn't I do to go to Miami and be with Tommy Atkins!

That we will go to Miami, there is no certainty.

"Their character changes with the light. They are brisk and sharp on sunny blue and white mornings, ancient and tragic when veils of rain stream from the balconies; voluptuous when a hot midnight is illuminated by lamps and vibrates with guitar music and the muffled heartbeat of an African drum.

Juliet Barclay, *Havana: Portrait of a City*

B Y TEN PM, ON NEW YEAR'S EVE, Daisy's husband, George Atkins, had already had too much to drink. Alcohol brought out his mean streak. Among other things he said he worked hard, made a lot of money, and could do whatever he goddamn pleased. Why would he have to limit himself to one woman when there were ten *gordas* out there standing in line for him? He worked hard and deserved his rewards. Daisy was upstairs putting Beverly and Herman to sleep while he said all those things.

Rebecca, who had had quite a bit of wine, kept saying, "I haven't felt this relaxed in ages!"

The New Year's Eve party was at Rebecca's and Tommy's. They had invited several couples with their children. By ten PM the youngest kids were getting sleepy, but the older ones planned to wait until way past midnight. The pre-pubescent girls—which included Daisy's eldest, the beautiful Sylvia, Hazel's twins, Hannah and Sally, Sarah's middle one, Ashley, and Conchita's daughter Belinda—were sprawled out in the family room either listening to Coolio and Seal, playing Jenga, or watching videos. As to Nell, she was roaming around with her best friend, Jessica Fish.

All through dinner Tommy had an endless *tête-à-tête* with Roger, Sarah's husband. Very recently, Roger had decided to give up practicing law to go into politics. His wife, Sarah, was a judge. The Nemeroffs lived nearby, on Pine Tree Drive.

Rebecca said again, "I haven't been this relaxed in ages."

After dinner Rebecca suggested that everyone adjourn to the living room and come back to the table for dessert later, after midnight. Tommy and Roger stood up and just kept on talking all the way to the bar. Harvey and Helen

Atkins sat in front of Dr. Stanley Fish the dentist, and Conchita, his wife. Daisy was coming down the stairs. Hazel and Bob were admiring everything in Tommy's and Rebecca's house, Hazel being an interior decorator and Bob a psychiatrist.

Rebecca was busy being the hostess; she was traipsing from the dining room, to the kitchen, to the living room, serving drinks, choosing CDs, making sure no one was sitting alone bored and ignored. She had also invited Selene Machado who came all by herself because she was having big marital problems. And since Selene was a very attractive woman with green eyes, black hair, great hands and a fabulous figure, George Atkins was all stirred up.

The minute he saw Daisy coming down the stairs George started to brag about all his sexual conquests and adventures right in front of her, but Daisy ignored him in a fury, so he had to look around for another victim, and chose Tommy. Immediately he told Selene, who was the only person listening to him, that he didn't know about letting Tommy become his partner in the business, you never know, first he runs into a little trouble and it could be downhill all the way. George hiccupped and laughed at his own thoughts. "First he runs into a little trouble . . ." George repeated. "Loses his business . . . and now he wants to take over my business." But then he immediately stopped being serious and said that they would have to spend all the money they made buying dresses for Nell at Miami Tent and Awning.

"Huh? Tommy!" he interrupted Tommy's endless conversation with Roger. "Don't you get all of Nell's clothes at Miami Tent and Awning? Ha, ha!" Then he turned to Selene again and said, "Now I know! Señor Father wants him to be president of the company so he can afford Miami Tent and Awning!" then he turned to Harvey and shouted, "Your wife should shop there too, Harv! You listening to me old man?" Then he demanded different music. Who's Zooming Who? Louder. "So my Nelly niece is already ten?" George shouted at Nell when she passed by on the way to the kitchen. "Going for the leftovers, Nelly? How time flies! Just the other day she only weighed six pounds and look at her now! Poor Tommy! Soon there will be twenty boys at his doorstep." Tommy heard; he momentarily stopped speaking to Roger and commented, "I sure won't have to worry about boys if she keeps on gaining weight. On the contrary I'll have to bring them here at gunpoint."

"Except that you'll be too broke to buy a gun!" George said and found this so funny that he just couldn't stop laughing.

Ana Daisy finally told George he was being a real asshole ("*comemierda*" was her word). He didn't pay any attention and started saying that men work to make money so their wives can buy books and spend the day reading. Then he said, "Hey! I just heard the sound of my own voice and I find myself quite clever!" He guffawed. He carried on. And where would the publishing business be were it not for lawyers, doctors and rich men's wives? "What do you think, Bob?" Men, after all, only buy paperbacks . . . they don't spend their afternoons browsing in bookstores. They buy paperbacks at the Publix Market! (By now Ana Daisy was really angry—"*encabronada*" was the word she used to describe how she felt). "Could we have the Trío Los Panchos so I can dance with Selene?" George demanded.

Rebecca and Daisy were taking dishes back to the kitchen. Daisy whispered, "Sometimes I hate him so much!"

"I'm relaxed tonight, teehee! and hey, maybe he's right," said Rebecca as she opened the cabinet underneath the kitchen sink and pulled out the trash can. She giggled some more.

Nell was at the kitchen table eating Key Lime pie.

Ana Daisy protested, "Right about what? Men not reading? Gimme a break. He's such an ass, I swear. I don't know why he's saying such an indecent *macho* thing since I work and I make a decent amount of money. He's probably about to fall in love with some *americanita* who doesn't work and spends her time browsing in the bookstores. Becky, what are you laughing about? This does not go with your personality."

Rebecca talked while she emptied dishfuls of empty stone crab shells and lobster carcasses in the trash can. "I think he was referring to me. George is convinced that I spend my days reading while Tommy's working fourteen hours a day in West East Jesus Palm Beach and plotting to take over the family business. Pass me that rice. And he's right, lately I do spend my days reading. This is changing the subject but Daisita, if I were you I wouldn't even consider the possibility of George falling in love with someone else again. It's bad luck. You can cover that with Saran Wrap, right behind you. Ask Yemaya *que te quite lo malo*. And anyway didn't George promise his Señora Madre that it would never happen again?"

Rebecca opened the dishwasher.

"Are you putting the Mexican plates in there?" Daisy asked. "Are you drunk?"

"No, I'm washing those by hand. Give me those other ones."

"Here you are," Daisy said while handing her the other ones. "You know George's really pissed about Señor Father wanting Tommy to be president of the company. Do you think it's fair? After all George has so much more experience and you have to admit that Tommy did run into a little trouble and lost his business," Daisy insinuated.

Rebecca, who was rinsing dishes said suddenly, "I know he lost his business. It's no use repeating it every time you see me. Anyway, it happens to be Señor Padre's company and it's up to him. If he wants Tommy to be president . . ."

"He'll probably lose the family business too," Daisy whispered before saying in a louder voice, "I'll be right back with some more dishes and food."

In turn, Rebecca whispered, "I know he lost his business . . ." Her lip quivered, then suddenly she caught a whiff of something, something that reminded her of all those years they spent running the club. What was that smell? She kept sniffing. Trying to sort it out, catch it again.

Oh, that smell, it was her.

It wasn't until late in 1984 that Rebecca decided to get pregnant. She was going to turn thirty in 1985 and thirty seemed so old, almost pre-menopausal. By February she was pregnant, but life went on just as before. They'd spend five nights a week managing the club, they'd sleep until noon or one, she drank a little less, she never once snorted cocaine while she was pregnant, but she did smoke a pack of Marlboros a day. They never talked about her pregnancy, but she thought he was as curious and as eager as she was, mostly curious, and she never suspected that anything would change in their relationship.

Nell was born in November of 1985. Suddenly Daisy's predictions came true. She was at home with her newborn, her episiotomy, and her hemorrhoids. Tommy went on with life as usual, except that he began coming home later and later each morning. He even stayed out those nights when the club was closed. When he got home she could smell Joy, 1000, Arpege, Shalimar, Opium, Poison, and Yves Saint Laurent's Rive Gauche. To make matters worse Rebecca lost the diamond ring he had given her.

One day when Nell was around five months old Rebecca finally asked, "Tommy, are you screwing around?"

"I sure am!"

"Why?"

"You figure it out."

If she stopped nursing Nell that very same evening it was because she was too drunk to breastfeed. Since they didn't have a nanny, Tommy had to cancel his engagements and stay at home. He went to the Publix Market, he purchased a few cans of baby formula and fed Nell for the first time. He even had to change her. For two days Rebecca was locked up in the bathroom, sitting on the floor, crying. Every few hours Tommy would knock on the door and ask, "Rebecca, are you still in there?"

"I am!"

Forty-eight hours later she opened the bathroom door and said, "I'm better."

Rebecca spent the next six months reading novels and feeding the baby. Sometimes they'd go through four jars in one sitting. While she read she'd spoonfeed the baby without even looking. She'd wake up, grab her book, fill the bottle, open the jar of baby food . . . The baby seemed to be doing all the eating for her, since she hardly ate and she smoked cigarette after cigarette while she read and fed Nell. One day Tommy came home smelling of Magie Noire, the next of Je Reviens, of Charlie, and after that of First, all this while Rebecca read, lost weight, fed the baby.

Then one night Tommy came home at eleven. "What's the matter?" she asked.

"Rebecca," he said, in Spanish, he said Rebecca in Spanish, he had not said it for a long time.

Standing there, putting the dishes in the dishwasher, Rebecca was just about to relive that moment so many years ago when Tommy and she became friends again. But the past disappeared like a spook the minute Daisy said, "Why do I defend George? He's such a jerk! Do you want to put the silver in there?"

Rebecca said, "Yep!"

"There you go. Who knows? If it weren't for the children—and just in case you haven't noticed, I get pregnant every three years to save the marriage—we'd probably have split up long ago. Sometimes I have the feeling that George is the type of guy who'll wait till the children are in college. Beverly's only six and Coleman's almost three so we got a ways to go . . . You'll see. You're right, I shouldn't even think about it. What's more I don't even know why I hang on to him, he makes me suffer, that's all he does. *Te lo juro que me hace sufrir, Rebecca.*"

"Thanks Helen," Rebecca said. Her other sister-in-law was bringing food back into the kitchen.

"George is about to take his pants off and show everyone his butt," said Helen.

Both Daisy and Rebecca shrugged.

As soon as Helen left Rebecca said, "Daisy, I just got a fantastic idea! Remember that invitation I wrote and never sent? When I wanted *las old girl-friends* here every Friday for a *tertulia* to talk and to rock and you said we needed a reason? With what George was saying about women reading I just found the reason! Let's start a reading group! We'll pick a book, get a bunch of us superficial useless bored rich men's wives together and meet, let's say one afternoon a week! That's how we can get all *las girlfriends* to come regularly! And we can even get new girlfriends! Even *americanas* like Hazel and Sarah! *¿Qué tú crees?* These days it's really fashionable to belong to a reading group. A lot of women are doing this instead of . . . instead of . . ."

"Doing lunch after the shoe sale, having lovers, and getting divorced," Daisy finished her sentence.

"I hate it when you finish my sentences and especially when you say something I would never say. Anyway, it sure would take my mind off Tommy. Since he lost his business and got a real job, I don't see him any more."

"By the way how's your father?"

"I spent the morning with him today. So what do you think about the reading group? Will you come?"

Rebecca poured the Cascade in the dishwasher, closed it, then walked over to some leftovers that Helen had just put on the kitchen table. Daisy took a *croqueta* and ate it while she nodded and moaned "un-hunh," meaning that she was all for the reading group.

"What kind of book will we read?" Daisy asked. "A long one?"

"I don't know. How many rocking chairs should I buy? Because I'm still getting rocking chairs for everyone."

"That's it! I'm full!" Nell said and stood up.

"Sweetheart, did you get enough to eat?" Rebecca asked, then she turned to Daisy and said, "Let's put that stuff away too. I don't want to leave Norma with such a big mess. We could ask Helen if she wants to be in the reading group, Hazel, Sarah, Selene Machado who's probably dancing with your husband now, *¡echa más champán amigo!* God, *Trío los Panchos me emputece!*" Rebecca laughed. "And we could ask Trudi Agramonte, and Lucy whenever she's not traveling the world, Annie if she's willing, but you know how busy she is . . . We could also ask Silka, poor Silka! *¡ay m'ija la pobrecita!* and Nancy . . . And we could ask Conchita, of course . . ."

"And Priscilla Drake," Daisy suggested.

Rebecca shrugged.

Helen walked in and said, loudly, "I think George is going to fuck Selene in front of everyone if we don't stop him."

"She's my age, he won't fuck her," said Daisy casually. Then Tommy walked in and said, "Rebecca" (in Spanish, he said Rebecca in Spanish), "why are you in here doing dishes?"

"I'll be right out, I swear. Please deal with George or he'll ruin the whole evening. Daisy, will you hand me the Mexican dishes? Oh, and Tommy! Take the Trío los Panchos off *porque me emputece* and I want to dance with you. Put Lucía's CD on. Please, Tommy, deal with George!"

"Ok. Any idea where Jimmy is?"

Daisy said, "Isn't he at Señora Madre's?"

"Yeah," Rebecca said. "She was going to buy him a new set of golf clubs so he's probably there still kissing her thank you. *¡Gracias abuelita linda!*"

"Rebecca, you're drunk!" said Daisy.

"I'll tell Harvey to call Mom and make sure. And Rebecca," Tommy said in Spanish, he said Rebecca in Spanish, "I'm going upstairs to bed if you're not out there in ten minutes. And you've got to entertain Hazel and Bob, they look bored."

After Tommy disappeared Rebecca said to Daisy, "First I'll buy five rocking chairs, we'll pick a book, invite everyone and we'll try it once! Just to see if we enjoy it, if we don't, we'll bag it and I'll have five new rocking chairs, but if we do enjoy it, we'll get together once a week or whenever's convenient. And I can buy more rocking chairs!"

"Ok," Daisy said. "Let's do it. And we could also ask Jenny Rincón if she want to join us . . ."

"Huh! Whatever you pick will probably offend her. It won't be feminist enough. Pass me that last dish," said Rebecca. "Oh and I'd also like to ask my cousin Alma to join us, it would probably do her good."

"Did I tell you I saw her the other day?" asked Daisy while she pulled up her stockings, scratched her belly, then adjusted her earrings and her emerald necklace. "You wouldn't believe how down she was! And I just flat out asked her, *Why did you marry poor?* She said she couldn't believe she'd made a mistake again. Alma's a mixture of upbeat and depressed, which is bad news. Those are precisely the people who do crazy things."

"Yes, Doctora Daisy."

"I happen to be in management, *m'ija,* I spend the day looking for money and it's just like being a psychiatrist or a priest. And I'm not kidding about

Alma and I pray to God that I'm wrong, you should too, she's . . . how would I put it? She can't forgive herself for not having some kind of great life right now. She went to see me for a job and I know she can be extremely upbeat but you can't emit bad vibes when you're in sales. Is she still self-medicating?"

"Probably," Rebecca said. "My mom and her mom have no problems getting drugs without a prescription on Calle Ocho."

"So you pick a book, and I'll call everyone and set a date. *¿Qué tú crees?*"

"Come to think of it I'll buy six rocking chairs," Rebecca said before turning to the kitchen door and yelling, "Oh my God!"

Daisy looked and then it was her turn to yell, "Oh my God!"

Then Rebecca asked frantically, "Jimmy, what's the matter with you?"

He looked at her then fell, then he started crawling on the kitchen floor, moaning.

Jimmy was Harvey's sixteen-year-old son. At that time in his life when all Harvey did was get in trouble, he'd gotten a fourteen-year-old girl pregnant, and Jimmy was the product. Jimmy lived in Oregon but was staying at Tommy's and Rebecca's for the holidays since he couldn't get along with Helen.

Rebecca repeated her question over and over again, "What happened Jimmy? Are you on drugs? Tell me what happened, Jimmy!" then she looked at Daisy and said, "Get Harvey and Tommy!" then she turned to Jimmy and asked again, "What happened, Jimmy?"

He moaned, "I took Señora Madre's vitamin C."

"What's wrong?" Tommy asked.

"He took your mom's vitamin C!"

"Oh fuck!"

"Shit, what's wrong?" Harvey asked.

"He took Mom's quaaludes thinking they were vitamin C. You know how she loves to hide her drugs in vitamin bottles and pretend she's taking vitamins. We've got to get him to Mount Sinai we'll swing by Mom's first and get that bottle of vitamin C. Jimmy! How many did you take, Jimmy?"

"I dunno, five six seven eight . . ."

"We're outta here!"

"He'll be all right," Daisy said after they left.

"Probably. Let's go join the others and pretend nothing's happened."

As they walked back into the living room Rebecca was asking Daisy, "Wicker or Mission rocking chairs?"

REBECCA CAME UP WITH THE IDEA of starting a reading club on New Year's Eve. On January 2, after making soup for Jimmy, who was still feeling terrible after having gotten his stomach pumped, Rebecca went to Books & Books on Lincoln Road to look for a book. She got so absorbed by her browsing that when she looked at her watch she gasped. It was time to pick Nell up at Conchita's on North Bay Road.

Conchita and Rebecca had been pregnant at practically the same time, they had given birth a few weeks apart, they'd both had girls, and as it turned out Nell and Jessica were best friends who had sworn eternal friendship to each other.

Rebecca returned to Books & Books on Wednesday January 3 when Nell was back at school. Apparently Daisy had already started calling everyone. Annie couldn't come and Hazel and Sarah didn't want to commit, but she had gotten four definite yesses so far. Even Lucy, the famous Lucía, thought it was a great idea. She was so sorry she couldn't come! But Silka said she'd love to come and that she could arrange for her nurse to drive her over in the van. "Poor Silka!" Ana Daisy exclaimed. "*La pobrecita* in that wheelchair!"

Conchita had serious qualms about this whole idea. Ever since she had started needing glasses to read, Conchita had quit reading. She thought that reading glasses were a sign of old age and slipping them on your nose a surly reminder that you were over the hill, so she flat out refused to read any more.

"It's like shaving your hair off to hide the gray!" Rebecca exclaimed.

"I've never heard anything as silly in my life! *¡M'ija estás loca!* If you don't read it's your brain's that's going to age! Oh come on! *¡Anda!*" Ana Daisy insisted.

"Let me think about it," Conchita said to Rebecca when she went to pick up Nell.

"Okay," Conchita finally agreed that evening when she was on the phone with Rebecca. "But I'm not bringing my glasses. Becky, will you read to me?"

So Daisy told Rebecca to go ahead and get a dozen books of her choice, had she already chosen something? No. When was she going to choose? Today. If there were any copies in large print maybe she could get one for Conchita so she didn't have to hold the book two yards away.

Not only has Conchita quit reading but she's also quit wearing a watch because of this lousy vision nonsense. Now she has absolutely no sense of time, or goes by her own, which amounts to the same thing. Guess what? Lucy said she'd come once! The famous Lucía is going to join us!

Rebecca said she was off to Books & Books, she had asked around to get everyone's opinion. Everybody prefers a long book, not too introspective, not too long either, interesting enough to be just as long as it's interesting, not too much book for too little a subject or too much of a subject for too little a book. A book that really cares about the reader and not just some brilliant author showing us how brilliant he is. Everyone's read enough of those authors. Something you want to come back to and that stays with you. That's what the quorum wants. Oh, and everyone's read Jose Martí, a whole bunch of Latinos and Latinas, Charles Dickens, Tolstoy, Dostoievsky. No one wants to re-read *Madame Bovary, Lady Chatterley, Jane Eyre,* or *Pride and Prejudice.* Camilo Jose Cela is out of the question, for he seems to be the most morbid and depressing author in the world, and anything remotely like him is out of the question too. Everyone is willing to read or re-read Jorge Luis Borges except for Jenny Rincón, who's convinced he's a woman hater and Trudi Agramonte who thinks he's too heavy and doesn't have time for that kind of thing.

All the girls agree that they want a book they can really get into and that will amuse and entertain them and change their lives forever. They want a book that becomes real, and that they can carry around with them wherever they go, either physically or in their minds, a book that they'll read while they're standing in line with a number at the deli or in the waiting room at the plastic surgeon's or just sitting poolside enjoying nice weather in Miami while it lasts.

A book that will make them forget the heat once it gets too hot, and the air conditioning that's always too cold, as a matter of fact they'd love a book that will transport them away from the eternal summer of air conditioning when they're feeling trapped.

They either want an imaginary book based on fact, or a factual book based on imagination, or both. But they also want a book long enough and interesting enough to take then from here to the end of summer, preferably in several different volumes (but one volume will do) with live characters preferably very tormented and passionate and profound, but not depressing or morbid. The only one interested in a morbid story is Alma, who can't stop reading biographies of Sylvia Plath and Anne Sexton. "Something weird's up with

Alma. *Ella no está bien,*" Daisy said to everyone she talked to. "I have the feeling she's going to do something awful."

"Oh course she isn't," Rebecca retorted. "She has two lovely children."

"So did Sylvia Plath! *Tú veras,* you'll see, I'm in management, I'm always looking for money, so I *know* people," Ana Daisy insisted.

Which reminded her, Friday late in the afternoon was the best time to meet. Ana Daisy had slow Fridays, Rebecca didn't have to worry about picking up Nell because *Señora Madre* did, and everyone else didn't have to do a specific thing that day. Friday, between five and six, everyone agreed.

THE NEXT DAY WAS THURSDAY, SO Rebecca asked Conchita to pick Nell up at school when she went to get Jessica and Belinda, that way she could take as much time as she needed to find a book.

She was at the Lincoln Road Mall book store at ten-thirty AM just when it opened. To the right of the entrance were the Florida and the Cuba books, picture books of Miami Beach in the fifties, books with great photos of Havana before Fidel, how a Cuban cigar is made in full color, tobacco vs. sugar or mulatto vs. white? Tobacco always being brown and the whole point of sugar being the lightening or purification of sugar. Sugar! *¡Azúcar!* The Everglades, the paradise that never was, should we save a stinky ugly slimy swamp? or, Why nobody likes the Everglades. Old Marjorie Stoneham Douglas books, President Clinton once mentioned her, she was a Florida specialist who discovered the beauty of the rivers of grass in the Everglades but admitted that she never spent much time there. *Victorian Florida, My Love Affair with Miami, Lemon City, Ybor City Cookbook, The New Latino Cookbook,* Silka's father's books, Miami Beach in the seventies when it was a dying city and when Rebecca and all her girlfriends were about to graduate from high school, that's when Alice Cooper was singing, "I'm Eighteen!," James Taylor was everyone's friend, Carole King felt the earth move under her feet, Carly Simon was dying of anticipation, weird things were happening in the Court of the Crimson King and everyone was saying good-bye to Miss American Pie. They went on a field trip to the Everglades and Rebecca saw old macaroni and cheese under a very yellow heat lamp, the food had a crack of dryness right down the middle of it, who's that person?

There was this incredibly angry person staring at her and waving a book at her. You're not supposed to stare so she couldn't just raise her head and look at that person in the eye, but from her vantage point she could see the person's arm, what book did that person choose? What book was that person waving at her? It seemed like one of those blank books. Then there was a loud little girl saying bad words. What foul language! And a cripple who rushed toward the person waving the book and grabbed it. Those two started to struggle while the little girl kept on saying bad words. What book were these two weird people fighting about, and were there others on the shelf? Was one of them the author? The angry one went to talk to one of the salespeople and waved the book around while talking. Rebecca moved closer. The cripple ran out of the bookstore followed by the foul-mouthed little girl.

"I could put a few of these in the front," Rebecca overheard the salesperson saying.

"I want to see it with my own eyes," said the angry one. Rebecca caught sight of the book but couldn't quite read the title at this distance. The person put the book back and stomped out of the bookstore making a lot of noise and also making it look as if quite a number of books had fallen down accidentally. Immediately Rebecca walked to the book shelf and counted five copies.

"I'd like to order a few more copies of this book," said Rebecca over by the cashier. "Who was that person who just walked out? The author?"

"No. This novel was written by some woman using the pseudonym of Trish Izquierdo, and that was one of her characters. So far we've only sold one copy, so we have quite a few signed copies in the back, how many do you want?"

"Do you have any in large print?"

The salesperson seemed surprised, as if she'd just asked for large print on a blank book, the salesperson seemed that surprised.

"If you don't have large print make it seven more."

"I'll bring them right out," said the salesperson, staring at Rebecca as if she were just plain mad.

Rebecca drove home with twelve copies of this unknown novel written by this unknown author whose characters seemed to get out of hand. *Playing with Light* was the title.

She drove straight to North Bay Road and as she got out of the car she waved the book at Conchita who was standing outside. "I got it," she said. "Let's start. Let's start the book. I can't wait!"

So Rebecca sat down to read the first chapter out loud to her friend Conchita. She did give Conchita a book, though, and told her to open it, in case she got tired of listening and wanted to put her glasses on and follow with her eyes once in a while.

"The novel we're about to read begins on the next page," Rebecca said.

> "Reading in the shops has begun for the first time among us . . .
> This constitutes a giant step in the march of progress and the
> general advance of the workers, since in this way they will grad-
> ually become familiar with books . . ."

Jose Antonio Portuondo
*La Aurora y los comienzos de la
prensa y de la organización en Cuba*

AFTER BEING SULLIED by Protestant worship during the brief occupation of Havana by the British, the old church of Santa María de la Luz, on Calle Aguacate between Calles Sol and Luz, was never again used as a church, becoming instead a chocolate factory and afterward a dress factory. *Moda Titania, la más Parisienne del mundo.* Titania Fashions, the most Parisian in the world.

The original entrance to the church had been condemned after the British left one hundred years before this story begins, and the new entrance to the factory was a wide arch through which fabric-laden horse-drawn carriages could pass by. Each evening they unloaded their goods in the courtyard. A heavy wooden door lined with panels of stained glass (which are called *luc-etas* in Spanish) was the entrance to the factory. Above the door was a semi-circular fanlight window which saturated the floors with shifting fans of carmine and azure light. Inside, hardly anything was reminiscent of the building's religious past, the place was busy and noisy. There were rows of tables and chairs where the seamstresses worked shoulder to shoulder. The old pulpit remained intact.

Don Gabriel María, the owner, had spent years looking for the perfect Reader and had never found one. He wanted someone who would read the entire day and take very short breaks to drink either cane juice or ice water and coffee, or to smoke, someone who would read until the church bells from all of Havana's churches rang six times. To be truthful, Don Gabriel María wanted to emulate González y Gutiérrez Fashions, his competitor.

It was rumored that very often at González y Gutiérrez the novel got so interesting that both Reader and listeners would disregard the bells and stay on. This was almost too good to be true! Don Gabriel María searched far and wide, he asked the lottery vendor, the greengrocer, the cane cutter, the liberated slave, the Negro woman with the basket on her head, the tavern keeper, the librarian, the cockfighter, "The perfect Reader, do you know him?"

The only answer he ever got was, "Huh?"

Titania Fashions was owned by the Santa Cruz family, who lived in a mansion a couple of blocks away on the corner of Calles Obra Pía and Aguacate. It was hard to believe that such an anxious and hysterical family lived behind the unassuming walls that gave out to both streets. It was breathtaking inside. The place was so gorgeous it was almost unbearable. You hardly knew what to look at or what to touch, it was exquisite. But one couldn't possibly imagine that something as splendid as this existed just from looking at the yellow stucco and at the many windows with the ornate bars and the curtains made of a material too heavy to flutter in the wind.

The front gate, through which everyone came (gentlemen, ladies, scissorsgrinders, prostitutes, beggars, interior decorators, greengrocers, hairdressers, liberated slaves, servants), was solid mahogany. It was heavy and noisy when slammed shut and beautiful with a complicated lock that had apparently had the most ornate of keys. As a matter of fact the Santa Cruz family still regretted having lost that key. They were perpetually looking for it.

Although the escutcheons of the family could be seen right above the door, the Santa Cruz family was not yet in possession of a title. They'd adopted the Santa Cruz name three generations ago and were still asking the Spanish crown for a title. In the meantime they'd had the Santa Cruz escutcheon engraved in the stone.

The house was built on two main floors. It had covered walkways, better known as *portales,* on both floors, and, once again, the arms of the family blazoned over each interior door. Every single member of the family loved to live here and that's the one point where they agreed, otherwise they were always arguing with each other.

Each relative seemed to either hate or envy the other relatives and always thought they were to blame for anything bad that happened. But they all agreed that La Casa Amarilla, The Yellow House, was a great house.

It had cool spacious rooms ranged around galleries and overlooking two different courtyards. Between the ground and the first floor was an *entresol,* where slaves used to live until the family discontinued using slaves, and where the servants now lived. The majority of these servants were either former slaves or the children of slaves working in the sugar cane plantations not too distant from the city.

There were also offices on the *entresol*. It so happens that each generation of the Santa Cruz family had produced at least one serious, hard-working money-maker.

Throughout the rest of the house there were elaborately carved window frames and banisters. The main purpose of the slatted doors and shutters was to keep out the sun, or to let it in with moderation, but they weren't only practical, they were also excessively pretty and a lot of fun to play with and touch. You could have the sunlight come in any way you wanted. On the floor, against the wall, in someone's eye . . . The half doors were marvelous too, and, once again, there were a thousand different ways to play with them.

This house had been built on a grand scale just when the Santa Cruz family was expecting a title "any day now" (that was eighty years ago). But, title or no title, the family used to entertain lavishly. There was a time when they considered themselves to be one of Cuba's oldest and most powerful families and behaved accordingly, as if they owned the whole island.

The main structure of their house dates from the seventeenth century. Soon after it was built it was remodelled in the baroque style. Then Don Gabriel María Cardenas y Santa Cruz invested 11,863 pesos beautifying it. He kept repeating as loudly as he could that he wanted the best, the very best, and that money was not an issue. He wanted class at any price. By the time he was through redecorating the house, everywhere you turned there was an obese cherub.

Don Gabriel María Cardenas y Santa Cruz was born a Spaniard, like most of the white people who lived in Havana *intramuros*. Indeed, this part of the city continued to be referred to as *intramuros* by its inhabitants although most of the walls had been torn down by 1850.

At the time of his death, Don Gabriel María Cardenas y Santa Cruz's life was a mixture of discouragement and confusion. He had been asking the Spanish crown for a title for the past twenty years. His contribution to the fashion in Cuba was extraordinary. He dressed the ladies of the highest classes, as well as the servants and the prostitutes (he said he didn't care where the money came from).

Of course the rich ladies imported their ball gowns and wedding dresses from Paris, but Don Gabriel María's genius had focused on the clothes that they wore every day, when looking good was still important. Don Gabriel María himself had determined what the ladies should wear to go to the store. He'd told them what to wear for the afternoon drive. And he'd even designed a comfortable stylish dress for the house, where the ladies spent most of their time.

He'd even created a dress he called "the *tertulia* gown," a little shorter than most gowns, with the skirt cut in a way so that it wouldn't get caught under the rocking chair.

Habaneras had these get-togethers called *tertulias* every single day at three PM. This was the highlight of many a woman's existence so she'd usually begin getting everything ready after breakfast. The little ham sandwiches demanded hours of preparation. Everyone wanted the fat trimmed off the ham as well as the whitest softest bread with no suspicion of crust whatsoever.

Once the food was under control it was time to rearrange the furniture in the living room. Two or three rows of rocking chairs were arranged, depending on the number of guests expected.

Since none of these ladies had a busy life, they'd usually arrive on time. The most talkative ones would immediately go for the *sillones* (rockers) in the middle while the quieter ladies were relegated to those on the periphery. The maid would then bring in *el cafecito*[1], *los bocaditos*[2], *los pastelitos*[3], and *el agua fría,* the ice water, as cold as possible. Before you knew it all the ladies were rocking and gossiping, some even smoked *puros*[4].

All Cubans had a particular attachment to rocking chairs. From the moment of birth the talcum-powdered Cuban baby was rushed to the rocking chair to be rocked to dizzy slumber. It was on a rocking chair that he would spend the next five years of his life.

When he wasn't sleeping in his crib, or being covered with talcum powder, or being force-fed in the kitchen, the Cuban baby was on someone's lap being rocked. This rocking life went on until the child was old enough and reasonable enough to sit and rock by himself, with no danger of toppling backwards or forwards.

Although the boys stopped rocking at around age thirteen, the girls kept on doing so throughout their lives, they were expert rockers, just as they were experts in the art of handling the fan.

They rocked while they sewed, they rocked while they talked, while they drank coffee and smoked, and while the church bells rang (which was always). And once they became shriveled up *viejitas*[5] who could barely walk, they'd be carried to their rocking chair next to the window the minute the woke up and they'd spend the whole day there drinking *cafe con leche*[6], rocking and complaining. This is the story of many many *cubanas.*

Don Gabriel María was well aware of these habits and had therefore created a shorter skirt so the lady wouldn't accidentally rock on the fabric and ruin it forever. For although party dresses were worn only once, a *tertulia* gown could be worn until the lady decided to pass it on to her servant.

Yes, indeed, Don Gabriel María also dressed the middle-class ladies. And even the liberated slaves and the lower classes (*la gente chusma*). He bragged that he was dressing all of Havana regardless of class and that if this didn't get him a title he'd move to the United States and become a Protestant. Just the thought of it made his nose turn red. *Coño*[7], he deserved a title of nobility more than anyone! For having demurred so long the Spanish crown was unjust, heartless, and unfair! His grandfather before him had already adopted the name Santa Cruz in hopes of expediting this wonderful event. But it never happened, *¡coño!* Generation after generation had died without becoming aristocrats. And this was not fair, *¡carajo!*[8]

"I do not want to be a book worm. If its book is taken away from it, the little blind head is raised; it wags, hovers, terribly uneasy, in a void—until it begins to burrow again."

Katherine Mansfield

"WHY'D YOU STOP READING, BECKY?"

Rebecca was muttering to herself, "What are these *numbers?*" and quickly turning the pages of the book until she got to a passage that said:

The numbers refer to notes that can be found in the end of the book. The author is planning to put these notes all over the place. What's more, the author will translate every single Spanish word in the text. This is a classical historical novel based on imaginary fact. Everything in it is true, including the author's exaggerations. The imaginary bibliography at the end will prove that nothing but the truth is being told and that all the characters, male or female, either have or could have existed once.

Conchita asked again, "Why'd you stop reading to me, Becky?"

"Mom, what's for dinner tonight?" Nell asked.

"Why don't you girls go check on the new kittens?" Conchita suggested. She then turned to Rebecca. "Was that the end of Chapter One?"

"Un-hunh."

"It ended with a bad word? Is *that* a way to end a chapter? Who's the author?"

"Some Cuban woman from New Jersey," Rebecca mumbled while reading the footnotes to herself. "But raised here."

"Is she our age or younger? Did she go to our school?"

"No. She went to Ransom-Everglades," Rebecca said.

"Let me tell you about my plans. I went today and Dr. Weinberger said he'd perform the surgery in the summer while the girls are at camp. Are you leaving already?"

Rebecca had just stood up. She retrieved her sandals from underneath the couch, and slipped her feet back into them. After searching in her bag she said, "I guess I left my keys in the car."

"Are we meeting tomorrow?"

"It'll have to be next Friday because no one can make it tomorrow."

"So you'll read me Chapter Two on Wednesday when we go pick the girls up?"

"Un-hunh, *ciao*. Nell! We're going!" Rebecca yelled as she kissed Conchita on both cheeks.

"What can we see, read, acquire, but ourselves?"

Ralph Waldo Emerson

IF THERE WAS SOMETHING THAT USED TO BOTHER Conchita, Rebecca thought, it was hearing people say, "Conchita Fish . . . Is that name for real?" And how could she possibly be Cuban with a last name like Fish? Oh! She married a Fish. Well that explains it! And her maiden name is Pérez. Conchita Pérez, that's more like it!

But wait! Something else used to bother Conchita, Rebecca just remembered, and this something else was being thought of as Cuban. Her name could very well be Conchita Pérez, but she happened to be French. She wasn't Cuban at all! She was French. One hundred percent. Her parents fled France during the war to escape persecution and ended up in Cuba, where she was born. It used to infuriate Conchita when people said that she couldn't possibly be French with a name like Conchita Pérez. For many years it made her scream. She'd yell it out loud, she'd insist, she'd pout. She was French, ¡carajo!

Conchita's French is terrible. Rebecca remembered how Conchita used to love to read Racine out loud and was convinced that her pronunciation was perfect. When Rebecca met her in first grade in the Academy of the Assumption right away Conchita said that she spoke French at home.

Rebecca rocked harder. Just trying out one of the four new rocking chairs she'd bought.

Then the family went to France one summer. Conchita looked forward to it all year. Speaking French. Being French. Rebecca chuckled. She knew her friend so well.

But when she finally arrived in France she realized she didn't speak French! She was only ten and this felt like the worst of humiliations. (Conchita did confess this to Rebecca years later, when it didn't matter any more.)

But the next few years of Conchita's life were spent with this obsession. She wanted to be French and to speak French like a native. It caused her so much grief, and there seemed to be no cure for it.

Then Conchita discovered mathematics and outgrew her obsession with being French.

Then she outgrew mathematics.

Rebecca stopped rocking, got up, and proceeded to test-rock rocking chair number two. The first one had passed the test, it rocked powerfully and smoothly.

Now Conchita keeps wondering, Can she possibly outgrow her latest obsession? She stops to think, then laughs. When you're obsessed about getting old, can you possibly outgrow that obsession?

It was never this bad. This is by far the obsession that's caused her the most grief. This business about needing glasses to see things that are near . . . It's not funny.

Conchita is quite eager to be part of this reading group, after all, reading groups have become so fashionable! and she has derived great pleasure out of reading all her life, but when it comes down to choosing between reading and accepting old age, it's the reading that has to go. A few months ago she even gave up on telling time, for the same reason. Rebecca suggested that she trade her Rolex in for a Swiss Army watch.

They were supposed to meet at noon on Wednesday January 10 to read Chapter Two together. And just because Conchita refused to look at her watch she arrived at half past two thinking it was noon.

Rebecca was quite annoyed. "I've been waiting for two hours! *¿Tú crees que yo no tengo más nada que hacer?*" she asked and immediately realized that she sounded like her mom. "It's too late now! We have to pick the girls up!" she shrugged.

"*¡Anda chica no te pongas bravita!* I can't see my watch!" Conchita coaxed. What if they took the same car? Rebecca could read Chapter Two and Conchita would drive. "*Mea culpa!*" said Conchita. "*¡Vamos!*"

Rebecca and Conchita are in the car reading chapter two. The girls attend the exclusive Gertrude Marie Paige School in Coconut Grove so they have quite a ways to go. Sometimes Rebecca says that her life consists of driving Nell around. They're on the causeway, she's reading aloud. They're on the expressway going downtown, she's reading. The downtown Miami skyline is on their left. Pretty soon they will pass the exit for Key Biscayne, and they just keep on going, until the expressway ends and becomes South Dixie Highway.

She continues reading in the school parking lot while they are waiting for the girls, she continues reading while they're driving Belinda to basketball practice, while they drive Nell and Jessica to ballet in Coral Gables. Daisy just dropped the graceful Sylvia off and waved, she had to run or Herman would be late for piano.

Throughout the ballet class, Conchita listens, Rebecca reads.

"She has a witching flirt with it that expresses scorn; a graceful wave of compliance; an abrupt closing of it, that indicates
vexation or anger; a gradual and cautious opening of its folds,
that signifies reluctant forgiveness."

Maturin Ballou

THE SANTA CRUZ FAMILY'S WEALTH and influence began to dwindle after
1854. By 1855 they had nothing but their mansion, their factory, some
sugar cane fields outside Havana, and so few members that they were starting
to feel less like a family and more like spontaneous generation.

The last of the grandparents died in 1850. The black vomit that decimat-
ed the population of the country from 1852 to 1856 had killed most of the
other relatives. Deadly diseases such as the black vomit ignored class and
color. Everyone in the neighborhood was shocked to hear that the non-dis-
criminating disease hadn't even spared Don Gabriel María, the creator of the
tertulia gown.

At the time of his death in 1855 Don Gabriel María still wasn't a noble-
man and of nobility he possessed only the name Santa Cruz which his ancestors had adopted.

Don Gabriel María had had no sons and his two daughters had both been
total disappointments. Not only were they female but they both had terrible
personalities.

There are not many ugly people in the world, and when it comes to
young women most of them can pass as pretty with a nice hairdo and a little
cascarilla, a mixture of finely powdered eggshells and egg whites. It was not
so with Don Gabriel María's younger daughter, Escolástica. It seemed as if
God had expedited her face, or as if some lazy painter had given up on painting it when he was halfway through, or as if he had thrown the canvas into
the fire in a fit of discouragement, and the oils had melted. There was an
unfinished quality to Escolástica's face. *Cascarilla* and kohl couldn't even
begin to make it look better.

But ugliness wasn't Escolástica's only problem. She was also a cripple,
and proud and arrogant to boot. To make matters even worse, that ugly little

blonde creature with a limp just wouldn't take no for an answer. So her good father, Don Gabriel María, had no choice but to hire three or four men to come to the house one morning while she was having breakfast, tie her up, shove her into a victoria, and drive her to a nunnery outside Havana.

Escolástica had put up quite a fight when her dad had forbidden her to marry Lolo Tacón, a moody architect with no talent. This was strictly out of the question because architects were of the lower classes. And who were these loud know-it-all Tacóns anyway? Were did they come from? They were *chusmas!* They were nobodies! This Tacón family just appeared out of nowhere one day saying that their last name was Tacón and that they had lived in Italy and that they were distant relatives of the famous Tacón after whom the theatre was named. Nothing they said about their past ever made any sense, which meant that they were making it all up. This could have been a family of convicts and atheists for all Don Gabriel María knew. In any case it was a fact that there was a Tacón family secret and there was no way Don Gabriel was going to allow his ugly uncooperative pig-headed daughter to marry a skinny effeminate insolent architect of the lower classes.

But Escolástica *did* put up a fight. She spent quite a few years throwing herself against the walls of the suburban nunnery in fits of rage. She wanted to be free! That's all she wanted! The nuns urged her to write her memoirs or to pick a book and read, either pray or learn something! Make this stay productive! Escolástica wouldn't listen. Every minute of those dark captive years was spent kicking and screaming and swearing that she'd escape and marry Lolo one day.

The older daughter, Catalina, was no better. She was always falling in love with the wrong men even if her parents had never—ever—let her go anywhere. She had absolutely no interest in reading or in sewing or in shopping or in praying or in going to the *parque* in her *volante*. All Catalina wanted to do was stand behind the iron bars at her window and look at men. It was precisely there that she met all the wrong men she fancied.

By age eighteen Catalina had categorically refused all the good bachelors her father had chosen for her. One rainy night she confessed to the cook that she wanted an affectionate man who could be a lover and a friend, strong and tender, somewhere between a prince and a botanist or a damsel-fly specialist who would always understand her. She said she was getting sick and tired of her father bringing her nothing but cocky *macho* creeps with nothing to say.

Right after her father's funeral Catalina went and told her mother that she wanted to move out of the house. She added that she'd rather be in that hole in the ground with her father burning in Hell than to spend another minute in her company. Mother and daughter did not get along. Catalina repeated, There must be some kind of way out of here!

María Eugenia just wouldn't have it. Since when did young women pack their bags and move out of the house? Everyone was going to think she was some kind of *puta!* Where would she go live? In a brothel? Those two just couldn't stand the sight of each other. They never bonded. Catalina was annoyed out of her mind by everything her mother said. She never even tried to put herself in her mom's place and feel sorry for her.

When she wasn't moping, Catalina was looking for some reason to pick a loud fight. Life was so boring and she had so few interests that quarrels were the highlight of her days. One day she finally found a worthy cause . . . Escolástica!

Her mom didn't have a heart! How could she keep poor Escolástica in that stiffling boring nunnery. Obviously, her mother would yell back. This was none of Catalina's business! Escolástica would be freed, in time.

María Eugenia, who was so fond of aphorisms, came up with two or three terse ones commending patience. The worst part was that they rhymed. María Eugenia regretted it instantly, she even tried to take it back. But things had gone too far. Catalina was so angry she could spit. After she heard the doggerel she immediately yelled, "This time *vas a saber quién yo soy!* You're going to find out who I really am!" To herself in a whisper she said, *I've got to get out of this place, if it's the last thing I ever do!* Both mother and daughter swore that they'd never talk to each other again for as long as they lived.

Exactly one week later, Catalina looked through the ornate iron bars of her bedroom window down at the street and saw Joaquín Aguasclaras exiting her house and getting into his fancy two-horse *volante.* He looked up at that very instant and saw Catalina who was like a prisoner looking down at him through the iron bars. Suddenly Petra the servant girl realized that her mistress was looking down at the street and pulled her by the hair back into her bedroom. She had her orders.

A single and pretty Habanera such as Catalina had to be protected from men, and every man was dangerous, whether he was a pauper, an aristocrat, a *criollo,* or a *peninsular.* Joaquín happened to be a *criollo hidalgo* womanizer with a heart, about as close as Catalina could get to her dreamboy damsel-fly scientist.

It so happened that Joaquín paid a visit to Catalina's mother every afternoon, but this was the first time he had ever seen the beautiful spinster daughter of María Eugenia.

It didn't take the intelligent Catalina many weeks to realize that this gentleman who owned the beautiful *volante* with the crimson wheels came to see her mother every afternoon. Soon, both the mother's and the daughter's life revolved around Joaquín's daily visits. He always arrived at two in the afternoon, and by that time Catalina's face would be covered with *cascarilla* and she'd be wearing a new dress just for these few instants when he'd stare up and look at her. The minute Joaquín stepped into the house, Catalina would immediately take the new dress off and give it to Petra the servant. She'd indeed be wearing another dress at five in the afternoon, when Joaquín left the house. They'd both stand there looking at each other with amorous desire until Petra pulled Catalina by the hair back into her bedroom. It was a miracle that Catalina didn't lose all her hair.

When the church bells rang six times, Catalina would roll on her silk stockings, pick yet another dress, pick some fine jewelry and a pair of lovely satin slippers, and rush downstairs where the magnificent but old Santa Cruz family *volante* was waiting. Before heading for the Paseo the postilion would pick up two or three of Catalina's girlfriends who lived nearby. Then they'd set out for the Paseo, fast! Puffs of either pink, white, blue or green muslin were flying in the wind over the sides of the *volante*. The sun was weaker at this time, and it was not quite so hot especially with the *volante* going as fast as it did, but the ladies continued fanning themselves. All ladies were experts in handling the fan and quite eager to use it when they dallied outside the walls of Havana.

The rickety *volante* was carpeted with a Persian rug. It had a solid gold foot rest, crimson velvet screens with blue and gold tasselled silk cords, and black leather seats with crimson velvet buttons. Since this *volante* was often parked out on Aguacate Street it was a miracle the foot rest hadn't been stolen yet. It was just a matter of time though. Havana wasn't what it used to be.

Lately everyone was complaining about Havana. People said it was noisy, dirty, muddy, ugly, smelly, and full of lowlifes, liberated slaves, aggressive dwarfish lottery vendors who loved to cast spells on you, homeless derelicts, pirates, murderers, and burglars. Both Habaneros and Habaneras kept mumbling to themselves, *We've got to get out of this place, if it's the last thing we ever do!*

Once they were outside the walls the women would choose a shady spot on the Paseo, order the postilion to stop, and immediately begin fluttering their fans with flirtatious naughtiness. This is how Catalina began communicating with Joaquín every day, and it didn't even matter if it was raining.

Invitation, enticement, outrage, reprimand, forgiveness, such was the language of the fan. Soon Joaquín could understand everything.

One evening there was a ball at the Palacio, Catalina was more beautiful than ever. Her black hair was pinned up on top of her head with silver flowers. Her face was plastered with *cascarilla.* As to her dress, it was a ruffled, puffed and tucked muslin. Attached to her bracelet and necklace were fireflies. The *cocullos* or fireflies had natural hooks on their heads, so they could easily be attached to the ball dresses. From Catalina's waist hung a little silver cage containing five *cocullos.* She seemed to be covered with diamonds. Her whole person sparkled. To be sincere, she always looked much prettier in the evening because she always put too much makeup on and it looked really cakey in the midday sun.

These days she was so happy and excited that she was even being nice to her mother.

She fluttered her fan, she was fluent in its language. Joaquín stared into her eyes. They were opaque black beads. The whites were a bit bloodshot. This is what Cleopatra must have looked like. Catalina always went to great lengths to outline her eyes with thick lines of jet-black kohl. Before Escolástica was relegated to the nunnery she'd kid her older sister and tell her she looked like an Egyptian mummy except not as pretty, but Catalina wouldn't listen and kept on thinking she looked good with all that kohl.

That night, after Catalina got home, she carefully unhooked the little *cocullos,* put them back in their little cages, gave them a little dish of sugar cane juice, then ran off with Joaquín Aguasclaras.

Her mother could not and would not forgive them. Society would not forgive them. Even if it was 1859 and the times were changing all the neighbors gossiped about them. Joaquín Aguasclaras was rumored to be illegitimate in spite of his aristocratic last name, and he was also supposed to be an indiscriminate womanizer. Catalina's mother couldn't believe it. How could she? All this time she'd really believed her daughter wanted an affectionate man, someone who knew all there was to know about damsel flies. Was Catalina really this stupid? Not only was Joaquín totally unaware of dainty insects, but he didn't even have money! Did Catalina really want to choose poor?

María Eugenia said all the bad words she could think of before she began to scream. She screamed so loud that it drowned the church bells, and it even drowned the voice of the lottery vendor, of the scissorsgrinder, and of the *güajiro* who was trying to sell his cow.

That very same evening, after she lost her voice, María Eugenia Aguilera y Peñalver de Santa Cruz, disinherited her older daughter. The next day at nine AM she had a court order barring Catalina from coming within two hundred yards of La Casa Amarilla.

When they realized what was going on behind those unassuming walls the poorer neighbors crossed theirs arms over their bellies and looked to the heavens. It was a tragedy, indeed, who would have guessed? Who would have imagined that it would happen to them, of all people? *Tan ricos.* So loaded.

Tragedy struck again seven years later in 1866 when Don Gabriel María's widow, María Eugenia Aguilera y Peñalver de Santa Cruz, was accidentally shot and mortally wounded during the ritual firing of harquebuses that she had organized at the Palacio de los Capitanes Generales.

It had been an age-old tradition that this house, La Casa Amarilla, The Yellow House, handed down from mother to oldest daughter, and it had been so for the past century, but María Eugenia de Santa Cruz had decided to break with tradition when her daughter Catalina eloped.

Exactly two weeks before her untimely death while disporting at the Palacio, María Eugenia had called for the lawyer and administrator whom she had put in charge of her estate, Manuel Tacón—father of the architect poor Escolástica wasn't allowed to marry (it was rumored that the mischevous María Eugenia had named Manuel Tacón as her administrator just to torment her dead husband in his grave)—and she made it clear that the house was to be bequeathed to Escolástica Santa Cruz y Aguilera, her younger daughter, who was still pounding on the walls of the high-security nunnery.

"1. It is forbidden to distract the workers of the tobacco shops, workshops and shops of all kinds with the reading of books . . ."

Edict issued by the Political Governor
of Cuba on May 14, 1866

CONCHITA FISH HELD THE BOOK at arms' length and tried to read the list of characters. She then tried to stretch her arm at little more and tilted her head back as far as it could go.

Characters from the oldest to the youngest (the numbers refer to the order in which they are mentioned):

1. Antonio Gabriel María Santa Cruz—father, died in 1855.
6. María Eugenia Aguilera y Peñalver de Santa Cruz—mother, died in 1866.
4. Manuel María Tacón y Tacón—attorney, administrator of the Santa Cruz estate.
8. Wencesla María—the cook.
5. María Catalina de Dios Santa Cruz y Aguilera de Aguasclaras—older daughter, born in 1833.
2. María del Rosario Escolástica Anacleta Santa Cruz y Aguilera de Tacón—younger daughter, born in 1839.
7. Joaquín María Aguasclaras y González—Catalina's husband, born in 1841.
3. Lolo María Tacón y Faber—architect who marries Escolástica, born in 1841.
9. Petra María Valdez—servant, born in 1842.

Characters yet to be mentioned:

10. María Fernanda Aguasclaras y Santa Cruz—Catalina's and Joaquín's daughter, born in 1860.
11. María Soledad Valdez—Petra's and Joaquín's daughter, born in 1868.

Conchita Fish said, "God! I sure am having trouble sorting through all these Marías! Couldn't the author come up with any other name? It's so confusing! Don't you think there are too many Marías? Even the *dad's* named María! Rebecca, will you keep on reading?"

"What hast thou, Cuban? Life itself resign,—
Thy very grave is unsecurely thine!
Thy blood, thy treasure, poured like tropic rain
From tyrant hands to feed the soil of Spain."

José María Heredia

ESCOLÁSTICA WAS REALLY SURPRISED that Christmas Day of 1866 when they simply opened the big heavy door of the convent and let her go.

Both her parents were dead, they told her. And she had inherited everything. She just stood there with her mouth wide open until Mother Superior said, "Go! Go!" Escolástica squinted, she was really suspicious, what kind of trick was this? And why didn't they just leave her alone? The more she thought about it the more she was annoyed.

It wasn't long before her skin twitched. She looked to the left, then she looked to the right. She lifted her right arm, and sniffed, she lifted her left arm and went through the same motion. The coast was clear. She was free!

Looking back, she didn't even have time to enjoy her new-found freedom. There was so much to do! Escolástica ran her fingers through her thinning hair, leaned against the south wall, took a good look at the house and realized that it was in urgent need of repairs and attention. And it could sure use a good cleaning! She ran her tongue over her front teeth. There was dust everywhere! It was gritty, she could taste it. And crud on the kitchen floor, looking in that direction. Not to mention the mice and the roaches that seemed convinced that her skinny legs were broomsticks. And where was that horrible odor coming from? She sniffed and followed her nose, then stopped abruptly and sniffed under her armpits, just to make sure. Reassured, she uttered, it isn't me, *no soy yo*.

First Escolástica had all the hardware of the mahogany doors either polished or replaced. Then she noticed that the paint was cracking and peeling everywhere she turned. So she chose a different pastel color for each room. After that ordeal she bought a new table and new chairs, and she had a fountain placed in the middle of the expansive courtyard.

The water gushing from the fountain cast figures, ghostly diamond-like creatures that looked like flames on the darker walls. They danced to the sound of the water, behind bars, for the curvaceous banisters cast their own shadows from above.

Finally Escolástica hired some local artist to paint a fresco on the darker walls that opened onto this splendid courtyard. The final product was titled "Life in One Hundred and Thirty Years." Lascivious red women with big heads were sitting on rocking chairs reading. The dancing shadows of the water gushing from the fountain made it look as if they were rocking.

Escolástica also loved *faux* finishes, especially the ones that made you think there was a shadow, when there wasn't! or a staircase, where there wasn't! or that there was no step there, when in fact there was!

The truth of the matter is that over the next year and a half Escolástica spent so much time and energy improving and embellishing the house that in the evenings she was always exhausted and in quite a foul mood. Her life was so hectic that she never had any time left to sit down and plan her wedding to Lolo Tacón. No matter how hard she tried to find time, there was never enough! The wedding was put off month after month, to Lolo's great dismay. It was put off so many times that Lolo was starting to get peevish about it. Given the chance, Lolo would allude to the wedding in a sarcastic way and invariably end up hurting Escolástica's feelings.

Escolastica was a compulsive, hard-working, control freak who absolutely refused to delegate. This explains why she was also running the dress factory two blocks away, and visiting the sugar cane fields once a month with Manuel Tacón and Lolo.

One fine February day when Escolastica really despaired about ever getting a title from Spain and felt awfully bitter and resentful about it, she threw her hands up in the air and liberated all the slaves in a fit of vengeful rage.

At first everyone thought she was mad, then they said she was downright stupid, after that she became an idiot, then they noticed that she was getting results and in two weeks' time she began to have the reputation of being a free spirit (which she liked), and finally one of a shrewd businesswoman.

By liberating her slaves, Escolástica had somehow managed to get cheaper labor. People scratched their heads and remembered a time when they'd called her stupid. So what if she volunteered to pay for labor? All her slaves stayed. And they began to pay rent. Escolástica seemed to make money even by doing stupid things!

Escolástica first came up with the idea of liberating the slaves early in January 1867 when she went to visit the cane fields for the first time and saw all the tools and machines available. She then realized that slavery was an expensive anachronism, so a month later she declared all her slaves free.

She did discuss this decision with her administrator Manuel Tacón, who agreed with her in many ways. For Manuel Tacón the abolition of slavery had always been synonymous with independence from Spain up until the day he read the works of the political thinker José Antonio Saco, who believed that a social revolution was the natural consequence of a political revolution, and that a social revolution, in turn, would be the ruin of the Cuban race.

After reading that Manuel Tacón hardly knew what to think! He re-read that sentence aloud so many times that the words flew off the page like a frightened flock of birds. And once he knew it by heart, political thought became pure sound. How did one see clearly and take sides? One moment Manuel Tacón didn't want a social revolution, and the next he'd be looking toward Saint Domingue and Puerto Rico and how those countries had let themselves be blackened by the presence of so many Africans. He would get so fearful at times that he wanted to send all the Africans back to Africa.

Escolástica gave his rantings some thought. They drank ice water, smoked, talked, argued, yelled, swore never to speak to each other again, and finally changed the position of their noisy wicker rocking chairs, made them face north, toward their powerful imperialistic neighbor, the United States, which had just had a civil war. The southern states, which happened to be the ones with the slaves, had lost. Slavery had apparently been totally abolished up north. Those were the facts, Escolástica and Manuel Tacón agreed up to there.

Now if one of these days Spain got really nasty, and out of spite the Cuban people decided to ask Ulysses Grant to grant them statehood, wouldn't it be better to have all the Cuban slaves liberated by then?

No!

Yes!

No!

Lolo overheard this conversation, puffed on a cigar, and protested, "I don't want to be annexed! I don't want to become a Protestant! They don't believe in saints! And I'm lost without my saints to help me . . ." Lolo puffed and puffed away, always smoking. "And they don't even know how to make love in Spanish," Lolo added.

Little did it matter if the Santa Cruz family fortune had diminished, that was the past and this was the present, and Escolástica was doing everything in her power to bring back the family's glory of yesteryear.

For some unknown reason, and in spite of being such a free spirit and quite eager to be independent from Spain, Escolástica did harbor this secret desire to become an aristocrat just like her father and grandfather and great grandfather before her. She daydreamed of being called the Countess of Morro Castle, to be an aristocrat, to be Spanish, but also to be Cuban, autonomist, Mambisa (revolutionary), manumitter of slaves, enlightened! And just when she was daydreaming about all this, she remembered!

Why not ask her estranged sister Catalina to come back and live in this house? How could she possibly have forgotten her? Escolástica was really ashamed of herself when she realized that she hadn't given her sister a single thought in years! What kind of person was she? No wonder she wasn't getting anywhere with her wedding plans! She had absolutely no family values!

Late in 1867, when Escolástica had this sudden realization, Catalina and Joaquín were living in poverty in the dress factory. Catalina had indeed gotten pregnant by Joaquín Aguasclaras out of wedlock, but he had immediately married the dishonored woman.

When Escolástica announced her intentions to those around her, everyone wondered why the younger crippled sister was so generous and kind. Anyone else in her place would have let the more beautiful older sister rot in poverty and disinheritance, but Escolástica was not a bad person like most of the other people in Havana, she had no interest in seeing anyone suffer or in taking Catalina's rightful inheritance away from her, so she invited her back with Joaquín and their young daughter, María Fernanda.

The marriage had gone sour. Being a social outcast had turned Joaquín into a rebel. He was soon more interested in politics than in Catalina, and he had this uncanny knack for falling in love easily. When they moved to the Casa Amarilla, he immediately fell in love with the black servant Petra. Catalina surprised them naked in a tiny cot downstairs next to the kitchen and bit half of Joaquín's nose off. He was therefore not quite so handsome anymore. But Catalina remained insanely jealous.

Lately Catalina had been suffering from severe hysterical melancholia. She was avoiding everyone and didn't even want her daughter near her. The only person she seemed to love and respect was Escolástica, whom everyone loved anyway. Oftentimes Escolástica was asked why she was so lovable and she'd reply that she knew that she'd live to be a hundred and one, and that this gave her incredible serenity. Also she was definitely not at all good-ooking. She was a washed-out delicate blonde with a twinkle in her eye and either red or brown birthmarks all over. People didn't think she was all that ugly unless they got up close. Maybe it was something about her nose, or the friz of her thinning hair. That's when people started really liking her: once they took a good look at her she wasn't a threat to anyone.

None of this mattered to Escolástica. Anyone in her position would have tried to play the role of the mean gossipy revengeful pious woman. Not her. She had never said anything mean to anyone (except to her father when he forced her into a nunnery) and she was almost relieved to have been born an ugly woman. She had also been born with hip dysplasia and always walked with a limp. Her face just wasn't pretty. It had not one thing pleasing about it. Her forehead was way too low. And it was as if she'd been close to being albino. All this gave her great freedom.

A pretty woman in Havana in the second half of the nineteenth century was in dire straits. Her only chance at pleasure was having a lover after she married. Habaneras could never go out by themselves, could never be alone, there was nothing for them to do. Escolástica had none of these problems, she was ugly, she was rich, she was crippled, and somehow this combination allowed her to go wherever she wanted and to do whatever she wanted. She was not good-looking enough to be a loose woman. She never worked on her appearance. She said she didn't care about her looks, and that she'd be wasting time and makeup if she did. She had a limp, but she was active all day. The doctors told her that with her dysplasia she could never have children and she had accepted that even though she absolutely adored kids. With Lolo's help she was raising the lovely eight-year-old María Fernanda, who had been rejected by her mother. Escolástica also loved Petra's little baby girl, who was crying for her mother's breast.

Escolástica also had a sense of humor. People would talk to Escolástica and then end up laughing hysterically. They couldn't stop! First they'd get the giggles, then a stomach ache, then they'd beg please please stop I can't stand this anymore, and then they'd roar with hysterical laughter again. *Tertulias* at the Santa Cruz house were a riot. At first the women would rock slowly, but then they'd end up rocking as fast as they could with the loudest ha ha ha's imaginable. Some women actually fell from their rocking chairs and kept on laughing even if their panties showed. Others would spit their coffee out with uncontrollable laughter. By the end of the *tertulia* there'd be cookie crumbs on the floor and they'd walk on them with their bare feet, giggling and giggling hysterically.

In the Fall of 1868, when Escolástica was finally ready to marry her beloved Lolo, the French sausage that was being manufactured in the nearby suburb of Regla was all the rage. Everyone seemed to adore this French sausage and the aristocracy was eating it morning, noon, and night.

Although Manuel Tacón, Lolo's father, had advised Escolástica not to eat the filthy sausage, for there was no way of knowing what kind of meat went into their making, once Escolástica decided to do something there was no stopping her. She was supposedly the most mule-headed woman in Havana at that time. If the aristocracy ate that sausage, so would she, and she couldn't care less if everyone called her a social climber.

So the stubborn, persistent Escolástica decided to send the servant Petra—with whom, you will recall, Catalina's husband had had a child—to Regla to buy some of this delicious sausage. Petra was a newly liberated slave, a *liberta,* who had preferred to stay on with the Santa Cruz family as a servant rather than to go and find a job somewhere else.

It wasn't that she was particularly attached to the Santa Cruz family. What Petra cared about were the perks that came with this job. Over the years she had developed quite a taste for fine clothing, and had such a closet full of once-worn discarded gowns, that she even wore gowns when she washed dishes, scrubbed floors, and nursed her newborn. She particularly loved to wear Escolástica's mother's wedding gown and had refused to take it off for the past two weeks.

"Petra, Petra *linda,* I have to ask you a *favorcito*[1]!" Escolástica said at breakfast. "Tomorrow I want you to go to Regla and buy that delicious sausage everyone's talking about. And listen, Wencesla, I want to have it for lunch tomorrow. Petra, are you listening? Yeah? So what did I just say?"

The arrogant Petra repeated everything Escolástica had said.

"Good!" exclaimed Escolástica. "And everyone can have the sausage for lunch tomorrow! Even you, Cascabel!" Escolástica yelled.

Cascabel was the nickname she used for Catalina's eight-year-old daughter María Fernanda. Escolástica wanted so badly for her sweet little niece to be happy that there seemed to be no nickname better for her than Cascabel, which meant *bell.* But there was no changing that little girl.

Every day Escolástica prayed that the poor little dear wouldn't notice her Mom, who had taken to spending her days in the chapel weeping. Escolástica would always come in and ask her what she was crying about, and Catalina would reply that she was crying about everything.

"Escolástica, I can't handle life, *no puedo con la vida.*"

"What about your daughter? Isn't she a reason to live and be proud and happy?"

"Are you kidding? *Esa sinvergüenza,* that shameless filthy loudmouthed ugly ungrateful creature? Escolástica, you've got to be kidding!" She'd end these diatribes of painful despair with loud sobs that would echo in the chapel.

At other times Escolástica would come across Catalina in one of the galleries and try to reason with her. They'd sit on one of the polished wood chairs near the obese cherubs. The water from the fountain would drown their voices and thus prevent the servants from eavesdropping.

Catalina said: *Me cago en el día que me casé con ese maricón de Joaquín. That puta chusma de Petra (ojalá que se muera)* will probably marry Joaquín after I die. Both his parents are dead so who's going to prevent him from marrying way beneath his class?"

Escolástica laughed. How could a man possibly want the servant woman Petra who's as crazy as a loon for his wife? "Have you noticed how ridiculous she looks always wearing our mother's old wedding dress?" So Catalina started to laugh. Before they knew it they were both roaring with laughter in the courtyard.

Escolástica did adore Joaquín Aguasclaras, but in a sisterly way. Oftentimes the flirtatious Joaquín would pass by Escolástica, pinch her in the rear, and utter, "I should have married you instead!"

"With these hips and this face?" was Escolastica's eternal comment.

"They're just there to hide your beauty from the world!"

Joaquín had two passions. The first was women—*all* women. The second was reform.

The evenings at La Casa Amarilla were all the same. Lolo said they were dull and uneventful and that you could hardly tell one evening apart from the other. Escolástica had quit going to the Cafe Louvre, the Palacio, and the theater every single night because of Catalina's angry illness. Now they only went out once a week just to satisfy Lolo and keep Lolo from having fits of self-pitying boredom. All the other nights Escolástica, Lolo, and Joaquín had supper by themselves in the large dining room, while Catalina ate alone in her bedroom.

After dinner Joaquín would go and attend clandestine meetings in a house nearby. Escolástica and Lolo would be left to themselves with no chaperone, free to talk about whatever they wished. They each grabbed a wicker rocking chair, dragged it out into the courtyard and, as they gently rocked, they sipped good rum, as Lolo smoked, Escolástica swatted gnats, they whispered sweet words to each other, until they were tired.

This is what Escolástica was saying during the last supper that she ever had with Joaquín: "Well, thanks to the excellent advice given to me by Lolo's *Papa que Dios lo bendiga*[4] we've been harvesting five times the sugar cane with a fifth as many men. Everything that dear Manuel ever told me turned out to be true, *que Dios lo bendiga.* First he said, Don't free the slaves, you never know, the United States could annex us, and they have a slave economy. But then the North won and Manuel said that this was a Copernician revolution as far as he was concerned. So we put off manumission hoping to be compensated for the loss of our slaves. That didn't work either, so dear Manuel shyly suggested that I modernize. It's all mechanized now. I absolutely love the modern world! *¡Es recio!* All our slaves have been manumitted that's about as radical as reform gets, what is it that you want now, Joaquín? *Ya yo he dado todito lo que puedo dar, que otro se ponga pa' su turno.*"

"Spain cannot absorb our sugar production. The crown keeps telling us that any kind of rebellion will automaticaly reproduce the fate of Haiti here and urges us to keep the slaves."

"Joaquín, *corazón,* you're getting boring."

"You don't have to listen but let me finish, *mi amor.* It's precisely by keeping the slaves that we'll suffer the same fate as Haiti. We don't want Cuba to get Africanized! Look at Saint Domingue! We don't want a black country! We want a white country!"

"Keep this up and I'll go to bed without dinner," Escolástica said.

"Listen, I'm almost finished. The biggest problem is that too many errors have been made already and we certainly can't send those poor Negroes back to where they came from, after having lived in Cuba they'll hate Africa! No other country even remotely compares to Cuba! have you ever seen a beach as beautiful as Varadero, or prettier *mulatto* women? We have to whiten this country and the only way to do it is by putting one foot in front of the other. [Lolo yawned loudly, Joaquín carried on.] That means that no more slaves should be imported and that the poor should be allowed to marry blacks. They'll never have pure blood but little by little they'll be whiter and whiter. Just like sugar! *¡Azúcar!* The white blood is thicker. The slave dealers have gotten too much power anyway. What's more, the manumission of the slaves is a precondition for our own emancipation. Am I making any sense? I don't know about both of you, but although I was born in Spain I feel like a *criollo,* not like a Spaniard. A lot of things are about to happen, Escolástica and Lolo, you two should get married as quickly as possible and be ready for the changes."

"You weren't born in Spain!" Lolo said.

"Yes I was!"

"No you weren't!"

"Yes I was!"

"I hate the name Escolástica, from now on I want to be called Rosario," Escolástica said right before she yelled, "Petra! We're hungry! Bring *la maldita comida* now!"

The soup was pumpkin soup, and Joaquín liked squeezing the juice of five limes into it. He looked ugly with his mutilated nose, but the doctors had done all they could to improve it.

"You're too much of an idealist," said Rosario (the name of Escolástica has just been changed). "Besides, Spain's the country of our ancestors. Maybe we can't be independent, Joaquín. I've been talking about this with Manuel Tacón so much that I'm getting sick and tired of the subject and I really wish we'd talk about something else. Last night I had this dream where God said, What's the use? The minute Spain leaves, the United States are going to step right in here. We're going to have President Ulysses S. Grant instead of Captain General Domingo Dulce which is so much easier to say that Ulysses S. Grant, saliva always pops out of my mouth when I say Ulysses S. Grant. And then what? They're going to impose their culture, their practical soulless architecture, their horrible food, and their boring Protestant ways upon us. We'll have to get all the angels and the saints out of our churches again just like we had to do a hundred years ago when the British were here. So maybe we should just remain the way we are with some reform. We're an unlucky nation that will never be free, that's all. El Generalísimo Anacleto Menosmal wants to be emperor, why not just vote for him and get it over with?"

"Obviously, you don't know a thing about politics. Listen, *corazón, tranquilita, escúchame mi amor. ¡Pero coño chica escúchame!* We want to collaborate with Spain. But Spain has to stop treating us like children," said Joaquín.

"Another tax and we'll be ruined! We'll all be paupers! We'll end up like Saint Domingue, full of blacks!" Lolo blurted out.

"Lolo, taxes have nothing to do with the country getting black. I have a plan for the cane fields. As a matter of fact I have all sorts of plans. It's going to be the dance of the millions, you'll see," said Rosario. "We'll be so rich we'll be able to pay whatever tax Spain demands. And they say that the United States is even worse than Spain with the taxes. At least Spain is disorganized, but apparently the Grant cabinet just sits there and counts beans all day."

"And they just had a war and annexed the whole South, why would they want to annex us?" Lolo asked.

"Petra! Can you bring the rest of the food, please? *Petra!* Did you hear me?" Rosario shouted.

"Of course she hears you."

Immediately Petra walked in with two chickens on a tray.

"We have to be independent!" Joaquín slammed his closed fist on the table and said. "Why should we have paid for the Spanish expedition to Mexico four years ago? Why should we pay for Spain's military campaigns in Africa? And why should we have paid for the naval war against Peru and Chile two years ago? Not only that but we're still paying the salaries of the entire Spanish diplomatic corps here in America!"

"That is so unfair! *¡Pero coño yo no te lo puedo creer!*[8]" Lolo yelled.

Joaquín carried on: "Spain should be defeated, not convinced! You're right I wasn't born in Spain and I'm glad I wasn't! Part of me is just so hung up on class origins that sometimes I forget I'm a revolutionary. You two get married and run this place and I'll change the world! I'll make Cuba a better place. Why don't you join the Mambises, Escolástica—I mean Rosario? We need women like you. And I suppose we need people like you too, Lolo. But to get back to you, Rosario, I can't repeat it enough, we really need people like you."

"With this face and these hips?" Rosario laughed.

"You are a very special person. It's just too bad you have all those defects! *Pobrecita tan feíta,* but I was just thinking, if you can change your name can't you change other things about you too?"

"It's too late, Joaquín."

Petra came in to clear the table before they were finished eating. As usual she was wearing the splendid wedding gown that she had inherited from María Eugenia, her former mistress, who had always treated her better than she had ever treated her own daughters. Oh it was a gorgeous wedding dress, it was yellowed and a bit wilted now, but it had had diamonds sewn into it when it was first used. Everyone had stolen the little diamonds one by one and there wasn't one single diamond left now, but all those empty little holes were nostalgic reminders of how beautiful the gown had been when it was first used. In another way the dress was as disappointing as an empty box of chocolates. What's more Petra wore it every day and she hardly ever washed it, so it was always looking a little gray.

Just when she saw Petra walk in the room Rosario reminded her about the sausage again.

"Petra *linda,* you're still going to Regla tomorrow to buy some of that French sausage all of Havana is talking about, aren't you? You can leave the little one with Wencesla. It shouldn't take you long."

"Yes, *Señorita* Rosario," Petra replied.

"How did you know I had changed my name to Rosario?"

"I overheard."

She walked out of the dining room.

"That woman is so arrogant! *Te lo digo, la negra esa se ha puesto tan arrogante que no le cabe un . . .* "

"You'll treat her right, won't you?" Joaquín asked. "And treat my daughter right too, she's the beginning of a new race."

"You sound as if you weren't going to be around any more," Rosario commented.

"I'm going to a meeting tonight. A very important one. I'm saying that just in case something happens to me. I might not be back tonight."

"I'll take care of her, Joaquín. She's treated like a queen already. If I get any nicer she'll make me bend over backwards. I just make her serve the table at dinnertime and give her an order once in a while so she doesn't forget that she's still a servant here. That's why I'm sending her to Regla to buy the sausage, I could send someone else, but I don't want her to forget that she's still a servant and that I give the orders."

Petra came back in and put a tray in the middle of the table. It was dessert.

"I love *mantecado!*" Lolo yelled. "Petraaa! Bring *churros* and *refrescos! ¡Tráelos rápido carajo!*"

When Catalina awoke on the morning of October 10, 1868, Joaquín her husband was nowhere to be seen. What's more, that scandalous and arrogant Petra had been sent to Regla to buy some sausage and by noon she had not yet returned. Catalina emerged from her bedroom in a frantic state. She was weeping, she was trembling, she was growling. "I'm going to do something crazy," she kept saying. "That whore ran off with my husband! *¡Me cago en la madre que la parió coño!*" she stood in the middle of the patio and screamed.

"I'm going to Regla right now to see what became of Petra," Rosario walked toward Catalina and said. "Don't say such things. Please behave, I'll be back soon. With Petra, hopefully, I hope nothing happened to her. God, aren't you ever going to let me taste those *malditas salchichas? ¡Catalina por Dios pórtate bien!*"

"What do you mean you hope nothing bad happened to her? I hope she dies a violent painful death, that's what I hope! That dirty scandalous whore ran off with my husband! And all my sister thinks about is eating those *malditas salchichas de mierda coño!*"[15] Catalina screamed again at the top of her lungs after Rosario had gone.

"What's wrong with my Mommy?" asked María Fernanda, who was having lunch in the kitchen. "I don't want to eat."

"In three days you'll be eight years old," said Wencesla the cook. "You have to eat so you'll get big like me."

"I don't want to be fat like you. And little do I know that my Mommy is crazy."

"Crazy in love with your father, that's what she is."

"Petra's dead," said the little girl. "And at this time little does everyone know that the good servant Petra who knew my father is dead."

Wencesla the cook made the sign of the cross.

María Fernanda was a weird little girl. She had been born at the intersection of the Calles Sol and Luz, right in that old church that had been sullied by Protestant worship and that had later become a chocolate factory and finally the dress factory. After Catalina and Joaquín eloped they had nowhere else to go so this is where they set up housekeeping. Those were the worst of times. Nobody wanted to be their friend, Joaquín became a social outcast, and Catalina was not invited to any *tertulias*. They lived like squatters in Catalina's family's dress factory.

It was no secret that they lived there, everyone knew. But Catalina's mother never went there and everyone allowed Catalina's daughter María Fernanda to roam around freely in the dress factory while the women were sewing and a novel was being read to them. All the seamstresses seemed to love this little girl. Poor little soul with such an irresponsible mother *que le caía a todo el mundo como una bomba!*[16] And all this went to show that money wasn't everything. Not that Catalina had any money, but even if she did, who would want to be in her shoes? With that Joaquín . . . *Con el desgraciado ese . . .*

This is where María Fernanda spent the first seven years of her life. She hardly ever left the dress factory where all types of dresses were being made with all types of fabrics. It was her world.

The most special thing about this world of hers was the reading of the novel to the dressmakers. Oh, the owners of Titania Fashions (The Most Parisian in the World) weren't the ones who came up with this idea of reading to the workers. It was a custom that dated back to the 1830s and that had originated in the tobacco factories where everyone seemed interested in knowing what was going on in the world of politics. Usually it was only the newspaper that was read to the workers. But at Titania Fashions most of the workers happened to be women who weren't really interested in politics, much less in Cuban politics. What did it matter to them if Cuba belonged to Spain or to the United States? They'd still have the same life anyway. Their only hope was winning the lottery, and they wanted to be entertained; it was already bad enough to have to come to work every day. That's when Rosario told Lolo to choose a good novel for them, a real page-turner, a *Cecilia Valdes* type of novel, but that took place in the future so that it wouldn't elicit any racial or social emotions. All Rosario wanted was to make it worthwhile for the seamstresses to come back to work early each day and work after hours. Nothing could do this as effectively as the desire to know what was going to happen next in a novel. The problem was that she didn't want to be bothered and hired the first reader who applied.

So María Fernanda had grown up playing with the light on the floor of the dress factory while listening to a mediocre reader. At times the light was just so and the scissors, the hands, needles, thread, cast distorted shadows on the floor. Taken by this shadow show, the little girl would reach out and grab the projection of the scissor, to see if it would cut, of the hand, to see if it could touch, the needle, prick, the thread, tighten around her finger. While doing this she never missed a word of the novel that was being read. "Read on!" she yelled often. "Read on!"

This child had begun to speak at six months of age, in almost perfect sentences. The daughter of Joaquín Aguasclaras and Catalina Santa Cruz had been raised with the word and by a few black servants from the dress factory. She was just as adept in the practice of Catholicism as in that of Palo Monte. She knew how to worship the forces of nature concentrated in that large cauldron in the room next to the kitchen, the Nganga. She herself had guarded the cauldron and played the role of the *muñeca de Talanquera,* a doll chained to a chair so that she does not run away while guarding the Nganga.

"Little do we know that today I will shout, Rosario will shout, and a man very far away will shout. Rosario will live to be a hundred and one and so will I, maybe. Little do we know all that."

The black cook Wenscesla made the sign of the cross again. She herself had initiated little María Fernanda into the Palo Monte, but for some illogical reason Wencesla always became very Catholic when she was afraid.

As soon as María Fernanda could talk, she said bad words. Not only that but she also threw tantrums and refused to eat. Either that or she only wanted to eat the specific things that her saint commanded her to eat. Another big problem was that she talked and talked and never did anything but talk.

"I don't understand how such a white child can be so black," Wencesla often said to herself.

"Finish your plantain soup, child, and stop conversing with the demon. Do you want eggs?" she asked and showed her a plate with fluffy white rice and two fried eggs. This *huevito*," she said and pointed to one egg, "was laid by a black and white *gallinita*[17] whose name was Edita."

"I'll eat it. And I would like custard for dessert and a *piñata* for my birthday and I'd like to put on my new birthday dress today before my mommy's carried away by the demon."

"*Ave María Purísima sin pecado concevida,* child don't scare me! That's good that's good, go play!"

"Little do I know that I will grow to be a madwoman with only two children! Read on, Umbertico Barrios! It's life or death now in that lopsided prison of yours!"

The cook made the sign of the cross again.

Midafternoon stillness. This was the afternoon light, the hottest part of the day. María Fernanda picked a skinny light pink hibiscus in the courtyard, took her shoes off, and put her bare feet on the red tiles. There was a bronze bull head with a ring hanging from his nose. There was a fancy lock in the shape of a slave probably made by a slave. The next door also had a fancy lock, this time in the shape of Shangó. Saint Barbara enraged. There was a heavy wooden door of polished wood, shiny, her mother's door . . . her mother, the unhappiest woman there ever was . . . or was it the angriest?

María Fernanda pushed the door, it opened. It was dark in the room, all the curtains were drawn. Then suddenly María Fernanda screamed as she had never screamed before. Her mother wasn't struggling. She wan't even trying! And the daughter couldn't do anything about it.

María Fernanda screamed again, "Oh God, she's letting it happen!!" Her mother's mind was being carried away by demons. They were evil, wiry, red-eyed, buglike, they smelled of crushed centipede.

At that very same moment the *volante* dropped Rosario off at the sausage factory, two miles outside the Montserrate gate. She felt so confused at that moment that she barely knew what to feel. Little did it matter if she raised an annoying cloud of dust with each step she took, her mouth continued to water every time she thought of those sausages. At the same time she seethed with anger at the thought of Petra having perhaps run off with Joaquín and not even bothering to get her *las malditas salchichas*. But she was deeply troubled by what Wencesla the cook had said. "Señorita Rosario, you offended Petra this morning, you treated her like a servant, and you know how the Lucumí people are . . . always ready to kill themselves because of some idiotic trifle."

As Rosario walked toward the factory, she wondered, could it be that Petra had killed herself? Would she ever taste that sausage? What was that foul smell? She quickly sniffed her armpits. It wasn't her. And why are all these people being rounded up? Are they closing the factory? Are they going out of business? What's going on here?

Go in and take a look for yourself, the town gossip (*la chismosa*) said to her.

Rosario stepped into the factory and screamed at the top of her lungs.

The only thing left of Petra was her head, and a blood-stained wedding dress.

There was so much confusion in the factory that was being raided that for a while no one paid any attention to Rosario. She screamed some more, and wept, and shouted and pulled her hair. Finally she sat on a stoop and *la chismosa* did the same.

"What happened here?" she asked.

La chismosa knew everything. Apparently the sausage manufacturers were a gang of European thugs who were using real people to make sausage.

Rosario put her head in her hands and tried to make sense of this. Can't allow grief to take over. Everything has to have a good solid reason. Stay out! She waited a few minutes. The answer! Stay out! No answer. And it didn't stay out. Slowly it seeped in. Grief. So she shouted.

And shouted.

And shouted. The skin on her cheeks was stretched to the fullest, it finally cracked, blood trickled out of the uneven tear, then her lower jaw fell out of her mouth, shattered like fine blue Venetian glass on the sidewalk, quickly washed downstream in the gutter by the flow of her tears.

La chismosa stared in awe, then stood up and ran, this tidbit was still warm and she couldn't wait to share it with anyone.

MARÍA FERNANDA WAS RIGHT, for there was a third shout, that same October 10, 1868, at midnight. It came from many miles away, from the eastern part of the island, from the Finca Demajagua, in the province of Oriente.

Three days later, instead of reading the novel to the factory workers, Umbertico Barrios read them the newspaper instead. The latest news was that Carlos Manuel de Céspedes had manumitted the slaves on his sugar cane plantation and declared Cuba to be independent from Spain.

"*¡Cuba libre! ¡Qué viva Cuba Libre!*" Umbertico Barrios shouted (he was simply quoting Carlos Manuel de Céspedes).

Umbertico Barrios read on. After the shout, the patriot Carlos Manuel de Céspedes set out for the village of Yara. "Yes!" Umbertico shouted. "The exact same village where the rebel Taino chief Hatuey was burnt at the stake by the Spaniards!"

"We don't need a history lesson!" one of the seamstresses protested.

When asked by a priest to repent for his sins so he could join the Lord God in the Kingdom of Heaven, Hatuey asked if there were Spaniards in Heaven.

"We don't care!" another seamstress shouted.

Of course there are Spaniards in Heaven, the priest replied.

"Then I don't want to go to Heaven!" Hatuey yelled.

"Long live freedom! Freedom or death! *¡Qué viva la libertad!*" Umbertico shouted (he was quoting Hatuey).

The factory workers were starting to run out of patience. They wondered where María Fernanda was, why hadn't she come in three days? "On with the novel!" a seamstress shouted. Why wasn't María Fernanda here to threaten Umbertico? "We don't care about politics!" another seamstress shouted.

But María Fernanda wasn't there, so Umbertico just kept on going.

Once again Umbertico shouted at the top of his lungs, "*¡CUBA LIBRE! ¡QUÉ VIVA CUBA LIBRE! LONG LIVE FREEDOM!*" (This time he was quoting Carlos Manuel de Céspedes again.) And his shout echoed throughout the factory.

The squall line was moving toward them fast. At home, María Fernanda looked up and saw a thread-fine zig-zag in the sky; it resembled a crack in fine china. In any case that's how she described it to the other household members sitting on rocking chairs and arguing, right behind her. Lolo was convinced that it was a strand of hair sticking to the window pane, and tried to remove it, in vain. Soon the zig-zag became a trickling gash in the sky, a raggedy tear that violently split open, letting ten years' worth of water gush down.

It had to rain that night, and the next night, and the next night.

The seamstresses sought whatever shelter they could find and really wondered about Umbertico Barrios. Was he totally out of his mind? What was that silly talk of war? Are all Readers mad? You have to be mad to take a job like that. No benefits, no vacation, no security. They didn't even have to whisper because the weather was extremely loud. Come to think of it, it did sound like war. The buckets of water falling on the sidewalk were the artillery, and when the thunder wasn't galloping toward Havana, it was a canon in D major, followed by a wild audience clappping.

The next morning Lolo was still insisting. "I am right, I am right, I am right." The thread-fine line in the sky was nothing other but a strand of hair sticking to the window pane. "It was water! It still is! Can't you hear it, you idiot?" María Fernanda yelled at the top of her lungs.

Then it was Rosario's turn to shout, "How in the world can anybody hear what's going on outside with your constant yelling?"

There was a moment of silence.

See what I mean?

I'm right.

No. I'm right.

No, I'm the one who's right.

So the waters of war had finally reached the Yellow House where the Santa Cruz family minus Joaquín, Petra, and Catalina continued being self-absorbed, ensnared in everyday life and its petty demands—superficial, money hungry, starved of tenderness, quick to anger. Not even the Ten Years' War that ensued could keep each member of the household from repeating, "I'm right, of course I'm right, I'm always right."

THE MOTOR WAS RUNNING, the air-conditioning was on. They were parked right under the giant banyan tree, in the parking lot of the Gertrude Paige School, waiting for the children.

Conchita sighed. "The part about the sausage is revolting."

"But it's true apparently, it's in the footnote. Oh, I'd forgotten, you can't see the footnotes."

"And who's that Rosario who pops up at dinnertime all of a sudden?"

"It's Escolástica who changed her mind about her name. The author probably decided she didn't like the name all of a sudden and didn't trust the 'Find and Replace' in her word processor. It always invariably leaves at least one of the old names in there. Has it ever happened to you, Conchita? I have seen it happen with my own eyes. I'm reading somewhere quietly and all of a sudden this unknown character pops up! And that's usually a character that the 'Find and Replace' left unchanged. I've really seen it happen."

"I never read that attentively any more," said Conchita. "And when I used to read attentively I'd read with the *Cliffs Notes* and when a character wasn't in the *Cliffs Notes* I just wouldn't bother. Remember when I was collecting *Cliffs Notes?*"

"Conchi, tell me the truth, do you think Nell's getting fat? Never mind, here she is. Nell! How was your day? *¡Besitos para Mami! ¡Linda!*"

"Becky, you're acting as if she just came on a freedom flight from Havana. Where's Jessica?" asked Conchita.

"She's right in front of you."

"Oh! Hi sweetheart!"

"Mom, what's for dinner tonight?" Nell asked.

"In other words, the Model Reader is a textually established set of felicity conditions to be met in order to have a macro-speech act (such as a text is) fully actualized."

Umberto Eco, *The Role of the Reader*

R EBECCA HANDED THIS LIST to her father and said, "These are the women who will be at my first *tertulia*."

1. Me, Rebecca Barrios.
2. Ana Daisy Santiago. Do you remember her? She's married to George Atkins, Tommy's brother. I know you're not very good with names.
3. Helen Medina. I'm sure you've forgotten her. She's married to Harvey Atkins, Tommy's other brother, the one who went to prison a long time ago. Helen makes tons of money and it's too bad she's so fat.
4. Trudi Agramonte. She had a big family tragedy when we were in twelfth grade. But she's an attorney now and really dedicated to her career. She's the only one of us who's never been married. Physically, she's the Cristina Onassis type, not ugly, but definitely not pretty.
5. Selene Machado. Another friend. You'd definitely like her. She had green eyes, a great figure, and still draws a happy face in the "o" of Machado.

"You don't have to learn this list by heart. I just wanted to bring you something different today. Mami hurt my feelings and I might never come back here again, so long as she's here."

6. Conchita Pérez. You've seen her plenty of times with me at the supermarket. She's married to Dr. Stanley Fish, a fantastic dentist, and there's much more to Conchita than this urge to get plastic surgery.

7. Alma Cuevas. You know her, of course. But what you may
   not know is that she's married to Rod Target now, and
   about to break up.
8. Jenny Rincón. It was Daisy's idea to invite her.
9. Lucía. The famous singer. But she's only coming once.
10. Silka Velásquez. The most beautiful girl in our senior
    class. Now she's in a wheelchair.
11. Priscilla Drake. You know her dad. That famous liquor fam-
    ily. I'm not tickled about her coming. She dated Tommy,
    and I still remember what it means to date Tommy. It's
    what keeps me going.

He said, "Too many people. That's a mistake."
"It's too late now. They've all been invited."

"The exactness of the textual project makes for the freedom of its Model Reader. If there is a *'jouissance du texte'* (Barthes, 1973), it cannot be aroused and implemented except by a text producing all the paths of its 'good' reading (no matter how many, no matter how much determined in advance)."

Umberto Eco, *The Role of the Reader*

"So I ENDED UP with four new rocking chairs," Rebecca told her father. "Instead of ten."

She was sitting on the porch stoop with her back turned to him, staring down at the ground. Leafcutter ants transporting green shapes across the walkway were headed toward the bitter orange tree. On their way there they unanimously avoided Rebecca's feet. The procession kept such a steady tempo that it appeared static. Here, movement was an optical illusion. The army of ants just a thin pencil line, a lost necklace, a delicate crack.

"Noisy ones," she added. "So with my old four, I now have a total of eight rocking chairs."

Everyone agreed to come on Friday January 12 between five-thirty and six PM. Rebecca said she left both gates wide open so everyone could just drive into the property and park. She spent most of the afternoon making sure everything was ready for the ten members of the new club.

"Too many people," her father said.

"And only eight rocking chairs."

Casting shadows on the walkway with her hand, Rebecca was playing with the ants, intent on drawing with them, forcing the parade to adjust and go on, bend, re-orient, this way, a little loop here, back, back, compromise. A pencil drawing of her feet was what she wanted.

"I wanted it to be perfect," she told her father. "So here I was, planning a simple gathering to discuss a book, and I was cranky, uptight, hyperventilating, in total panic . . ." The list would have been endless had he not interrupted.

"What do you mean that's how I usually am?," she chuckled.

She said she ended up going to the liquor store twice and to the market three times. And it was a good thing that Norma the housekeeper was there to lend a helping hand. She couldn't have managed by herself, she wanted it to be perfect, it was too important, the beginning of something, of a lifetime of *tertulias,* ice water, friends on noisy rocking chairs casting big jumping shadows.

It was incredibly cool yesterday and Conchita arrived at half past four wearing her famous fur. The minute the thermometer plunges down to fifty here on the Beach, Conchita immediately hops in her car and gets the coat out of storage.

"Poor coat," Conchita herself says. "It doesn't get out enough."

The fur is famous indeed. Critters seem to love it. That fur has been through a lot and it's definitely a conversation piece. The year Stanley bought it for her Conchita loved it so much that she left it in her closet over the summer, and it got fleas! Not one flea, not two fleas, it was flea heaven. The coat seemed to have a heartbeat. It was so bad that Conchita had to put flea powder on it, stick it in a deadly dry cleaning bag, and wait a month. "My coat can't breathe!" she kept whining.

Every winter Conchita makes Stanley (her husband, who also happens to be one of the most popular dentists here on the Beach) fly her to New York because she's supposedly dying to see a Broadway show. In fact it's so she can wear her fur coat.

They go to Aspen every February for the same reason. But they're not going this year because Stanley wants to play golf.

By the way Conchita is way too short for that coat.

"Are we close?" Rebecca repeated her father's question. "Conchita and I? Yes, I guess we are," she said unwillingly. "We're good friends. I like her, she likes me, we don't feel threatened by each other . . . Does that answer your question?"

"No."

"Once I helped her comb lice eggs out of her fur coat. And we giggled."

Yesterday Conchita picked the three girls up at school, and swung by her own house first so her two could change into something warm.

When they got to Rebecca's at four-thirty, Nell rushed into the house freezing and giggling. Rebecca admitted that she was annoyed by the sight of her. Why was she so fat? Nell ran upstairs to take off her school uniform and slip into her never-used and enormous Gap fleece-lined sweatsuit. They bought it for summer camp in Maine last July, but as it turned out she never once needed it. By now it was undoubtedly too tight.

When Nell came back downstairs the size and price tags were dangling on her back. Of course the sweatsuit was too tight! She was still giggling and Rebecca felt like running after her with a sharp kitchen knife, to cut those tags. Rebecca admits to herself that she's terribly annoyed by Nell's giggles, they make her sound like an idiot.

"Were you cold too?" her father asked.

Rebecca, who had just broken a dead twig off the bitter orange tree, said she was wearing brown leather pants and a thin yellow cashmere sweater. Her stomach was really flat yesterday, she remembered. She couldn't find lipstick to go with the yellow sweater. She leaned forward, brushed her hair, and tied it all on top of her head. Some strands were falling on her face.

"God, you've got such great skin!" Conchita said to her. She had just taken her sunglasses off and left them on the buffet. "Which vitamin is it?"

"Grief," Rebecca said.

"How is your dad?" Conchita sounded concerned. She tossed her luscious leather handbag behind the couch.

"My mom wheels him out on the porch every morning and he spends his days reading out loud to a stray cat. He insists that it gives him a sense of fulfillment. But I don't think this is going to have a happy ending."

"Who's Conchita?" her father asked.

For a split second Rebecca looked exasperated. With the tip of the twig she disturbed the leafcutter ants' line.

"You don't remember? She's my girlfriend! The one who's married to the good dentist! The one who appears so shallow, but isn't. She really isn't. It's just like Mami being nice and nasty. Conchita's smart and stupid and deep and shallow. She's the one with the fur coat, the one who can never keep track of her stuff."

While Rebecca was saying that the ants were regrouping, fast, and the unfinished pencil drawing she'd managed to get of her feet was gone now.

Yesterday it was freezing in the house. Before Conchita arrived Rebecca was looking everywhere for the heater. She had even called Tommy on his cellular and told him she was freezing. They live in a big old Miami Beach house full of drafts, which is great most of the time. Rebecca doesn't really like air conditioning because the sound of it is addictive, and most of the rooms in this house will stay comfortable most of the day with a ceiling fan.

Whatever girlfriends had children were going to bring them along and they could all play together in the back. There were swings back there, as well as a rope to swing from, a turtle, a new kitten, a tree house, the neglected, obnoxious, lusty dachshund, and a massive, intricate banyan in which to play hide and seek. Either that or they could go watch videos or listen to music in the family room. Too bad it was so cold or they could have gone out on the boat or jumped in the pool.

As soon as the three girls scampered out Rebecca said to Conchita. "Sit, let's chat before everyone arrives. Brrr! Take your coat off and here's a blanket you can put on your legs. Tommy will be bringing a heater. So tell me, is that creepy man still harassing you?"

Those strappy high-heeled sandals worn with pantyhose made Conchita's feet slide forward when she walked. She took her fur coat off and dumped it in a corner of the Florida room, on the floor.

"He sure is!" Conchita sighed.

Rebecca, who was already seated, urged her to try one of the new rocking chairs.

"And I don't know what to do," Conchita said as she sat down. But she didn't rock. "He keeps calling me, he keeps threatening me, he keeps following me . . . When I was driving here he was following me! Last night he called me and said he was going to destroy my marriage and my family and that he wasn't going to stop until he had me. I swear I'm telling the God-honest truth."

Rebecca seemed alarmed, "Conchi, don't you want to call the police?"

By now Rebecca had quit rocking.

"What would I tell the police?" Conchita said in a whisper. "It would be his word against mine. He's a very respected obstetrician here on the Beach. He could say I'm making it all up. I don't want to go through that type of embarrassment! Where's my purse?" she fretted.

"In back of the couch."

The conversation was cut short when Tommy arrived with the new heater. After he greeted Conchita and kissed Rebecca he sat on the red tiles of the Florida room and began taking the heater out of the box. There seemed to be several intricate pieces to it.

So Conchita said, "I can't believe they used fireflies as jewelry!"

Rebecca was worried. She glanced at her watch. Wasn't anyone else going to show up? "I want this to be perfect," she said to herself and then stood up. This was no time to be sitting, idle, in a rocking chair. Besides, whenever Tommy was around, Conchita and she had absolutely nothing to say to each other.

"Tommy, why'd you let the dog in?" she asked, sounding annoyed. "He's going to give Conchita's coat fleas! I don't want him in here!"

It was a good thing that Daisy arrived at that very moment.

"Of course you know Daisy!" Rebecca said to her father. "You've known her for ages! She's family! Daisy's married to Tommy's brother George who committed bigamy twice."

"Daisy . . . *la chismosa* with the yellow eyes?" her father asked.

With her back still turned to her father, Rebecca nodded. When she explained that Daisy has always been very strong and athletic she felt the need to flex the muscles on both her arms, as if she were lifting weights. And she has big, sinewy legs and calves this big around, Rebecca said, making a circle with both thumbs and index fingers. She still had her back turned so her father couldn't even see. Chunky feet, she carried on. . . and such a tiny waist! (About as big as her calves, according to Rebecca's hands.) Such a flat stomach! Such fat thighs! (As big as the world.) Which suddenly reminded her . . . Daisy's daughter Sylvia seems to get prettier each day. Why can't Nell look like that?

"Are we close?" Rebecca repeated her father's question. "Let's put it this way, we can get spitting mad at each other and then let go of it. We do that all the time."

Daisy's son Herman wanted to go outside and play. She had left her two younger children with the nanny who said she'd leave as soon as George got home.

"Who's George?"

"I told you! He's Tommy's extremely successful brother. The one who committed bigamy twice and got away with it. They swept the whole thing under the Persian rug. Tommy's family's perfect, they're not like us. Nell's fat and stupid, Mami's a wicked witch who's always saying ugly things, you're paralyzed, and all I do is fret and read! You can't sweep all that under a Persian rug! And that's why I wanted to have this *tertulia* in the first place! It was important for me!"

"So what happened?"

"It was ruined."

He said, "Turn around, look at me."

"No."

Daisy walked into the Florida room saying, "I got some census figures in case anyone's interested, about the population in Cuba at that time. Boy were they hard to get! Anybody interested?" Then she sat down next to Conchita and said, "Oh I love this rocking chair! Oh, hi, Tommy! I didn't know you were here! What are you doing on the floor?"

"Trying to figure out this heater. There, I got it! Rebecca, sweetheart, maybe it'll work better if you turn the ceiling fan off!"

But Rebecca was off, screaming, "Who let the goddamn dog in this time? He's full of fleas!" And she kept praying, "Oh God, I want everyone to come!"

"Where's my purse?" Conchita asked no one.

After Rebecca slammed the kitchen door shut and was yelling, "Out, you nasty creature!" another voice was coming from the opposite side of the house, "Hello! Anyone home? It's me!"

"You'll never guess who it was," Rebecca told her father. "The famous singer Lucía!"

"Lucía? Never heard of her."

"Of course you have! Everyone knows Lucía . . . Are we close?" Rebecca suddenly turned and repeated her father's question. "Oh no, not at all. Lucía's too famous."

Rebecca was back in the Florida room in no time, and the famous singer Lucía said, "Hey *m'ija Rebecca linda como siempre.* Your house is so gorgeous! *¡Daisita mi amor! Conchita linda* look at your hair, I can't believe it! Great perm! Oh my God you did your eyes! *¡Ay pero qué bellos están! ¡Fíjate que quedaste bien!* Sometimes they leave the eyes with no expression whatsoever. My dear you look like *una quinceañera!* Have you lost weight, Daisita? So are we going to have rows of rocking chairs and rock and talk like in the *tertulias?* You really look great, Becky, have you been working out a lot? Real motivated, hunh? I can tell. Tommy! *Un beso.* I haven't seen you out in the boat in a while and I want to hire your company to redo my house. *¡Tan guapo como siempre!*"

"Remember those bags I had under my eyes?" asked Conchita while Tommy said, "I'll be upstairs," while Rebecca asked, "Would anybody like a glass of ice water?" while Lucía repeated, "I can't believe how gorgeous this place is! It's got such character!" while Daisy opened the French door and yelled, "*Herman!* Stay away from the floating *deck!*"

"Don't let the dog in," Rebecca said before she turned and walked back toward the kitchen.

So Conchita repeated her question. "Does anyone remember those bags I had under my eyes?"

Daisy closed the French door and said, "Boy *do* we! That's all we ever talked about! Those *bags* under your eyes!"

Conchita took this seriously. "Weren't they ludicrous? Now I'm going to try to get this done," she said and touched the lower part of her jaw. "As soon as the kids are away at camp. Then the tits, then the thighs, then it's time to start all over again! I wonder if I left my sunglasses in the car?"

After Conchita said all that she began to rock fast.

Lucía said, "These rocking chairs are great!"

Everyone noticed that Rebecca had disappeared.

But Rebecca did overhear Lucía saying that she seemed uptight, "not relaxed like when she first fell in love with Tommy." So Daisy came to her rescue. "Well that was a hundred years ago! What do you expect?" And of course Rebecca is uptight! She's been having all these personal problems. Tommy lost his business. Nell's too fat and has learning disabilities. Her father had a stroke. And now she wants this gathering to be perfect and she's probably making herself crazy over it, drowning in a drop of water, praying to God that everyone shows up. She'll probably spend most of the evening in the kitchen making sure everything is going smoothly. She is a perfectionist, and gets quite upset if things don't quite turn out the way she plans. Not only that but she wants everything to be like one of her eternal page-turners with a beginning, a middle, an end, and a binding. To make a long story short, she's never been out in the real world. A reader, that's all she is. "What's more," Daisy whispered. "She's been trying to get pregnant for three months."

"Hum!" Rebecca uttered after she overheard all this. "Is that the sum of me?" she asked her father.

In turn he asked, "Did I hear you say the evening was ruined?"

By now Conchita had lost interest in the conversation because it didn't concern her. She took off one of her high-heeled sandals and inspected it closely.

They were all rocking like little girls whose feet couldn't touch the floor.

"Don't remind me of 1982! That's the year I got pregnant with Sylvia," Daisy was saying. "I have such bad memories of that year. Do you remember, Becky?" she asked.

Rebecca had just come back from the kitchen with a tray full of glasses.

She said to Daisy, "We still weren't talking to each other that year."

"You know what? You're right! Nineteen eighty-two was a bad bad year!" Conchita said as she threw her sandal on the floor. At times Conchita was so self-absorbed that she seemed to have conversations all by herself. "They're all the same I tell you, I think I have dated the whole American Medical Association and the whole American Bar Association and at the end they all end up being, *lo mismitico,* the same," Conchita said.

"Don't you hate it when she brags like that?" Rebecca asked Lucía and Daisy.

By now everyone who had a rocking chair was rocking steadily.

"No one smokes any more?"

"Becky, how long has it been since you quit?"

"Nine years."

"Nine years!"

"That's right, no one seems to smoke any more."

"Not even pot."

Anyway, far out, that book. Especially the part about the fireflies. Great idea! Sure, I'd love some water! Is that all there is to drink? Too early to start drinking alcohol? Hunh?

It's good water though. Cold. What are we going to talk about if we just drink ice water?

The author really went a little too far with that part about the sausage. Frankly there were many other ways of getting rid of that servant!

But the part about the sausage is true!

Who cares? Truth does not always need to be told.

Conchita grinned and held on to a thought for a little while, then she said that since Rebecca had been reading this novel out loud to her in the car for the past two weeks, the pages of the novel seemed to be scattered all over Miami. Pages one through five, for example, were on Alton Road, six through fifteen on the Julia Tuttle Causeway, the rest of that chapter on the expressway with Miami on the left. And from now on traffic jams on South Dixie Highway would forever remind her of Chapter Two; as to Chapter Three, it began under the banyan in the car facing the Paige School. No matter how much the author insisted on that Calle Aguacate, for her that weird family's house was in Coconut Grove, but the inside of their house made her think of Rebecca's house. Did something similar to this happen to anyone else or was she the only one?

Daisy said that it got her into doing research. So she had numbers that concerned just about everything that happened in Havana in 1868, like how many people got married, how many were born, how many died, how many tourists came, how much the hotels cost, was anyone interested?

Lucía said that the part about the demons carrying Catalina's mind away is probably true. And what about that little girl that the cook *tiene haciendo el Palo Monte*? The cook has that little girl involved in the Palo Monte religion, that's black magic! She thinks Trudi Agramonte had a cook like that who did all that horrible *brujería* to her family.

"Who's Trudi Agramonte?" her father asked. "I'm having trouble sorting through all these women."

"Wait, she's going to show up any minute."

At last Rebecca started to relax, but where were the seven others she'd invited? What if they didn't come? She jumped out of her rocking chair and fretted silently. "Is that fleazy dog back in here?" she wondered out loud.

Norma, the maid, brought out more water and finger sandwiches and pastries and more *croquetas*. She said to Rebecca, "Your mother's on the phone."

On her way to the phone Rebecca said that ever since she'd been reading this novel she'd been giving much thought to what the famous semiotician Umberto Gomez had said about reality being parasitically dependent on fiction.

"It really makes me feel like going to Cuba," she said from the next room.

"For me the novel takes place in this house too, for some reason," said Daisy.

"They've done a great job decorating it," said Lucía.

Before she picked up the phone Rebecca overheard Daisy saying, "It's all Tommy. He's the one who comes up with the decorating ideas. All Rebecca does is read." She also overheard Lucía saying, "Well look who's here! If it isn't Trudi Agramonte my attorney herself in person! You are so hard to get on the phone, *m'ija!* Gimme a kiss!"

Trudi said, "I'm not going to be able to make it on Fridays this early. Can't we change this to Saturdays? I can't take half of Friday off to come to some reading group. Can't we do it on Saturdays or later on Fridays and then have dinner together with the husbands, the boyfriends and the what-nots. God, what a nice place!" she said and probably stopped to look around. Rebecca was overhearing all this and couldn't see what was happening. "They must be *loa*-ded!" Trudi went on. "By the way my boyfriend's coming in two hours. I hope it's okay with everyone. And I don't know about the rest of you but I didn't have time to read the third chapter, so someone's going to have to tell me what happened. I'm going to ask Becky to tape a whole bunch of chapters for me so I can listen to them in my car and not hold you girls up."

"We're in no hurry. It's not as if there were going to be a quiz," said Conchita.

"How did you overhear all that if you were with your mother on the phone?" her father asked.

"I can handle two conversations at the same time."

"Who's Trudi?"

"The girlfriend who looks like Cristina Onassis."

"How many rocking chairs is that so far?"

Trudi asked everyone where Rebecca was and Rebecca yelled from the kitchen, "I'll be right with you, Trudi! Pick a rocking chair, make yourself at home!"

Daisy suggested that they just rock Rebecca's empty rocking chair in the meantime. Lucía stared at the three remaining rocking chairs and asked who else was coming.

Rebecca asked her father, "Is this *tertulia* a success so far?"

"For a *tertulia* to be truly successful, everyone has to talk at the same time."

Meanwhile Rebecca was on the phone with her mom. "Well Mom if you think something's really wrong then why not go to the doctor? It could be nothing!"

"No, what for? I have nothing to live for, and I know they're going to discover something really bad and then what? Chemotherapy, humiliation . . . I don't even have proper health insurance and nothing to live for and I should have had more children, it's been three days since I last spoke to you and yesterday I got a hold of Nell and she told me she was too busy doing her homework to talk to me, is that what you teach her, to have absolutely no love for me? Irma was really lucky, she gets to see Almita's kids all the time and they go to lunch together and Almita has time for her, but you, you're always busy, apparently Frankie's buying her a car and I don't even dare go to the supermarket with mine, one of these days it's going to die on me right in the middle of a bad neighborhood, but I can't afford a new car, but anyway I'll probably die first, what's there to live for anyway?"

"I've gotta go Mami I have company."

"Oh wait I forgot to tell you, that's why I called. I went to Marverde Travel today and you'll never guess how much money I spent sending stuff to Cuba. You remember I told you I had to send some extra stuff to my aunt Ramona because when I went to Cuba and saw the poverty she was living in

I swore I'd send her something every month. So I made *una cajita,* a little box and filled it with a can of Klim, that's powdered whole milk, a bag of Texmati brown rice which is really delicious, a bag of Fig Newtons that everyone in Cuba loves, three envelopes of Kool Aid, which were so heavy! what else? Hold it . . . I said Klim milk, Fig Newtons . . . Oh yes, the Goya seasoning with the *achiote,* chocolate chip cookies, melba toast, a bottle of oil, a box of pasta, I think that's about it, guess how much it cost, just guess! One hundred and forty seven dollars! Ten dollars a pound. Those agencies are exploiting us, *nos están chupando la sangre,* they're the real *chupacabras,* no wonder they want Castro to stay in power! They know we have no choice! And Menosmal probably owns all those agencies! He doesn't have family in Cuba so what does he care? Then I thought, now that I'm here I might as well send the little shoes for La China's daughters, Becky you're not going to believe this, they're charging twenty-five dollars a pound! It cost me seventy-five dollars to send four pairs of *apéame uno* shoes, can you imagine? They were just cheap vulgar *chancletas!*"

"Mom, I really have to go now, I have company, I'll call you later."

"Yes, of course, no time for me," Rebecca's mother said and hung up.

The dog was back in the house, which meant that someone else had arrived. Thank God!

It was Selene Machado. She'd shown herself in and was kissing and hugging the four girlfriends in the Florida room.

Selene said, "What is it with this horny dog?"

Daisy reminded her that at the New Year's Eve party it was her husband George who had played the part of the horny dog.

"Don't remind me."

Rebecca's father said, "Isn't she the one who used to draw a funny face in the 'o' of Machado?"

"Apparently she still does," Rebecca turned around and smiled at her dad. Immediately she turned right back.

Right away Selene said that the first couple of chapters had given her courage. Everyone seemed interested in what she had to say. Isn't this what a reading club is about? A group of people get together and try to determine how the book they're reading affects their lives. "So I did a very courageous thing today," Selene said.

So now that Selene had a captive audience she proceeded slowly. She really hated the part about the sausage. That was so sick! But she loved the novel! She said she was one hundred percent into it in spite of, or thanks to, her Attention Deficit Disorder.

After they were all seated, and Selene had blurted out that she definitely didn't care for ice water, Daisy asked, "So what courageous thing did you do?"

Selene cleared her throat. Everyone waited. She finally said that she'd made a decision.

Everyone stopped rocking, stopped breathing, stopped drinking, it was a moment of total suspense disturbed only by the sound of the obnoxious dog's claws on the granite floor. He liked Selene and he was going to hump her leg no matter how hard Rebecca kicked him.

Talk, Selene, talk.

Rebecca's dad asked impatiently, "So what was it?"

"Nothing." Selene had simply decided to get a permit for a handgun in order to shoot her husband.

Everyone was let down. You could tell by the way they resumed their rocking.

"You don't need a permit," said Rebecca.

Lucía suggested, "Perhaps we do need something other than ice water to drink."

Selene turned to Rebecca and said, "What do you mean, I don't need a permit?"

"You can just go and buy one. You don't need a permit in Florida, I tell you. You're free to carry," Rebecca said before she turned her rocking chair to face Trudi and Daisy.

"It can't be that easy! We'd have all these lunatics running around with guns," Selene turned to Lucía and said.

"We do," said Lucía right before she moved her rocking chair into Rebecca's group.

"Once I get a permit, *and I'm sure you need a permit,*" Selene said to Conchita, "I'm going to buy a gun and I'm going to shoot them both, him and his girlfriend."

Conchita then proceeded to tell Selene all about the obstetrician who was harrassing her. Selene couldn't place another word.

In the meantime Rebecca, Trudi, Daisy and Lucía were discussing the semiotician Umberto Gomez's theory that reality was parasitically dependent on fiction. They were all talking at the same time.

When Jenny Rincón got there late she said she really had a lot of questions. There were things she didn't understand about what was going on in Cuba, and also things she didn't approve of, like the racism, the way women were mistreated. Did the author agree with all this? Wasn't the author painting some kind of *macho* society where only money and war counted? Jenny Rincón had exactly the same hairdo, those thin wiry bangs, and that low ponytail right at her neckline. She was thin, and not very pretty, her hands were deformed, and she had hair between her eyebrows. One more thing, does the author ever openly condemn slavery? Jenny wondered out loud.

Priscilla Drake didn't get there until seven. She said she had had to wait until her husband got home because she hated to drive after sunset and that's why she was late. By the way, was it all right if men came? Because her husband had come along, he was still outside, trying to get the baby out of the car seat. So much for those quick-release seats!

"Is that him?" Rebecca asked.

But the footsteps and the panting were George's. He was carrying their two youngest children and saying that this was a woman's job and that never again would he stoop this low. "I'm kidding, of course," he said. "Where's Daisy?"

Rebecca offered to take one of the babies.

By the way there's a man outside struggling to get a baby out of a car and the car seat's putting up quite a fight. "Where's Daisy?" George repeated. "I need for her to take this other baby."

"Shut the door. Don't let the dog in!" said Rebecca.

Tommy came downstairs. The doorbell rang. It was this man with a very southern accent. Trudi's boyfriend.

"Shut the door!" Rebecca repeated.

The doorbell rang again. This time it was Priscilla's husband.

Rebecca didn't take her eyes off Priscilla until she was through saying hello to Tommy and Tommy was shaking hands with Priscilla's husband, Guillermo Ros.

Rebecca touched one of the thick thorns on the bitter orange tree and said, "Alma and Silka didn't show up."

Silka Velasquez called and told Rebecca that she hadn't been able to begin reading the novel because she wasn't able to turn the pages. Lately her illness had been making a turn for the worse.

Then Alma called to say that she couldn't come because she had a very bad cold.

After everyone left and Tommy had gone to bed, Rebecca poured herself a glass of wine and taped as many chapters as possible for Silka, who was too weak to read; for Conchita, who was too vain to read; and for Trudi, who said she didn't have time to read.

"What about Helen?" her father asked. "You skipped Helen. Did she come?"

Rebecca had lured a few leafcutter ants onto a twig and was inspecting them closely. "Yes, she also came late. And she ruined everything."

"The view of Havana from the entrance to the port is one of the most picturesque and pleasing on the northern equinoctal shores of America."

Alexander von Humboldt

"There is nothing attractive about the town of Havana; nothing whatever to my mind . . ."

Anthony Trollope

"I was in a constant puzzle, on first visiting Havana . . . for there seems to be no 'west end' . . ."

Samuel Hazard

ROSARIO SANTA CRUZ WAS HOLDING a sheet of paper at arms' length with her head tilted back. She tried stretching her arm a little more, tilted her head back as far as it could naturally go, and squinted. Finally she shook her head and frowned. "I don't know," she uttered. "And you can't really tell much from a list of characters. Is this by order of appearance or of importance? And why eleven women? Does that number have a meaning? And wait a minute, is it going to make all my seamstresses think they deserve to be rich and demand more free time, as well as sweet employers and husbands? I don't want anything that makes them class-conscious or overly proud. What's more, I don't want them to miss a stitch because they're listening too much."

Lolo Tacón shrugged with impatience. "Trust me, it's a great novel! It'll open their minds and they'll work more intelligently. Every one of the seamstresses at the factory is going to love it! You'll see, this story will force them to come to work early in the morning to get a seat by the pulpit so they don't miss anything, and then they'll work overtime. Why? you ask . . . Because they can identify with each one of these women, Am I getting too fat? Is my hair falling out? Do I look old? Is my husband going to cheat on me? What is it that I live for? What's more, Rosario, I have it all arranged with the reader. Every evening at quarter to six there will be a turning point in the story, so they won't want to leave! They will all stay there an extra half-hour just to see what's going to happen. Now you go ahead and multiply an extra half-hour by thirty-five seamstresses! Go ahead! And then multiply that by the six days in the week . . . I know numbers is all you care about, so go ahead and multiply! I'll wait. Rosario, *corazón*, what it all comes down to is that even the reader will want to work overtime! It's a page turner! Who cares if González *y* Gutiérrez Fashions pays a few *centavos* more per hour? As long as we read better novels to our seamstresses we have nothing to fear from the competition! Not only that but we've managed to lure Umbertico Barrios's son away from there!" said Lolo.

"What's his name?"

"Umberto Junior."

Rosario protested. "How much will we have to pay this Junior?"

"Only a few *centavos* more than what he was getting at González *y* Gutiérrez. All Umberto Junior wants to do is spend his day reading. He doesn't care about politics like Umbertico, his father. We just have to give him enough to feed his family and to keep his wife from nagging all the time! I heard her the other day when I was sitting at the terrace of the Cafe Louvre and they were walking by with their three daughters and two sons. She was shouting at the top of her lungs, 'Look at *fulanito*, look at *menganito*, and look at *you*, you lazy bum! All you ever do is read books and reading does not put food on the table for your information. I regret *el maldito día* I married you!'"

"They must have been walking very slowly." Rosario commented.

Lolo begged. "Be serious, Rosy . . ."

"Well, if you assure me that the reader isn't going to cost us a fortune . . ."

Lolo was confident again: "Umberto Junior is a flake as far as money is concerned. Of course I've promised him the world! But he's not going to get it. What's more he wouldn't know how to ask for money if he were starving! Listen, Rosy, *corazón*, it's a novel that takes place in the future, over one hundred years from now. I liked it the minute I realized the action takes place in Florida where we'll be spending our honeymoon. Maybe I'd like to move there one day. What do you think, Rosyposy? What if we learned English and moved to Miami or Tampa? We can open another dress factory there, everyone needs to dress! Say yes, say yes, Rosyposy!"

"You're so cute, Lolo! Come here, gimme a kiss!"

The lovers hugged and kissed. Only six months had elapsed since Catalina's mind had been carried away by demons, since Petra had been murdered and since Joaquín had disappeared, but Rosario and Lolo didn't want to put their wedding off any longer. It seemed as if some strange force had always been trying to keep them apart, and this frightened them. They really wondered if fate would always get in the way. Worse yet, would something horrible happen each time that they swore eternal love to each other? They ended up getting carried away with their suppositions and before they knew it they were in a total state of panic. Was this part of the curse? They both got hysterical. Where did the curse come from, God or the demon?

Finally Rosario realized that this panic wasn't getting them anywhere. She was the more lucid of the two, and she was the one who set a date. "April 10, no matter what!" She slammed the cutting board with her fist and yelled.

Their wedding was exactly two weeks away. Bishop Espada himself would be performing the ceremony in the chapel of La Casa Amarilla, where so many of Rosario's ancestors had received their sacraments. The couple planned to honeymoon in Florida before returning home and settling down to raise their two little nieces, María Soledad and María Fernanda. It was obvious that Rosario and Lolo could never have children, so they might as well treat these two as if they were their own.

"In two weeks we'll be out of danger," said Lolo. "Once we're married no one can make us take our vows back!"

Rosario said: "What we're doing has probably never ever been done before. I know we're crazy but I can't help it!"

"Oh, I'm sure it's been done before, everything's been done before, Rosy, absolutely everything! And don't worry, no one will ever find out, only my family knows, and you know how prudish they are, they'd rather die than tell anyone."

By 1869, only two dressmakers at Titania Fashions worked with the traditional fabrics imported from Spain, and this was usually to fill the incessant orders for curtains. Since an incredible number of hours were spent daily trying to find cute innovative ways to keep the sun out of the house, curtains played a very important role in Cuban lives, and it so happened that the Spanish fabric was perfect for making curtains.

Quite a lot of work and creative energy went into the making of Spanish fabrics. The result was indeed a beautiful but also heavy, itchy, and thick material that was extremely difficult to work with. Besides, with the gold, silver, and copper thread that was so often woven into the fabric, some outfits could weigh over a dozen pounds.

For almost one hundred years the tyrannical and uncaring Spanish crown had made all Cuban dress manufacturers use exclusively the Spanish fabrics and had thus forced the law-abiding and fashion-conscious Cuban men and women to swelter in outfits that did not at all correspond to the Cuban climate. According to the newspapers and to the political thinkers of the time, Spain didn't care if the Cubans were hot or if they got heat rashes from so much sweat accumulating under their clothing. All the Spanish Cortes (Courts) did in crises such as these was advise these poor people to import more talcum powder.

More talcum powder, *más talco!* This is how The Ugly Duckling talcum powder flooded and monopolized the Cuban market. Whatever happened to the Cubans, Spain profited. It was no coincidence that The Ugly Duckling was a Spanish-owned company.

These Cubans covered with talcum powder were merely pawns in the chess game of attrition that Spain was playing with Great Britain in the Caribbean. It was for this reason that the Cubans weren't allowed to import anything but Spanish fabrics. Spain even went to great lengths to impose the embargo on foreign fabrics.

Anyone ordering their gowns from Paris had to pay a scandalously high tax. Anyone importing fabrics from Italy would be fined. Anyone importing fabrics from Jamaica would be fined and then imprisoned.

Jamaica was the biggest threat. Those cool, colorful cotton fabrics from Jamaica were a constant reminder to Spain that England was still lurking nearby.

Indeed, Spain had not forgotten that the British had successfully invaded Cuba in 1782. So Spain was going to make sure that nothing even remotely British ever sneaked onto Cuban soil again. Seeing those wonderful fabrics from Jamaica on Cuban soil resembled a new and also subtler British invasion.

But there was no Morro Castle strong enough to keep the fabrics out and no cannons strong enough to kill the taste for them. At first Spanish propaganda tried turning the Jamaican fabrics into vulgar cottons for convicts, peasants, and the lower classes. There was negative advertising everywhere, so much so that it made everyone laugh at the subterfuge. What's more, the propaganda was at its peak during that sweltering month of July when even the thought of wearing the lightest cotton was pure torture. All people ever did during the dog days was rock, fan, and repeat, "*¡Pero qué calor Dios mío!*"

Jamaica wasn't the only threat. Cubans had always had this inalienable and inalterable taste for French fashions. The Cubans loved anything that was French. They loved French perfume, they loved French names, French novels, French panties, French architecture, and, most of all, French fashions. If you weren't wearing a gown imported from Paris at the ball, then you might as well not go. The predilection for things French was so intense that if some women had been shown a rag and told it was French they would have worn it. Spain tried to get this out of their system but to no avail, the Cubans continued absolutely adoring everything that was French, so much so that any attempt on Spain's part to put an embargo on French products, would have precipitated the unavoidable, a revolution.

With Jamaica the situation was completely different.

Before 1850 Rosario's own maternal great great uncle-in-law, Antonio María Jesús Tirry y Tirry, began smuggling from Jamaica fabrics that were called Indianas or Zarazas, made of cotton that was either hand-painted or dyed different natural beautiful colors. Needless to say, the minute these Indianas made it to Cuba, men, women and children were ready to lie, cheat, and steal for them. At last something that was cool, comfortable, pretty, and didn't itch!

This stroke of business genius was, of course, at the root of the family fortune. Cuban women love bright colors and never in their life had they seen such preciously bright blues and reds and yellows and purples. Even widows started wearing these Indianas in the privacy of their own homes.

When Spain caught wind of this they had the clergy look into this and declared the import of Indianas totally illegal. The Spanish crown felt so threatened by Jamaican colors that they declared an embargo. Nothing Jamaican could come on the island and nothing Spanish could be exported to Jamaica, to do so would signify trading with the enemy which was punishable by a fine, imprisonment, loss of nationality, and even death.

The colorful comfortable wearable cotton fabrics became so illegal that everyone wanted them. Parties would be thrown were everyone would be playing with fire and wearing these fabrics.

This was in fact British infiltration. The British had enjoyed being the masters of Cuba so much, that they never got over it, and kept on dreaming the impossible dream of overthrowing the Spanish crown on the island and of getting Cuba back. If that meant not having anyone buy those heavy hot and itchy Spanish fabrics, that's how it would be.

Finally so many yards of the Jamaican fabric were smuggled into Cuba that Rosario's great great uncle-in-law was still selling it by the meter ten years after the port of Havana had been hermetically sealed tight against anything that even remotely resembled Jamaican cotton.

Spain even tried adding brighter colors to their fabrics. Nothing could change the Habaneras' taste for the transparent, the light, and the flashy. After that Spain tried to make black appear fashionable and high class, but even the widows continued hating to wear black.

While all this was going on Rosario's grandfather, who had just inherited the business, decided to make pink and blue the colors of the summer of 1810. With the help of his son-in law, the young Gabriel María, they flooded the market with transparent pinks and light blues.

The following year Gabriel María started making simple white blouses made of Dutch fabric and socks made of Scottish thread for women. The countess of Merlin wore this for the first time and the next day everyone wanted to look exactly like her. Fashion was a great business to be in and a surefire way of getting rich. Habaneras absolutely refused to wear the same dress twice. Even if the dress was imported from Paris and of Thousand and One Nights quality luxury with precious stones sewn into it, an Habanera would rather die than wear it twice.

As to the linen dresses that they wore in the morning to go shopping, the rule was that once linen was washed it had to be given to a Negro woman, either the cook or the housekeeper. The same went for the silk stockings. Which meant that you had a whole island absolutely obsessed by clothing and not wanting to wear anything twice.

The shrewd Gabriel María noticed this and soon began buying used clothing from the Habaneras' servants who were also refusing to wear dresses twice, and why not since they received more dresses than they could wear in a lifetime?

So Gabriel María began buying these once- or twice-used dresses, cleaning them, changing them a little, putting a tag that said "Titania Fashions the most Parisian in the World" on them, and selling them back to whoever wanted them. It was too bad that his father-in-law was dead at that time, for he would have been proud of his daughter's husband.

So this is how this family's fortune had been made. The first ancestor came shortly after Columbus discovered this world. His name was Medina. He was Cuba's first tailor.

When asked why he'd left a thriving fashion business in Granada to come and dress the adventurers of the New World, the first Cuban tailor had cited the Spanish Inquisition. With a name like Medina and his accent he didn't stand a chance! All he wanted was to make money and get fat, why did they have to pick on him?

Before we start feeling sorry for Medina it must be said that it was in fact debt and scandal that had forced him to flee to Seville, pay up front, and then and wait his turn to get on one of those rickety-rackety caravels headed for the other side.

Medina's little cottage industry had turned into big business even before he had time to adapt to life in Havana. The day he opened his tailor's shop there was a long line of people waiting outside on the sidewalk to have their measurements taken and to put in orders for new clothes. It soon became a tradition that the man who married a Medina woman would take over the business make it thrive, add new blood to it.

After Medina came Machado, then Santiago, then Cuevas, Ruiz, Velásquez, Rincón, González, and so on until the family decided to adopt an aristocratic name.

This is probably why the business thrived. Each generation would bring in new blood, a new last name, new ideas. It wasn't long before other companies, seeing how well a business thrived when it was handed down from father-in-law to son-in-law, started doing the same.

The problem now was that the family seemed to be at a dead-end street. The only adult left was Rosario, and she was marrying an architect who wasn't at all interested in business. All Lolo wanted to do besides choosing the novels that would be read to the seamstresses, was to remodel and refurbish La Casa Amarilla. They had terrible arguments each time Rosario tried to get Lolo involved in the serious money-making aspect of the business.

Lolo would then throw a fit and yell that money was a vulgar thing for mediocre peoople. Lolo was extremely proud of being an aesthete. Lolo was the proudest of aesthetes, and also the most stubborn person that ever lived. Even more stubborn than Rosario. Not only that, but Lolo could really pout. Lolo could pout for days and weeks when annoyed or contradicted. Living with Lolo was like walking on eggs. Rosario did not have it easy at all, Lolo was the moodiest person she had ever met.

What was Rosario to do? She looked to her dead ancestors for advice, they remained silent. She scratched her head in desperation, sniffed her armpits. The thought of doing something new was overwhelming for such a conservative person. All she wanted was to follow in her ancestors footsteps and continue making lots of money for the family, but fate seemed to want it some other way. Something kept telling her to come up with her own answers. Or should she just throw her arms up in the air? (She always took a quick whiff of her armpits when she did that.) Should she wait for María Fernanda to marry? But María Fernanda was only eight years old! That's when she decided that she herself would run the family business. If Lolo refused to run it, so be it! *¡Carajo!*

". . . and this prattling text is then a frigid text, as any demand is frigid until desire, until neurosis forms in it."

Roland Barthes, *The Pleasure of the Text*

YOU CAN MAKE A ROCKING CHAIR TALK. It depends on the floor, whether it's tile, or wood, or linoleum, or bluestone, and on the person who's rocking, their personality, how hard they rock, how quietly, the language or languages they speak, how bad they want to say something, their accent. But in the beginning, when the rocking chair is new, young, *un silloncito*, a baby rocking chair who's new to the surface and to those thighs, those feet, those legs, that mind, those haunches, its vocabulary is limited to two syllables at a time. Soon it gets the hang of you. He-len, He-len, too-much, to-drink, last-night. She came, late and, had not, bo-thered, to read, the first, chap-ter. Dark mood. De-mon. She bit, Har-vey. Ea-ting, drin-king, ea-ting, drin-king, con-tra, dict-ing, Har-vey. She-e, ven-bit, Har-vey.

For the past two days she'd been so mad at Helen! Ruining her first *tertulia* like she did.

The rocking chair was new and Rebecca liked to play with the way they talked. This one had a funny accent. She was sitting on the back porch by herself having breakfast with the phone and the novel on her lap. Too bad the sun was in her eye. So when the phone rang she decided to sit somewhere else and get acquainted with all four of her new rocking chairs. What's more, she could see the bay from here, and the morning shadows.

Right away Conchita said, "I gotta talk to you now!" She sounded shaken. Her voice had quite a tremor to it. Rebecca glanced at her watch. It was half past nine and Tommy was still upstairs asleep. "I'm all by myself," she said. "It's a wonderful morning, come on over."

Conchita was probably going to tell her that she'd changed plastic surgeons. So the minute she arrived Rebecca started doing her own talking. "I'm so mad at Helen! I hate her! Ruining my first *tertulia* like she did . . ."

Conchita sat through that whole diatribe without interrupting, so Rebecca got curious. "What's up?" she asked.

"Is Tommy here?" asked Conchita in a whisper. "I don't want him to hear."

"He didn't get home till five AM last night so he'll be sound asleep for a while."

So Conchita told her everything.

Rebecca thinks she held her breath for a while. She was so shocked and dismayed that she let her rocking chair prattle. Still holding her breath, she looked at Conchita. Size-four, size-four, some-times, size-two, de-pends, on-the, gar-ment. So tiny, so bad, so tiny, so bad. Tiny-bad-tiny-bad.

Rebecca uttered a simple, "Wow!"

Conchita closed her eyes. Now they were sitting face to face. Never mind the sparkling diamond shapes floating on Biscayne Bay. Never mind their shadows lying on the green lawn. This was serious. With round eyes Rebecca stared at Conchita and resumed her rocking.

Conchita is barely five feet tall and she is already shorter than Jessica, her twelve-year-old, who plays basketball. They live in a three-story white stucco house on North Bay Road facing the bay, barely a five-minute drive from Rebecca's.

Stanley, Conchita's husband, is a dentist. He's never home. He's either working or playing golf. He's always busy. He never stays in bed with her in the morning. He's up and gone at dawn. They don't have anything in common. Conchita spends her days taking care of her house, her body, her girls. She used to like to paint.

Maybe it's all Stanley's fault. Yeah, let's blame Stanley! Her eagerness acted like a drooling doggy dog.

"Wow!" Rebecca sighed again.

After Jessica's birth when Conchita had quit working she discovered great pleasure in painting tiles and lampshades but one day for no reason at all, she decided to quit, suddenly.

Rebecca was rocking slower, still staring at Conchita with utter dismay. No, Conchita is never bored, she refuses to admit that she's ever bored. There's always something to do, but sometimes she wonders what exactly there is to do, especially since she doesn't really get anything done, and doesn't even need to do anything. She has a maid and enough money to pay for any help she needs. All she has to do is spend the time looking for the help. So what is it that takes up so much time? A few months ago she was so busy that she even had to quit her *faux* finish classes.

Whose fault is this? the rocking chair asked. And do we need to find fault? Rebecca wondered if Conchita could hear how it talked. Do you think it's better in the book? Life, I mean?

Conchita's tone was acerbic. "Right, let's change the subject. Let's talk about the book now!" She didn't even bother to open her eyes when she said that.

Let's run to that other world where bugs are gems! Tiaras! The real world. Fireflies are jewels! Someone threw them in the bay. There they go! Tennis bracelets!

No! We've got to get to the heart of this. Proceed slowly.

What is it about Conchita? Isn't she just another rich Miami Beach housewife? So bad . . . Where does that leave me? Rebecca wondered and the rocking chair wondered.

Conchita picks up and drops her daughters off at school and at their other activities, but are all her days taken up by this chore?

"Get out of here!" Rebecca yelled.

So Conchita opened her eyes and said, "Why don't you get rid of that dog if you hate him so much?"

The rocking chairs prattled on.

At least her friend Rebecca was a volunteer reader at an old people's club. Rebecca loves to read, whenever she isn't doing something with Nell or taking care of the house or shopping, she's reading. According to Tommy the first thing Rebecca does each morning is grab a book and disappear into the bathroom, where she remains at least half an hour. Then she walks back into the bedroom with the book in her hands, her head down, reading. She continues reading all the way downstairs and only stops for those few seconds when the preparation of the coffee demands all her attention. She continues reading while she waits for the coffee to percolate, she reads while she yells at the dog, and even at red lights. The people behind her always have to honk their horns so Rebecca will get going. Rebecca reads so much that sometimes she even reads books in secret so people won't think that she's trying to escape reality. Whenever he decided to pick on her, her brother-in-law George asks her what she plans to do the day she will have read everything. "I'll start reading people's minds," she says.

Rebecca's life is totally different, yes indeed. Rebecca doesn't seem to worry about getting old or about not being smart or pretty enough. Her skin is fantastic and she is certainly smart and pretty enough. Sometimes Rebecca used to help Tommy in the office when certain matters called for discretion.

Conchita isn't sure what she meant by that and if it had anything to do with Tommy losing his business.

Conchita closed her eyes again.

It was Rebecca's turn to stare.

So back in December Conchita asked Stan if she could help him in the office. Stan said, "I told you not to quit your *faux* finish classes! See! You're bored now!"

Is all this the dentist's fault?

Stan left very early this morning to go play golf with his friends, and Jessica and Belinda spent the night at Daisy's who has volunteered to take all the children to the Everglades today. Rebecca confessed that she was more than glad to get rid of Nell. January is after all the best time to visit the Miccosukee Indian Reservation and to go on the airboats. Most of the year it is quite a buggy, humid, sweltering place.

So Conchita was having her breakfast all alone when she couldn't keep the secret any more and decided to call Rebecca. She had to tell someone. What if she got in trouble? Someone had to know what was going on. She was having black coffee and melba toast, nothing sweet or pleasant, that was out of the question. Everyone told Conchita she was the last person in the world who needed to go on a diet, she only weighed ninety-six pounds! "Look at this!" she said while squeezing a chunk of flesh from her thigh. She didn't want breasts, or thighs, or buttocks, or a belly, or a waistline. She wanted to look like an eleven-year-old boy, but she never told anyone. All she said was that she was so short that she had to watch out. "And these damn breasts!" she thought. "Ugh!"

None of that mattered any more.

After her Spartan breakfast she usually goes out for an hour jog, then rewards herself with a medium glass of fresh-squeezed orange juice. Right after that she goes to her tennis or aerobics class. The minute she gets home she runs upstairs and inspects her body to see if she has developed more muscle.

She always skips lunch.

"Rebecca, what are you thinking about?" Conchita asked.

"Things I'm going to tell my father when I go see him this afternoon."

Mind if I water the plants while I read your mind?

Conchita regrets her breasts. Before this happened, what she told Rebecca today, she couldn't stop thinking about it. She should have adopted her children! With all the starving children in the world, she went and got pregnant . . . *twice!* There was plastic surgery, and she'd already had yards of skin stretched and cut and tucked, but for some reason it frightened her so to get her breasts done. At first she thought that if she got other things done perhaps she'd lose her fear, she didn't. So far she'd gotten her eyes, her nose, and the cellulitis in the back of her arms done.

Love the shadow of water.

She is scheduled for her face and her throat in the summer while the girls are away at camp. By the time they get back they'll have a new mom! A prettier mom. But never pretty enough, of course. Never smart enough. Never good enough.

Rebecca turned the hose off and walked back toward Conchita. The novel they were reading was lying on the third new rocking chair. Rebecca picked it up and sat down.

The minute she opened her mouth it sounded reproachful. Conchita said, "You always have to be holding a book."

Rebecca didn't let go of it. It wasn't that she was going to read it, but she liked its size, she liked the cover and she liked checking to see how much she had already read to Conchita. She opened it to Chapter Four, and she remembered how it was in school and in the university when she used to read so much, and how Conchita liked math and painting.

Rebecca rocked quietly. Conchita leaned forward and put her head in her hands. "Go ahead and read," she said. "Please. Read anything. Or I'll fire you! My mind or whatever! Please read."

What about some ice water?

What seemed like a lifetime ago Conchita was so good in math that she ended up in the London School of Economics. There were so many men there, and so little competition. She was one of the few girls in her class. She met Reza in London and it was love at first sight. They were mad about each other and could barely stand to spend ten minutes apart. The only problem was that he only spoke Iranian and French. He was a great mathematician, but he sure was having a lot of problems with the English in class. His government had sent him there. And he did learn the English little by little, but in the beginning she had to use the little French she had learned as a child. She understood everything he said to her in French, but speaking was quite another story. She would spend her days smoking and drinking coffee, by the time 6 PM came along she still hadn't eaten a thing and she could smell it in her breath while they were making love, she could smell her own stomach juices, but he smelled the same so it didn't matter at all. She really wanted to marry him, they were meant for each other and would have been a loving couple with strong chemistry. Everyone at home kept saying, "Are you crazy, you really want to marry an Iranian?" She told them he was as smart and intense as a man could get. What's more, they would talk for hours! "And what is it that usually frustrates us in men?" she asked anyone. "That they refuse to talk!" Of course she wanted to marry him!

What happened was that he never planned to marry an American girl.

He was straight with her.

Rebecca, how did you know? And whose shadow is that?

The seventies, Rebecca thought while she rocked, light years away from the squeaky clean nineties and the fresh breath gel caps, the internal deodorant, the fresh out of the shower air . . . But you can still see vestiges of old Miami Beach when it was still all right to play with your life. It was considered normal. Light up outside the movie theater or the market. Play with your life, throw it all in the bay, along with the bugs, those gems, even the praying mantis paper money. Was that what happened to Conchita now? Why did she go and do a thing like that? Hubris? Nostalgia?

Now the hotels that used to be full of old Jews in the early seventies when Rebecca and Conchita were in high school have been painted pastel pink or green or blue and are full of beautiful people as far away from old age as possible. "The News Cafe is so expensive!" Rebecca said the other day. "I went there with Tommy and he kept looking at the women . . . and when I protested he said he had always looked at pretty women! I think I preferred South Beach *cuando estaba lleno de viejitos!*"

"My rocking chair keeps prattling!" Rebecca chuckled.

"It's shocked and shy. Where did I put my sunglasses?"

"You left them over by the bagels."

The whole place is indeed swarming with beautiful bodies. Just twenty years ago those same hotel terraces were full of rickety armchairs in which old and sick people would spend their days, talking about the past, hoarding bread, living on half their dividends, never knowing whether they were proud or sad to have lived this long.

Conchita's father, who used to own a hotel on Ocean Drive, always said that the old get introspective but they don't have the necessary attention span to get anywhere in their thinking. The result was a vicious circle of thought. Mr. Pérez had catered to the old for so many years that by the time he sold his hotel and was old himself he had this deep ruthless prejudice against anything that was old.

"This is our town," Rebecca said. "We've seen it change."

"My father died here."

"And I will lose mine here."

They saw the end of a generation. They were teenagers snacking at Wolfie's after school, their parents were still young and restless, downing Valium and Ritalin with Chivas Regal, and the Miami Beach oldsters were between eighty and one hundred years old. They had seen both wars in Europe. They used to eat matzo ball soup either at the Wolfie's on 21st street or at the old one on Lincoln Road, the one that's a Burger King now; no more Danish pastries, chicken livers, borscht, Yiddish.

"Now the Beach is full of beautiful people," said Conchita. Stupid beautiful people. One thought led to another. It wasn't enough being skinny. She just didn't feel pretty!

And she was so ashamed of herself.

"Do you think I'm going to get in trouble, Becky?"

"I don't know."

"Will I go to jail?"

Conchita closed her eyes. Rebecca read her mind.

Conchita lived the crazy life in Boston trading foreign currency and traveling, and lots of cigarettes, lots of money, lots of cocaine, lots of men. She was so exhausted! And proud of it . . . Then one fine day when she was 27 she returned to Miami Beach to visit her parents and her old girlfriends.

The toothache started on the airplane on the way down. Who was it who recommended that dentist on Arthur Godfrey Road?

Daisy, of course. She's the eternal matchmaker who always regrets it.

A week later Conchita said to herself that she might as well marry a dentist, and before she knew it she was married to Dr. Stanley Fish.

During the wedding reception her mother kissed her and said, "All that math you studied . . . for nothing." That was after her Mom had heard that she was giving up her job in Boston. "Mom, I'm tired of working so hard, believe me, I'm burning out." Her Mom could not believe her, she shook her head. "I didn't raise you to be a housewife. Conchita, after all the sacrifices your father and I went through to let you have a proper education. All the money we spent . . . It's all gone down the drain. Conchita, not only have you betrayed us, but you've also betrayed yourself!"

This is how they had both been taught to think. *A woman's sole aim in life is to have a career and be self-sufficient. Marriage brings distress.* And, "Wait until you have children of your own . . . then you'll know what it is to suffer, just wait until you have children of your own . . . Your life will no longer be yours."

Both Rebecca and Conchita have always felt guilty about being mothers, only mothers. This town that shelters them. Maybe the only problem is midsummer when it gets too hot. Addicted to air conditioning.

Conchita thought of having more children to keep her busy and make her forget all about her good career going down the drain, but having Belinda had ruined her breasts. While Rebecca's rocking chair prattled and squeaked Conchita regretted the whole thing. She should've kept it all to herself. Never tell anyone your secrets. But this secret had been killing her . . .

Instead of telling the truth she should've just stuck to the story she made up. Blame the dentist, her parents, the sixties, seventies, eighties, nineties, time fast time.

"Get out of here!" Rebecca yelled.

It started with the grief. Last summer, suddenly the girls were at camp up north and there didn't seem to be anything for her to do except pamper her little body. So Conchita went to Epicure and was eyeing the squash blossoms and wondering how to make them when she heard this voice, this familiar voice, squash blossoms are delicious. Oh my God it was Steve an old boyfriend from the good old days, first from high school, and later from when she was going to college up north and would come and spend the summers here in spite of the heat, but what can you do when you're from Miami and you've been gone all year? He looked good! All tanned. Of course he had turned into the doctor he had planned to be, they all did. He looked great. They recited the headlines of their lives to each other. They both had great spouses, magnificent children, they were as happy as can be, both of them, he told her she looked great but of course he didn't mean it, but she thought he looked great and she meant it, and she wanted him. She was so tired of Stanley, sometimes she'd kid him and tell him he made love like a dentist, which he did, the whole thing was like pulling teeth, she could only joke about it, once she said to Rebecca that all the petroleum jelly in the world wouldn't do, and of course, Becky, who hates intimate conversations, suddenly heard the phone ringing. But Steve looked so good. Conchita said she'd love to meet his wife and boys, oh she'd love to meet them wasn't it incredible to meet this way again? Both of them happily married? But deep down inside she was saying remember what you used to do to me Steve? What I did to you? How intimate we got? In your Dad's car, parking over by Beach High . . . Once she screamed so much that a police car stopped and caught him with his face between her legs.

It only took a few days for Steve to become an obsession. He'd given her his numbers both at the clinic and at home. She waited for him to call, he didn't. Three days after she first saw him by the squash blossoms she called his home and introduced herself to his wife. I knew Steve from way back, when we were kids! She invited them to dinner. Gail was her name. Steve married a girl named Gail, of all names, Gail! Why isn't she dead? If she were dead maybe Steve would marry Conchita who used to do all kinds of things with him when they were both seventeen and he swore that she gave the best blow jobs.

Gail, Steve's wife, was so unsuspecting. Some of these women don't seem to have any blood in their veins. They came to dinner and Gail and Conchita talked about children and about being happily married. Was it better to be a dentist's or a gynecologist's wife? What do you do when you're trying to seduce a gynecologist? Exactly. So Conchita went and spread her legs apart and he walked into the examination room with his nurse and examined her. Then he told her to get dressed. She was fine. Then she returned. This is what was bothering her. A nagging pain right here. Just won't go away. She wanted him! He said he was in love with his wife, that his wife was expecting another child. Conchita didn't care. She told him to his face. Again and again. She was going to have him no matter what! Just one more time? One more time! He refused to fuck her one more time. Immediately she began harrassing him, calling his wife, making up all sorts of stories, such terrible ones that a week ago she even made Gail break down and cry at the Publix Market. Conchita saw her parading her belly, taking a number at the deli. Conchita walked right up to her. Conchita wanted her dead. Conchita never knew Hell could flow so easily out of her mouth. She was a dragoness, dying to kill the lady. Gail left her shopping cart and ran out of there.

Yesterday, he got the police involved, and his lawyer involved. Here he was, supposed to be following her and harassing her and dying for her. It was a good thing that Stan had left for golf at dawn and that the girls had slept over at Daisy's. The sheriff had handed her some papers this morning. Sunday morning!

Conchita is stealing the show!

Rebecca tightened her belly and her thighs. "Wow!"

A-bind, a-bind, trou-ble, trou-ble, what-if, Stan-ley, finds-out? Will he divorce her? Maybe he'll kick her out of the house and keep the girls. And she won't even have Rebecca as a girlfriend because Rebecca does not like having divorced or single women around Tommy. She might, after all, steal the show.

By now the light had changed and Rebecca was rocking steadily. Light-dark, light,-dark, with her eyes having to adjust each time. Light-dark, light,-safe! Reading Conchita's mind. Maybe it isn't too late and she can undo everything she has done wrong in her life. Should she try to forget, just bury it, pretend it has never happened? How can she be such a bad person? Was she damned? Was she lost? Was she damned? Rebecca stood up and stepped out into the intense sunlight. "Conchita, will you please get out of my mind?"

Now Joaquín Aguasclaras is fucking Petra the servant. If she were Petra she'd bend over the kitchen table when everyone had gone to bed, no! feeling indecent and loving it she'd do it in the middle of the afternoon when everyone was taking a nap, and they could be discovered, yes!, and he would pull her skirt up and pull down her panties and push it into her, hard!, and keep on thrusting, hard! Now the cook *obeah!* awoke from her nap and hearing her screams and his grunting, she saw him and he kept thrusting harder and harder just using her taking advantage of her and calling her all sorts of names talking dirty to her. Then he noticed that the cook was watching and he pulled out of Petra and just left her there and penetrated the cook with one thrust. Just pulled her skirt up her panties down she was obese she smelled like onion she had a world of cellulitis on her buttocks and he pushes her into the laundry room and made her bend over the sink and her rear end was enormous and open and soft and flabby he went in and thrust and thrust, everything was so big he didn't know where he was. One moment Rebecca was Joaquín, the next Rebecca was the cook, the moment after that Rebecca was the other woman, and all the other women Tommy had ever had, the little girl, herself, even Conchita, watching watching being watched taken hard nothing like being taken hard she didn't let him withdraw there was no way she was going to let him come out she held on and the phone rang. And the answering machine. "Hello, hello! It's me. Will you pick up? You know what I told you a little while ago? Hello, I know you're there, will you pick up? I need to talk some more. I was making it all up. He's the one who's harassing me. He's following me. He wants me more than anything in the world. I'm scared. What's going to happen to me? I'm telling the truth for real. And I need for you to read the next chapter to me." Rebecca didn't let him withdraw she kept on holding on and taking pleasure in deep spasms.

"The tropics suggest color and demand it."

Julia Louisa M. Woodruff

"**I**F I WERE YOU I would definitely stop bending over backwards for Lolo. Lolo wants Lolo's way and will never have it any other way or it's the tantrum. *Le da la neura.* I am Lolo's father so I know. Lolo had been a pain in the rear end ever since I can remember. We have done everything we could, we have bent over backwards, forwards, as a matter of fact you know that we have even done the unthinkable to please Lolo, but there is no pleasing Lolo. What have we gotten from Lolo thus far? Disrespect and ungratefulness. I like to work ten hours a day and come home late in order to forget Lolo, and so does Lolo's mother who didn't deserve this. Now I see the same thing is happening to you. Listen to me, *yo te digo esto de corazón*, so if you don't want to hear me, *yo no me ofendo, allá tú con Lolo.*

Rosario and Lolo had gotten married on April 10, 1869, the exact same day that it had been decreed that all the inhabitants of the Republic of Cuba were free. It was a real coincidence.

After Manuel Tacón had finished telling Rosario the worst things about Lolo, he turned to the cane field and said, "That's *la niña linda.* Cuba's pretty little girl. In November she's fat and just asking to be cut. Just look at her! You just have to know how to cut it. I'm glad you finally decided to come in the fall and take a look for yourself. Now tell me, is there anything as beautiful as a sugar cane field?"

Rosario Santa Cruz was with Manuel Tacón, the administrator. They had both gone to inspect the Santa Cruz family's sugar cane fields in the province of Camagüey, quite a few hours away from Havana by train. Rosario absolutely hated to venture outside the limits of the capital. When she was in the country she had but one desire, to get back to the city, but somebody had to do this! It was November, the cane was ready, the whole field was white. Cut me! cut me! it was saying, I'm Cuba's pretty little girl and November is my month.

One year had elapsed since the tragedies that seemed to have struck the family on the same day. Catalina had gone mad and the family had had no choice but to send her to Mazorra, Petra had been brutally murdered, and

Joaquín had vanished into thin air. Every once in a while Rosario would put her arms akimbo and say, "I wonder where Joaquín is . . ." Each day brought a little less hope of ever seeing him again.

Six months ago Rosario Santa Cruz had become the wife of the architect Enrique Tacón, better known as Lolo. The newlywed couple was left alone to manage the family's estate. Initially they had planned to honeymoon in Florida right after the wedding, but war was raging in Cuba, and nothing around them really seemed conducive to a honeymoon. Furthermore, Rosario had no time to sit down and plan a trip to Florida, there were just too many things going on.

This got Lolo really angry and discouraged. For days Lolo pouted and wouldn't say a word to Rosario. Lolo had to be begged and begged and it seemed as if there'd be no end to this pouting. Lolo just kept repeating, "I want to go to Florida!"

Then Lolo got over it, finally! and Rosario swore with her hand on the family Bible that they'd travel all over Florida next year. Lolo smiled a little and then finally gave in.

In the meantime, they'd spend their honeymoon in La Casa Amarilla. Already the servants had begun to gossip about this couple. There was a lot of gossip and too many rumors that no one believed. It couldn't be! Things like that don't happen! The servants insisted, they had seen for themselves. Still, no one believed. Had they seen it with their own eyes they still would not have believed.

The small town that had grown around the cane field was called the *batey*. The houses were palm-thatch huts that belonged to free men. Many of the slaves had been liberated by Gabriel María Santa Cruz before he died of the black vomit in 1864. There were mostly Jamaican families (who had helped the ancestor smuggle in the light, colorful, cotton fabrics), who were all paid wages. There was a mill nearby but it didn't belong to the Santa Cruz family.

"Jamaicans are the best," said Manuel Tacón. "No one can cut sugar cane like a Jamaican. If ever I'm not around anymore, remember, Rosario, don't let them burn it, it won't yield as much. It has to be cut just right. You have to give her time, good soil, and water. You have to wait for the right moment. Look! Look at how strong and fat she is. If you wait until December it won't be any good. Don't let them burn it and choose only the cutters who will cut it well."

Rosario said she couldn't take care of it and didn't really want to. This field was way too far from Havana and she wasn't about to make these trips every month to supervise. All she wanted was to go back to Havana and oversee the goings on at the dress factory and spend her time with Lolo embellishing La Casa Amarilla.

Lolo the architect was absolutely crazy about La Casa Amarilla and had all these ideas for improvements. Sometimes they were crazy ideas but oftentimes architects just don't want to consider reality. More than anything Lolo wanted to play with light.

Lolo had supposedly been educated as an architect in Spain and therefore insisted on putting this knowledge to good use in La Casa Amarilla. A good part of this knowledge concerned, precisely, using light as an element of architecture. In Spain light was as important as a window or a door or a staircase. But Havana light was not at all like the light in Salamanca and, alas, Lolo learned this through trial and error. It cost Rosario quite a few *pesos*.

Rosario's comment was always, "Why waste so much time making ornaments with light that are just illusions. It's like Plato's cave!" But no matter how much she argued Lolo kept on playing with light.

Lolo then proceeded to tell Rosario that she was nothing but a really stupid and superficial person and didn't even deserve to be listening to all these bright new ideas of genius. Light and shadows on a wall are no less real that some kind of Ching or Ming porcelain ornament imported from China that can fall down and break and just sits there collecting dust! An ornament with light is forever. Besides who was Rosario to allude to Plato? How dare she? She who hadn't even read him because all she cared about was money, yeah, that's all she cared about.

"Tell me it's not so!" yelled Lolo.

Lolo started pouting again and it got so bad that Rosario had to go to put La Casa Amarilla in Lolo's name so Lolo would even consider talking to her again.

It was this kind of behavior that Manuel Tacón could no longer tolerate. It annoyed him, and he was Lolo's own father, so it's easy to imagine how much it annoyed other people. What's more, Rosario was really stupid to have put the house, her family house, her patrimony, in Lolo's name. In one of those fits of rage Lolo could kick her out and have the locks changed and never let her in the house again. Rosario would be left under the rain on Calle

Mercaderes with *una mano delante y otra detrás* (one hand in front and the other in the back), as they say. And Lolo was quite capable of doing such a drastic impulsive selfish thing. It was enough to get Lolo's goat, Lolo would do anything unreasonable.

Rosario mentioned that she was really getting sick of this conversation and could they please talk about something serious and important? What she really cared about was making more money and that Casa Amarilla was really becoming a burden so if Lolo wanted it Lolo could keep it. The question is, who is going to take care of these *malditas* sugar cane fields?

Manuel Tacón said he would. He volunteered right away. He'd promised Rosario's mother *que en paz descanse* (may she rest in peace) that he'd help whoever it was who inherited all this to squeeze the last black *centavo (kilo prieto)* out of it whatever it took, even if it meant lying cheating and stealing (Manuel Tacón could get out of hand with his promises sometimes). And he'd do everything in his power to really exploit this place or he wasn't Manuel Tacón and his mother wasn't an honest woman.

Oh, it could definitely use a lot of exploiting. Times were difficult though. Ever since Carlos Manuel de Céspedes had yelled *"¡Cuba libre!"* from his Demajagua farm on October 12, the country had been in chaos.

The Mambises revolutionary group, struggling for the independence of Cuba from Spain, had organized themselves better than ever, and since their first victory had been at Yara, they referred to Carlos Manuel's initial shout as *"El Grito de Yara"* or "The Yara Shout."

La Demajagua, the property that belonged to Carlos Manuel de Céspedes, was a sugar mill near the beautiful cobbled-stoned historic city of Santiago de Cuba that British and American travelers loved. You could see them wandering with red sunburns, bright eyes, and pen and pencil in hand.

It so happened that Joaquín Aguasclaras who didn't yet know of his wife's dementia or of Petra's murder was tediously on his way to Oriente province the moment Carlos Manuel shouted *"¡Cuba libre!"* They had formed a group of thirty-five men with few weapons and called themselves the Mambises.

But Joaquín finally got there on October 27 when Céspedes had demanded the abolition of slavery and the Mambises had enjoyed triumph after triumph. Six months later all the slaves were declared free men.

In spite of all this Manuel Tacón said he would take over the cane fields if Rosario wished for him to do so. He'd start cutting tomorrow and get quite a crop. It was no problem at all. He could get enough *libertos* to do the job in no time. The problem was deciding what his share of this treasure would be. He showed Rosario the palms of his hands, as if he were Jesus Christ, and said he hated to talk about it, and by it he meant money, *pero tú eres tan pichirre mi vida*, he said to Rosario.

Rosario agreed. Manuel could do whatever he wanted, it was up to him, except that she wasn't about to put the property in his name, she'd already done that with Lolo just so Lolo would quit pouting but she couldn't have the whole Tacón family owning everything she owned. What if they stopped liking each other? It's easy to trust someone when they're your friend and you're their friend but what do you do when all of a sudden the friendship ends? Rosario was ready to give Manuel Tacón a generous portion of the profits though.

"And what will you do with the rest of the money?" he asked.

Rosario was planning to take it to Key West or Tampa and put it in a bank there. It was something she had dreamt and absolutely had to do. Except that Lolo didn't want to go to Tampa, Lolo wanted to stay in Key West and eat conch and drink rum from morning till night, and they hadn't found a compromise for this argument yet, except that they could go anyway and Lolo would stay in Key West having fun while Rosario continued on to Tampa and did whatever it was she had dreamt of doing in Tampa, it was something she had to do!

Something kept telling her that in the United States her money would be safe and this had nothing to do with her being convinced that the United States was a greedy vulgar hypocritical imperialistic country just waiting for Spain to cough or clear her throat to assault her and grab hold of Cuba. At least her money would be safe in the United States.

"Don Manuel, this is changing the subject, but you won't tell anyone will you?" asked Rosario, almost pleading.

"About what? Oh, that," he remembered. "Don't worry about it! I'm probably more embarrassed about it than you are!"

In the months that followed Rosario and Manuel Tacón made so much money that they could barely conceal their satisfaction. Everything was going smoothly, everyone had their own responsibility. Manuel Tacón was obsessed with the cane fields. They were his life! Just mentioning a cane field would put a twinkle in his eye! He cared about the money of course, but he was one of those men who like to spend their lives working and planning and doing what they like. Sugar cane fields were what Manuel Tacón liked.

Rosario, in turn, was really interested in the dress factory. She loved the fabrics and she loved gossiping with the seamstresses and she loved creating new styles and imagining that some new color or look suddenly took and that it was suddenly the *dernier cri* all over town.

As for Lolo, Lolo was mainly interested in remodeling the house and in choosing novels to be read to the workers at the factory. So no one was interested in what the next person did, which made everyone wonder why there was so much fighting going on. It was probably just due to the stress of daily life. Havana was such a smelly dirty city that a few hours sufficed to put anyone in a bad mood. The streets were full of garbage and reckless young men and women would speed by on their *volantes* and practically run you over if you were on foot.

And it was noisy! Often it was difficult to get a good night's sleep. That's probably why there was so much fighting and bickering at La Casa Amarilla. Besides that, each one of the adults minded their own business and went about their daily tasks with egotistical self-absorption. Once they were into their thing there was no getting them out of it. The problem is that no one seemed to be interested in the two children, Petra's baby, María Soledad, and María Fernanda, the mad Catalina's child. Even the cook Wencesla was sometimes so absorbed in her cooking and in tasting her own food that she didn't even care what the girls were up to.

The following year Carlos Manuel de Céspedes became president and the new Cuban flag became official. Rosario and Lolo kept bickering about when it would be the best time to travel to Florida. In May of 1869 they had the worst of arguments and it seemed as if they'd break up. Lolo said that it was already too late, by the time they reached Florida it'd be sweltering and Lolo really didn't want to spend so-called belated honeymoon days drinking rum and eating conch in a mosquito-infested place. January was the best month in Florida and if Rosario hadn't kept on putting this trip off they'd have been there in January and coming back home now.

At the end of June they were still giving each other all this grief about the trip to Florida, and the heat in Havana didn't put them in any better a mood. It was smellier and noisier than ever in the city.

The political situation in Cuba had radically changed once again. Spain had suddenly decided to increase repression. The United States offered Spain one hundred million *pesos* for Cuba, but Spain refused. No way! They wanted to keep the power there was no way they were going to hand it over to the United States. Meantime the Cubans in Florida were making a big fuss. They were all for a total embargo. Joaquín Aguasclaras (who still didn't know about the tragic fate of his wife and mistress) was one of them.

They wanted to starve Cuba in order to force Spain out of there and make it a United States colony. It wasn't that they actually said it would become a United States colony, they actually believed it would be an independent nation once Spain was out and the United States took over. As all overconfident, self-righteous people who got it right once, and live on that one time they were right for the rest of their lives, they were deceiving themselves!

Rosario and Lolo were too angry at each other to even stop and consider politics. Rosario was making so much money that she didn't really care which way the country went, and Lolo was doing the craziest things with the house and having the craziest story read to the factory workers by Umbertico Barrios Junior, the best of readers.

They couldn't even have a meal in peace. Rosario's mere presence would annoy Lolo, and finally during one of these quarrels Rosario did the unthinkable and threatened to tell the world the truth about Lolo even if it ruined her own reputation. But life had gotten so unbearable with Lolo that Rosario was at her wits end.

"Lolo Tacón!" Rosario yelled at the top of her lungs. "It's over between us!"

Lolo could keep the house, but that meant that Lolo could keep the two little girls too, that meant raising María Fernanda and María Soledad who came with the house, it's in the will, *¡carajo!*

"I'm not keeping those two witches," Lolo protested. "I hate those little girls. They're rude and dirty and nasty."

"Oh yes you are!"

"No I'm not."

"Yes you are, they happen to come with the house, like the cats."

And this also meant that Lolo would no longer have the architect's license, because Lolo had gotten it through fraudulent means, yes sir, Rosario was going to tell the world that when Lolo was a little girl she wanted to become an architect so badly and she was so spoiled by the parents that they all started pretending she was a boy. Lolo was no boy! Lolo was a girl!

Rosario had married a girl. And now that she wanted to get this marriage annulled that's exactly what she intended to do, she'd go and tell the Church. They could go take a look for themselves. Even the servants knew! Lolo is a girl and now that everyone knows she's a girl she can't be an architect anymore because girls can't be architects, girls can't be architects! There are hardly any professions for girls! Now she's going to get to keep the house and raise the two little girls María Fernanda and María Soledad all by herself while Rosario spends her days at the dress factory.

The next day, Rosario bought a mansion in El Cerro, and moved out.

"Notice the peculiar manner in which the chairs are placed. You see two rows of chairs, parallel to each other, and, perhaps, a large rocking chair at each end, or very possibly all are rocking chairs."

Samuel Hazard

THEY WERE SITTING OUT ON THE PORCH, side by side, both gazing at the heavy curtain of rain in front of them. He was on his wheelchair and she was on a rickety wicker rocking chair that hadn't even seen better days. The four loose springs inside the tattered cushion all seemed to have a directional will of their own, and this made her feel a bit lopsided. She kept trying to contain one of the springs with her thigh. This was by far the most querulous rocking chair there ever was, even worse than Lolo, that character. Once white, Rebecca herself had spray-painted it Chinese red many years ago, without even bothering to wipe the intricate mold and the accumulated grime off with a damp cloth. So there were several layers of brown and green both underneath and on this highway of weathered old red, especially at the cross points, when two pieces of wicker going in different directions, touched.

It kept raining hard, which was unusual for the month of January. The rain was splashing on the granite, trying to reach her feet, and succeeding.

"I don't want to get wet," he said. "If it keeps raining this hard I want to go inside."

"Mami won't turn on the air conditioner, it's too sticky inside. Anyway, as I was saying, I want to be important! After all I'm the one who came up with this idea of having a reading club, so I want to have some control over it. Don't you think I should? Or am I just there to serve ice water and pass the little sandwiches around? I swear, the whole thing seems to have a mind of its own, 'cause this is not at all how I envisioned it. First of all, I thought I'd be at the center of things, and as it turns out there's always someone to steal the show."

The reading club met for the second time on January 26. Rebecca appraised the afternoon light before she placed four rocking chairs in a row, side by side. With the precision needed to hang a fine painting on the wall, she fine-tuned their orientation, and once she was happy with it, she dragged out the other four rocking chairs, and also put them side by side, facing the initial four.

The majority was prompt, there were no major snags, Rebecca did her best to be more relaxed, the ice water and the finger sandwiches got passed around, and by five pm seven rocking chairs were occupied. Rebecca did try to protect the druidic orientation she had given the rocking chairs, but to no avail, before long her home-made Stonehenge was in total disarray, and disregarding the quality of light, the girls were facing in any direction.

As soon as she arrived Helen swore by bell, book, and candle (in a discreet whisper) that she'd be good (no drinking, biting, or punching). So Rebecca breathed more easily. Then it was Daisy's turn to promise to do her best and not say anything mean to George, no matter whom he tried to pick up. That settles that, Rebecca ouffed. Then finally Conchita crossed her heart and hoped to die that she wouldn't mention plastic surgery, but that was after she redrafted her story about the obstetrician and made Rebecca call Heaven to witness that she solemnly believed this here last version to be true (the obstetrician was simply pursuing Conchita, and Conchita was, let's say, somewhat fond of him).

The minute the girls arrived they started talking about the book, so Rebecca didn't have to make any efforts to drag the conversation back to where it was supposed to be, let alone remind anyone that this was a reading club and that they were here to discuss a book, *this particular book* (said with a wave of the book). The problem was that everyone was either on a different chapter, paragraph, page, line, word, punctuation mark, and quite eager to discuss a different theme.

Soon Helen, whose chair was facing the house, said that the most urgent matter was whether those two women were lesbians or not and she wanted to know right away because if they were lesbians she'd just plain stop reading the book. She said she hated homosexual literature.

Jenny Rincón, who was almost facing Helen, wanted to know exactly why Helen had said something as bigoted as that.

Immediately Helen replied, "I'm not interested in lesbians and I never will be and if that shocks your sense of fairness, tough!" She then turned to Rebecca and said, "I'm sorry but I just don't like lesbians, I find them disgusting."

Jenny was annoyed. "What you're saying is so bigoted! It's almost illegal." She stood up and made her rocking chair face another direction.

"And why are you defending lesbians? *No me digas que tú también*," said Daisy, who was now facing Jenny.

"I most certainly am *not!*" said Jenny, with the sun in her eye.

Daisy stood up for a second and shouted at her son Herman who was trying to jump out of the tree house. When she sat back down she said that surely Rosario hadn't known about Lolo being a girl until she married her. And has anyone noticed that Lolo is never referred to with so much as a single pronoun?

Silent Rebecca, facing the bay, gazed at Daisy from the corner of her eye, and wished she had been the one to point that out. She then glanced at her cousin Alma who hadn't yet said a word. And her rocking chair said, Am I responsible for everyone?

Conchita, who was braiding Belinda's hair, argued that they did a whole bunch of things together and touched each other all over before they were married. But apparently that didn't mean a thing. Touching each other all over could have meant that they touched each other in the kitchen, in the living room, in the courtyard . . . Rosario was obviously a virgin, how could she know? The little girls giggled when they heard the word *virgin*. Three of them were waiting for Conchita to braid their hair. In the meantime gorgeous twelve-year-old Sylvia was putting light blue nail polish on Jessica's nails.

Helen insisted that she just hoped they weren't lesbians (the girls giggled again), that would be really ironic to get the majority of the last graduating class of The Assumption together after a quarter of a century in order to read a lesbian book (the little girls giggled, Sylvia smudged one of Jessica's fingers).

Jenny Rincón argued that just because there were lesbians in there didn't mean that this was a lesbian book. Nell took a huge chunk of Brie. Daisy said to her, *"Te estás poniendo muy gordita."* As a matter of fact, Jenny added, having a homosexual experience didn't mean you were a lesbian either.

"A ésa le viene bien cualquier cosa," Daisy whispered as she dragged her rocking chair over by Conchita's.

Rebecca said to Helen: "Some of you have exactly the same opinions about female homosexuality as your moms did." Immediately she regretted saying that. Couldn't she have come up with anything more interesting? What's more, this was going to turn the conversation away from the book, exactly what she didn't want. Hate-you-hate-you-hate-you.

"My mom, may she rest in peace, had to be right about something," Helen said casually as she rocked.

"My mom thinks that all homosexuals are spies sent here by Castro himself to undermine this country," Daisy commented while she rocked, slouched, with one leg sticking out.

"I don't even like undressing in the girls' locker room," said Trudi as she picked one of the *bocaditos* from the silver tray.

Rebecca realized that Trudi hadn't talked until now either. She'd forgotten Trudi! So she swore she'd be more alert, a social shepherd dog, making sure that all the quiet sheep talk. Quiet-sheep-talk-talk-talk.

"That's because you think they'll make fun of your figure," said Conchita who couldn't free her hands from the French braid she was making. Rebecca immediately stood up and offered to put a sandwich in her mouth. "No, thanks, I can do without the extra calories!"

So Trudi said, "Maybe you're right. I've always hated to undress in front of women."

"If they were lesbians the author was really discreet about it," said Conchita. "Unless Becky skipped and made me miss things."

"I never skip."

Trudi then commented that what she found ridiculous was these two women marrying. They couldn't possibly have married and she really blamed the author for having taken it a little too far. She believed that you can't just write a book and stretch a readers credulity like that. Who's going to believe that a thing like that happened in Cuba in the 1860s?

So Rebecca interrupted and said that the author had not made anything up. Something like this had really happened. It was in the newspapers, it was a scandal.

Yes but the truth is not necessarily credible either. Who cares about the truth?

Rebecca stopped rocking and repeated to everyone that this was an historical novel based on imaginary fact. She stood up with the tray in one hand and the book in the other. The author explained everything in footnote 6B. She put the tray down. It's right here in a testimony. She read out loud. *Enriqueta Faber y Caven who was born in Lausanne, Switzerland in 1791, was left a widow at eighteen and she fled to France where she told everyone she was a boy just so she could study medicine. Once she became a doctor she left for Havana and continued pretending to be a man. At age 28 she married Juana de León but the marriage went sour after three years and Juana revealed to everyone that her husband was in fact a woman.*

"This is really wild," said Trudi, "Let me take a look at that."

Rebecca handed her the book distractedly. She was happy that the focus was on her, at last, so she kept on talking and told Trudi, Alma, and Daisy that apparently Bishop Espada didn't really find it scandalous. He only forced this woman who pretended to be a man to work for five years at a woman's hospital named San Francisco de Paula for free, which Enriqueta Faber didn't mind because medicine was what she liked to do anyway. Then she moved to New Orleans, became a nun, and wrote a book about female oppression in the nineteenth century.

Daisy wondered out loud if there were any statistics on this kind of incident.

As for Helen and Jenny, who were facing each other again, they were ardently discussing homosexuality and the Revolution and how some people thought there was more homosexuality since Fidel Castro took over the island. More hurricanes too. And the heat!

Did you hear the last thing he said? Helen turned and asked Conchita. "If I have to give this island back I'll give it back in a pool of blood, didn't he say that?"

"*Dios mío eso de Cuba no se va a resolver más nunca.* We'll all die of old age and that island will still be Communist," said Daisy, still rocking the same way. "I'll never get to see the place where I was born."

"But now you can go *como si nada*," said Conchita who had just finished a braid. "Rebecca's planning a trip to Cuba. Tell them, Becky."

Just when Rebecca was about to speak Daisy said, "*Ay no pero yo no voy mientras esté ahi. ¡De eso nada monada!*"

Rebecca had to interrupt. Wherever she was this Cuban Daisy had tons of charisma and she'd surely steal the show. Quickly she said she was more determined than ever to go to Cuba. As a matter of fact she had already bought the tickets to Cancún.

"When are you going?" Trudi asked casually.

"Maybe in July when Nell's away at camp," said Rebecca, who felt she had stolen the show once again.

But Daisy had to go and speak Spanish, "*Hace un calor de madre en ese momento.*"

Oh no she isn't.

Immediately Rebecca said she wanted to go to Cuba so badly she could almost feel the moment when she'd board the plane to Havana in Cancún. Tommy was dying to go too. As a matter of fact he'd love to start a business there. Tommy's family was in business in Cuba for nearly a century, isn't that incredible? So anyway she had already bought tickets to Cancún this far ahead of time because there was so much to plan and so many things to take over there. Rebecca's mom had told her to start filling suitcases with stuff. All kinds of clothes, aspirin, vitamins, everything . . .

"You can buy a lot of stuff at the Diplotienda," said Trudi.

"When did you go?" Jenny asked.

"Two years ago."

"Just when I went."

Now Jenny's saying that she absolutely despised the mentality there. In spite of all that ideology the women remain Marías. They'll pick up a man and screw him just for pantyhouse and lipstick.

"Remember when we were in third grade and your mom was still in Cuba? *Te teníamos tanta lástima,* Jenny," Daisy said.

Rebecca felt the need to say something. "Maybe it's too bad they tore down our school."

"I don't want to talk about that summer," Trudi said.

"But the Diplotiendas are quite expensive." Rebecca then said.

"So is excess luggage, they make you pay and pay and pay, I'm just warning you. You can do whatever you want with what I told you. Take it or leave it. *Yo no me ofendo, allá tú,*" said Trudi.

Daisy wanted to get off the care packages to Cuba subject, she said she had gathered quite a few numbers concerning Havana *intramuros* at the end of the nineteenth century. She took out a little notebook out of her handbag that was lying on the floor right next to her rocking chair.

"Are you ready for this?" asked Daisy who resumed her rocking.

In 1862 the population of all of Havana was 139,640, but 180,000 if you included the homeless. Between 1792 and 1862 it increased 250 percent.

"That's an annual average of 3.60 percent," said Conchita.

"She was always such a genius at math!"

"Becky, it didn't take genius to figure that out!"

Now Havana *intramuros* that we call Habana Vieja or Old Havana had an area of 2.9 square kilometers.

"Conchita how much is that in feet?" Rebecca asked.

And the population of Havana *intramuros* in 1862 was 46,445.

Again, Rebecca asked, "What percentage of the whole population of Havana was it, Conchita?"

So when they're talking about the entire city of Havana it's as if we were talking about Miami plus the Beaches, Coral Gables, Hialeah, Coral Springs, and so forth . . .

By now Rebecca felt completely left out. In her own house. Own-house-own-house. This is my reading club, her rocking chair kept saying. Mine, mine, mine!

"This is what makes a novel such as this interesting," said Daisy. Just figuring out the raw data that comes with it and then trying to imagine what that means. What do 46,445 people not including the homeless and the transients do in an area of 2.9 square kilometers, "Conchita what did you say that 2.9 square kilometers was in feet?" Daisy turned to her and asked.

Fortunately Conchita said this was getting really boring, and when they mentioned this reading club she thought it was to read a book for pleasure not to go and do research on it, then going and accumulating census figures and then deconstructing the whole thing. If it was going to be like this they might as well tell her now because she'd been out of school for a long time and she wasn't about to start behaving like a schoolgirl again. As a matter of fact she hated The Academy of the Assumption, it was a bigoted concentration camp, the lousiest place she'd ever been to in her life. If she went there in the first place it was because some Pedro Pan *exilio* group who felt sorry for her offered to pay her tuition if not you wouldn't have caught her near that God-forsaken place, and as far as she was concerned all those nuns could . . . Suddenly Conchita turned to a glaring Rebecca and said, "I'm not talking about plastic surgery, am I?"

Quickly Rebecca changed the subject, "I wonder what happened to Priscilla and Selene . . ."

"What about Silka?" Helen asked.

"She's supposed to come."

Rebecca was staring at Jenny's hands. When Jenny's mother was pregnant back in the fifties she had taken a miracle drug that kept women from having morning sickness and Jenny had been born with deformed hands, only one pinky finger on her left hand, and a nailless thumb and forefinger on the right. "Anybody want ice water?" Rebecca asked.

"*¡Ya me tienes hasta el copete con el agua fría!*" said Daisy.

"Am I late?" asked Priscilla who suddenly appeared. "By the way there's a dachshund out front who's wrapped his leash twenty times around these gigantic rose bushes and he's practically got thorns in his eyes now . . . "

"Damn!" yelled Rebecca and stormed into the house.

"What is she worried about? Losing the dog or the roses?" Priscilla asked disjointedly as she kissed one girlfriend after the other. She then picked one of the two empty rocking chairs. Incredible book, huh? She's a little bit ahead of everyone else now but she wants to tell you that a little further ahead they even mention her family the Herrera y O'Farrells, isn't that neat? The foul-mouthed little girl . . .

The others said, "Don't tell us we haven't gotten there yet!"

"Look who's here!" Rebecca said as she wheeled Silka out onto the porch.

"Silka!" two or three girls said simultaneously.

Then Rebecca said, "You girls have fun, I'm going inside to tape Chapter Six for Silka, Trudi, and Conchita."

"So you left," her father said.

"I was feeling peevish, But I did overhear their conversation, my bedroom's right upstairs."

They didn't even gossip about her, what were they going to say? She doesn't look pretty today. She doesn't have anything interesting to say. Instead they wondered what had become of Joaquín Aguasclaras. Had the author forgotten about him? Don't you just hate it when a character vanishes into thin air? He'll either vanish into thin air, which would be surprising because with a published book you'd expect an editor to catch that, or, what will most probably happen is the author will not know what to do with him or not be able to keep up with his activities along with everyone else's, there are already enough characters to mind. Writing a novel must be like playing several chess games from memory with several different opponents, so of course what the author is probably going to do is just plain kill Joaquín Aguasclaras.

"And what became of the famous Lucía?" Rebecca's father asked.

"Unfortunately we've lost Lucía."

"Imagine if you were characters in a novel and an author, not knowing what to do with you, or not being able to keep track of so many women, would get rid of you little by little . . . Lucía was the first to go . . . Who's next? and who's last? I'm getting wet, let's go inside."

"And Alma didn't say a word all evening. I should've paid more attention to Alma," Rebecca said as she pulled the screen door open. She then wheeled him in. "I know I was a bad hostess, but they kept stealing the show," she added when she was halfway in the house. "So I was feeling peevish."

Her mother overheard from the next room. "Peevish? Were you talking about me?"

Rebecca shrugged. "See what I mean?"

"Isabella color is very common in Cuba."

Julia Louisa M. Woodruff

PERHAPS JOAQUÍN AGUASCLARAS WAS A WOMANIZER, and a snob, and perhaps he had never had one clear thought in his life, but he was also a brave man of political commitment, who knew no envy. It was alongside the rebels who would later become the great heroes of the revolution that he fought, and no one noticed him, his name was not destined to appear in one single history book, he received no kudos, no medals, no words of encouragement or praise, yet he kept on fighting, and it was to his country and to liberty that this emotional patriot dedicated the last five years of his life.

Joaquín Aguasclaras died of tuberculosis in New York in January of 1873. Indeed, Cuba was five years into what would be an endless struggle for freedom when Joaquín, deformed by the illness that had attacked his bones, took his final breath and expired. The superintendent of his shabby building told one of his neighbors that he died alone, *como un perro*, like a dog.

Ever since that early autumn evening of 1868 when he left La Casa Amarilla after dinner never to return again Joaquín had been active in several different revolutionary groups. After leaving Havana he went to Bayamo where he joined a military faction, then he went to Santiago de Cuba and joined another faction, after that he went to Key West where he was very active, then to Tampa, and finally to New York, where he spent the last two and a half years of his life.

These paramilitary groups were ready to do anything to undermine the Spanish crown. Furthermore, they were willing to be colonized by any country other than Spain. Any other country would do! You name it! As the years passed and they got no satisfaction the grass got greener and greener on the other side. At a given moment the other side was so green that it was almost blinding.

Thanks to the money they'd earned from the ever-growing tobacco industry in Key West, Tampa, and New York City, these Cuban revolutionary factions had gained quite a bit of political influence in the United States. Some of these pressure groups were actually trying to force Washington to put an embargo on Cuba and to firmly maintain this embargo as long as El Generalísimo Anacleto Menosmal remained the Maximum Leader. The moral behind this was that Spain was being too imperialistic.

The United States government was therefore quick to react and to condemn Spain for its imperialistic ambitions. There was much talk of an embargo. They talked, they threatened, they had meetings, screaming matches, more meetings, more talk. All the groups to which Joaquín belonged had code names such as Alfa One, Beta Two, Theta Three, Omega 68, and so on. They'd get together once a week to scream and talk.

Most of the people who belonged to these groups were ready to let all their relatives starve in Cuba if this meant independence from Spain. El Máximo Líder Anacleto Menosmal had become the Demon personified so there was no possibility of a reconciliation and no middle ground.

It is really a coincidence that Rosario and Joaquín never crossed each other's paths while in South Florida. Embittered by a marriage gone sour and determined more than ever to make money to compensate for being so unlucky in looks and in love, Rosario started traveling to Key West twice a year in order to deposit money in a bank account she had so intelligently opened there.

She'd then proceed to Tampa, where she had shrewdly and once again quite intelligently invested in the tobacco business. But then again Joaquín's life was so clandestine that often not even the leader of his faction knew where he was. What's more, Rosario much preferred Key West to Tampa and would spend as little time as possible in Tampa which she thought had absolutely no character.

As to her relationship with Lolo, once she had threatened to denounce Lolo to the authorities and told Lolo that she hated Lolo Tacón more that anything in the world, that the name Lolo Tacón had become like vomit in her mouth, and that all she wanted was to see Lolo with some incurable disease that made the skin hurt like Hell and rot, Rosario decided to forget about it and not tell anyone. The problem was that everyone in the household had overheard the whole quarrel. But then again they already knew the truth, having surprised Lolo naked several times.

Denouncing Lolo would have been a whole big deal, it would have meant summoning Bishop Espada and proving her own innocence to him. Indeed,

Rosario would have had to get in front of the tribunal and tell them that she had no idea that this man was a woman until she married her and saw her naked, and Rosario was too busy for that type of thing.

The legal system was long and tedious and who knew how long something like this would take. To make matters worse lawyers were quite expensive and as far as money was concerned Rosario was very cheap and conservative. What's more this had been one more quarrel and like all quarrels once you get all the nasty things you have to say out, you're over it and you're even a little ashamed of having been so mean and petty.

But this state of temporary sanity didn't mean that those two were back together again. They had finally parted good friends agreeing that life with each other was impossible, they were just too different! Their interests were different, their hobbies were different, their outlook was different, they just weren't made for each other! Lolo could keep the house and the two little girls and Rosario would move out.

Rosario therefore rented a house in Havana *extramuros* and ended up loving this suburb (El Cerro) so much that she had a mansion built there for herself. This way, Lolo and the little girls could come visit on the weekends and get out of Havana *intramuros* that was so noisy and smelly and polluted.

In December of 1872, knowing that he didn't have much time to live, Joaquín had decided to return to his country and be buried there whether or not Spain still ruled, but he was penniless and never managed to pay his way back to Cuba. What's more at that time he had already moved to New York, where many other Cuban rebels also lived, so there wasn't the slightest chance that he could accidentally bump into the business-minded Rosario and that she'd either give him or lend him the money to return home.

Poor Joaquín didn't know a soul in New York! So he died alone and in poverty the following month without ever knowing about his wife's death in Mazorra or seeing his daughters, María Fernanda the legitimate one, and María Soledad the bastard child, again. Since no one knew him or cared about him in New York the body wasn't discovered until a month later when the landlord told the superintendent to call the fire department and knock the door down and evict that Latino for nonpayment of rent. It was January 27, time to pay or to leave!

All they found was a cadaver surrounded by cockroaches and eaten by rats, cats, and worms. Nobody had noticed the smell because that building always reeked of garbage and cat spray.

According to Lolo, and to the cook, and to Rosario, and to anyone who knew them, even the scissorsgrinder, the two half-sisters María Fernanda and María Soledad were the two most unpleasant, most smelly, most naughty, and most overall exasperating little girls in the world. Nobody liked them. Everybody just about hated them. And some people went as far as wishing them dead. Everyone tried to avoid them. What's more their language was appalling. They used the foulest, most vulgar, most *chusma*, most embarrassing words imaginable.

By the time she was three years old the little green-eyed blonde mulatta, María Soledad, could in three sentences or less probably embarrass and shock the most vulgar and lowly of whores, *una puta mala* as they're called, and the worst part is that she'd learned it all from María Fernanda, her older sister, the legitimate one.

Where María Fernanda had learned this foul language no one knew, but everyone was being blamed for a while, quite a few accusations were made, quite a few fingers were pointed.

But anyone could have put up with the foul language and finally gotten used to it, this wasn't the worst aspect of these little girls. One of the nastiest habits of the weird sisters was using the fountain out in the courtyard as a toilet. When asked why they insisted on doing this, they'd simply point to the statues of the fat cherubs who were either urinating or spitting water in the fountain. They'd do it every single day rain or shine.

One could understand little María Soledad doing it, she was only five and a half years old in the spring of 1873, but María Fernanda was almost thirteen and still using the Baroque fountain imported from Venice as a toilet.

At first Lolo told the servants to get the excrement out of the water, but the servants got tired of doing this three or four times a day, and finally Lolo had to do it. Lolo didn't want these lovely fountains to turn into cloaques or cesspools. Lolo loved sitting next to them on a favorite rocking chair to meditate and come up with new ideas for improving and embellishing La Casa Amarilla and to think about the next chapter that should be read to the seamstresses at the dress factory. So the screaming and yelling at La Casa Amarilla was terrible.

All María Fernanda would say to Lolo was, "*Chingado* or *chingada*, whatever it is you are, clean it yourself!"

At age thirteen most Habaneras were preparing to become delightful young ladies. They'd practice the language of the fan and look forward to afternoon rides to the *parque* on the *volante* and to going to the theatre and to balls and to other events at El Palacio de los Capitanes Generales. This was also the age at which they'd start to get invited either by older girls or by women to those famous afternoon *tertulias*.

Life for the Habanera was simple and superficial to the point of being boring; and this is why Lolo had pretended to be a man for so many years. Girls' days were exact replicas of one another except for Sunday when they went to church service or when there were special events such as baptisms, weddings, funerals, scandals, or first holy communions.

This is how a typical day in Havana *intramuros* began and ended for a pretty or plain looking girl of high society (it didn't necessarily have to be this way if you were ugly or crazy):

A servant usually came to wake up *la Señorita* or *la Señora* of the house at around eight in the morning. This servant would just walk into the bedroom without bothering to knock, and little did it matter if this happened to be a *señora's* bedroom and if this *señora* had decided to sleep with her husband that night. The servant would just walk across the room shouting good morning and then pull the curtains open with one violent gesture and let in the unbearable sunlight.

By then the *señora* or the *señorita* who had been sleeping had turned in her cot and was facing the other side and had put her hands over her head as if she were being tortured and already seemed in a really bad mood. Everyone had big beautiful canopy beds but those were just to make the room look European. Rich or poor, married or single, black or white, Habaneros and Habaneras slept in cots. It was usually so hot at night that the only bearable place to sleep was in a lightweight cot with a cotton pad on it. They would cover themselves with a flimsy mosquito net that served as a cover and as a sheet. The little cot was put away during the day only to be taken out at siesta or at bed time.

Breakfast consisted of eggs, white rice, *mameyes*, pineapples, melon juice, buttered toast, coffee, and chocolate, a whole feast set out in the informal dining room. By then it was so hot that no one was hungry.

Then came the morning ablutions and the rest of the morning was spent either reading in the courtyard or sewing or standing at a window looking out at the street.

These houses were beautiful but there was little to distinguish them from prisons, except that the iron bars were curly and fancy. The fate of many women was to stand there all morning holding the bars, staring out at freedom.

DID YOU GET ENOUGH TO EAT at your *abuelita's*, sweetheart? Did she make chicken?

Nope, pig's feet.

Why don't you have a tall glass of milk with Quick and a chocolate pudding before you go to bed, *mi vida*?

Okay. Mom! It's Sunday night! Haven't you finished my homework yet?

I'll get to it as soon as I finish taping this chapter, sweetheart.

For some Habaneras the dream of freedom came in the form of a gentleman who would notice them and talk sign language to them. But freedom could also mean something as simple as greeting the scissorsgrinder, waving to the traveling greengrocer, asking the fruit vendor if the bananas or the *chirimoyas* were good today, making fun of the farmer with his stubborn pig, laughing at someone who didn't quite make it across the street, who had either gotten run over by a fast *quitrin* or *volante* or had fallen in the mud.

Freedom was most of all a dirty muddy smelly street with loud busy people coming and going. Once in a while a foreign white woman could be seen walking alone in these streets. Standing behind their fancy curly bars, Habaneras young and old often wondered with their hearts full of envy what it felt like to be out in the world and do whatever you pleased *(hacer lo que te dé la gana)*.

But envy was continually being replaced by laughter, sooner or later that very same woman who knew freedom so well would end up stepping in a nasty slimy puddle and, while trying to pick up her leg, she'd lose her shoe in the miasma. Ha ha ha! It was in times such as these that freedom was funny.

Roads had always been a problem in Havana. The city was way too busy and populated to have dirt roads but nothing had worked so far. When the rainy season came the streets were invariably washed away. In the beginning of 1872 the authorities had begun putting mahogany planks on the streets, but this had proven too costly.

It is around this time that Lolo Tacón came up with a new invention for roads. Lolo proposed a mixture of stone, coconuts and mud. The authorities, who were so desperate that they were ready to jump at anything, went head over heels for this idea. A month later the Tacón Miracle™ was used in several streets. But once again, when hurricane season came every single one of these roads was washed away. There was nothing but a malodorous, disappointing bog left.

In the spring of 1873 just about every street in Havana had a big problem and was being worked on. There really wasn't one worthy street in the whole city. Tired of scrimping and skimping for nothing and of taking one step forward and three steps back, the authorities finally gave up and decided to have cobblestones laid on half of the city *intramuros* no matter how much this cost and even if the money had to come out of someone's pocket.

When she stood at her window behind bars looking out at a humid boggy freedom, the world of liberated slaves, prostitutes, and lottery vendors, María Fernanda could see cobblestones being laid on Calle Aguacate, her street.

Where was freedom?

For a pretty girl such as María Fernanda, freedom was in insanity, nowhere else. Escolástica, who had changed her name to Rosario, had her ugliness, and Lolo pretended to be a man. All María Fernanda could do was be crazy because what awaited the good-looking woman in Havana was an utter nightmare. Before she knew it she'd be married, and marriage in most cases was a fate much worse than dressing saints (dying a spinster).

The married woman was expected to become an insipid superficial sex-less greedy harpy who catered to this womanizing peacocky conceited black-bean-fed fat boy who worshipped his own penis. María Fernanda thought about it and wept. She saw her life going by, in sheer idleness, just waiting for the day to waste into night and for night to become the next same day. She didn't want this! She didn't want to lead a selfish useless life!

María Fernanda usually spent her mornings looking out through the iron bars and yelling profanities.

Lunch was at one, and since María Fernanda did love to eat she did act like a normal person at lunch time.

Lunch was followed by siesta time. This was the hottest part of the day and nobody felt like doing anything. Even María Fernanda kept quiet. It was generally at this time of the day that she'd use the fountain as a toilet. The sun was at its zenith. Suddenly Havana was quiet, even noise itself seemed too oppressed by the heat to make noise, it wasn't even this quiet in the middle of the night. It was indeed at siesta time that everyone got the best rest. They'd fall asleep out of pure exhaustion and not wake up until half past four or five, in a pool of sweat.

Indeed, nobody slept in those European beds. Their only purpose was to adorn the stately rooms. Sometimes newlyweds tried to sleep in a real bed on their wedding night, but who could sleep under all those heavy covers and under a gold and wool canopy? Furthermore, little did it matter if a mattress came from Europe, the minute it arrived in Cuba it was a home for bedbugs or *chinches*. So whoever tried to sleep on a mattress would invariably get up in the middle of the night scratching all over, especially between the fingers and behind the knees, drag the cot (better known as *el catre*) out from its hiding place underneath the bed into the middle of the room, open it up, lie down, ah! a sigh of relief! The last part of the cot ritual was the tucking of one's self, head to toe, in a sheet of transparent mousseline that usually protected against mosquitoes, spiders and scorpions *(alacranes)*. But scorpions did manage to climb into the cot under the mousseline. The only thing to do then was to get out of there and run and yell, *¡Alacrán! ¡Alacrán!*

The postilion would usually appear half-dressed and beat on the critter until it was scorpion paste. While he was doing this the cook would be preparing hot chocolate for those who were so upset that they'd never be able to sleep again.

After the *siesta* it was time for the women or the girls to get ready for the *tertulias. Tertulias* were as much a part of being a female as menstruation.

Friends would organize them, they took place every day at someone's house, usually one person would have a *tertulia* at her home once every three or four days, depending on the number of friends who regularly attended. If there were five women, then they'd receive every fifth day, and so on.

Tea, coffee, ice water, fruit juices, finger sandwiches, and very sweet pastries were served at the *tertulias.* For the past fifty years the wealthiest homes ordered their finest foods, especially the pastries, almond and egg yolk nougat, candied fruit, guava jelly, caramels and hard candies with soft fillings from Herrera y O'Farrell Confectioners, the same family that owned the liquor company. Their prices were outrageous but anyone who sank her teeth into anything that came from La Casa Herrera y O'Farrell would necessarily spend the next ten minutes producing orgasmic sounds such as "Uummm! oooH! yum! ahh! OOOmmm!" What's more, everyone adored the pink box in which these goodies came, and at times the mere thought of the color pink was enough.

It was that good, and everyone would have been glad to pronounce the words "*¡Riquísimo!* Delicious! Succulent! Delectable! *¡Exquisito!*" except that most of these edibles were too gluey and glutinous. They remained stuck to the teeth.

For the daily *tertulias* rocking chairs were put in a circle. In the middle of the circle was a fancy mahogany or Chinese table on top of which all these goodies were displayed for everyone to sample and enjoy.

The ladies would sit and rock and eat and talk for two hours. Sit and rock and talk. Sit and rock and gossip. You could hear them rock and talk. It was something you could almost become good at. It almost called for a certain talent.

After that the older women stayed home and the younger unmarried ones would dress up all over again and get on their *volantes* or *quitrines* and off to the park they went just when the sun was no longer as hot but there was still daylight. The men would either pass by on their *volantes* or walk in the park, this is when it was crucial to know the language of the fan.

There were plays almost every night, and a ball every two or three nights. It was at night that Havana came alive. It was at night that it was cool enough to have a good time or move around, it was best to spend the afternoon sleeping and then enjoy the night. By the time an Habanero or an Habanera turned thirteen or fourteen he or she and the chaperone were going to bed at around three AM.

This is how María Fernanda's life went except that she didn't want to participate in any of the *tertulias* and absolutely refused to do anything with a fan except fan herself and absolutely hated being dragged to the theater by Rosario and Lolo. It wasn't that Rosario and Lolo particularly liked going to the theater, but they'd tried to do it for appearances' sake.

By now they were pretending to be a separated couple who had parted on good terms. Each and every attempt at a social evening and to act like everyone else in town had resulted in a total fiasco. It would happen to Rosario once a month, she'd suddenly decide that they should try to be like everyone else and if that meant taking their meals together, going to the theater and to the ball, well then *carajo* that's what it would be!

Evenings out at the theater were always a catastrophe. First of all Rosario and Lolo could never agree on the play they wanted to see. Rosario would always be the one to give in, after all who was she to judge a work of art? she who had never been interested in art! Lolo would tell her to stick to her thing—supporting this family—and she'd stick to hers, giving it an artistic dimension that money alone would and could never ever buy. No wonder the Spanish crown had always refused to give a title of nobility to the Santa Cruz family. The only thing they were any good at was making money! They had absolutely no sensibility whatsoever! In any case this was Lolo's opinion and this was what the screaming and the shouting was about before they decided to go and see the play Lolo wanted to see.

After that they'd have to flip a coin to determine who'd go and tell María Fernanda that they were taking her to the theater. Nobody wanted to do this because María Fernanda would always throw a fit and threaten to disrupt the play. The worst thing that ever happened was when María Fernanda crawled out of the theater in the middle of the play and couldn't be found for days.

When she finally showed up she announced that she'd lost her virginity and both Rosario and Lolo, who had been worried sick, became hysterical. They were weeping and wailing and threatening to die of grief. Finally María Fernanda anounced that it was a joke, that she *hadn't* lost her virginity. Couldn't they take a joke?

"Oh thank God!" Rosario and Lolo sighed with relief.

Another big problem was that time was passing and that María Fernanda would turn fifteen in just over a year. What would they do about her *quinceañera* (or sweet fifteen) party? She said she didn't want one and that if they tried to force her to have one she just wouldn't wear panties. A week later they decided to drag her by the hair to a ball if they had to. Perhaps a ball and the good-looking *macho* men there would give her an idea of how great it would be to have a *quinceañera* party. "Besides," said Lolo, "in most good novels a woman's outlook on life changes with her first ball."

"I'm not going to no goddamn ball. *¡Cabrón de mierda vete p'al carajo!*" she yelled at Lolo. *"Me cago en la madre que te parió."*

"Very well, no pork rinds, no milk candy, no *coquitos*, no caramel flan, no *turrón* and no guava pastries for a week!"

"Okay I'll go, but I won't be happy there."

"Promise not to shit in front of everyone."

"Just this once, but I really hate it when you threaten me with the pork rinds and the milk candy. Oh and the *coquitos*, I can't live without my coconut macaroons!"

The dress was another problem. Of course they'd have one sent from France. There was a branch of the family business that did nothing but import dresses from Europe. They even had a catalogue and the ladies could either pick the dress they wanted or have one custom-made. María Fernanda said she wanted hers custom-made and she wanted it to make her waist appear enormous, her chest flat, her *derrière* flat, her legs skinny and her feet as big as Queen Bertha's in the fairy tale. If any man so much as approached her she'd . . . she'd . . .

Very well she would not lift her skirts in front of everyone and show everyone her *derrière*, she had promised Lolo she wouldn't, but she could very well whisper in his ear that he was *un jodido de mierda* and could he please get the fuck out of her sight.

Once they got that straightened out, María Fernanda needed a dress. What color did she want? She insisted on black orchid, with black lace, and black gloves. And a little red to make her look like a whore (those were her words).

"But that's a woman's dress, not a *quinceañera's*-to-be dress!" Lolo screamed.

"*¡Quiero lucir como una puta, carajo!*"

"Mafer, *coño* watch your goddamn language!"

It took so long to agree on the dress that it wasn't until early December that the pink gown finally arrived from France and that María Fernanda was all ready to go come out in society.

They finally decided that María Fernanda's first ball would be on December 31, 1873, exactly the last day of the year, but not for any symbolic reason, Lolo argued. Granted, it was a bit late to make a debut, Mafer was already past fourteen years of age. But this wasn't Lolo's worst nightmare. Lately María Fernanda had been eating so many pork rinds that Lolo feared she wouldn't fit into her gown. Finally a few days before the ball they had a three-inch panel added to the pink gown at the waist and María Fernanda was all ready to go.

Ernesto Tirry y Sotolongo was twenty-seven years old. He belonged to the aristocratic and very wealthy Herrera y O'Farrell family who made all kinds of fine foods and liquors and exported them all over the world. The family had been doing this for several generations. They were even wealthier than the Santa Cruz family.

What was curious and bizarre about this family, and about many other Cuban families in business, is that the family business would not be handed down from father to son, but from father to son-in-law. As a matter of fact, no son of the family had ever taken over the business, it had never happened. Each generation brought new blood to this business. One of the Herrera y O'Farrell women would marry that special man from the outside and he'd take over the business. Ernesto's father, Pedro Tirry y Tirry had married an Herrera y O'Farrell, Isabel Sotolongo y O'Reilly, and had taken over the thriving candy business. Isabel's father, James O'Reilly y Pérez had formerly been president of the business and had married one of the Herrera y O'Farrell women. This is why the last name itself, after which the candies and sweets were still called, had not been anyone's for three generations. There was always a new name at the head of the business, name that would only last as long as the man.

It was obvious that one of Ernesto's three sisters would find the right man to take over the company and that this brother-in-law would feel threatened by him and offer him lots of money just so he'd stay out of his business. Ernesto's own father had done this before him and he'd already advised Ernesto not to even think of participating in this business. He'd be paid handsomely, of course, and he never had to worry about money for the rest of his life, he could just have a good time until he died.

Ernesto was healthy and strong and at age nineteen he'd gone to study philosophy in Salamanca, Spain, and then traveled all over Europe, and gone further, to Greece, to Palestine, to Africa, to China. At age twenty-seven he was back in Cuba and wondering what he'd do with himself now that he'd seen it all and done it all.

"Hello, Fatty!" he said to María Fernanda at the ball. His exact words were, "¡Hola, Gorda!"

IT IS ON THAT HIDDEN STRETCH of Brickell Avenue where there are still dilapidated Spanish mansions with proper names, empty fountains, coral benches, and sunken gardens tucked behind walls of either pink hibiscus or magenta bougainvillea that Rebecca parked her car. Elegant elderly women they are, with a dainty handkerchief, just enough mauve, a violet scent, but a little too much pressed powder. Another side to Miami, no aqua, no pink, no vice, quiet, still a distance from the breast implants, and the young athletic commercial zoning that is approaching, like the squall with a million raindrops. Just north of here the look has been redefined by outrageous buildings. The old landmarks were not air tight enough, precious Freon was being wasted on them. Have to stay cool. For a second there was dead silence. The aporia of the morning, right after the rush. "*Ay,*" Rebecca mumbled as she groped for her sneakers and her socks that were on the floor behind her seat. She knew how to say that Flamenco "*ay, ay, ay*" in her mind, but not out loud.

Today she planned to bicycle all the way to the lighthouse, and back, with the gear as high as it goes, she promised herself, as she gently pushed aside a few pink hibiscus in order to catch a glimpse of one of her favorite houses. The windows were so huge that you could see right through the house, all the way to the glittering backdrop of ocean behind. She wished she could just walk in there and be absorbed by the house, become a white curtain in the breeze, being gently blown out. And she could get wet when the squall came. Reluctantly she turned away, went back to her car, pulled the bike out of the back, and walked her bike all the way to the corner.

Were it not for the heat, the humidity, the glare, bicycling in Miami wouldn't be worthwhile, because it's too flat, she thought as she pedaled slowly toward the entrance to Rickenbacker Causeway and fussed with the gears. It's level all the way to the bridge where the causeway does swell, but then it dips again.

Past the Seaquarium all the way to the lighthouse it's a piece of cake, except for the traffic. Quite a few drivers are afraid of the narrowness, they squint and drive, and when the bridge swells they panic because their eye is telling them that a fast fall awaits them right after the top. But the danger they represent is still nothing for these legs that need real challenge. Is there any way to make this harder? More painful? What if she threw herself under a cream and gold Infiniti, would that do it? Care to be numb enough, *tertulia* woman? Brace yourself for the impact. She could almost feel what it was, to hurt, and die.

Muggy weather, the morning sun is weak and it will indeed rain soon. *Tertulia* woman, like Umbertico Barrios before her, she is nothing but a reader, can't even talk good, she simply goes by the book. She's always telling herself that she isn't good enough. For what exactly? Come here, tell me all about it. Hurt and die hurt and die hurt and die, she pedaled. Those few people in the water will run out of there fast, collect the red and white cooler they left on the weathered picnic table, and rush to the safety of their cars. It's not the lightning that scares them. They simply hate getting wet. Swimming's a willful act, so it doesn't count. What exactly is causing this painful anxiety? she wondered. Tommy? Her father? No baby? Why am I being so cruel? Why don't I talk and what do I want to hide? What if lightning struck, would that hurt the *tertulia* woman bad enough? Self-hatred, who does all the hating? The self or the hatred?

The toll collectors know her. They always tell her to have a great ride. Hey, she's just one more of these women who can't live without exercise, who can't live without, who can't live, who can't. Sometimes she even holds her bike between her legs and stops to chat with them. How's your dad? Bad. Dad-bad-dad-bad. Can't you see I'm being as bad as I can? And it's not even that bad, just like Umbertico Barrios. Clumsy and tidy. Nothing compared to Lolo, Conchita, María Fernanda, and Helen; the novel is bleeding all the color she once thought she had in her life, inhaling, drawing it all in, swallowing.

How can María Fernanda talk like that? And what about Conchita? How could she dare? Almost lost it all, now she's content, she got away with it, so she's wondering what she'll do next.

Ever since evil visited them, this time disguised as a stroke and as a nightclub that had to be closed, hardly a day goes by without Rebecca going up a notch in the scale of self-discipline. It's my contrition, contribution, convocation, conversion, she pedaled. Confection, convection, convulsion, contraindication. It was a prefix day. How far will it go? Can't take away my sugar, don't take away my wine. The rest can go to Hell. Oh, and don't take away the baby I want to have. Condition. And when she went to see him in intensive care on Saturday he asked, "What's happening with your marriage?"

Fine, wine, dine, fine, wine, dine, mine, mine, mine! Talk! What are you hiding?

In the hospital she overheard the doctor telling the nurse that from now on he needed a diaper. What's happening with your marriage? asked the man who needed diapers. Those things shouldn't be said, just like the rest. Don't think don't think don't think don't speak. Muggy buggy muggy buggy. It happened right when the reading club was meeting for the third time. Time lime time lime. Key lime. Her mother called, hysterical. Comes from the uterus, hysterical. If you squint you can see the uterus right in there. He's having another one! Conchita volunteered to keep Nell. See you later crocodile in a while alligator hop on the bus Neil what's the deal, Gus? Daisy and Helen had already an argument in front of everyone and Helen had stormed out of there yelling, "Count me out of this reading club!"

"We've lost Helen now," she told her father.

"Who's Helen?"

Good question, who's Helen? Can't keep track of all of them. How do you make ten women talk at the same time? But that's not all, how do you make ten women read? You can lead a woman to the rocking chair, but you can't make her . . . Helen, *for your information*, happens to be the other sister-in-law. She's the woman who makes so much money. Not only that but to this day she kicks, screams, punches and bites. It's the child in her which never got educated out. Like Mami, if the line's too long at the supermarket she'll throw herself on the floor and have a tantrum. Like María Fernanda when the reader stops. Like Papi, before time began to swallow him. Rebecca wondered if he remembered how loud he could yell, anywhere, especially in public places. Oh the scenes he made! How it embarrassed her. How she swore that he'd never make her suffer again. And there she was, at the hospital, taking big gulps of what seemed to be all the grief in the world. It made her stomach feel cold.

"What are you thinking about?" he asked. Bad Helen. Harvey's wife. Harvey, who went to prison. No, not for bigamy, you're confusing him with his brother George. Harvey was a successful attorney here in Miami who thought he could get away with everything.

Rebecca said she'd gladly tell Harvey's story where it not swarming with stereotypes. The job, the money, the power, the girls, the toys, Harvey had it all, so he decided to go for the wrong clients. Tommy? Of course she isn't talking about Tommy! My Tommy? Tommy isn't like that at all. Granted, he lost his nightclub for all the wrong reasons, but we were different. I'm a reader! I'm deep deep deep. I'm not some kind of moll. So anyway, we've lost Helen, Rebecca changed the subject. Who's Helen? Who's Daisy? Who's

Rebecca? Who in the world are those three sisters-in-law? Three women in one law.

"I got some great numbers if anyone's interested," Daisy said after Helen left. " . . . concerning rent, taxes, purchases, remodeling costs because they loved to remodel, I think they probably spent much more in the 1850s than we do now."

"I'd like to take a look at those numbers," Conchita said. "Were those in the novel too? Or is Becky skipping again?"

Daisy barely allowed her to finish asking her question. "Of course they're not in the novel, *artistes* get criticized if they're that thorough. Besides, readers don't want a history lesson or an economics lesson, much less a novel with numbers in it, not even for addresses. I went and researched them myself because I get very curious when I'm reading."

"And I've got a map of Havana," Rebecca said. She took another sip of red, placed her glass on the coffee table next to the couch, sat down, and began to unfold the map.

The minute she arrived Priscilla said she was tired of drinking ice water and went straight for the bar where Tommy was fixing himself a drink and assuring everyone that he'd be out of there in no time. Sitting with the open map on her lap Rebecca momentarily turned her head and gazed at the beautiful Priscilla asking for some vodka.

Rebecca confessed to her father that she liked to do something else besides reading, and that was to move people around in her mind, and make them do whatever she fancied. Did that call for any talent? Just a little? Because she definitely had this power of visualization, as a matter of fact she could even handle the unbearable. It even used to stimulate her jealousy, back when she was still jealous. Didn't that mean she was profound? Tommy and Priscilla. She smiled before she looked back down at the map, as if the memory were a comforting one.

Then Selene arrived. Rebecca caught a glimpse of her kissing Tommy on the lips. "Why is everyone inside?" Daisy asked. And this made Rebecca pick her head back up and look around. Then it was Conchita's turn to ask, "What made Helen so angry? God! She's so rude. She just plain stormed out!" Meanwhile, Rebecca was carefully folding her map. Daisy urged her, "Becky, will you please tell everyone to step outside?" She then walked away mumbling to herself something about what a pity it was not to take advantage of the winter. As early as April we'll all be confined to air-conditioned rooms and drawn blinds. So Jenny said she refused to have an air conditioner, she absolutely wanted to know how hot it was outside, it was a matter of principle. Besides, didn't the first settlers in south Florida do very well without? And she couldn't believe that man had the nerve to simply walk up to María Fernanda and call her Fatty. A woman should have the right to be fat.

By now Alma was in the dining room talking to Selene. It was when she walked by them urging everyone to step outside and enjoy the outdoors before it was too late that Rebecca overheard a good part of a sentence. So she gulped down the last of her wine and interrupted. She happened to have several pistols, they could help themselves, she even had a .38 Special with a rubber grip that sheltered the hammer. That means you can fire it in your pocket without the hammer getting caught. But it's the .22s that are perfect for shooting someone in the head, the bullet stays in there and destroys the brain. Alma looked her right in the eye when she said that. "I really need one," Alma said. "For self-protection."

"Come over this weekend and help yourself. I'll even teach you how to use it," Rebecca said distractedly since she was watching Trudi wheel Silka all the way outside. Down those three steps, a bumpy ride.

"So what are you going to do with all these friends?" her father asked.

Shoot them.

Outside, at last, with the eight rocking chairs rocking to different rhythms, Daisy suggested that they talk about the economy in Havana in the latter part of the nineteenth century. "She's like a good student who always does her homework," Rebecca told her father. Maybe she deserves to be shot first.

"I detect envy in your voice," he said.

Rebecca watched Daisy as she took her little notebook out of her handbag, held it close to her heart for a second, then caressed it, saying, "This is full of treats." In 1862 there were 624 clothesmaking establishments in all of Cuba and 203 in Havana alone that were making an average annual profit of 10,000 *pesos*. That meant that . . . Rebecca noticed that Trudi hadn't said a single word. She seemed so bored, and so did Silka, sitting there, in her wheelchair.

I can't keep track of everyone!

So Priscilla turned to Silka and said, "Your mom looked just like Cher. And you, my dear, were gorgeous! When I heard about what happened to you, I wrote a poem!"

Rebecca sighed with relief.

Then Selene said to Priscilla, "Don't tell me you still write poetry?"

"Of course I do! I can't stop. Even my internal dialogue rhymes!"

Pedal, pedal, pedal, harder, faster, almost in Key Biscayne now.

Priscilla then said: "Didn't I tell everyone about some of my ancestors being in this book? That man Ernesto Tirry y Sotolongo who dared call María Fernanda a fatty was a member of the Herrera y O'Farrell family which I'd do anything not to belong to anymore."

"The other day I read a little bit about it in the paper, and it seems like a really nasty family quarrel." Selene commented as she watched Tommy walking with Nell all the way to the treehouse. Rebecca, in turn, had her eye on her.

Just listened. Couldn't get into the conversation. What's going on with Tommy and Selene? Smell a rat. Priscilla's monologues go on and on, what's more her sentences are so abundant and so close together, with such brief punctuation, that it's practically impossible to get a word in. Why couldn't I have an interesting family like Priscilla's? Rebecca wondered.

Out of the blue Selene announced that she was planning to change her name. What did everyone think of Paige? Paige Machado.

"With a happy face in the o?" Rebecca asked.

This is Priscilla. "As I stand in front of you (the quickest of commas) the way you see me now (another one of those heartbeat commas) appearing normal (short period) *Como tú me ves ahora* that I seem normal (necessary repetition) and even joining this reading club and acting as if my life was just OK (period) Well I happen to be on medication and I am really fragile (no punctuation here) I can't eat 'cause I have to run to the bathroom right away (reluctant semicolon) I shouldn't drink because it just enhances my depression (semicolon) I'm having vaginal problems (long period) Anyway *ésto no tiene fin* (she caught her breath) My father had my husband fired from the company."

Rebecca was watching, listening, and Priscilla was talking with all her fingers.

Apparently that has never ever happened. It's just like the novel. *Lo mismitico.* The family business has never stayed in the family, it has always gone from father to *first* son-in-law, with the word first italicized, and now they're changing all the rules. The excuse was that Guillermo and Priscilla were squandering the family fortune, Rebecca explained to her father. The real reason is apparently that everyone was against Guillermo, Priscilla's whole family hated him because he was prematurely bald and really possessive of her. Wait until he finds out that Tommy screwed her. All her sisters hated him, they wanted Monica's husband to be the president of the company. You know why? Because, according to Priscilla, Monica's husband behaves like a friendly waiter. He's sticky sweet. "You want something?" he asks, "Just name it you got it! It's got your name written on it." You tell him, "Let's meet tomorrow at two," he replies, "You got it! Two o'clock has your name written on it." Whereas Priscilla insists that Guillermo is just like that man Ernesto in the novel. This signifies that Priscilla has not only gone and left everyone chapters behind—as if this were a footrace—but also that she is beginning to think the novel is hers. She's appropriating it! "How dare she compare Ernesto to Guillermo!" Rebecca thought to her most secret self.

"And Priscilla just went on and on," Rebecca told her father.

In this novel the author explains how it's always one son-in-law who becomes president. So Priscilla married that particular son-in-law and you should have seen her father and Guillermo for the first few years you would have thought that they were the ones who had gotten married and were on their honeymoon. Her Papi adored Guillermo. Then all of a sudden Monica who had always hated Priscilla because she's always been prettier and smarter (all the Drake sisters are pretty though, Rebecca admitted), she marries this candied apple who has pink cotton candy for brains (according to Priscilla) . . . does a *brujería* on her Papi and her Papi starts suspecting Guillermo of stealing and of making bad decisions . . ." And although nothing like that happens in the novel . . ." she said, but Rebecca didn't let her finish her sentence.

"What's happening with your marriage?" Rebecca asked Selene, really loud.

"Papi, are you awake?" Pedal, pedal, pedal. And the sweat's dripping into her eyes. "Can't handle all these women," she told her father. "They'll suck me up. Don't forget I'm a reader, that's all I am, and I'm too empathic."

This here is Selene. "He wants a divorce as soon as possible so he can marry his girlfriend right away and have children. After all these years all of a sudden he can't stand the sight of me and thinks I'm a terrible person. If I could only get a gun, I'd shoot them and that way I wouldn't even have to think about it anymore! But it's so *embarrassing* to get a gun!"

"I said I'd give you one," Rebecca said casually.

"I walked in the store and I told them I wanted a license as quickly as possible and they said I didn't need a license but I just kept on talking about how I didn't care what I had to go through and that I was ready to get bonded and to take safety classes whatever it took and they kept on repeating I didn't need a license. Isn't that ridiculous? Isn't that dangerous that anyone can just walk into a store a buy a gun? No wonder there are so many holdups in Miami!"

"And so few crimes of passion," said Rebecca.

"Have you talked to his mom?" Priscilla asked shortly after she finished reciting her poem to Silka. All eyes turned to her.

"Each time I get a conversation going I am immediately left out," Rebecca complained to her father. What's more, I didn't get a chance to ask Selene if she was screwing Tommy.

This made Selene curious. She turned to Priscilla. "No. Why should I talk to his mother now?"

"Daisy does it and it always works," Priscilla said casually.

Daisy stopped rocking and glared at her. She then looked at Rebecca and raised her eyebrows. Rebecca in turn shrugged.

Lying there on his hospital bed, her father closed his eyes, so she stopped talking. He then said, "I'm still listening."

Pedal pedal pedal, we'll be at the lighthouse soon, before the squall line.

Alma said she wanted to talk to Rebecca, alone, inside, so Rebecca missed the second catfight.

Right on the other side of the window, right inside, they were sitting side by side on the upholstery couch. Alma was asking Rebecca about divorce and Rebecca kept saying that she didn't know anything about divorce but that she could recommend someone. Alma had already started the whole process but she said she needed more than five hundred dollars a month for child support.

With her back straight and one hand inside the other Alma said, "I feel I can talk to you about this because we're family, almost sisters, and we were raised together . . . My problem is that I can't believe I made a mistake again. I just can't believe it. I don't know if you know what I mean. Lately my life seems like one mistake after the other," she said while she exposed the palms of her hands in a Jesus-like way when she said that.

"*M'ija*, it's none of my business but from what you told me on the phone the other day . . ." Rebecca said with her back against the armrest and her arms crossed.

"Oh by the way thank you so much for letting me talk to you, I really needed some advice . . ." Alma slouched.

So Rebecca said, "And sorry I had to run. But feel free to call me any time, as I said I don't know if I can be of much help and it's none of my business but if I were you I'd just let go of it, you can't dwell on . . . on . . ." She bit the tip of her thumb. "Almita, you can't dwell on things that aren't even there. *Lo que yo no comprendo* is why you want a divorce, he seems like a pretty decent guy."

"I'm really disappointed with him and I can't get over it. He's just . . . he's just . . . he's so . . . nothing . . . he's like a dime a dozen . . . there's nothing special about him and I can't be in love with a man unless he's special . . . like Ernesto! The one in the novel."

Everyone's been reading ahead!

After she scratched her chin with her shoulder, Rebecca's forehead began to itch, then her breasts, then her stomach, she pulled her bra, jiggled it, scratched her head, rubbed the corners of her eyes.

"Are you all right?" Alma asked.

"Yes, it's the dog. Fleas. This is kind of embarrassing and I don't know your husband but I suppose he was like that when you married him, so I don't see why you don't like that about him now," Rebecca suggested. "Don't mind me scratching. It doesn't mean anything. But it is catching. Can you scratch me here, under my shoulder blade?"

"I changed, I matured, and I thought it'd be different," Alma said as she scratched her. "I want so much. I don't want an amateur show of a man any more. I was meant for something else. Like in this novel. When I talk about it it seems naïve and it's hard to explain, but I needed something like a life where I wore gowns all the time, and something very precious about my life, I would have liked to go to balls, to the theater, to have gowns, and fine jewelry, lots of it, like in the novel!"

Rebecca was really trying to fight back the embarrassment. "That's fine. You can stop scratching."

Alma kept on talking. "Maybe I was just born at the wrong time. God! Every time I try to express myself it never really comes out. Sometimes I want to write a book and put everything I feel in it, and all my experiences, and it could really help a lot of people, but I just don't have the time with the kids and I hate my environment, I hate living in the neighborhood where I live, the people are so . . . *vulgares, chusmas,* do you know what I mean? If I lived in a place like Coconut Grove or here on the Beach or on Key Biscayne and if I could afford childcare maybe I could finally sit down and read and write. I have so much ambition but everything seems to be against it, even my own personality. I make all these efforts to be happy and full of energy, but it's right there, discouragement is right there. It's like when heroin addicts talk about the monkey on their backs. But if I don't get more child support I'll have to move in with my mom and I'd rather die than move in with my mom. This would be my third failure!"

"Maybe we could mingle a bit," said Rebecca. "We'll talk some other day, tomorrow."

"What about the gun?"

"Swing by tomorrow afternoon, I'll teach you how to use it."

Rebecca went to join the others. "You know how I hate to hear things like that," she told her father on Saturday afternoon. "I think I'm going to catch it."

"Did you give her the gun?"

"Not yet. I'm here instead."

Outside, before her mother called, Rebecca once again unfolded the map of old Havana and placed it carefully on her lap. It was a crinkly gown from Titania Fashions, the most Parisian in the world.

She told everyone that her cousin Juan Carlos lives on Bernaza, she searched for Bernaza, right in old Havana, Havana *intramuros* as they used to call it when Rosario moved to El Cerro. "That's where my father lived," Rebecca said. "In El Cerro. His family had a house there." She was already living her first day in Havana. Breakfast at the hotel and a taxi to the Plaza de Armas. Obispo Street to . . . oh look! what do you know, Calle Tacón, there's a street called Tacón, could it have been named after Lolo? Palacio de los Capitanes Generales, that's where Rosario's mother was mortally wounded during the firing of the harquebuses, that's where they had all these events. She's actually going to a place where Rosario and Lolo and María Fernanda have been. Rebecca kept on sliding her index finger along the streets of Havana *intramuros*, the corner of Obrapia and Aguacate, that's where they live! For a week now she has been studying the map of the city and trying to imagine what each one of these streets looked like. O'Reilly, Obispo, Obrapia, and much further down, Sol and Luz, where the dress factory is, in an old church, if she ever gets to Havana she will definitely search for it.

Now she likes to think that just when she had her finger on Calle Amargura her mom called.

She was sitting on the stone wall facing the ocean and Stiltsville, four houses standing there on stilts, right in the middle of the ocean, way over there. With her back turned to the lighthouse she was looking at her map, because she had managed to get here before the squall line.

When it finally started to rain her primal Havana instinct urged her to run and get out of the rain. But run where? To her bike? So she stayed there and let the raindrops drip down her face. They came fast, drop after drop on the map, on Calle Amargura, on Calle Sun and Light, on the words she loved to touch, on the paper she wanted to slip into, between the lines, into the a's and the o's, absorbed forever, sucked into the vacuum, disappear like light into a crack.

Conchita came over later that same day. She was in charge of picking the girls up at school on Monday so she'd usually be at Rebecca's by four, to drop Nell off and chat a while.

The girls went to play in the back yard, so Rebecca and Conchita sat on the back porch. Rebecca dragged another rocking chair next to hers and placed the tape recorder right where the seat dips. After she sat down she turned to Conchita and asked, "All set?" Just to make sure she looked around, was anything going to disturb them? She then groped for the ON and the REC buttons and immediately began reading Chapter Seven. She was taping it for Trudi who loved to listen to the novel in her car, and for poor Silka who couldn't hold a book in her hands.

Indeed, Rebecca always forgot to turn the recorder off when she couldn't help but yell out-of-context phrases such as, "Go away! Keep that damn dog away!" or "Stay away, *carajo*!"

THE MINUTE SHE GOT TO THE DRESS FACTORY Rosario sensed that something was not right. She sniffed, smelled her armpits, put her nose back up, felt the air with her fingers, no lint, her nose finally told her. Bad sign. Rosario was ready to be angry. Her ears were also telling her that something was wrong. Was it the loud whispers of many excited women? No! Something was missing! The sound of scissors. Which meant that no one was working!

That day, when she surprised the seamstresses sitting around a map of Miami, Rosario had to put her foot down. Not a single one of them was working and they were all talking at the same time, in loud whispers. They couldn't find her island, they couldn't find the Seaquarium, what about Tommy's nightclub? They wanted bikes! I want Tommy! No he's mine! How dare you? I prefer Harvey. Nothing like a man's who's served time! And what about George? He'll marry us all! I prefer the quiet dentist. And what about Guillermo? The bald one! One shameless strumpet even wanted all five of them!

Rosario was fuming. Right away she told Lolo that Umberto Barrios Junior had to go. Bring back his father! Either that or no more reading in the workplace. Now those women want bikes! And get rid of a few, there's too many of them. Make them work twice as much, cut the work force in half.

Now they want bikes.

"The first female I saw in Cuba . . ."

James Williams Steele

FOR TWO YEARS María Fernanda didn't want to have anything to do with Ernesto, and she called him every name you can imagine, the insults went from *perro de mierda*, to *jodido* and *vete p'al*, she even yelled "stay away you damn dog!" But she couldn't so much as make him wince, he was determined to have her no matter what. She even told him that not only was she not a virgin but that she was *una puta asquerosa* and a *chingada* nymphomaniac and that she wanted to fuck everyone she saw except him, *¡jodido cabrón!* she yelled at the top of her lungs. "Go away, *carajo!*" He insisted that he didn't mind at all, and that she'd learn to love him and that he'd be willing to wait and to be a good husband to her.

Each time he mentioned marriage María Fernanda would turn blue with rage. She threatened to do a *brujería* on him where his whole family would die of the worst virus ever, one that's going to show up in a century, a futuristic virus like the one they talk about in the novel that's being read to the seamstresses, and then he'd get it and his dick would fall off and then she broke down in tears but continued yelling get the Hell out of my sight I never want to see you again. Go away! *¡Vete, coño, vete!* Go away!

Her war with Ernesto who came to her house every day was like the war that the Cuban people had been waging against Spain for the past seven years. Some battles were won, confidence returned, other battles were lost and confidence was lost. She seemed to yell the same thing the Cuban people did, "I want freedom." She'd taken to dressing in white and blue and putting five pointed stars all over her dress to show that she was for freedom.

Ernesto said he'd fight for freedom along with her. She didn't believe him. She was convinced that all he wanted to do was take her freedom away from her. He insisted that she was wrong. With him she could do whatever she wanted. He swore. She was only fifteen years old and needed someone to protect her when she went to the streets to demonstrate.

"To protect me against what?" she yelled turning blue in the face again, with rage.

166

"Against someone hurting you, I don't want anyone to hurt you."

"Protect me so you can lock me up and take my freedom away from me, no way! I hate you, why don't you just drop dead? Can't you understand that I hate you? *¡Vete, coño, vete!*" she uttered between her teeth when they were sitting by the fountain out in the courtyard.

Lolo was walking back and forth in the galleries pretending to be busy inspecting some corners of the house. In fact Lolo was simply trying to eavesdrop and was ready to intervene if Mafer insulted Ernesto. So when Lolo was around, Mafer had to whisper. If not Lolo would intervene and would start yelling and they'd start pushing each other and Ernesto would be in the middle saying *por favor*, please, let's be calm, let's discuss this like civilized human beings, we're not monkeys!

And sometimes Rosario would arrive and join the fight and the cook would run out and before you knew it Lolo was looking for something to break and finally Lolo would start to cry. This was something that Lolo would always save for the last minute as a last resort. If there was something Mafer couldn't stand it was to see Lolo cry.

Ernesto had already asked Rosario for María Fernanda's hand and Rosario gladly gave it to him if he could somehow manage to grab it and hold tight. He could definitely carry that nuisance of a girl away on a big white horse and get her off their hands. They could elope, they could do whatever they wanted as far as Rosario was concerned.

Rosario kept repeating that she'd taken enough shit from the world and from María Fernanda.

It did take quite a few years for Ernesto to get Mafer to utter at least two words that weren't insults.

In 1877, on María Fernanda's seventeenth birthday, Ernesto, who had a big bouquet of pink miniature roses in his hand, ventured to ask Mafer why she was always cursing. He turned around and said hello to her half-sister, the ten-year-old María Soledad. "Go to Hell!" said María Soledad. "Go away!"

"I curse because I can see into the future," Mafer replied. "If I weren't cursing I'd be seeing the future, you idiot!"

"Could you please explain this a little better?"

She sat at the edge of the fountain and replied. "No! When I'm cursing loud I don't know what's going to happen." She was wearing yellowed wrinkled linen and didn't have any shoes on.

"I don't see what one thing has to do with the other," said Ernesto.

"That's because you're a moron. I can't see the future when I'm cursing loud. It keeps me from thinking. Can't you understand that, you imbecile?" she said and stuck her toe between two cobblestones.

"Do you see bad things in store for you?"

She looked down at the grown. "Not necessarily. I see good and I see bad. And they're both frightening and they both take away from life. And it's none of your business."

"Am I in your future?" Ernesto asked.

"Yes. But it's none of your business," she replied while she sadistically stepped on a line of leafcutter ants.

"Am I your husband?"

"Yes. Go away!"

"Am I a bad husband? Do I lock you up? Do I make you move to the country? Do I cheat on you? Do I take your freedom away from you?"

"No. Go away!"

"So why don't you want to marry me?"

"Get away from me you creep you dickhead *maricón de mierda cabrón!* Go away!"

"Listen to me, Mafer, the day you have a man, listen, that day, at last, at long last, you will see less clear! The future won't matter. All that will matter will be the moment! The orgasm!"

He said that so loud that Lolo came running with mad round eyes. "How dare you say disgusting things in front of my niece!"

Mafer yelled: "Leave him alone, Lolo!"

WHAT'S FOR DINNER, MOMMY?

Cuban chicken, rice, and broccoli.
And for dessert?
Chocolate pudding.
When are we going to eat?
Not for a while.
I'm hungry now!
Get a slice of salami out of the fridge, dear. Can't you see I'm busy reading?

E ITHER THE CUBANS LOST THIS WAR, OR they felt they had.

By 1878, when the end of war was signed and declared, Cubans had not achieved independence for their nation. But there was no more slavery, all the men on the island were free men, and many of the women had demonstrated out in the streets wearing blue and white dresses with pointed stars, many of them, even from the aristocracy, had had their possessions confiscated, but they kept on fighting for freedom. *Libertad.* Liberty. *Libre.* Free. For what?

Oh but it is one of those concepts that acquires a new meaning as time passes, with each different situation. Freedom can never be something that has already been said and that has already been talked about. *¡Libertad! ¡Cuba libre! ¡Qué viva Cuba libre!* That's what they kept shouting. Perhaps not as loud. They kept shouting it in their minds. Long live Cuba *libre*. Even if it's not for now.

In January of 1879, María Fernanda Aguasclaras y Santa Cruz was married to Ernesto Tirry y Sotolongo. The wedding took place in the chapel of La Casa Amarilla where the couple will reside with the bride's uncle Lolo.

Mafer had the most beautiful dress you could imagine. Lily white with tiny diamonds sewn all over the bodice. Fireflies all around the low neckline, competing with the diamonds. It gave her face an expression of pure light.

Her half-sister María Soledad who was eleven threw a fit, she didn't want Mafer to marry, but Mafer threw the eleven-year-old her garter and promised to give her the wedding dress so she could play bride with it whenever she wanted.

Lolo got hysterical during the ceremony. Right when the priest asked if Ernesto would accept Mafer as his lawful wedded wife Lolo began to sob and the sobs kept getting louder and louder until they couldn't even hear the priest. Then Lolo started screaming I'm going to lose my beloved niece, so Mafer turned around and said that they'd still be living in the same house and that as soon as they returned from their honeymoon in Florida everything would be the same as it was except that Ernesto would be there all the time and that he'd be taking over the dress factory.

This seemed to calm Lolo down. But then immediately Lolo turned to Rosario and asked Rosario why she'd spread the rumor that the newlyweds were moving to El Cerro.

Rosario said, "I said no such thing."

"Yes you did."

"I said no such thing."

"Yes you did."

And before you know it they were arguing but luckily the priest accelerated the ceremony and the bride and groom walked up the isle and the party began.

While they were dancing Ernesto finally got the courage to ask María Fernanda.

"Sweetheart, don't get offended," he said shyly, "but your uncle Lolo, is he . . . I mean . . . does he have a sexual preference for men . . . is he . . . like . . . effeminate? Pardon the word sweetheart and I hope that my using a word like that doesn't offend you."

"Didn't I ever tell you?" Mafer asked.

"Tell me what?"

"I guess I didn't. Lolo's a woman. My uncle Lolo's a woman. Can't you tell?"

"Oh . . . hum! . . . oh well that explains everything," said poor Ernesto with a puzzled look on his face.

The most beautiful room in the house was prepared for the newlyweds. It had windows that gave out to the interior courtyard and a balcony that gave out to the noisy Calle Aguacate, and a door with many mahogany slats which you could slant whichever way you wanted. It had a great bed with a heavy silk and golden bedspread.

Ernesto said, I know you're going to be a little nervous. We haven't so much as . . . and then he looked at Mafer and she was stripping off her bridal nightgown. And he couldn't believe his eyes what a beautiful body she had. These wide full hips these milky young girlish breasts that made him think of hormones and milk and menstrual blood and wet dogs, her belly, her slim torso, where her little belly popped out, and her black pubic hair. She was looking at him like a hungry wolf, coming toward him as he took off his robe. Being the intellectual he was, Ernesto had prepared this whole speech about how she'd be somewhat afraid because she'd never seen a man naked but before he had the time to say any of that she was already kneeling in front of him and putting his erect penis in her mouth.

He groaned with pleasure and he pulled it out of her mouth fast because he knew he was going to come right away if he didn't, they didn't make it to the bed or to the little cot or to the couch he entered her hard and fast right there on the wood floor. He couldn't tell whether it hurt her or whether it felt good. When he tried to ask he got his head pulled back by the hair with one hand and his butt squeezed with the other. She seemed possessed.

It was so quick, he was about to apologize for coming so fast, but this was totally unexpected, before he knew it she was on top of him, yelling so loud that it could be heard down the block and all the neighbors that had been invited had a moment of silence and said to themselves, that's María Fernanda. *Gracias a Dios*, she likes it. The cook heard it, María Soledad heard it, Lolo heard it and really wondered, for the first time ever, about men. Could it be that good? And Lolo had all the liberty in the world. As usual Lolo could go out wearing men's clothes and pick up a mercenary soldier leftover from last year's war who was hungry for a boy and then, surprise! Lolo would be willing to act both parts. Lolo got so excited that Lolo couldn't sleep all night. It would have been impossible anyway with these newlyweds screaming and yelling.

They did it four times. The first time on the floor with Ernesto on top. The next time on the cot with Ernesto on top. Then Mafer went on top. Then they did it standing up with Mafer bending over the oak veneer table with the cherubs.

Was María Fernanda cured? Had Ernesto's love finally managed to get that possessing she-devil out of her head? No. That person would always be there. The great thing about their love was that he kept her crazy and that he kept her sane, so as long as he was around both sides of her would be satisfied, the madwoman and the sane one. She did the same thing to him, she answered every prayer that had so far been left unanswered in his life, she was the quenching of his thirst, she was food for his soul and for his belly. I am so privileged to know you, he said. Whatever he wanted from a woman at any given moment, a mother, a whore, a wife, a nurse, a tormentor, she had the capacity to turn into, in the blink of an eye, in a heartbeat. This was the love of María Fernanda and Ernesto.

No NEED TO ORIENT the rocking chairs on February 9, for just about everyone seemed to have something else to do. Priscilla said she had to take Javier to a party, Rebecca said out loud. She was sitting all by herself outside with the light in her eye. What if this were just another story being read? Daisy has an important business dinner, Rebecca kept on pretending. Trudi is visiting her boyfriend in Atlanta. What does it sound like? Alma called at four to say she had cried and would not show up with swollen eyes. Maybe Alma should go first, just to add a touch of drama. Selene is finally shooting her husband tonight. Kidding! It's Selene's grandmother's birthday. Can our story be read out loud? Does it lend itself? Just a list of excuses.

As to Rebecca, she stood up and decided to drop Nell off at Conchita's then . . . what could she say? How could she steal the light from María Fernanda? How could she get the novel back before Daisy, Alma, and Priscilla usurped it.

So Rebecca put on some tight blue jeans and a tight white tee-shirt, no! A flowery dress that flows, a dancing dress, sexy sandals. As soon as Tommy got home they didn't even quarrel, simply got on the boat, turned the motor on, and went to have dinner in an outdoor restaurant by the bay.

Monty's, where the Jamaican band jams all night. How does that sound, María Fernanda? It was all true. But what was it placed next to the thought of getting on a *volante* and telling the postilion to get you to the Cafe Louvre, or the Tacón Theatre. Or getting in that tiny cot with Ernesto. She wished Daisy were here with some kind of computer graph. Here's this compared to that. Oh, she should've married Ernesto instead! The mousseline of her dress flowing in the wind, going fast, running over jaywalkers, talking with the fan. I get to fantasize too, if not they're going to take the novel away from me, *esas otras,* those others.

Back to earth.

The problem is that no one called Jenny Rincón and that apparently she canceled something else to be at the weekly reunion. When she showed up at Tommy's and Rebecca's house with her little boy, Justin, on Friday evening February the ninth, the gates were closed and no one was answering the intercom. She waited until seven thirty and her kid was so hungry that by the time she left she felt extremely humiliated and offended.

She called Rebecca the next day and swore she'd never come back again. They could count her *out* of the reading club.

They were on the phone for a long time. Rebecca, who had a nasty hangover, must've gotten tired of saying, "I'm sorry." But Jenny could not let go of it. She argued that this had gone way past the point of forgiveness, too far, way too far. "Come on, Jenny, let go of it," Rebecca said. To this Jenny replied, "You girls have done this to me before! Many times!" Indeed they had, ever since she'd known Jenny the *leitmotif* had been, "Did anyone remember to tell Jenny?" The party was canceled, the movie was canceled, the pool party was canceled, we're no longer meeting at the donut shop, or at Lums, or by the water, the picnic's off, did anyone remember to tell Jenny?

It's as if everyone went out of their way to forget Jenny. Or ignore her! As if she didn't exist! She was invisible and had always hated that! And she was right, especially that it happened all the time. Rebecca told Jenny to hold on, she had to get some Excedrin.

Rebecca had seen it happen often, someone could be talking to Jenny at a party or at the skating rink and then they'd just walk away as if she weren't there. So Jenny Rincón was really touchy about this. She was a bit paranoid because of the deformity of her hands and because her husband hadn't had a job in over two years. She had often overheard jokes about him and who knows exactly what went on in Jenny's mind.

By the end of their phone conversation Jenny had come to the conclusion that the only reason they asked her to join this reading club was to make fun of her. A shocked, and nauseous, Rebecca insisted, "How could you say something like that? Oh, come on!" she urged Jenny while she rubbed her temples.

"I had too much to drink last night."

"Celebrating my humiliation?"

"Now you're beginning to sound like my mother."

The truth of the matter was that Jenny had been so unlucky in general that she had lost her sense of humor very early in life. Terrible things were always happening to Jenny. Trays were dropped on her head when she was at a restaurant. If she'd buy a dress she'd take it home to discover it was defective and then she couldn't find the proof of purchase. Just about everything had happened to Jenny, so when she went to Rebecca's and found the place tightly shut she decided she didn't want to be part of the reading club anymore unless someone apologized and really meant it.

Rebecca apologized.

Daisy apologized.

Rebecca called her back on Saturday evening to apologize, and left her a message of apology the next day on her answering machine.

But Jenny could not forgive, she said she didn't feel they were sorry enough.

So Rebecca kept on apologizing. No luck.

During one of these interminable phone calls Jenny blurted out that she didn't even like the novel they were reading, because the author seemed to have willfully decided not to talk about how the slaves and the women were mistreated in Cuba at the time.

Jenny even wondered if the author was racist or something because Petra was made fun of at the beginning of the story. The author had talked about how she was always wearing the wedding dress she had inherited from her mistress. And then she was turned into sausage, and Jenny thought that even if it was true who cares? The author could have abstained from giving us such gory details. Not all truths are worth telling anyway.

On Monday Jenny also told Rebecca on the phone that the characters in the novel she had chosen were totally oblivious to everything that was going on around them and that all they cared about were their little lives and their own problems without so much as mentioning all the injustice that was occurring at the time. Apparently slaves were given very severe punishments and Habaneros had really low opinions of slaves, which the author should have pointed out and condemned.

Some Habaneros thought that all Africans were dangerous barbarians, others were convinced that all blacks cherished the idea of being accepted by Havana's upper social strata, and some even said without the slightest trace of embarrassment that freed negro women put on airs. And last but not least if the author was going to base everything on fact why didn't she mention the hardships of the slave Juan Francisco Manzano who taught himself how to write and was forced to work when all he wanted to do was write poetry?

"How should I know?" Rebecca replied a bit annoyed.

"You live in a little microcosm," Jenny said to Rebecca. "You have no idea of what's going on around you."

She really thought they should have read a book condemning Castro's prisons instead.

But Jenny just hadn't read far enough because Chapter Eight dealt precisely with the question of slavery. As usual Rebecca read it to Conchita and at the same time taped it for Trudi and Silka, who was really disappointed that the February 16 meeting was canceled too.

Rebecca did promise Silka that they'd meet on the twenty-third, rain or shine. Everyone would be there except Lucía, Helen, and, of course, Jenny.

"Who will be the last to go?" Rebecca's father asked.

"May the main character win."

"Who's that?"

"The one who steals the light."

THE CORNER OF CALLES AGUACATE AND OBRAPIA, where La Casa Amarilla stood, was noisy and bright. Farmers would come with their pigs and try to sell them. Other peasants or *guajiros* would come with their donkeys laden with angry chickens hanging by their feet. The scissorsgrinder just wouldn't keep quiet, he'd yell and scream just to hear his own voice and annoy everyone, so would the other peddlers with their mules and vegetable baskets. Carts pulled by oxen carried other merchandise, making quite a racket, but this was nothing compared to the strident voices of the carriers carrying water from the public fountain to the houses that didn't have water. They would haggle at the top of their voices with the sulfur vendor for pieces of sulfur that they desperately needed, for without sulfur there was no possibility of selling dirty water. It was the sulfur that purified it.

Then there were the horses, the fast selfish *volantes* who killed and scared quite a few people a month, the squawking parrots, the caged birds, the fountain splashing, the beggars, the acrobats, the cripples, the gamblers, the prostitutes, everyone trying to make a living.

To all this atonal din could be added the sound of María Fernanda's pleasure on three afternoons a week and almost every night. Everyone was sure that she would get pregnant right away. After all, they did it all the time and her hips were nice and wide and her breasts seemed to have been made so that they would leak with milk, but she kept on bleeding, month after month.

It would have probably been the best time for her to get pregnant though. The peace had been signed with Spain, and she knew, since she could foretell the future, that they had seventeen years of peace ahead. Not that this peace meant the people's happiness, for there was an undercurrent of frustration and a deep feeling of injustice.

María Fernanda was very busy fighting to put an end to slavery. For little did it matter if all Cubans had been declared free men, little did it matter if slavery had been officially abolished, it still went on.

Ernesto and María Fernanda would organize demonstrations against the slavers when they arrived at the harbor. The three main slavers were the Duquesa de Braganza, the Grandes Antillas, and Socorro. They were coming and going so often that everyone knew them by name just about as well as they knew the *Niña*, the *Pinta*, and the *Santa María*.

Back home, Mafer spent hours writing pamphlets condemning slavery and describing the different kinds of tortures being inflicted upon slaves and writing to the president of the United States begging him to intervene and to ban slavery in Cuba and put an embargo if need be.

Lolo, after having turned La Casa Amarilla practically into a museum and painted an enormous mural in the courtyard called "Florida, Where I've NEVER Been," had decided that there were two things in this life that were interesting. The first was checking the material that was to be read by the seamstresses by Umbertico Barrios, who had been hired back after his son was fired, and the second was painting cigarette labels.

It was fine to paint cigarette labels but the problem was that Lolo had chosen to record the fate of the mulatta on these labels and that both Mafer and her half-sister María Soledad considered these labels racist and offensive. Oftentimes they'd go and tear up Lolo's work, but that would make them feel really bad and they'd both end up apologizing to Lolo so they were left with no option but to scream and to shout which seemed the only way to get your point across in that house.

Each one of these labels that Lolo painted had a little story to it that essentially went like this:

One label showed a very pretty mulatta wearing a fancy pink dress, or sometimes white dress to really get it across that she was still a virgin. Another label was of a this same innocent mulatta admiring the good looks of a white gentleman, and this made María Soledad really furious.

María Soledad, whom everyone called Marisol, was a mulatta indeed but she wasn't at all interested in white men and she was always repeating it to everyone. She seemed quite proud of finding black men absolutely luscious. She said she wasn't about to repeat her mom's mistakes and go to bed with some white man then be constantly reminded that he could never marry her because of her impure blood. Marisol took it as far as saying that she'd rather be the mistress of a black man than the wife of a white man, in this life, and in the next! And whenever Lolo had someting to say about the color of her latest boyfriend's skin Marisol would yell at the top of her lungs that she wasn't going to let herself get pregnant by any white *hidalgo* fag and have everyone say that there is no sweet tamarind and no virgin mulatto girl and that's the two things in life one can be sure of. So there'd be a big fight at home every time Lolo chose to paint the mulatta falling for the white man.

Since María Fernanda and her half-sister Marisol had always been very close, they would both gang up against Lolo. Once Mafer went as far as to hit Lolo, so Lolo started to cry and Mafer began to cry, all this while Ernesto was in his study reading a book. Ernesto put his book down to go and find out what all the crying was about, and there he found the three of them saying they were sorry to each other.

So Lolo would invariably go back to painting the cigarette labels, this new-found and adored hobby. There was also a label showing the white gentleman flirting with the mulatta and saying, *How pretty you are*, and there were pink hearts coming out of his heart and some other pink hearts coming out of the mulatta's heart. A red label showed them kissing. The purple label showed the mulatta pregnant, and it said, *As you sow so shall you reap*. A green label talked about the end of pleasure. A final one showed the mulatta's daughter about to begin the same life as her mom. María Soledad kept repeating, "This is not going to happen to me."

A typical day at La Casa Amarilla would go like this. They would wake up at around nine AM and stay in bed until ten or so. One half hour was dedicated to morning ablutions, then they went downstairs for breakfast. Three rooms were occupied upstairs. One was Lolo's, the second was María Fernanda's and Ernesto's, and the third belonged to María Soledad, who was turning into a beautiful young lady.

They would have breakfast together at eleven in the morning, take their time, have several fruit and many cups of coffee, and then stand up and say that it was time to get to work. Work meant a favorite activity. Lolo liked painting the cigarette labels, María Soledad loved writing letters to the president of the United States, Ernesto adored reading, and Mafer spent her time writing pamphlets condemning slavery.

These activities would go on until two in the afternoon when lunch would be served. Ernesto did none of the things gentlemen of his social rank did in the afternoon after the siesta. Usually the man, *el hombre, el macho*, would either go to the bullfight or to the cockfight or to a bar or cafe or to see his mistress. Ernesto of course had no mistress, he only had eyes for Mafer and he wasn't interested in all the other activities, so he'd spend his afternoons either making love with Mafer or working at the museum or overseeing the work at the dress factory.

Lately Ernesto had gotten quite interested in what Umbertico Barrios was reading to the seamstresses in the dress factory. So much reading was going on and the seamstresses loved it so much that many hours had to be spent seeking out new stories to read. As usual there'd be a vote regarding the choice of theme, and it would invariably be a novel about life in Florida in an incredible future.

Marriage had indeed changed Mafer. Not only was the future more difficult to see, but stories about an incredible future in south Florida didn't seem to interest her any more. It was difficult to believe that this same Mafer had been such an avid listener in her youth. She said she had other things to do now, like have babies, learn to be a nurturer, and deal with reality. Besides, wasn't Umbertico Barrios much happier without her around? As a little girl she had indeed tormented his days, and he still refused to mention her by name, she was simply one or two of his seven demons, an unhappy ending, the worst that could happen.

Some of the men working in the factory complained about these being women's books but the seamstresses were the majority so they always got their way. Often there would be debates during which they'd try to determine if there was such a thing as a man's book or as a woman's book but they never came up with any good answers. Needless to say these debates would always end up being very loud with everyone talking at the same time and Lolo would invariably get quite upset.

Lolo insisted that there was absolutely no difference between men and women, absolutely none at all. Once someone came up to Lolo and asked the question, Chico, shoot straight with us, ¿tú eres maricón o tortillera? and Lolo went into a quasi-epileptic fit of rage. "I am none of those things!" Lolo yelled. "I'm just someone who wants to be free! ¡Quiero hacer lo que me da la gana!"

The evening would usually be spent at home, a quiet dinner in their lovely dining room. Rosario, who had changed her name back to Escolástica now (Tica for short), would join them and they'd talk about politics and art and personal family matters. Tica was more and more against the idea of annexing Cuba to the United States. She yelled that they'd all be sorry if Cuba became a boring Protestant country.

Sometimes they'd go to the theatre but they only did that because of social pressure and also because the theatre had been named Tacón after one of Lolo's relatives. Nobody in this family really enjoyed the theatre, but there was so much pressure on you to go and see the latest play that once a week they'd give in and really make an effort.

Ernesto hated to go because he preferred to stay home and read. Tica hated to have to sit down in the same position for several hours. She said she'd always been uncomfortable sitting down especially in those uncomfortable theatre seats. Mafer would always get a terrible urge to talk while she was in the theatre so everyone would end up spitting "Sssshhhhh!" at her. But she just couldn't help it, the theatre seemed like the ideal place to talk. As to Lolo, Lolo always said that the only reason to go to the theatre was to people-watch, and that seemed like a really interesting activity.

Once Lolo had even bought binoculars, better known as *prismáticos,* in order to spend the whole play people watching. That week Lolo just couldn't wait to go to the theatre. Lolo tended to get terribly excited about anything. But to Lolo's dismay, the minute Lolo began to look at everyone in the theatre, Lolo discovered that all eyes were on Lolo, and since Lolo could read lips what Lolo read on their lips was the eternal question that would invariably be asked when Lolo was around, What is that? Is it a man? A woman? A lesbian? A fag? Lolo wanted to shout, I am none of that! I'm just someone who wants to be free! *¡Quiero hacer lo que me da la gana carajo!* Very soon Lolo stopped wanting to go to the theatre.

Mafer and Ernesto had organized their lives in such a way that whenever Ernesto was at the dress factory or helping plan the new museum, Mafer would organize a *tertulia.* Lately Mafer had been trying to be a totally normal person. Ernesto insisted that it really wasn't necessary and that he liked her the way she was, crazier than a she-goat and all, but she insisted on putting out all the fires in her past she was intent on erasing that madwoman she had been most of her life.

She was dying to get pregnant and kept counting first the weeks then the months then the years since they'd been married and had been making love passionately and wondering why nothing was happening. She'd was so disapponted every month when she'd bleed and even prayed upside down so that it'd happen. Sometimes she'd go into the chapel and get angry with God who wasn't allowing her to be normal, and she even threatened Him a couple of times, but He remained as silent as God is when He refuses to answer prayers.

One day, finally, she yelled at God so loudly in Havana Cathedral that she did manage to embarrass Him and they made a deal. They both agreed that she'd conceive the day slavery was really and truly abolished in Cuba. She was so happy with the deal that she even promised God to name the child after Him.

Once she knew it was going to happen Mafer was much more relaxed about it. They had a great life anyway, and many good things happened. The demonstration she organized against Governor Dulce was a great success.

Then in 1886, at the age of eighteen, María Soledad married Antonio Gomez, a freed slave who was a postilion and a tailor. When he was a slave he had been one of those rare slaves who had been spoiled rotten by their mistresses, so he had always been accustomed to fine clothes and a relatively comfortable life.

Mafer, Lolo, and Rosario planned the wedding and in spite of all the bickering and the tears it turned out to be the best, the most beautiful and especially the most fun wedding, right there in La Casa Amarilla. Everyone left that reception with a smile on their face and saying that that was the best party they'd ever been to and that they wished Marisol would get married every day, and how handsome the groom was, it wasn't his fault if he was so black.

At first this had caused enormous problems in the household. Tica had put her foot down and said that it was out of the question that Marisol marry someone so black especially when she was so light-skinned that she could easily pass for white. All Marisol had to do was marry someone white and no one would even remember that her mother had been a black servant. Antonio, the fiancé, overheard this quarrel and he interrupted Tica to say that as a child he had never been allowed to play with *negritos* so he couldn't understand why she was treating him like such a black man. All the women in the family told him to stay out of this and he heeded their advice, he never said a word again and just did whatever Marisol said.

After they got through with Antonio, the women went back to their fighting. Marisol reminded Tica that she only liked black men. Tica then threatened to take this to the authorities because a marriage such as this could affect the family.

It was hard to believe that all this bickering had preceded the wedding where everyone had so much fun! And they laughed! Tica was in a great mood and when Tica was in a great mood everyone would go crazy laughing. It was during the wedding that Tica announced that from now on she refused to answer to the name of Rosario and preferred to be called by her other name Escolástica, Tica for short, and that this was it! She'd never change her mind about her name again! So everyone had to start calling her Tica. Oh and by the way she was going to move back into La Casa Amarilla because she was getting awfully lonesome in El Cerro and she and Lolo were going to try once more, and if it didn't work out this time then there'd really be a scandal and a divorce.

After everyone had eaten cake there was one minor incident when Tica and Mafer got into a terrible argument about the United States. Mafer told

Tica about how she was writing letters to the president and practically begging him to go into war with Spain and to annex Cuba, either that or put an embargo on Cuba and really make Spain suffer and Tica barely let her finish her paragraph. She was dead set against the United States imposing their ways and mores and culture and especially their tasteless food on this country. Before you know it there'll be a million tourists here who think they own the place and they'll be speaking English everywhere in Havana and eating their terribly sloppy fast food with relish and ketchup. And the place will be totally Protestant and money-minded. Tica admitted that she loved to make money but that she was not a worshipper of the dollar like those Protestants, she was a worshipper of the *peso*, which is different, not only that but they'll tear our churches down and they absolutely hate angels and saints because angels and saints are not serious enough for them.

Tica had lined her driveway in El Cerro with cherubs and she didn't want to see them torn down! No way! And once those people impose their food on you there is no way out. They eat fast and they get fat. They boil their meat and take the joy out of eating and plain Protestant food is all you eat and before you know it you start worrying about eating too much and getting fat and the more grease you take out of your food the fatter you get and the drier your hair gets the rougher your skin gets and every meal will make you feel guilty that you ate. There is so much food there that they are full of eating disorders. They have to keep themselves from eating instead of spending their days anticipating the joy of the next meal, like we do. They talked about it in the novel they were reading at the dress factory, Tica reminded them.

Lolo couldn't remember there being any mention of eating disorders in that novel. Yes, some women are worried about being fat and others are worried about not being perfect. There will come a time when you can go to a doctor and have your whole body redone. Lolo suddenly remembered, Yes, that was indeed in the novel they were reading in the dress factory. Then suddenly Lolo remembered that they never went to Florida and got all upset. Then Mafer remembered that she wasn't pregnant yet. But after Lolo reminded Tica of that unkept promise Lolo let go of the rancour and wasn't too upset. Lolo simply begged Tica to behave herself, and Tica said, Okay.

Slavery was finally abolished in 1886.

C AN'T WE JUST ORDER PIZZA TONIGHT, MOM?

No! Can't you see you're interrupting me? Shut up!

I don't want salmon.

God dammit! Quiet! I'm in the middle of reading!

Why can't we have pizza?

Because you're too fat, you need to go on a diet. Now leave me alone, I'm reading!

Nell began to cry. I'm going to tell my father! All you do is read and you don't take care of me. And you want to have another baby, start over, from scratch, be a better mom this time. I heard it when you had a dream out loud.

A T THE END OF THAT YEAR, on Christmas Eve, Azucena—reputedly the best midwife in Havana—was called to La Casa Amarilla. Mafer didn't want just anyone to deliver the baby. Lately so many babies had been dying in the first week of their lives that Mafer wanted to make sure that she had a midwife who had studied at the Midwives School in San Francisco de Paula Women's Hospital. Mafer had even sent for Azucena the week before so they could meet and Azucena said that she should have no fears for once the baby was born she'd cut the umbilical cord and put oil of *copayba* on the belly button and the baby would be sure to live to a ripe old age provided he or she didn't have any terrible accidents, didn't eat poison by mistake, or get yellow fever from not resting after meals, hanging out too long in the moonlight, or eating too many fruit at night. Right then and there Azucena gave Mafer and Ernesto her bill and asked to be paid in advance:

One dose of oil of *copayba*	16 *pesos.*
Fast and safe delivery	26 *pesos.*
Cutting of umbilical cord	8 *pesos.*
Total	50 *pesos* to be paid to Azucena Martínez in advance.
Extras:	
Night delivery	10 *pesos*
From 4 in the afternoon to next morning	16 *pesos.*

It took Mafer only two hours to give birth to a son, whom she named Teofilo Anacleto Immanuel de Dios Tirry y Aguasclaras. She kept her promise and named him after God. With this baby Mafer's hips got really wide and they would never ever be the same again, but she didn't mind. With each one of her pregnancies she'd gain twenty pounds that she'd never shed, all in her hips and stomach and thighs. Actually, the plumper she was the tinier her feet and ankles and waist became, and the more Ernesto liked her.

REBECCA WAS TELLING DAISY that it was interesting to read about the garbage in the streets of Havana. In a never-ending footnote the author had actually supplied a list of late nineteenth-century garbage: pineapple rinds, orange peels, pieces of coconut shells, corn cobs, egg shells, pumpkin rinds, chicken bones, fragments of melons, *malanga* peel, yucca peel, sugar cane pulp, chili stems, and the list goes on and on. Daisy interrupted to say that it was nothing compared to the information she had, but Rebecca just kept on talking. And what about the list of odors: *tasajo* (beef jerky), *bacalao* (dried fish), garlic, donkey excrement, horse, cow, coffee, tobacco, and negro (yes, negro, the author explains in another one of the footnotes that the travelers to Havana were all racist, narrow-minded people except for Samuel Hazard).

Conchita said, I don't know why Rebecca never reads the footnotes to me. All I remember is this girl going to the bathroom in a nice fountain surrounded by cherubs, this man's penis covered with lipstick, this lesbian painting cigarette labels . . .

Rebecca protested. She had read the footnote concerning the cigarette labels.

What did it say besides *Ibid*?

That labels were indeed hand-painted, and no matter who the artist was, it was always the same story, the mulatta falling in love with the white man.

Must have something to do with the collective subconscious.

Sugar and tobacco. Black and white.

They didn't believe in brown sugar yet.

Brown sugar was in the making.

Conchita said, Okay, I admit, Becky did read a footnote to me once. But now I forgot what it said. Couldn't remember for the life of me.

It said *Ibid*.

Doesn't that Marisol woman's bridegroom seem handsome? He reminds me of Denzel Washington.

Who's Marisol? Priscilla asked.

. . .

Right, the half-sister. The medication I'm taking is the death of my memory.

Once again, Rebecca felt left out of the conversation.

Hey, Priscilla, what's wrong with your husband? He's sitting inside all by himself, moping. Daisy was the one who was wondering. Then Rebecca heard Trudi say that she'd be really surprised if they had all these different races living peacefully under the same roof. They fight all the time, they're not living peacefully. But what is typical? Alma asked. Typical is only someone or some family you don't know. But there aren't really any happy families, are there? Did you hear about the Isabella color? That was Daisy talking. Wencesla the cook said that María Fernanda's panties were Isabella color, then in a footnote the author explains what Isabella color is. Legend has it that once upon a time Isabella La Católica asked a special favor from God and promised not to change her panties for a year if the favor was granted and guess what? The favor was granted. She didn't say her *panties*, she said her *linen*. Back then you couldn't say the word *panty* in front of God. Anyway that's where we get Isabella color. Tommy made a face. So Daisy asked, "What's he doing here?" We shouldn't say these things in front of men.

What if he wants to join us?

No way.

I was just stepping inside. What's wrong with Priscilla's husband? Conchita asked.

The minute Tommy went inside Guillermo stepped outside and walked across the lawn, all the way to the bay. Is he going to jump? And there goes Priscilla. Something's going on. Priscilla's out there talking to him right now. Now that we mentioned the hygiene, Rebecca said, there's that other footnote where the author explains that the morning ablutions consisted of wiping your face, neck, and hands with island rum. Can you imagine? Tommy, who just stepped out because he forgot something, and who's back indoors for good, likes that idea. And he's getting used to the Isabella color panties. I'm ready not to ever change my panties again in my life if it means that George will never cheat on me again. Hey, you never know! That's right, what he does isn't cheating! It's called falling in love. The minute he falls in love he runs and tells me he can't wait to share his happiness with me. Apparently Tommy cheated on Rebecca a few times but it was nothing serious, Rebecca heard Daisy saying to Trudi and Silka. He didn't cheat, he screwed around. Don't say it in front of Rebecca or she'll . . . you know how she tends to react . . . Alma is definitely the only person who would have enjoyed living in those times. Alma says, That's right. Wearing long gowns and going to the theatre, the ball, the *paseo*, having this real romantic courtship. Here comes Priscilla now. But her husband still seems upset. Is he going to jump? Conchita was still complaining that Rebecca wasn't reading the footnotes to her. She could only remember the part about this woman giving her husband a blow job and getting lipstick all over his penis.

Sssh!

Sssshh!

Mom, can we order pizza?

Aren't you going to eat some of Abuelita's *croquetas*, dear?

I hate Spanish food. What's for dessert?

Apples and pears, dear.

Nell ran off crying.

Who thinks Nell is losing weight?

Actually she seems to have lost a little weight since Tommy started being sweet to her the other day. It took him ten years. A lifetime. Do you know why? No. Maybe Tommy and Rebecca are trying to patch things up. Life takes its toll on relationships.

Who told Priscilla's husband that Priscilla dated Tommy years ago?

Selene said innocently, "Did I say something wrong?"

Trudi said, The author isn't really painting the portrait of a typical Cuban family in the second half of the nineteenth century. I don't think women gave blow jobs at the time. You mean with the lipstick detail? No, that's not what I mean! But maybe it is your typical family, Priscilla argued. The wine is delicious. And so are the *croqueticas. ¡Ay qué ricas!*

By the way, Rebecca said, Jenny Rincón has decided not to come back. But she just called and is really angry because she feels that apparently her choice of not returning has not affected this reading club at all. She has the impression that no one is even going to feel her absence, no one's going to ask, *Hey, where's Jenny?* So she's really resentful about that. So she kind of wishes we were all dead or really sick and unlucky. In any case she's adamant, she's not coming back and she never wants to hear from us again in her life.

Daisy really hates it when people commit to doing something and promise that they're going to show up every Friday no matter what, then the slightest thing happens like Jenny coming and no one being here two Fridays ago, because that's what it amounts to, and then all of a sudden that's it! They back out and all the plans are no good any more. These *croquetas* are so good where did Becky get these *croquetas*? Becky! *¿De dónde vienen estas cro-*

quetas? Oh no wonder. Her mom made them. The minute you have a good reading club going someone decides it's time to break it up and try to sabotage it. That's why reading clubs never last! He's all upset now. Who? Priscilla's husband! Does he prefer being called Bill or Guillermo? He can't stand the thought of his wife being within fifty miles of a man she dated once. Who told him? Ssssh! Rebecca doesn't know. Of course she knows. I think she's the one who told him.

Selene was sitting next to Tommy inside the house and those two seemed to be having an endless conversation. And Daisy was just about ready to utter some mean remark but every time she opened her mouth Trudi would interrupt and ask her for details concerning the Zanjón Treaty that ended the Ten Years' War with Spain or for some more numbers concerning the population of the island of Cuba at that time. Was that in the novel too? Conchita asked. Rebecca kept glancing inside the house. Then Trudi was wondering if slavery had been abolished in 1886 or in 1888, it's hard to tell because history books give both dates. Some books even say that slavery was abolished in 1860. Would anyone like some ice water? Rebecca asked. She said she had to go to the kitchen anyway. And why are Selene and Tommy having such a long interesting conversation? Don't you hate it when men do that? Sometimes they are so compulsive and they don't even do it on purpose. There is this other footnote where the author explains what courtship was like in Cuba a hundred years ago. *Ay pero chica, Dios mío,* Becky, I don't think I've had one single footnote read to me! said Conchita. Where's Becky? She went to get some ice water. You said you hated footnotes! I said I hated *Cliffs Notes!* Priscilla, where's your husband? We quarreled and he left. He doesn't want me to be here. So the man has to make everyone aware of his intentions if he wants to come and visit his sweetheart every day and from that day on he HAS to come every day if not she'll send her brothers after him, this is what Rebecca was saying when she stepped outside. And he can't dance with anybody else at the ball and he can't look at anyone else or stand out in the street talking into an iron grate. Apparently Cuban women at that time were extremely jealous. Thank God we're different now! We're much more reasonable. Daisy went over to Rebecca and whispered something in her ear. They don't seem to remember that there's a world around them. Hey, Selene, Rebecca said when she stepped back inside the house, Have you changed your name yet?

Now she's planning to change it to Catherine, but she wants it spelled K-a-t-h-r-h-y-n-n-e. Either that or Caitline, spelled . . .

Designer spelling.

And Selene also said she wasn't going to buy a gun after all, and before you know it she was back to talking to Tommy. So Rebecca went and sat between them.

What's with Selene and Tommy? Trudi asked Daisy. I sure hope Tommy isn't planning to do The George Thing, if you know what I mean. Selene's so vulgar. I know that Rebecca gets on my nerves at times but I'm quite used to having her as my sister-in-law. Apparently Guillermo's sitting all by himself in the car, said Conchita who had just returned from the bathroom. He's upset because Priscilla once dated Tommy. You know how Cuban men are. He can't stand the thought of someone else having screwed the mother of his children.

Rebecca, who had momentarily disappeared, came back to where Selene and Tommy were sitting and said, Look at these photos, Selene. My Mom just received them. These are my relatives in Cuba. Here's my great aunt Malva, and she can't wait until we visit one day, she's going to make coconut maca-roons, *raspadura*, sweet potato pastry, and milk candy for when we get there, she saw me once when I was three, and that's it. That's my great aunt Malva when she was fifteen sitting next to her sister who's my Abuela. She's the one who died last year, when my mom and dad were visiting Cuba, before my dad had his stroke.

Selene yawned.

Next week I'm sending my great aunt Malva a pair of *chancletas*, pow-dered whole milk, Fig Newtons, Kool Aid, plantain soup mix . . . And here's a picture of my cousin Amapola whom everyone calls La Rubia. She's my uncle Rodrigo's daughter, you know the Marielito who got shot in the head by that horrible Elsa woman whom I met at the Fountainbleu ice skating rink when I was sixteen. Did I ever tell you that story? One day when I got back from college up north my mom tells me Rodrigo's getting married to this Elsa I met at the ice skating rink. At first I thought it was great since Elsa had a house on Royal Palm Avenue and that would give my uncle Rodrigo a little stability, he was a Marielito you know, but the marriage only lasted two months then he moved out and she lived with her parents and after they divorced they'd still meet once in a while in her bedroom but it was a big secret since she lived with her parents, so he'd climb in through her window and one day she just plain shot him in the head as he came in the window and told everyone she thought he was a prowler. It's pretty obvious that she had Isabella colored linen. My cousin Amapola whom I've never met (she's still in Cuba) is Rodrigo's daughter with some woman who now lives in Alberta, Canada. She has two daughters, Leidys and Leidys, here's their picture. I'm sending the cutest shoes in the world to them and a whole bunch of Nell's clothes. Here's another cousin of mine, La Gorda they call her. Oh there you are, Daisita! Isn't it incredible, Daisita, that my mom has been talking to me about these people for years and that I've never given them any thought? Selene yawned. Rebecca put her hand on Tommy's knee.

Priscilla's leaving.

That's terrible. Do you have to go too, Selene?

No.

And here's a picture of my cousin Malva sitting on the couch she bought with some money my mom and dad sent her six months ago. And here she is with the car my mom and I helped her buy . . . I have this whole itinerary of all the places I want to visit if ever I go to Cuba because ever since we've been reading this novel I've been reading up on the history of Cuba and I also want to visit all the streets that are mentioned in the novel and the Palace of the Captains General and the Tacón Theatre that really exists and the corner of Obispo and Aguacate Streets where the family in the novel lives and the Calles Sol and Luz and El Cerro where Rosario, or Tica, or whatever her name is, moved to, is that the phone ringing it's probably that obnoxious Jenny again. She's going to tell me that the author is skirting the issue and not talking about the horrors of slavery or what it feels like to feel grief and anguish. What do I care if she never returns! Then Jenny or some other fool is going to tell me that I probably don't even know what grief is. Daisita, Trudi, Conchita, Almita, good-bye Priscilla! Tell them, Tommy, as if I didn't know grief . . . But is there any other way to deal with it? So what if I read? What's wrong with that? You tell me, you too, you know what it is, is there any other way to deal with it? Confront it? Just plain talk about it and not open a book and read? Every time it comes really close all I can do is push it to one side and keep on going even if that means reading out loud. And it comes every day and it's always right here next to me, like a twin.

So Priscilla isn't coming back.

Too bad. Then Rebecca asked, Has everyone seen the map of Havana *intramuros*? See how it's shaped, like a broken piece of coconut shell, or like my fantasies, I've looked at this every day now for the past month. Here's La Plaza de Armas. You can't see the end of Armas because I've put my finger on it so many times, that's where my walk begins, I suppose a horse-drawn *volante* will drop us off right here, and we'll walk to the old Tacón Theatre named after one of Lolo's uncles, see Tacón Street? Then we'll take O'Reilly Street and see El Palacio de los Capitanes Generales. I want to walk up and down all these streets, this "O" neighborhood, I've even learned it by heart like a poem, O'Reilly, don't you just love those Irish names? They're from the British occupation, Obispo, Obrapia, then there's Lamparilla, Amargura, and Brasil, and all the way up here there's Empedrado Street, that's the first street that was cobbled. Look here, Bernaza, near El Floridita where we'll go and have a drink. Every day I make myself little and walk up and down these streets.

Daisy pointed to Rebecca and said, She's the Madame Bovary of going to Cuba.

Conchita asked why.

Didn't they tell you in the *Madame Bovary Cliffs Notes* that Emma likes to get the map of Paris out and pretend she's going to different places?

Why are we all sitting indoors now? Is anyone aware of the fact that Silka has been left all alone. And so has Alma, who's standing on the edge, looking at the water. Will she jump?

Conchita said, I don't remember that part. I'll probably have to get my *Madame Bovary Cliffs Notes* back out. Let me take a look at that map.

Suddenly Rebecca exclaimed, Conchita!

Even Daisy, who was putting her little notebook back in her handbag, suddenly said, Conchita!

¡Ave María! said Trudi.

Conchita had actually put on a pair of reading glasses and was inspecting the map of Havana *intramuros.*

Cuarteles, Chacón, Tejadillo.

Empedrado, Progreso.

O'Reilly, Obispo, Obrapia, she read.

Lamparilla, Amargura, Brasil.

Muralla, Sol, Luz, Jesús María.

¡Merced!

"Who endures contradiction without shame? Now this anti-hero exists: he is the reader of the text at the moment he takes his pleasure."

Roland Barthes, The Pleasure of the Text

REBECCA TURNED OFF THE JUICER and picked up the phone that was ringing. Immediately her mother asked, "Did you hear the news?"

"Yesterday Fidel cold-bloodedly shot down three or four small Cessnas that were being piloted by Brothers to the Rescue, a group of completely innocent young boys who weren't even flying over Cuban air space!" her mother said. "Can you believe it? Doesn't Fidel have any limits? Becky, I hope Clinton gets really tough with him. Apparently Mas Canosa is sending a delegation to Washington so there can be a real retaliation. This is the most powerful country in the world and they're not doing anything about it! Becky, are you there?"

Rebecca was sitting in a rocking chair with the phone cradled between her shoulder and her jaw. While her mother talked she examined her skin in a little vanity mirror. "Un-hunh," she replied.

"You've heard of Brothers to the Rescue . . . They're a group of patriotic volunteer pilots who mind their own business and periodically fly over Cuba to throw food and propaganda for those poor people who are starving and have nothing but Communist literature to read. Becky, who knows maybe Clinton's going to start a war against Cuba, maybe Mas Canosa, who is so powerful, will force him. Why doesn't the United States intervene once and for all and take over Cuba? Did everyone really like the *croquetas*?"

Rebecca finished her carrot juice. "I told you, they were absolutely out of this world. There wasn't even one left! But I heard that these Brothers to the Rescue were provoking the Cubans who told them they were getting too near Cuban air space, and that they had already been in Cuban air space, had insulted the Cubans, telling them they were going to overthrow the government and were flying back when they were shot down."

"Precisely! They weren't even on Cuban air space. Was the yucca really that tender?"

"It was perfect. What do you suppose the U.S. would have done if a bunch of Cubans had flown over Washington D.C. and threatened to overthrow the U.S. government?"

"What about the *platanitos*?"

"The fried bananas were marvelous. I told you yesterday and I'm telling you again."

"So what are you saying, Becky? That you're glad those boys lost their lives?"

"That's exactly what I do every Sunday afternoon, mom, I wake up from my nap wishing some innocent boys innocently piloting a Cessna will die!"

"Your father and I want to talk to Nell."

"She's at Daisy's. Hello? Are you there?"

Immediately, the phone rang again.

But it wasn't her mother to say she was sorry for having hung up on her.

Daisy said she couldn't believe this Cessna thing has happened. Just when things were getting so easy and Cuba was getting so open and Fidel was allowing cottage industries to be set up all over the island, and now this Cessna incident all of a sudden! She says she's convinced that someone doesn't want Cuba to open up, and it's either Fidel or that Mas Canosa fellow. "Are you there? Swallowing vitamins?" That megalomaniac Fidel probably got scared that all of a sudden Cuba was becoming capitalistic, and Mas Canosa the Great probably got worried that Cuba would open up without him being king or emperor, so they probably got together and said, "We don't like this." Daisy told Rebecca that she had just said that to her mom who got so furious! She even called her a Communist. So Daisy said, "Mom, the word Communist does not mean anything any more. It's 1996 and can you guess what the biggest threats are for my mom? Exactly . . . Hippies, Martin Luther King, and Communists. She still thinks Jimi Hendrix is alive and that one of these days when George falls in love with his next *americanita* I'm going to pack my bags and run off with Jimi Hendrix. It sounds terrible in English and it's awfully embarrassing, but my mother talks this way, she refers to him as *el negro ese*. As a matter of fact for my mother *all* black musicians are *el negro ese*. The other day when she came to visit and I was listening to Bob Marley she thought it was Jimi Hendrix. And she said, Do you still have a crush on *el negro ese*?" Suddenly Daisy said, "Becky, I'm going to change the subject but . . . you know that the three years are up, if George falls in love with someone else again, I'm not going to do anything about it. This is it. Selene called a few days ago to ask me how I had gone about it, getting his mom involved and his *abuelita* involved, and how they all manage to pull him back by his you know what, and I told her how much I regretted ever having gotten him back. Becky, sometimes I wish I had known other men before I married George. All I ever did was go out on a few chaperoned dates. You know I've never had anybody else. I'm proud of it but maybe that's what gives him all that power over me. He says he respects me too much, and that's why he falls in love with all these bad blonde *americanitas*, he says they're really hot in bed whereas he respects me too much because I'm like the Virgin Mary as well as the mother of his children. He swears he doesn't respect them, but then he wants to marry them! What do I care about being abandoned and respected! Nobody else will have me now, I have four kids and I'm too old! I don't want to go and dress saints in some Godforsaken chapel!"

"Tommy and I have spent this whole week without quarreling."

"That's beside the point, Becky. I know we're into faithful times but while everyone was experiencing free love I was madly in love with George and determined to be a virgin the day I married George. Twenty years later, even after having fucked George last night I'm feeling sick and tired of worrying about George's antics."

Rebecca wishes her problems with Tommy were as easy to describe. She seems to be angry at him all the time. Lately he's always getting on her nerves. "Not only that but when I'm ovulating I get really nervous and uptight and we fight! Maybe deep down inside I don't want to have another child!"

"I really wish you'd stop interrupting me without having anything of any significance to add to my problems. You had other guys before Tommy, it's different for you."

"You just reminded me of the summer of 1979."

"Well let's not dwell in the past I was probably upset because of something else. I'm sorry I ever said anything mean to you or meant you harm, I think we . . . we're all bad at a certain time of our lives and then we spend all these years regretting it and trying to fix it. In any case if this hell of a time I've had with George is some kind of punishment for having been snobbish and bad, I get the picture, I'm sorry, *mea culpa*, I'll be good from now on and I'll never do it again. But you've been bad too, haven't you? Remember how you used to keep Tommy on edge all the time, do you still do that? Remember all the mean things you've said to him? When you wanted to hurt his feelings . . . And remember how you hated me? And you hated Helen, and all the in-laws and you didn't like anyone really. You scared my children for years, they thought you were a real witch. I'd tell them, She's just confused and possessive and I had a little bit of something to do with it, I loved to make you feel bad. Sometimes I'd sit in front of you and imagine you dead or sick, three times I stole your wallet, I was the one who destroyed your passport three days before you left for Europe with Tommy, remember the panic? I hid your diamond, and you felt I had something to do with it, but you could never prove anything."

"My diamond ring? When I lost my diamond ring ten years ago?" Rebecca was so astonished she could barely speak.

Daisy said, "Yep!"

"Where is it?"

"Don't turn this into a big deal, Tommy got you another one right away. It's safe. I've got it. Do you want it back? You're kind of like María Fernanda in that novel who can read people's minds, and if they're hating you or just not caring about you, you feel terrible for no reason at all, just some vibe, that's why you're such a crazy girl. God, *mujer*, you can really hold a grudge!"

"Imagine that!"

"Don't be sarcastic. Remember when Ernesto told *her* that she'd stop seeing clear the minute she had a man, it never did happen to you, did it? You can see the future and you can read people's minds and, Becky, I'd like to know, what would you be tormented about if you couldn't see into people? And why do you want to get pregnant? You want another chance? Does it torment you each time you get your period? Does it feel terrible? Are you jealous of me because I have four gorgeous children and you have one fat daughter? But what would you be suffering about if it weren't for this? Something shallower or something deeper? It's not that I care, I just want to know out of curiosity. All of a sudden I feel like hurting your feelings. You must have annoyed me. It just went away. You know what, Becky? I remember when you decided that you were nobody's friend. You said you didn't like anyone. You said worse than that. You didn't want any acquaintances or fucking in-laws around, you just wanted Tommy and Nell and your book, everything else was a painful let-down."

"This here is my effort."

"What do you mean by this here?"

"What I'm doing here. The reading club. This is my effort to be in the world."

"It was my idea, and so far so good."

Rebecca protested, "It was not your idea."

"But I'm the one who's doing all the work."

"With my effort."

"And what effort is that? Reading out loud? You're certainly not leading the debate because every time the group meets you're off talking to your mom."

There was a moment of silence.

"You're beginning to get on my nerves, Daisy, and I want my diamond ring back!"

"Don't worry about it! Do you think George can't afford to get me one?"

"So what did you do with my diamond ring? Witchcraft?"

"So what do you think about this Cessna scandal? What do you think the U.S. is going to do about it? How can the U.S. threaten Cuba now? Tighten the embargo? The people have no medicine, nothing to wear and nothing to eat, so *por favor!* From what you told me they don't even have any toothpaste. Oh by the way yesterday I ran into Jenny Rincón at The Tu Tu Tango Cafe in Coconut Grove. You know how George loves to go there and we bumped into Jenny who was having an early drink. I didn't know she drank. Anyway she was really aloof and said she was glad that she wasn't part of our reading club any more and was considering starting one of her own. She said she finished reading the whole novel already so the thought of going back to your house and talking about chapters she'd already read and enjoyed bored her. Anyway she feels she can't really relate to anyone in that book. Isn't she weird?"

"I can't believe you were the one who took my diamond ring!"

"I even had it appraised. I wanted to sell it for the Hell of it. Then I kept it. Oh Becky, I forgot to tell you, I was reading some more Cuban history to prepare us for our next meeting and I read that when the U.S. government passed the Wilson Tariff on sugar imports, Cuban sugar exports to the U.S. fell from 800,000 tons in 1895 to 225,231 in 1896."

"Don't forget to bring me my diamond ring back."

"Hold it, your daughter wants to talk to you."

. . . .

Mom . . .

Yes sweetheart?

What's for dinner tonight?

Grouper and broccoli.

Can we order from KFC?

No.

And what's for dessert?

Either pears or apples. Will you please tell Daisy to remember my diamond ring?

The phone rang immediately after Rebecca finished talking with Daisy.

This time it was Conchita, who didn't even say hello, right away she blurted out that she was really depressed. Could she come over? She had indeed purchased reading glasses, but would Becky read Chapter Nine for her out loud? She had to tape it for Silka and Trudi anyway . . . Rebecca glanced at her watch. Conchita could come over in . . . a few hours.

Tommy was upstairs in the bedroom. The windows were open, letting in a soft breeze. Palm fronds were gently scratching the window panes. It smelled like Miami Beach. You can see the water from here, and a boat going by, fast. Inside this room, it is calm. Tommy lying there naked reading the Sunday paper on the unmade bed. Most of the sheets were on the floor, at the foot of the bed. You can also see swimming pools from here, and green lawns. He had gotten up very early this morning and gone out on the boat by himself. After he came back he went to the market and came back with all sorts of goodies for brunch. They ate outside. You can also see bougainvillea trying to cover walls. From this window. Lying on the bed he had one leg stretched out and the other bent, one foot touching his knee. Everything about his body is tight. They had tried to make love last night, but they had quarreled, and they had had too much to drink, he lost his hard-on at the last minute. What are the words for this? How do you talk through this? Talk me through it. In English there are Saxon words like *balls, dick, cunt, fuck.* In Spanish there are words that are either embarrassing or funny and that you were not supposed to say, *las bolas, la pinga, los cojones,* and what about the verbs? and she never did learn her advanced Latin words, all those declensions! What would Mafer say, that bad girl who has no trouble with the good words? He has balls that are big and heavy. His penis resting on his thigh is beginning to react to her taking her clothes off. He's pretending to read. Breasts and this abdomen that can be so good looking and pubic hair that she once shaved off because she discovered a magazine of his where they had shaved it off, and her legs that are supposed to be world-class. This body that she had worked on so hard. She likes it when she puts her hand on his penis and it reacts right away, stiffening. What about a kiss? He does not have skinny thighs. And she does not necessarily need foreplay. She kissed his knee, his thigh, his balls, his abdomen. The palm frond gently scratching the window panes. She's got him. Just wants to talk through it. Lying on top, and now he's getting on top, spreading her out with his knees, and he's inside her, his body is the place of pleasure, she is one with the man, and she wants to talk through it, so she can take it to the limit, if it can be done. Do this to me with the Anglo-Saxon words and the Spanish ones too, with all the nouns and their declensions, the verbs and their conjugations, every tense, the prepositions, the adjectives, the adverbs! So the verb may reconcile her to the earth and to her mind and allow her to be, at least for a few safe splendid moments, at peace. María Fernanda and Ernesto making love on a cot, his penis covered with lipstick, thrusting into her hard and could she feel his . . . balls? testicles? whatever word she used, against her spread legs, and he was inside thrusting and pushing her knees down toward the mattress the disorganized sheets and he entered her harder in and out until she screamed it was happening outside she was coming like a man and still wanting to talk through it all, and the words he uttered were Oh, God! I'm coming, he came, both tenses, and it was her turn, and D.H. Lawrence hated the women who kept on coming and coming after the man came. He said they weren't feminine. But D. H. wasn't the one on top of her. She felt almost too strong, she pulled his hair and when she said she felt she could hurt him in so many verbs, he laughed with more pleasure.

"I do not see the danger of our extermination by the USA . . .
If that happens, history will judge them . . ."

Máximo Gómez

TEOFILO TIRRY, WHOM EVERYONE CALLED TEO TIRRY, was born in 1888.
Mafer's waist was history but she turned to God and said she wanted
another baby right away. Knowing God, she had to wait a whole year. Then,
when she gave birth the following year the little girl succumbed after three
months to what was called the seven-day evil. They named her Juana. Mafer
refused to let the infant be buried in the Espada Cemetery and insisted that she
be put in the childrens' crypt in Espíritu Santo Church. Everyone in her family except Joaquín, her father (who had apparently been buried in a Queens,
New York, cemetery) had been buried in this church which hadn't interred
anyone for the past ten years. When Catalina, Mafer's mother, had been
interred there it had cost thirty *pesos* to be buried underneath row two plus
fifty *pesos* for a name plaque. Ten years later Mafer had to bribe so many cler-
gymen to have little Juana interred there that the whole funeral, name plaque
and all, cost over one thousand *pesos*.

Hı Mom! When's dinner?

Honey, can't you see I'm taping this chapter and reading to Conchita?
I just wanted to know at what time we were having dinner.
I don't know! Leave us alone!
When are you going to do my science project?
After I'm through with this chapter.
Yes! Oh, and here's your diamond ring.
My diamond ring. Give it to me. Oh my God I can't believe it!

> "One cannot express his admiration of a breast pin, an article of dress, or anything else, without receiving an answer that it is at your command; with such sincerity of expression that the stranger is half tempted to accept . . ."
>
> John George F. Wurdemann, *Notes on Cuba*

FOR THE NEXT FEW YEARS THE FAMILY had big loud arguments just about every day. They screamed, they shouted, they fought, they wept, they stomped their feet, and it seemed as if there would be no end to it. They quarreled over politics, or because Lolo had had too much to drink, or because Tica was in a foul mood, or because Mafer was dealing with her hormones, or just because someone felt left out, neglected, or misunderstood. Without exaggerating, they really quarreled every single day, and nothing was sacred once they got angry. They'd bicker and complain at breakfast time, they'd yell at each other in church, and they'd even fight during the *paseo* time, between five and seven in the evening, when they'd all hop into their old *volante* and ride to the Paseo del Prado.

The *paseo,* or promenade, or ride, was a daily habit of most Habaneros. It was part of their day, and just as natural as *tertulias,* or the three meals. But this family had neglected the daily Paseo for so many years that it was no longer a second nature for them. Instead, it was a big deal, and difficult to plan, and an ordeal to finally get out of the house. Someone was always holding everyone else up, and by the time they were all in the *volante* and riding away they all seemed to hate each other. Since Teo Tirry's birth they all agreed that they had to be like everyone else and swore that they'd succeed in this effort.

Mafer hadn't changed much with Teo's birth, and she'd handled little Juana's death as well as could be expected, the only difference being that she could no longer read minds and could no longer see the future, but Teo's birth and the death of Juanita had greatly changed Lolo and Tica who both turned fifty-one in 1890, the year little Teo Tirry turned two.

In the course of the past two years the two great aunts had progessively become sentimental doddering old ladies, and it seemed to be intensifying by the hour. Tica did remain the businesswoman she had always been, but she seemed to have no difficulty leaving this persona in the dress factory, for the minute she got home all she could say was *goo goo* and *ga ga*. As to Lolo, Lolo no longer knew if Lolo wanted little Teo to know Lolo as a man or as a woman and spent the next four years going from men's clothes to women's clothes. The problem was, What would society think? Would everyone start saying that Tica had married a woman and that the marriage should therefore be annulled? That was out of the question. Of course they could say that the marriage had turned sour because Lolo (born a male) had suddenly decided to begin cross-dressing. No, that was too much. Finally the idea Lolo came up with was to send the male Lolo to Paris forever and to have Lolo's long lost twin sister (*also* called Lolo) come to live in Havana after having spent all her life in France. That was Lolo's only way out if Lolo decided to become a woman after all. She would pretend she was Lolo's long-lost spinster twin sister separated at birth who had come to settle in Havana after all these years and dedicate her life to raising little Teo Tirry. What do you think, Tica? Lolo asked. Tica thought it was a great idea. That meant they were family and they could live together without anyone thinking that they were lesbians (but the word they used was *invertidas*). For little Teo's sake the two women were scared to death of being called *invertidas*.

All Tica had to do was go and complain about her husband of so many many years suddenly leaving for Paris and loving it so much that in his last letter he said he was never coming back, he'd fallen in love with the Boulevard Saint Germain, and by the way, he added that Paris is all a Cuban could ever want.

She could tell everyone it happened suddenly, one day, Lolo woke up, and was determined to spend the rest of his life in Paris. He woke up and said, *Me voy pa' Francia, pa' siempre*. And that was it. He got on one of those big boats and promised that he'd write from the Café de la Paix, which he did, and he said, I'm never coming back, from now on I'm a Cuban in Paris.

So Lolo had plenty of choices, but Lolo had to decide quickly for little Teo's sake. Finally in 1894 when little Teo Tirry turned six, Lolo decided that from now on she'd be a great aunt, Great Aunt Lolo, separated at birth from her brother Lolo who was now a Cuban in Paris. So what if they were both named Lolo? Lorenzo and Lorenza. That day Lolo donned a purple dress with flowers and white gloves and a little white handkerchief and a purple hat with a net and dressed like that until the day she died.

There had been so much speculation about Lolo being a woman dressed as a man for so long that when Lolo started to pretend Lolo was a woman everyone started to wonder if in fact Lolo was a man dressed as a woman or a woman dressed as a man. What was Lolo? And did anyone really care? There were so many other things to talk about. People in Lolo's social circle realized that they had wasted so much time wondering about this that they ended up getting tired of the whole nonsense. Besides, they only liked to gossip about people of a certain age, and that was preferably a young age, Lolo was fifty-five when she finally decided to be what she was, a female.

But this wasn't the real issue. What mattered more than anything was becoming a normal family so that Teo Tirry could grow up in totally normal surroundings and have a promising future and become the best at everything. If this meant having to do all kinds of boring things, so be it! They'd go to church if they had to, and they'd go for the daily ride on the *volante*, they'd have *tertulias,* they'd say their prayers before dinner and spend their evenings reading either poetry or Pascal's *Pensees* out loud, or reviewing Aristotle's logic, classifying syllogisms, Barbara, Cellarent, Darii, Ferio? Rethinking the Pythagorean theorem and Leibniz's monads.

Teo was sent to the best private boys' school in Havana. The abbot assured them that by the time this fine young man graduated he would know everything there was to know about Philosophy, Literature, History, Logic, Science, Geography, Greek, Latin, and Mathematics. The boy would not only have become a flesh-and-blood encyclopaedia, but he'd also be totally prepared for the world that was waiting for him out there.

When Lolo heard that she got all emotional. The thought of a world waiting for her darling Teo out there was too much to bear.

Cuban History was one of the most demanding disciplines. The children were expected to learn every single little detail from the moment Columbus landed in the New World to the mid-nineties.

With everything that was going on, current events became extremely difficult to study. All sorts of things were happening in Cuba in the nineties, and this made history something almost impossible to study by rote. The truth today was the lie of tomorrow as everyone, even the scissorsgrinder, loved to say.

José Martí, the poet, the revolutionary, the exile, was already quite well known by the Cuban people. He'd been living in exile in New York and Tampa for quite a few years and felt that the time was now. His mind approached the island of Cuba as would a rebel army. They would avoid the mistakes they had made during La Guerra Grande. This new war they were preparing would be quick and there would be several attacks all over the country happening simultaneously.

This is the atmosphere Teo Tirry grew up in. It was difficult for him to concentrate on anything but the daily news that everyone kept reading out loud. Teo Tirry was a fervent partisan of independence ever since he was seven years old. He spent hours reading about the present with his father, the studious and thorough Ernesto.

Ernesto said he'd go and join the rebel armies if need be. Teo Tirry said he would too, but he'd always say that in a whisper because each time his great aunts overheard him saying something like that they'd yell and run to him and hug him and not let him go for hours. And when they'd finally let him go his hair would be wet and oily with their concerned tears. Some of these tears would even fall in his eyes. From the time he was three years old Teo realized he was loved in an exaggerated way and that only death would change this, so he started being really careful about what he said.

He absolutely hated it when his aunts' tears fell in his eyes. And it was at age three that he expressed his feelings openly for the last time. Lolo got so upset that she blew her nose in his shirt. Teo Tirry had simply yelled, ¡Morir por la patria es vivir! (To die for the country is to live!). Everyone in the house agreed that Teo Tirry couldn't die, ever. They all wanted to hug him and hold him and were pulling his arms and legs and getting tears and nose drippings all over him.

Martí's death came as shocking news for the whole household. Tica didn't really care because she was pro-Spain and still asking the Spanish crown for a title. She explained to everyone that a citizen with a title was totally exonerated from debt, and with the way she liked to play with business and money it would be a good idea to be sure that if some venture ever went wrong they wouldn't lose anything at all.

Of course everyone in the household started criticizing her for being so obsessed by money, especially Lolo, who even called her a boring person. As usual Tica defended herself, if she weren't there making money all the time Lolo wouldn't be able to dedicate her life to so-called art, especially not with a father like Manuel Tacón who turned every fortune he ever touched into black pennies (kilos prietos).

Yes indeed Tica admitted she'd been stupid enough to put him in charge of the cane fields, and what had happened? You name everything bad that could possibly go wrong and that's exactly what happened. They ended up losing the cane fields. So if anybody else had something to say about Tica being tight and shallow and disdainful of the profound things in life, and behaving like someone from Cataluña, they should just speak up right away.

Ernesto said that he knew that without Tica's money he couldn't spend his days reading and writing pamphlets, and that Mafer couldn't spend her days taking Ernesto's dictation and eating and trying to blackmail God into letting her get pregnant again, and Teo Tirry wouldn't be assured such a great future.

"And if it weren't for me you wouldn't have Teo Tirry to love!" Mafer yelled.

Ahh, little Teo Tirry, he was the holiest thing in the house. The two older women seemed to drink the elixir of life and love at the Teo Tirry altar. If a little boy could have had an altar erected in his name it was Teo Tirry. Everything of his was preserved as a relic by Tica and Lolo, who even fought over the little clothes he had outgrown. Never was there a child so adored.

Which brings us back to the problem of being normal. These were not normal times. While Generals Gómez and Maceo were invading Havana and Pinar del Río, Spain was sending a tougher general with very large reinforcements to Cuba. And although General Valeriano Weyler was rounding up peasants and exterminating them, the rebels kept on fighting.

Every enlightened mind agreed that the Cuban people are, and of right ought to be, free and independent. But this freedom and this independence that was as much an inalienable right as fresh air and water, seemed like something they had to tear out of fate's hands, because fate seemed stingy with it. The fighting went on and on but in December of 1896 General Maceo, the hope of the revolutionary government, was killed during a small battle in the province of Havana. Teo Tirry was eight years old and he himself read this terrible news to his father, who had him read the newspaper to him every morning after breakfast.

General Anacleto Menosmal was another problem. He was the most powerful general left after the death of Martí and Maceo but the problem with Menosmal in the year 1896 was that he was a power fanatic. Everyone had the feeling that all Menosmal wanted was his own personal power, he would do anything for power, and what good would it do to spend years struggling to free Cuba from Spain if it was to see this tyrant, this egomaniac, this self-worshipper, immediately take over.

Coincidence had it that Menosmal's only son had died at Menosmal's side and Menosmal used this to add all the more aura to his reputation. He had a street named after his son, and then another street named after himself, then a street named after his mother's side of the family, he wanted to change the name of the Paseo del Prado to Paseo Menosmal, as a matter of fact he wanted *several* parks named after him, and the cemetery where his son was buried he wanted renamed Camposanto Menosmal. General Menosmal was so unbearably full of himself that many Cubans fled to Tampa at the time just so they wouldn't have to hear the name Menosmal.

Menosmal even wanted to have the Tacón Theatre renamed Theatro del Generalísimo Anacleto Menosmal.

Lolo asked, Why does an intelligent president like Grover Cleveland believe everything that crazy Caligula *maricón* of Generalísimo Anacleto Menosmal says?

In order to be a normal family, the ladies organized *tertulias* every afternoon. They'd get together and arrange rocking chairs on each side of the formal dining room and rock and rock and talk about the war.

The family had even taken to going to church every Sunday just for Teo Tirry's sake. But even in church the talk was of politics. Sometimes it got so out of hand that there'd either be applauding or whistling.

But most of the talks would take place during the *tertulias* with little Teo Tirry listening. Independence began to appear somewhat utopian when President Cleveland began to favor Spain because Spain could better protect American interests in Cuba.

Tica kept saying, All those Americans care about is their interests here, the rest they don't care, we could all die, they don't care! God, I'd do anything for a title!

Lolo interrupted, Look at that butcher *maricón* Weyler that Spain sent, does Cleveland care? Of course he doesn't. But you'll see one of these days a U.S. expansionist *cabrón* will be president or will have some kind of power and he'll convince everyone that Cuba is strategic and that Spain can't protect their interests here and that day we'll be invaded by the U.S. They're going to invade us! I know they are! They're going to invade us! We'll never be free, ever! I agree with Calixto García when he says that we are not fighting to become a Yankee factory and that Americans have no reason to interfere in our affairs. As a matter of fact if any of our governments, whether it be rebel or not, gives up the freedom we've always struggled for, for any reason whatsoever, that will mean that all our martyrs have died in vain!

Stop shouting, Lolo!

We'll never be free! Lolo carried on. And after the U.S. invades us who knows what other country will decide that they want to come here and plunder and pillage and sit on us with their big fat imperialistic colonist ass. Some Generalísimo Menosmal from Russia, maybe! Before you know it they'll be teaching our children Russian in school. And why is it that every politician or every rebel or any illiterate *chusma guajira* who has the slightest victory starts thinking he's Caesar or Alexander or Jesus Christ all of a sudden? Are we to be cursed with Generalísimos Anacletos Menosmales for the rest of our *malditas* historical lives!

Stop shouting, Lolo! We can't even hear the rocking chairs with your shouting.

Then Tica would say things like, It would have been good to get a title from Spain though. Think of it, not having to pay any debts, ever! Oh well, it wasn't meant to be!

Teo Tirry listened to these conversations so much that by the time McKinley became president of the United States the nine-year-old would say things like, McKinley will never recognize Cuban belligerency. And Teo was right.

These were troubled times but for this family they were also very special times. They finally realized who they were, as Cubans, as individuals, as women, as men, as a family.

Mafer was a good mature woman who knew what she wanted. She finally blackmailed God so badly that her prayers were answered. In 1897 at age thirty-seven she was pregnant for the third time and she was so happy that it made her complexion glow.

Three days after the battleship *Maine* exploded in Havana harbor, Mafer gave birth to a little girl whom she named, indeed, Maine. So a blonde and hungry and screaming Maine Tirry came into their lives on February 18, 1898.

Lolo was hysterical. She kept crying and screaming and sobbing and blowing her nose and shouting thank you's to God. A little girl! ¡*Una hembrita!* I can't believe we have *una hembrita!*

Everyone agreed that Mafer had been right to put her foot down with God. If you insist you'll always get what you want, but why does he always take so long?

One gorgeous starlit evening when little Maine was only a few days old the family turned to Tica and told her she had been right in dedicating all these years to making money. Everybody thought that her business sense had made her awfully shallow and vain, but it sure came in handy in 1898 when the island was devastated after three years of war and hunger was rampant and the economy was about to collapse. The tobacco industry had practically ceased to exist, the sugar production had dropped two-thirds, and almost all the island's cattle were dead.

One would have thought that in difficult times such as these the Santa Cruz clothes business would also have collapsed, but once again Tica had given the times much thought and went along with them. War or no war people still had to dress and Tica's latest fashions were exactly what a country in war needed. They catered to everyone! Rebels or conservatives, blacks, mulattos, expresso, *café con leche*, Cubans, Spaniards, cream of the cream, *guajiro*, *chusma*, everyone's money was good! Many Habaneros and Habaneras had never stopped going to the theater or to fancy balls at the Palacio, and they kept on buying the expensive clothes that Moda Titania, the most Parisian in the World, was selling all over the island. So there was no problem there, and Moda Titania was still making profit. But why limit yourself to the eternal rich when you have all these other people out there who are really affected by the war and still have to dress? Once money is in the bank it is of the highest social class no matter who handled it.

Tica said she wasn't prejudiced and would never be so, even if she managed one day to get that goddamn title. She provided the underprivileged with cheap, easy-to-wear, cool, comfortable Jamaican cottons with such pretty colors that people could forget the war for a few minutes while they looked at their clothes.

So the family became more normal than ever. They survived the economic hardships and survived them very well until American capital began to control almost the whole country. Even when this occurred the family was happy and normal and full of love, and with a new addition to the family that they adored, this is how they lived right in the middle of the little war, rocking chairs and *tertulias,* talking about the peace treaty ending Spanish domination. No Cubans had been allowed at the Spanish surrender in Havana. Cuban rebels were considered by the American government to be an illiterate bunch of lazy black-bean-fed *guajiros* with tobacco, rum, and expresso breath. And no mention was made of the rebels' assistance at the Battle of San Juan Hill (this is where Tica always reminded Ernesto that the six thousand Yankees could have very well done without the help of four hundred Cuban rebels to defeat seven hundred Spaniards, and Ernesto agreed).

But why was it that the American flag and not the Cuban flag was raised at the ceremony of Spanish surrender? The only Cuban invited for the lunch afterwards was that traitor Generalísimo Anacleto Menosmal. Lolo swore that she'd leave for south Florida in a heartbeat if that sadistic grunting Menosmal pig became president of the Republic.

Even the gentle Ernesto would lose his cool. And why were no Cubans accepted in Santiago naval base except for washing, cooking, cleaning out-houses and landscaping? For the first time in his life Ernesto raised his voice: Can anybody call this independence?

It is with all these never-ending, passion-inciting discussions that the family stepped into the next century. During the first minute of 1900 everyone compared ages. Tica was sixty going on sixty-one, so was Lolo, Mafer was thirty-nine, Ernesto was fifty-three, Teo Tirry would turn twelve that year, and Maine Tirry would turn two, *si Dios quiere*, God willing.

"**L**ONG LIVE WOMAN!" Umbertico Barrios yelled (it was in the book). "Long live passion! Long live freedom!"

"What did he say?" one of the seamstresses asked.

Umbertico Barrios was getting old, so he couldn't yell all that loud.

Then he had a bad coughing fit right after he yelled, "*¡Qué vivan las gordas, y las flacas!*"

Ice water! Ice water! Quick! For the Reader. He's falling! What's happening? Is he dying?

He's paralyzed.

"A Cuban woman is timid and guarded in the presence of every man."

James Williams Steele, *Cuban Sketches*

A LMOST A MONTH PASSED without Rebecca spending any significant amount of time with her father. She did go to her parents' house every other day, but her visits were brief, she'd simply make sure that everything was all right, then leave. So when she finally sat next to him for one of those long talks, he chose to ignore her, even the cat ignored her and didn't even jump and run. He just kept on reading out loud, but as if she weren't an audience at all.

So Rebecca sat there and rocked.

Selene showed up sometime in the middle of last week to pick up the cassette tape of chapters five and six of the novel because, Selene confessed, her life had been so hectic lately that she hadn't really been keeping up with the reading, but she said she would like to continue reading with the club and asked Rebecca for the tapes that Trudi and Silka had already heard. So she dropped in on Wednesday evening wearing this short tight dress, as a matter of fact she arrived at the same time Tommy did, and they walked in together talking, and, this is where it gets annoying, they continued talking to each other for the next two hours.

"Selene has to go," Rebecca told her father as she groped for her handbag that was right at her feet.

Each time Rebecca tried to get in the conversation either Tommy or Selene would answer politely and go right back to whatever it was they were talking about.

"You're all dressed up, Selene, aren't you supposed to be going somewhere?"

"All dressed up? Me?" Selene said innocently as she crossed her legs the other way.

Rocking next to her dad, Rebecca stuck her own leg out. Me? she said to herself, and crossed her legs.

So Rebecca went upstairs to help Nell with her homework and when she came back, there they were, still talking. First she stared at them, arms akimbo, and was just about to say something, but ended up simply crossing her arms in front of her. As she walked into the kitchen she shot sideway glances at them. After she poured herself what was left of a bottle of red wine she went to put Nell to bed and when she came back downstairs they were still talking!

In the kitchen she opened a bottle of good wine and gulped down a whole glass. Before she walked back out into the living room with another glassful of wine she squinted and smiled. She said she was going to bed and proceeded to walk up the stairs. That's when Tommy gave her a perplexed stare. To bed? "Oh well, so am I," he said. And that's how they finally got rid of Selene.

Upstairs in the bedroom, Tommy asked, "What's wrong?"

She could barely utter the word, "Nothing!"

"Rebecca, I know something's wrong. Talk to me!"

She just couldn't keep quiet. "So did you fall in love with Selene, is her conversation that interesting? What in the world were you talking about for hours?"

"Rebecca, what did I do now? Why are you drinking like that? What are you accusing me of? Rebecca, you're starting to act like the women in that book! You're jealous, why are you so jealous? Rebecca . . ."

"Leave me alone, I hate you and I hate Selene, and I never want her here again!" Rebecca screamed as she tore all the sheets off the bed.

"Rebecca, you just tore off all the sheets! You really are starting to behave just like the creatures in that book."

"Mommy!" Nell said out in the hallway. "What's wrong?"

"Oh *fuck!*"

"Rebecca, you're beginning to swear like that character, what's her name, used to swear."

The next day, which was Thursday, Rebecca couldn't quite decide whether she hated Tommy or whether her behavior embarrassed her.

"Selene has to be the next to go," she told her father again.

"You hardly come to see me anymore," he said.

"What should I do with Selene?"

"Weren't you going to give her one of your guns?"

"I gave one to Alma, but Selene didn't want one."

"You're going to have to shoot her yourself then."

Rebecca said that she was not going to have anyone monopolizing Tommy. She didn't want Selene near him again. She couldn't care less what they were talking about. She didn't know what to do last night! She felt like a stranger in her own house. They just wouldn't stop talking!

Rebecca kept taking her feet out of her shoes and putting them back in. "God, Papi, I got so jealous last night. I hate it when I go crazy like that. So you think I should tell Selene not to come back?" she asked her father as she pulled a little mirror out of her handbag.

"Do you think my hair's falling out? And am I getting crows' feet? It's always a mistake to look at yourself in a mirror when you're sitting outside. Do you think I'm too old to have a baby?"

It's that woman in the novel, she's the one who started it. And my fault too, because I wanted to melt into the words and wallow in them. By the way have you noticed that right now it's taking place in 1896 exactly a hundred years ago, do you think it has anything to do with the end of the century? Is it mine? Am I in it? Who's the main character? Bleeding, all the color out of my life. "What should I tell Selene?"

Her father didn't answer, he had quit reading, he looked dead, but he was asleep.

She stood up, went inside momentarily to say good-bye to her mom, and went home.

⚬⚬⚬

The phone was ringing when she walked in the door. Her heart felt tight, coldness dripped into her stomach, perhaps it was her mother telling her that her father had died. She picked it up.

For a moment she felt relief. Long live the Reader! He's only asleep. It was Selene.

She wanted Tommy's cellular phone number because he'd asked her for some information and she had it for him. It was business-related, of course, and Selene just couldn't find Tommy's cellular phone number.

"Oh, what is that number?" Rebecca said several times. "Oh, I'm so bad with numbers!"

Selene said, "Never mind, I'll try to reach him again at his office."

Rebecca said that Tommy wasn't in the office anyway, if Selene wanted she would have him call her back tonight. "By the way," Rebecca added, "the reading club has been called off." They wouldn't be meeting any more, it wasn't such a good idea anyway.

Selene couldn't believe it. "You mean we're not meeting tomorrow?"

"I mean we're not meeting *again*. Too many people are dropping out. First Lucía, then Helen, then Jenny. Now Priscilla won't be coming back either and Silka's saying that it's a big strain on her. Trudi's just too busy on Fridays, my cousin Alma's having psychological problems . . . So . . . you know . . . it's over . . . it was fun while it lasted, though. Maybe we'll get another reading club going some other time, I'll certainly call you." Rebecca was inspecting her lips while she talked.

"Oh, I'll be in touch with Tommy anyway."

"Selene, are you there? What about that gun you wanted to get? Still interested?"

"No. While reading that novel and being part of the reading club I realized that nice men existed, so why go to jail because of someone like Jim? Look at that man Ernesto in the novel, how he loves Mafer, and look at Lolo and Tica, and look at Helen and Harvey, Priscilla and Bill, you and Tommy, that's the way I want it for me. So I'm not about to commit murder and go to jail for a man who isn't even nice. Remember that man Joaquín in the beginning? He was no good. Look at him compared to Ernesto! Now I've decided that I'm going to find myself a good man, like Ernesto, like Tommy, like Harvey."

"I see. Well, good luck."

Rebecca continued feeling jealous for the next few days. She was still a bit upset on Friday so she decided to cancel the reunion and have it the following Friday.

WHEN THEY MET AGAIN there were three empty rocking chairs. Silka had called to say she just couldn't make it any more because she was too weak, and Jenny was no longer welcome.

Rebecca was quiet. Without being aware of it, she was acting like a guest in her own house. Gently she rocked and looked at the bay, not the least bit jittery. For once she wasn't looking around, overstrung, wondering if anyone was being left out, or bored. Now she was playing the role that had made her so edgy before, quiet, aloof, maybe bored, in any case not making any efforts to mingle.

For once Alma was in great spirits. She said the novel they were reading was hers, definitely hers, she could've been the main character! and that she could identify with just about every character, even the minor ones.

Daisy asked, "If we were those characters, who would we be?"

Suddenly everyone wanted to be Mafer, and, to make matters worse, they agreed that Rebecca was definitely not Mafer. Who was Rebecca? Umbertico Barrios. They even have the same last name! Are there too many coincidences? Priscilla, who won't be coming back, is a descendant of Ernesto's family, Rebecca comes from a long line of readers, "and I'm a reincarnation of Mafer!" Alma interrupted. Rebecca took a gulp of her wine, glanced at her with what seemed like indifference, squinted. Alma had promised to bring hot dogs and hamburgers and bread this time so they could have a barbecue.

When Tommy stepped outside Rebecca said indifferently, "Oh, Tommy, will you help Alma light the barbecue?"

She rocked and looked the other way. We can grill Alma right here. Alma has to go! She wants to be the main character! Rebecca squinted and smiled. Very early on we seem to develop these infernal patterns. She remembered when she was ten, and absolutely wanted the leading part in a school play. But Alma got to be Snow White, Trudi was the wicked stepmother, Daisy was the prince (there were no boys), and what was she? The narrator, the one who stood outside and explained what was happening. She rocked. I want my part.

"I don't want men in the reading club," Daisy said, looking at Tommy.

Conchita asked, "Why?"

"George will join and before I know it he'll have fallen in love with one of you. Rebecca, make yourself at home," Daisy said sarcastically. "Why are you so quiet?"

Before she went into the kitchen to season the hamburger meat Alma was standing there amusing everyone with the way she complained about the Publix Market, it seemed to be the slowest nastiest supermarket in the world. Why are the inhabitants of Miami Beach so ornery? She also said she was standing in line for such a long time that she bonded with the people standing in front and in back of her. She had gotten tons of meat.

Rebecca followed her into the litchen and asked her how much she owed her. Alma insisted that she forget about it, it was her treat. No really. No really. "We have salmon too," Rebecca said.

"So we'll all be in our mid-forties in the year 2000," Alma said. Some of our characters turned fifty in 1900.

Alma seemed all excited. She checked to see that no one was listening. It was all settled. On Thursday she'd drop the kids off at her mom's and she was going to have her stomach and her breasts done.

"You too?" Rebecca blurted out. "Has coming to Miami Beach every Friday contaminated you?"

Alma took no notice of what she was saying and explained that she'd been going to the gym ever since she last gave birth but there was no way of getting her stomach to go in. The muscles seemed to have torn and she wasn't ready to be old yet and a fat stomach was a sign of old age. It wasn't even for sex or to please her husband, it was for her own satisfaction. She said that every time she took her clothes off and saw her breasts she felt like crying.

"Have you been talking to Conchita?"

The problem of course was the money. Regular insurance doesn't cover plastic surgery so she'd had to borrow six thousand dollars to get this done. Conchita, who had just walked in, thought it was a bargain. "Why, the plastic surgeon that everyone went to around here practically charges six grand for a visit!" Alma went to mind the barbecue and left Rebecca and Conchita by themselves.

"Yesterday I dreamed that a scoop of strawberry ice cream fell on my map of Havana *intramuros* and stained it," said Rebecca. "It wasn't as if I'd been in bed sleeping in the dark and dreaming, it's a vision I had while I was awake. It was strawberry ice cream from the Havana ice cream parlor called Coppelia."

"And then what?"

"That's all. My map was stained right at Obispo, O'Reilly, Obrapia. I know them all by heart now. All those streets. And I have this whole itinerary planned. Tonight I'm going to get lost in a very old colonial city called Trinidad."

At that very moment Trudi barged into the kitchen.

She blurted it out right away, "Two nights ago he proposed and I accepted him! I'm getting married! I'm getting married! I can't believe I'm getting married and I am so happy! I'll be forty-four by then but it doesn't matter I'm glad I waited all this time and found the greatest man in the world. Isn't he spectacular? I have the impression that every single woman who sees him suddenly starts seeing all other men in the world as dull or black and white like Judy Garland saw Kansas." This was all so sudden that Rebecca and Conchita didn't know what to say.

And Trudi just kept on talking. She said she wanted bridesmaids and a cake and a great big fluffy dress, a real wedding! She wanted to be happy and she kept repeating that it was her day and that she could have any kind of wedding she wanted, she said that at times she'd like to have several of them. The wedding would take place in Atlanta because he had lots of family there and it's not that Trudi's friends weren't important but she didn't have any family. Her mother was in an insane asylum, her father had disappeared. Suddenly Rebecca's mind stopped wandering through the streets of Havana *intramuros* out of the words, the map, and returned to what she considered to ber faded Miami, her dull, numb life.

"But let's not just stand in the kitchen!"

They stepped outside.

To the summer of 1973. They had just graduated from high school and Trudi's kid brother was in the ninth grade. Trudi lived on Old Cutler Road. She never moved away from that house. Once the tragedy occurred and her family was destroyed everyone thought they'd sell the house and move away, but Trudi stayed. On the day it happened they went to Key Biscayne, Daisy, Becky, Trudi, and Conchita, and smoked dope in the car, going fast. They remember the last time they saw Trudi's brother, Alejandro. Trudi had shouted to him, Mom wants you to clean your room! She'll be back any minute, stay out of trouble. When they came back at the end of the day Trudi's mom asked them where Alex was, no one knew.

They'd left Trudi's house at ten AM and he was fixing himself a sandwich. It wasn't until nine PM that they called the police.

The police thought that perhaps he'd run away. The next week was sheer torture. The Agramonte family was sitting next to the phone waiting for news, any news. Nothing came. One month later there was still no sign of the boy and the family commenced a long painful journey into Hell.

Trudi's parents blamed each other. Trudi's father left at the end of summer and Trudi's mother's only solace in Hell was alcohol and drugs. They'd never found the boy. Everyone urged Trudi to sell the house and put her mom in some kind of institution. She didn't. Instead of going to the Ivy League school she had been accepted into, she chose to stay in Miami living with her Mom in that same house on Old Cutler Road. She attended law school here in Miami. For many years she had no social life, at first she'd study then come back home and wait for Alex to return, and get the family all right again, and once she became an attorney she continued with the same pattern. Work as long as she had to then come home, take care of her mom, and wait for Alex to come back home. A few years ago she did have to institutionalize her mom. It was a tough decision but her mom just couldn't be left alone and she was so nasty that no nurse would last.

Rebecca! Are you falling asleep in your rocking chair?

The same goes for the Cinderella play, the Christmas play, the Easter story, always got to be the narrator.

"My little brother Alex isn't ever going to come back," she said. It took me all these years to realize it. "In truth he sent me Jim so I quit waiting for him. The house is already on the market, I'll have my mom transferred to a clinic in Atlanta, and I'm out of here . . ."

After a moment of silence Trudi added, "And I want you to be my bridesmaids, and I want this wedding to be as fun as Mafer's and Ernesto's, the wedding in the novel where everyone had so much fun . . . Maybe we'll do it around Thanksgiving, and we'll get dresses for you girls, and you'll fly to Atlanta, and . . ."

"I'm sorry, but I definitely don't feel up to being a bridesmaid!" said Rebecca.

Conchita added, "I know my girlfriend. And being a bridesmaid is not her idea of a happy ending."

"So when are you leaving?" Rebecca then asked.

"In a month. I'll be coming back here regularly as long as the house isn't sold, but I'm pretty much out of here."

"What about our reading club?"

"I think you're down to four women now."

"Doesn't everybody just love reading that novel?" Alma interrupted.

Conchita turned to Rebecca and whispered, "I thought she was in deep depression."

"She's self-medicating."

Alma rambled on. "I have to admit that I've read a little further ahead because I just can't put it down. Whenever I'm doing something like housework or driving the kids to school I just can't wait to get back to it. I just can't put it down! And at the same time I really dread finishing it. I'll probably finish it by Wednesday and I am absolutely dreading it. I feel it'll be the end of my life. I feel I'm in it! Does that happen to any of you?"

Daisy replied, "Not really. Don't get me wrong, I do like the novel. Actually I came up with some interesting numbers concerning the sugar production, the population, and the depression they had after the war with Spain. And that's what interests me most. I like to compare those times to these times and Cuba's relationship with the USA back then and its relationship now and then find incredible coincidences. I've drawn all these parallels between Castro and Generalísimo Menosmal and between Clinton and Grover Cleveland and Clinton and McKinley and Spain and the USSR, I've even put the similar events and incidents on a spreadsheet in my computer. It's as if history were repeating itself. But maybe I am forcing the graphs and the issues. Since I work in advertising I've always done that."

Rebecca then turned to Alma who said, "I like it for totally different reasons. We have such great money problems that when I read it I have the impression that I live in one of those beautiful colonial mansions with beautiful furniture and tile and paintings and gowns. Anyway I forget for a while that we can barely make ends meet."

"That's what you get when you marry *un muerto de hambre* with nothing but a job," said Daisy. "*M'ija*, it is really a mistake to marry poor. So I can't believe you made the same mistake three times."

"But anyway that's not the only reason I like the book . . ."

This time Rebecca interrupted, "Let me guess, the other reason probably has to do with the feelings and the atmosphere and how this book allows you to escape to another world and forget your *muerto de hambre* husband and your childish children who're not gifted the way you expected them to be and who don't appreciate Mozart in spite of the fact that you continually played Mozart while you were pregnant."

"I'd love to travel but I just couldn't leave my children," Alma replied. She had crossed her arms and seemed intimidated now.

"You can leave them with your mom, can't you?" said Rebecca.

"Even so, I'd still be too worried. I've never spent a night away from them. Although one of these days I plan to check into a hotel and spend the night with a bottle of wine and a pack of cigarettes."

"Doing what?"

"Thinking, and writing."

"I didn't know you wrote, but then again everyone writes these days," said Rebecca with a bit of sarcasm in her voice. "Pretty soon I'm going to be the only reader left."

"Ours is the Cuban flag, the one for which so many tears and blood have been shed . . . We must keep united in order to bring an end to this unjustified military ocupation."

Máximo Gómez

THE CURE FOR YELLOW FEVER was finally discovered by Dr. Carlos Finlay, a Cuban, and the United States flag flew over El Malecón, over El Castillo de la Punta, over El Castillo del Morro, over El Castillo de la Real Fuerza, over La Plaza de Armas, over the Tacón Theatre, everywhere you turned there was a United States flag undulating in the wind. What Generalísimo Anacleto Menosmal had tried to do for twenty years, that is, become an idol, or a God, and to be worshipped and feared and respected by all, or at least to be present everywhere one turned, the United States succeeded in doing in a few hours. Apparently the Yankees had merely replaced all the Spanish flags, but Tica swore that there had never been as many Spanish flags. Mafer and Ernesto tried to reassure themselves as well as the great aunts. The United States had no interest in taking over Cuba, this was just temporary, just to make sure that Spain wouldn't turn around and conquer Cuba, Puerto Rico, and the Philippines all over again.

For once Lolo agreed with Tica and insisted that this was no reason the decorate the whole city with Yankee flags. "Pretty soon all the awnings will be made out of Yankee flags!"

There was even a U.S. flag over the Café Louvre! That same Café Louvre where Lolo used to love to go eat finger sandwiches, smoke, and drink tea. Lolo said, A while ago our alphabet soups spelled nothing but Anacleto Menosmal and lately all they spell is YANKEE.

"At the Café Louvre they even took down the French flag!"

"They must've mistaken it for a Spanish flag."

Máximo Gómez had refused to go to Havana for the raising of the American flag over Morro Castle, and he represented what most of the Cubans felt, a feeling that the occupying army never thought they would feel, since they had judged the Cubans to be a motley group of lazy illiterates.

The invading army thought the Cubans would be glad to have their country taken away from them once again and just live on the island without having to worry about anything, not even having to bother about governing.

In a letter to President McKinley, Ernesto Tirry wrote that he was awaiting the execution of the Joint Resolution. Mafer took the letter down in dictation. And it probably reached McKinley, but who knows if he read it. In any case, Mafer's handwriting remained throughout her life quite neat and easy to read.

Poor Mafer. Nineteen hundred was her downfall. She never really got over giving birth to Maine. The hormones never went back to their place and nothing was ever the same again. Oh those hormones our best friends and worst enemies, this time they decided Mafer's time was up, they were going to tear her to pieces, and the minute she fell asleep she could see and feel those little beechnut-colored beings coming out of her body and invading her brain.

They had bristly hair and the brightest eyes you could imagine. They'd even try to tear her eyes open and shine the light of their own eyes in hers. It blinded her and she resisted. She had succeeded in keeping them at bay all these years thanks to Ernesto's lovemaking, but Ernesto was no longer the man he used to be, he was much older and his weak heart had also taken some of the stamina away from him. From making love twice a day, they went to making love every day, then every other day, then every three days, four, five, every week, every ten days, and there was no promise in the air.

By the time the United States had approved the Platt Amendment, giving them right to intervene in Cuban affairs, Mafer and Ernesto were only making love once every two weeks, and madness and depression were rapidly letting their poison seep into Mafer's brain. At first it was a trickle and it ended up a waterfall.

Máximo Gómez refused to run for the Cuban presidency, Anacleto Menosmal was dying to become king or emperor or czar of the island. For this reason he bought a soldier's uniform, grew a beard and went to the *sierra,* where he assembled a group of revolutionaries fighting for Cuban independence trying to oust the U.S. and once the U.S. was out Generalísimo Anacleto Menosmal wanted to be crowned king and called the most maximum of leaders. Luckily or unluckily it was Tomas Estrada Palma, who had U.S. backing as well as that of Gómez, who was elected on May 20, 1902. The whole family went to the inauguration where the Cuban flag finally replaced the American flag on Morro Castle. That very same day the U.S. troops began to evacuate.

Mafer had a panic attack that day on the Malecón, the coastal boulevard. Ernesto kept hugging her and begging her to be reasonable, but it was in vain, she had begun to be able to see the future again and she didn't like what she saw. She knew that one day they'd be separated forever and the thought was intolerable. She also knew this day was approaching, her hormones had told her. I never want to be separated from you, Ernesto, she screamed and sobbed right there on the Malecón, the waves were high and kept slamming against the sea wall and spraying her face with foam, I can't take this pain, Ernesto, I can't! I can't live with this grief! I can't live with these thoughts! The light shone on the water, glittering images appeared and disappeared, Ernesto held her tight. Tica begged Mafer to control herself. Mafer wouldn't listen. Lolo shrugged and uttered that Mafer was merely hysterical because of her woman's problems. Lolo even suggested that Mafer should take up smoking, you never know. One passion could replace another. How did everyone think Lolo had gotten over that lifelong sexual identity crisis? Of course Teo's existence had a lot to do with it, but so did tobacco. From now on Lolo swore that where Lolo was, tobacco was, and that as long as there was Lolo, there would be tobacco, no matter how stinky some people thought tobacco was. It was nothing compared to the smell of stress, of boredom, and of *bacalao*. Mafer continued screaming in spite of Lolo's ranting.

Finally after much begging and urging Tica and Lolo went back home with shy Teo and blonde Maine who thought she never got enough attention because of Teo. Indeed, at first Tica and Lolo thought they'd be crazy about the little girl but right away they realized that their love for Teo was something out of this world. It was as if it was with Teo Tirry that these two old ladies had finally discovered the endless charms of the male sex. Tica even admitted that she would have married a male if there had been more men like Teo Tirry around.

Ernesto stayed on the Malecón with Mafer. There were several beggars nearby who seemed very curious about her outburst. One of them even approached her and introduced himself. He said his name was Pulguita. Mafer stopped a minute to greet Pulguita and tell him she was pleased to meet him. Her face was wet, the sun was shining on her face. Then the light began to descend, the crisis was not over. It started to get darker and darker, and night fell, they sat by the ocean in total darkness, the lights from the houses, the street lights, images in the water, I can't stand this pain Ernesto, I can't live with this grief, she kept repeating, the moon's trying to scratch the water and it hurts.

He said, We'll just sit here until it goes away.

The next day they all agreed that the city life was too much for Mafer. There were too many sights and sounds to stimulate the senses in Havana *intramuros* and the last thing Mafer needed was stimulation. There were too many tourists too. And too much stimulation. Too many superficial temptations. They'd have Mafer moved to the house in El Cerro that Tica abandoned quite a few years ago, the house with the long driveway lined with cherubs.

The problem was, should they all move there, or just Mafer and Ernesto? Tica feared that Mafer may do something crazy one day and absolutely wanted to preserve the kids. She said she didn't want history to repeat itself. She assured Ernesto that she and Lolo were far more capable of raising the children. Didn't they disturb him in his reading anyway? Didn't he often wish that there'd be total silence in the house so he could just keep on reading and reading? Affirmative. They could both go live in El Cerro and take some servants. Ernesto said he'd have to discuss it with Mafer.

Mafer categorically refused to leave Havana *intramuros* without her children.

"I'd rather die than live without my children!" she said every weekend.

It so happened that the family took to spending every weekend in the house in El Cerro trying to convince Mafer to move there. The problem was that the house was in a total state of disrepair and the gardens were overgrown and neglected. The house was beautiful though, but it looked eerie in its abandonment. Lolo decided that if they were to convince that stubborn Mafer to move there the place would have to look a little more appealing, not like a desecrated cemetery.

Lolo went to work at remodeling the house. At first Lolo thought it would just be a matter of months and the place would look wonderful, but once the construction got started it was one problem after the other. There were plenty of workers though. Thousands of Spanish immigrants were pouring into Cuba every year. So they always had a crew of twenty to twenty-five Gallegos working there, the problem was that no one really took Lolo seriously, so the place was more like the Tower of Babel than a construction site.

Not only that, but Lolo didn't really have a talent for visualizing things. It was only once the idea was there in front of Lolo's eyes that Lolo realized what the idea was all about and then Lolo would decide it wasn't such a good idea after all and have the whole thing, whether it be a stucco wall or a window, torn down. Then it was back to the drawing board. And so on . . . The biggest problem was that once Lolo had an idea, no matter how crazy this idea was, there was no convincing Lolo that maybe this or this should be changed, or that it was something impossible. Lolo was, after all, the most stubborn person in the world, and one of those few people on earth who refused to admit that you can't always have it your way.

When Lolo wanted something Lolo had to have it and as long as Lolo didn't have it Lolo would have a tantrum. Once Lolo overheard Mafer telling Maine that one of the hardest lessons in life is realizing that it's not going to give you what you want when you want it and Lolo went into a frenzy screaming "How dare you?" at Mafer. Lolo thought Mafer was poisoning the children's minds by telling them lies of this nature. Of course they can get what they want. Each and every time!

In 1906 when Teo Tirry graduated from high school the construction was still going on in the El Cerro house and it was interrupted at that moment because of the insurrection.

After Umbertico Barrios' death Mafer took over and spent her days reading to the workers at the dress factory. She continued doing so even when full rebellion broke out in August. Estrada Palma resigned, so did his whole cabinet, and Cuba was left without government. Once again the United States had to take control of the island, but Mafer refused to read the newspaper to the workers at the dress factory, she continued reading them a novel that they all seemed to enjoy.

Who cared after all if the U.S. flag was once again flying over Morro Castle? Mafer said to Ernesto that this just went to prove that Cubans were incapable of governing themselves. For once Ernesto lost hope. Perhaps Mafer was right, perhaps this would never be a free and independent island, perhaps he should adopt the Plattist mentality. Why struggle so hard? Let the Magoon administration keep on stealing. Maybe their affairs were not in their own hands but they were simply a U.S. problem. José Miguel Gómez, also known as the shark, will make a great president, he promises to bring back cockfighting and the national lottery.

In November of the following year Mafer's half-sister and her second husband, Martin, moved to the house in El Cerro. Marisol confessed to Mafer that her husband was in the process of forming an extremist group that he called the Independent Party of Colour and that hopefully one day one of their members would become president and, who knows, maybe Cuba would at last become an independent nation. There would be no Generalísimos Anacleto Menosmal to threaten it from the *sierra*. After all, if the choice was between the United States and Menosmal it was because no one had bothered to make more choices possible. The Independent Party of Colour was this third choice.

Mafer protested. How could they hope to win in a country that was seventy percent white? Marisol agreed, that was indeed a problem.

Then the inevitable happened. Mafer knew that Ernesto would leave her one day. She knew it from the day she met him and that was why she tried to run him off for so many years, it was to avoid the pain of this separation, that would take place, sooner or later. But up until November 1907, she didn't know any of the details concerning this separation.

Then one rainy day in November while she was reading to the workers in the factory, she realized at that very moment that she would never see Ernesto again. She kept on reading. It was too late, for it was happening, as she read.

B ECKY? Your voice is hoarse, were you napping?

No, I was reading. Out loud. And I was crying.

Just to tell you that the package finally got to Cuba and now they're fighting over the coffee and the Goya seasoning. La Rubia says the little shoes were too big and that she would have preferred to receive some coffee and seasoning instead. Do you want us to go together and we'll send it?

Sure Mami, I'll pick Nell up at school then I'll swing by and fetch you.

Your father wants to come too. Tell Tommy to come by later and we'll have dinner here.

Okay, see you around four thirty. At what time does the packages to Cuba office close?

Late.

See you then.

O N THE NIGHT ERNESTO DIED, Mafer went to the Cathedral and threw her- self against the walls yelling, God! I want him back! The police were summoned. They had to take her out of there in a straitjacket. And she kept yelling, I want him back! I want him back now! God, damn you, God! I want him back now! Give him back, you can't take him!

She had to spend several days at the insane asylum. There was talk of making her have brain surgery. Tica was all for it, but Lolo said it was out of the question. They'd have to shave off her hair! She went to fetch Mafer at *la casa de locos*. She'd help her heal. Mafer had already shown signs of insanity anyway. "*Lo que necesita es un marido* (what she needs is a man)," Lolo whispered to the doctors. "*La última vez que estuvo loca así como la ven, se le curó cuando tuvo marido.* (The last time she was crazy like she is now, she was cured the minute she had a man.)"

They'd have one of the rooms in La Casa del Cerro padded if they had to. She'd heal. Lolo would help her. Lolo would go and find a new man for Mafer, if it came down to that.

On Ernesto's tombstone Mafer put, *Here lie the remains of Ernesto Tirry y Sotolongo, an avid reader who departed this life too soon, with a book in his hands, beloved father of Maine and Teo Tirry, beloved husband of Mafer de Tirry.*

Next to his tombstone she had another tombstone put. It read:

This warm Cuban earth awaits the remains of Señora de Tirry, but here lie her heart, her soul, and her sacred lust that died with her beloved and adored Ernesto Tirry. Her heart, her soul, and her lust hope to be joined back to her physical body soon, for her flesh can no longer hope for any pleasure up here and has lost all desire to walk the earth and to dwell among the living.

It took several months to have these two tombstones put up after the burial. It seemed to take forever. But late in the spring they were finally ready and Mafer organized a get-together at the cemetery with a priest there to bless the tombstones and several people singing or praying.

After this ritual she went all by herself to the Cathedral and prayed to God to take her. She told God she didn't want to be here any more. It just wasn't interesting enough. She knew that He would urge her to wait a few days for her mood to change but she had already waited several months, and her mood had not changed, on the contrary, she'd gotten even sadder. Please God! she said out loud. She tried to convince Him that life was wasted on her. Give it to some baby! Give it to someone else! By that time she was screaming and disturbing the wedding taking place in the Cathedral. She'd learned this yelling and screaming and stomping with Lolo who always got her way, and who had told her way back when she wanted to get pregnant that she had to put her foot down with God or He won't give you the right time of day.

Please God! Give me what I want right just this once! I beg you! God? Are you listening, God?

Of course He wasn't! It seemed as if the only person who could really intimidate God was Lolo.

What's more, Mafer was the one reading those novels about the future to the workers at the dress factory, and God was very resentful about that. As a matter of fact He was so resentful (which came as no surprise) that He had condemned Mafer to catch up to the characters she was reading about. The problem is that she had so much catching up to do that she couldn't possibly be allowed to die.

That evening, after Mafer had informed Lolo of the scene she'd made at the Cathedral once again, Lolo said, "You were wrong to beg, the more you beg, the prouder He gets, you forget that He's the role model of Anacleto Menosmal and company so you have to treat Him the ways He deserves to be treated and that means not giving Him an inch! He starts behaving like a male turkey the minute He thinks you're intimidated. But I wouldn't have allowed you to die anyway, Mafer. If you left me alone with Tica, she'd go crazy."

E VERYONE CANCELED. ALMA WAS THE LAST to call. First she thanked Rebec-ca for having asked her to be part of the reading club. "Is this some kind of good-bye speech?" Rebecca asked. It certainly sounded like that. "As a matter of fact . . ." said Alma. By the way, Rebecca couldn't have picked a better novel. It touched her heart, deeply. Yes, she had read the whole thing. A happy ending? Rebecca sat outside by herself and rocked and read out loud to the cassette player and the seven empty rocking chairs.

She knew what Alma was about to do, and her heart felt so tight that she had to hold back the tears. Oh she'd tried, even God had tried, but there was no way out of this. Rebecca had her back turned to the setting sun. What Alma wanted more than anything was to be a character in a novel. A great house with antiques and heavy expensive fabrics with a gold weave, with many servants, and many evenings spent either at the ball wearing a new gown or at the theatre.

And *las tertulias*, she really liked the idea of *tertulias,* a group of women meeting every day to drink tea, eat finger sandwiches and chat while rocking constantly on those rocking chairs. Cuba had always been very keen on rocking chairs. In this other life she wanted, she'd be very intelligent, a pioneer at something, perhaps she'd be the first woman poet, or writer, or scientist, and the most important thing is that she'd have made a great wedding and an even greater marriage.

Umberto Barrios Junior got up on the podium, cleared his throat, had a drink of water, and read.

Ever since Alma could remember she'd looked forward to her wedding day. Her parents separated when she was still an infant and on those days her dad said he'd come visit she'd get all dressed up and pretend she was a bride waiting at the altar. That was her recurrent daydream, her wedding. By the time her family left Cuba, when she was ten, she'd had at least ten thousand weddings, but the bridegrooms never had a face.

The seamstresses were asking, "Who's the main character?"

"Is that what she does all day? Sit in a rocking chair?"

Once they got to Miami, the weddings got put aside for a while, she gave them much less thought with all that was happening. Her aunt, Rebecca's mother, put her right away in The Academy of the Assumption and she had to learn English, and she had to adapt and, most of all, she was in the middle of quite a quarrel between grownups. Not your ordinary quarrel, not a quarrel between a husband and a wife fighting for their child. The two people who quarreled over Alma were her mother and her aunt. All of a sudden Alma was the center of attention, two women were vying insanely for her ownership and meanwhile her cousin Becky was beginning to hate her for her presence.

"Oh to be rich like that! Not have to go to work every morning! Just rock to your heart's content!"

Becky's mom suddenly began to brag about how she loved both girls the same and how Alma was like her own child. Whatever Becky got, Alma got. Becky's mom kept repeating that she loved them exactly the same, and perhaps she even loved Alma a little more in the sense that she'd saved Alma from dire poverty in Calle Ocho and Alma needed her a little more. Moreover, Alma knew how to flatter her aunt, whereas Becky was the quiet resentful sort, who'd just shut herself up within herself.

"She's a murderess!"

"You can't just kill people!"

It's incredible how many years this unhealthy situation lasted. Everyone in that family was perpetually quarreling. Becky's mom and dad had earth shaking fights every night after cocktail hour. Becky and her mom weren't getting along. Her mom kept saying, This is my house, my decision, you have to accept her, and Alma always overheard. Alma and Becky weren't getting along for the obvious reasons. But even Alma and her aunt didn't get along, and this time for not so obvious reasons. It goes without saying that by considering herself Alma's saviour, Alma's aunt, Becky's mom, expected total loyalty from Alma, which she never ever got. In the end, Alma always loved her own mom much more. But this was just another facet of these long prisms of darkness.

"Give me those scissors, I'm going to stab her in the heart!"

"Give me the gun!"

"Doesn't Umberto Barrios Junior sound like his father at times?"

The most immediate and the most visible was that Becky was always furious. Morning noon and night her mom bragged about how much she loved Alma and what a great aunt she was. As to Alma, she didn't dislike her cousin's hatred, on the contrary. She had always envied her cousin and her cousin's hatred meant that she, Alma, she was important, different, destined for a great future, like Cinderella or Snow White or the Ugly Duckling.

"Look! It's Umbertico Barrios getting up from the grave!"

"He's buried in Camposanto Menosmal, under the ceiba."

Yes indeed, it started innocently. When they first arrived in Miami in 1965, Becky's mom thought that it'd be a good idea to have Alma stay over at their house since they were better established, had more financial stability, and were better able to give Almita everything she needed, dresses, accessories, school, a room of her own in the big house on Brickell Avenue, summer camp in Switzerland, frequent trips to New York, Caracas, and Puerto Rico.

"The rich suffer too!" Umbertico Barrios yelled (it was in the text).

This was paradise compared to what Alma's own mother could give her. A cot in a corner of a sweltering one bedroom apartment near Calle Ocho, public school, a stepfather she didn't like, no dresses, no trips during the Easter holidays, no pretty shoes, no princess life, and by the time she'd lived with her aunt for two months she could no longer live a life other than the princess life.

"The mistake was made quickly and it was irreparable," Rebecca read.

Both women thought they had a right to Alma, both sisters began to hate each other. Alma's mom began to hate her sister with heart and soul, Who was she to take her daughter away from her? As to Alma, the subject of contention, see the Bible, she had the best of both worlds, When her aunt displeased her she'd run to her mom and when her mom displeased her she'd run back to auntie's.

"They cut her in half!" Umbertico read with soul and heart. That's the way she lived until she turned sixteen and met Frank and decided she wanted to marry him as soon as they both graduated from high school. They were both sixteen and Alma fed Frank all her dreams.

"I love love stories."

By that time her own mom had more freedom and more material things to offer. Her stepdad was doing much better, they'd just bought a new house where she could have a room of her own while she planned her wedding. What's more, she could do whatever she wanted with her mom, who was ready to bend over backwards to be a step ahead of the competititon, it was a question of getting her daughter back and winning one over her despiteful control-freak of a sister.

"Give me my scissors. With a sad ending."

All the elements of tragedy were there, even a cast of characters full of good innocent blind selfish stupid women.

"Do cats really listen?"

"Where's Rebecca?"

"How come she doesn't come and see her father any more?"

"Planning a wedding with a sad ending!" Umbertico yelled.

So Alma moved back with her mom and began to plan her wedding to Frank, it was a wedding that took two whole years to plan, all the elements of the fairy tale were there. Frank's wicked mother who was against it (once again the hatred made Alma feel special), Alma's remorseful father who'd just arrived from Cuba and wanted to get to know the daughter he'd abandoned, Alma's kind and generous mom ready to help the young lovers financially as best she could and to encourage them the many times they needed encouragement. This is how it was supposed to happen.

"But she married poor!" he shouted.

Alma and Frank had a big fairy tale wedding at Vizcaya with at least threee hundred guests. Rebecca didn't attend. "This is what really happened," Rebecca read.

They couldn't afford the Vizcaya or a Christian Dior gown or a wedding for three hundred guests, they didn't even have three hundred people to invite in the first place. Disappointed, Alma tried to commit suicide and had to have her stomach pumped. Finally, they had to settle for a Catholic church in beautiful Coral Gables. They invited eighty people, sixty of whom showed up. The reception took place in the bingo hall adjacent to the church. The cake wasn't as delicious as Alma hoped it would be, but the *croquetas* were great. Her dress was not perfect. She had designed it herself, and had wanted the sleeves to fall beneath her shoulders, the problem was that the whole thing kept slipping down and she spent the whole ceremony and reception having to pull it back up. There's nothing worse than clothes that you have to fix all the time, especially when you're the center of attention.

"Four months later they filed for a divorce."

Alma still dreamed of a wedding though, and of another white dress, and so what if she'd made a mistake once? She begged God to give her one more chance, she even changed religion. She became a Methodist because being a Methodist she could marry in a church again.

"Alma loved going to Europe every summer."

It wasn't that she had a particularly good time there, it was more the thought of going there and of being there that she enjoyed. The minute she landed her thoughts were of the return. She'd try on shoes and finally buy them because there was a whole scenario going on in her mind of how she'd show them off in Miami. She'd buy this or that with the same daydream in her mind. She'd go to the museum and could almost feel the culture on her skin.

"On her skin?"

"Give me those scissors. What's the matter with the reader?"

"Then she married again, with a white dress, in the Methodist church."

Then with Rod Target, God gave her a third chance for a big wedding and she promised that she'd give up if this time if didn't work.

"What's so bad about making three mistakes? Give me those scissors so I can cut my heart out."

When she fell in love with Rod, Alma gave up her dreams of becoming a great psychologist and decided to get a master's degree in Teaching English as a Second Language instead.

"Fire Junior! Now the seamstresses want to learn English."

"And they don't wish to marry for love any more!"

Everyone said that Rod didn't really have much of a future. He wasn't really ambitious. He was never going to make much money. How did Alma feel about it? It was okay to marry humble but should Alma do it with her regal tastes? Didn't she love to travel and to buy expensive clothes? Didn't she tell everyone that she was always one shoe ahead of Imelda Marcos? Didn't Alma want to live the rich life? Shouldn't she think twice before marrying Rod Target?

"Now they want the best things in life."

She did have to have her stomach pumped once, but no one gave it much thought. The rumor was that Alma was an eccentric. Everyone agreed that she should have been an actress. She always wanted to be the center of attention, that was the reason she tried to commit suicide. Alma knew what they were thinking about.

Alma's so secretive.

Alma's pregnant. Can they afford to have a child?

"The baby's welcome," Alma told everyone.

"Now they want to commit suicide because they're unhappy."

"They can't have bikes."

"Does Rebecca still want her man?"

"Did she cool off?"

"She used to be so crazy about him."

When Jessica was born Alma sent out cards that read:

"Our family is growing, and so is our love . . ."

But the marriage did not survive. Alma made a mistake, for the third time.

"I can't believe I've made a mistake again," she told her mom. Alma was proud.

"What's so bad about making mistakes?"

"Cut! You're supposed to learn from them."

Lately she'd taken to going to her cousin Rebecca's reading club. She wasn't part of it, she knew, she didn't feel like part of them. All those women had such bright lives, they were not dirty girls of darkness. Tonight she would not be there with them. Would they wonder what happened? Where's Alma? Did she have her stomach and breasts done? She had indeed, last week, and still felt some discomfort.

She called Becky to tell her she wouldn't be there that evening.

Becky said: "You sure sound upbeat! Are you looking forward to being real skinny?"

"I sure am! There's still some minor discomfort, but soon! Soon!"

"Well, have a nice evening. I'm all by myself with my seven empty rocking chairs."

Alma has finished reading the book anyway, there is no reason for her to return.

She took her heavy handbag and left the house.

At five PM, after she bought a bottle of wine and two packs of cigarettes, Alma checked into a Holiday Inn near the airport.

From the grave Umbertico read.

Alma drank and smoked and wrote letters and wept. What was Rebecca reading now? About Mafer's desire to die, no doubt. About how God didn't let her die. She has to catch up to the characters she's reading about. Stupid woman of the past, when people still asked God for permission to die!

At eight AM the next morning she stopped to remind herself that it was a Saturday morning, she even said it out loud, just to hear what it felt like. Then Alma took out the .22 caliber pistol she had brought in her handbag, she lay down on the Holiday Inn bed, put the gun to her temple, and shot herself. She didn't die right away.

WHY? WHY? WHY? No reply would be satisfactory anyway. And it wasn't really the question Rebecca felt like asking. Rather, could it happen to her? Did she contribute in any way? For example, should she blame herself for having hated Alma when they were both young girls? Should she feel guilty about being alive? Too many thoughts were going through her head, and lately Rebecca would shake her head in exasperation, as if to be rid of them.

For the past two weeks she'd seen her mom every day, and her mom kept repeating, I can't believe this. They talked and talked and kept retelling Alma's life up until the last day that they tried to reconstitute over and over again. Rebecca even compared that last Friday of Alma's with their own Friday.

So when she was checking into the Holiday Inn, I was pushing a cart around the Publix Market, I thought she was coming to the reading group that night, she had said that she'd come, and show off her new flat stomach and smaller breasts. Why do you get plastic surgery one week and kill yourself the following week? Isn't that a waste? Did she think about her children when she spent the night at the Hoiday Inn? She seemed so upbeat! So that's what she had been hiding all her life! We made so much fun of her for having such a church wedding fetish! We shouldn't have, we were insensitive. So that Friday morning when Rebecca was driving Nell to school and Rebecca's mom was arguing with the man who was about to mow her lawn, and Rebecca's dad was reading to the cat, Alma had already decided to brutally leave this world, to walk the earth no more, she had realized that she wasn't interested, not at all!

Then she checked into the Holiday Inn while Rebecca was shopping at the Publix Market. After the Publix Market she went to Epicure to get smoked salmon, and to the fish market to get a big fish, and to El Palacio de las Frutas to get *cherimoyas* for Tommy's breakfast the following morning. And Rebecca remembered that she was really depressed that day because she'd just gotten her period and was hoping to be pregnant. She called her mom right before the reading group started and felt sorry for herself. Rebecca remembered that she'd said, I'm getting gray hair, I'm starting to need glasses to read, and now I'm sterile! What else is life going to take away from me? I've been trying for three or four months, I'm not telling! I must be sterile now! I want a baby! Like Mafer, I want to be pregnant more than anything! So she was ranting and raving while Alma was writing her suicide notes and drinking wine, and apparently she'd smoked a whole pack of cigarettes. Did she sleep? The doctor said that if it had been a higher caliber the bullet would have gone right through her head and she could have been saved. The problem is that a .22 caliber wasn't strong enough, so the bullet had been slowed down considerably when it penetrated the skull and it had advanced quite slowly and flipped over itself when it was transpercing the brain and it had finally lodged itself in the middle of Alma's brain and kept turning and destroying everything.

By the time she got to the hospital she was brain dead. They put her on a respirator in the hopes of getting the organs but the minute they saw Alma's mom they rushed toward her and said sign here for the heart, sign here for the lungs, and this really shocked her mom.

On Saturday morning when Alma was blowing her brains out Rebecca was taping the end of the book for Silka, Trudi, and Conchita.

At one, when Tommy and Nell went out on the boat and Rebecca stayed home because she was so upset about her period, she sat down on that couch by the window over there, the window whose light puts stripes of sun and shade on the page she's reading, and she went back to her reading. The phone rang several times, she didn't get up to answer it, and the answering machine was off. Little did she imagine that it was her mother calling to tell her about Alma, whom they'd found in the Holiday Inn at 10:23 AM with a pool of blood next to the white pillow, Alma who was already brain dead. And while Alma was in the hospital dying, Rebecca kept reading. But that's the way it goes, one of these days, when Rebecca's dying, someone will be comfortably seated in this corner overlooking Biscayne Bay and the downtown Miami skyline, maybe at that very same place, with a book. This house will have other occupants. Other readers, just like when Ernesto is dying, Mafer is reading. And when Alma died Rebecca was still reading Chapter Ten. Out loud.

She counted with her fingers, she asked herself the question out loud, "How many of us are left now?"

"But that one difference makes all the difference—between an uncomfortable, unsettling experience in which the gradual dimming of a fact is attended by a failure in perception, and a wholly self-satisfying one in which an uncertainty is comfortably certain, and the reader's confidence in his own powers remains unshaken, because he is always in control."

Stanley Fish, *Is There a Text in This Class?*

WHENEVER SOMEONE ASKED Teo Tirry a simple question such as, "Hello, how are you doing?" before replying "fine" or "not so fine" Teo Tirry would look both ways, as if he were about to cross the street. His great aunts' hysterical concern for him had made him extremely shy. What's more, if he had a headache or was feeling a bit under the weather, before he admitted it he'd first look both ways just to make sure that his aunts weren't within hearing distance.

Teo Tirry was gentle. He was a boy who later became a man of few words. A modest man who always preferred to remain quiet. Perhaps he was born this way and it wasn't some sort of reaction to his circumstances. Or maybe he couldn't deal with all the extremes. Even his lullabies were too loud, too exaggerated, his family was more than he could handle, and, if you take all the meanings of irresistible, his city, Havana, was irresistible. The greens were too green, the flowers were too bright, and what is that noise? Is someone being murdered? No, just someone trying to sell eggs, or pastries, or *malangas*. The smells and the life were just as irresistible as everything else, as strong and as unbearable as the beauty of the late afternoon sunlight on the lawns, on the plants, or flowing in through the iron bars, into your house, as sweet as sugar cane juice, as strong as coffee, as salty and as pungent as *bacalao*, as present as the people around him. He could barely stand it.

His eyes were always watery, he coughed, he stuttered and, when asked what he wanted to be, he replied that he'd go to the university and study to be an accountant. Tica said, Isn't that wonderful? Lolo said, Our Teo! An accountant! Come here and give me a kiss, *¡Teo lindo chi chi lindo chino lindo* *chicho chicho Teopu!* Is it true that Maine hit you? Maine ugly Maine bad Maine! *Fea mala* go away! *¿Teolindo de Lolo?*

By the time he turned eighteen Teo would whisper, Please, Aunt Lolo!

All he wanted to do in his spare time was ride over to the Malecón and look at the sea splashing against the sea wall. The waves would hit so hard! It seemed harder and harder each time, and the ocean spray would splash his face then evaporate into a thousand rainbows.

This is what Teo loved the most, and the sound of the waves was the only sound he loved. Both he and his sister Maine were bored by the hilarious intrigues of their family.

By 1910 Havana *intramuros* was no place to live. It was dirty, loud, dangerous and definitely not a place to raise a twelve-year-old like Maine. For a while it seemed as if immorality were the only thing Havana was about. Everyone seemed out to lie, cheat, and steal at all costs. The city got so dishonest that even the government officials who were dishonest themselves had no choice but to paint the *intramuros* lampposts red, the intermediate ones blue, and the ones in the outskirts green so that the victoria drivers would stop charging the tousists for enormous distances. Everyone was out to get the tourists' money and there was no reason whatsoever for the drivers to get it all, right at the beginning. Some tourists didn't even have any money left by the time they got to their hotel, so it was thought that painting the lamp posts different colors was the best way to prevent this.

In a city that had degenerated so much tourists weren't the only people at risk. Maine couldn't be allowed out of anyone's sight for fear that she might be kidnapped for a ransom. The Havana *intramuros* streets were so dirty anyway that it was dangerous to step outside the house on Calle Aguacate. There were times when the garbage wasn't picked up for weeks so the place was proliferating with rats and disease. At last everyone in the family agreed, they'd move to El Cerro where the lampposts were green.

The city had grown to such an extent that El Cerro could barely be considered a suburb. It was an hour drive by victoria, but then again it took at least forty-five minutes to get out of Havana *intramuros* because of the traffic. This traffic problem had even affected the work at the factory. Sometimes it would take them hours to receive some supplies because of the traffic jams. Tica really gave it much thought and finally decided that it was time to move the dress factory out of what she called that cloaque of a city.

Each member of the family had their own personal quarrel with what was soon to become old Havana. Lolo couldn't stand the thought of the children being in danger. Tica wanted to have her supplies on time. Mafer had quarreled with God in every single church or cathedral in the area. Teo had started working in a cigar factory in the newer part of town. He disliked the city anyway. He wasn't interested in bars, in gambling, or in nightclubs or in brothels, he simply enjoyed getting his work done every day, going to the ice cream parlor, and then looking at the sunset while sitting on a park bench. He had inherited his father's love of reading and could often be found in Pedrito Barrios' bookstore in El Vedado.

Pedrito Barrios, who had been Teo's best friend ever since grade school, was the grandson of Umbertico Barrios, a faithful employee of Titania fashions who had dedicated his life to reading to the workers at the factory.

Those times were gone now. No one would even conceive of paying someone to get up on a podium and to read to the workers all day. After Umbertico Barrios died, Mafer was the one who had done this, but lately she'd taken to dressing in black and walking from church to church, rosary in hand, to pick a fight with God in every church He had.

Sometimes she'd scream so much that she had to be dragged out of the place of worship. To spite God, Mafer had also decided to stop washing and to wear the same black widow's dress until it rotted. She liked to walk along the Malecón, where she was convinced she'd encounter Ernesto's ghost. Many tourists mistook her for a beggar and offered her dollars. One day she returned home with so much money that Tica was surprised. That evening over dinner Tica said to Lolo, "This is the first time in her life that our poor *loca* Mafer has made any money!"

As to Maine, she was the most conventional little girl in the world. At first all she wanted was to be a little girl and to wear pretty dresses and pretty shoes, play with pretty dolls, say cute things, collect tea sets, collect girlfriends, touch soft things. When she turned thirteen in 1911 she started planning her *quinceañera* party, her sweet fifteen. She'd wear a pink dress and pink satin shoes, and they'd have finger sandwiches, meringues, all the varieties of *turrones* in the world, *croqueticas*, coconut macaroons, candied fruit, waltzing. She spent the next two years planning.

By 1913, when she finally turned fifteen and they had the party, they had moved to El Cerro.

When Maine discovered that Marisol, who had been living in the El Cerro house for the past few years, was not a servant but in fact her mother's half-sister, she just couldn't take it. This is one time she got quite hysterical and wept in front of her two great aunts until the skin around her eyes cracked and she actually looked ugly. What was going to happen when she finally found a *novio*, a boyfriend, and this *novio* realized that this Marisol with the *café con leche* colored skin was her aunt and that Marisol's husband who was as black as night was therefore her uncle. Would any *novio* bother to marry her then? How would she explain and finally convince the future *novio* that their children wouldn't come out as black as jet?

"Is that my daughter talking?" Mafer asked.

By 1914 all of Mafer's hair had fallen out. Not only the hair on her head, but also her eyelashes, eyebrows, and even pubic hair.

Maine was so upset that Tica had no choice but to tell Marisol and her family to move out. She gave them some money but Marisol and her husband were so used to giving it away to the rebel groups that they ended up out in the streets. Soon after that Marisol's husband and her two oldest sons fled to Mexico after having organized a labor strike in Havana. They were soon found murdered in Mexico along with one of the founders of the Communist party.

With Marisol's husband's death also died all hope of an Independent Party of Colour. Marisol soon went to beg on the Malecón. Marina, her youngest daughter, opened La Casa Marina on the ouskirts of the city, a house that catered to even the most outlandish sexual fetishes, and Gloria, the firstborn, went to work as a chambermaid in the Hotel Inglaterra.

With this dark part of the family out of the picture, there was no longer anything standing between Maine and her future *novio*, all she had to do was to meet him.

In 1915 when Mafer's breasts shriveled up and turned to dust, pretty Maine still had no *novio*. Little did it matter if she went to balls almost every evening and wore the nicest gowns and looked absolutely fabulous, nobody even asked her for a dance.

In 1916 Mafer woke up one morning to find herself covered with warts and Maine wondered how in the world she'd introduce her mom to her future elusive *novio*, who still wasn't in the picture. And how could poor Teo stand to have her present at his wedding to Lucy, one of the Barrios grandaughters? Maine was miserable at her brother's wedding. Not only had her brother married beneath himself, but he'd invited the cream of Havana, just where Maine expected to find her *novio*, but how could she possibly meet her *novio* when her mom was covered with warts, her brother was marrying a plebeian, and the mulatto cousins were out there dancing the waltz as if they were as white as everyone?

In the next few years all the normal things happened. Teo and Lucy had four kids, Lolo had a stroke and was confined to a wheelchair. One side of her was paralyzed, but she could still smoke, and eat and scream that Cuba was never going to have a just government, that it had never happened, that it never would!

In 1925, when Gerardo Machado was elected president and seventy-six-year-old Lolo was still confined to the wheelchair and spent all her days out in the porch smoking and complaining about corruption, Mafer stepped outside, tripped on the wheelchair, and hurt her foot. She still had scars all over her body from all the warts she'd had. Her foot hurt. She was on the floor and looked at it. There was a small open wound where she'd hurt herself on the wheelchair. "This is never going to heal," she said to Lolo.

"Where's my baby Teo?" Lolo asked. Teo was thirty-seven years old by then, but he remained her baby Teo.

"Did you hear me?" Mafer asked. "It's never going to heal. And I've still got years to go before I die." There was a warm ray of sunlight right where her leg would be cut off.

"Give me a needle and thread," Lolo said. "I'm going to make a party dress for Helen."

Helen was one of Teo's and Lucy's three girls.

"You don't know how to sew, Lolo!"

"Get me a needle and thread! And sugar. I want a spoonful of sugar. And a cigar. *Y un cafecito.*"

"*Ay,* Lolo!" Mafer yelled. "I can see the future."

She saw what was going to happen. This little wound here would fester and she would have to have her leg cut off. Sloppy Joe's Bar for tourists. Woolworth's five-and-dimes that would be called *el ten cen* (ten cents), Casa Marina, an institution, anything you want, just name your fetish, Batista's coup, here comes another Anacleto Menosmal, oh those Americans are supposed to be so sweet, Teddy Roosevelt they call him, Teddy, like a Teddy bear. Teddy! This Teddy didn't approve of Ramón Grau San Martín because Ramón Grau San Martín wanted workmen's compensation and partial control over electric rates charged by U.S.-owned companies, imagine a Teddy who's against workmen's compensation, didn't he act like a daddy to America? *Norte América, Estados Unidos de América,* this here place, this one night stand of a place, this whore of a place is just what it is, a place to shop, to gamble, to eat, to have sex with children and with animals and with either pretty or ugly girls or with men, you pick, it's your fetish, in 1940, when

Batista will run for the presidency and will win, Tica dies, one hundred and one years old. You know when they will bring back Grau? When he will be the end of hope for Democracy. Sloppy Joe's, Woolworths, all in the name of love, all you need is love, in Norte América don't they always use the word love? Does Teddy love? Oh! Meyer Lansky loves to cook! Learned everything from Wolfie Cohen! Cheese danish! *¡Azúcar!* Coconut macaroon a/k/a *coquito con chocolate ¡Azúcar!* Wolfie's on the beach. On Collins Avenue. Her greatgrandaughters will eat a cheese danish and brownies at Wolfie's on Collins Avenue, sugar! and he will teach Meyer Lansky everything there is to know about cooking. Sugar! Lolo's going to die any minute now! Lolo's going to die! Who taught you how to smoke? How to love it? How you dislike it now! You changed, *m'ija.* Now it's for the lower classes, the smoking. Sugar. And Maine's going to walk in right now and say, Mom, if you can see into the future, tell me, am I ever going to have a man? Or is my vagina just going to shrivel up and fall off one day when I'm walking to the park eating vanilla ice cream? *¡Mantecado!* It's going to fall on the sidewalk and break like glass. Crystal. I'm in love with Tommy. I want to go to Miami to see Tommy. Will I take my grandaughters to Wolfie's on Collins Avenue? Will we make it to Miami? Oh my God, time flies! Carlos Prio, another Batista coup, it's 1952, Mafer is running and she's already had a leg cut off, look at what's left of her after all the great things that happen in life, look at what's left! Go ahead, take a little look! Little bones, *huesitos,* remember when you reached your peak in life? She's going to catch up to her characters. They're going to be born any minute now. Will Rebecca ever make it back to Cuba? Will Maine ever have a *novio*? Will Rebecca get pregnant? Or is it too late now that she realizes what it's all about? Why learn so late? Hurry up and be born, girls. Meyer Lansky's having a New Year's Eve party at the Riviera Hotel and you're too young to attend. We're going from fifty-eight to fifty-nine, M-26, he's coming he's coming, he'll be coming round the mountain when he comes, he'll be coming round the mountain, they're *all* Anacletos Menosmales. Who ages well? God, keep my role models at a distance. If not I'll really lose all hope. Marisol's grandaughter works as a waitress at the Riviera. They started whitening that family way back when, but then you get someone like Helen. That's what it's all about, you gotta lose things, each generation has to recover something lost. Imagine all the *basura* we'd have if we'd kept everything we ever inherited. Tons of garbage. Each generation has to start all over. They all canceled at the Riviera and the next morning the workers walked off their jobs and Meyer Lansky made breakfast for all the guests, this is a true story, while Teddy, Meyer's wife, did the dishes, another Teddy! We're going, we're going, take whatever you have, we're going, we're rushing to Jose Martí Airport, we're going to Miami, now? Now! My diamond ring! Tommy's already been born in Miami, he's not only in your hand, in your empty hand. But I'm an old woman, he'll never want me, it doesn't matter, you have to catch up to your characters, you have to catch up to my characters, there are already several little girls at the airport, the little girls who will go to The Academy of the Assumption, leave the sugar, the tobacco, sugar of my heart and soul, ¡azúcar! ¡sabor! scream as loud as you can, ¡azúcar! We're going to Miami. We'll meet at the airport. We're going to catch up. Catch up. Ketchup. We're going to Wolfie's on Collins Avenue. And Tommy's waiting in Miami, for us, for all of us, we just have to catch up. Sixty-two-year-old Maine was pushing her hundred-year-old mother's wheelchair in Jose Martí Airport. That Mafer is the one doing the reading, there is no certainty. There is no certainty that Mafer is the one doing the reading. That Rebecca is the one doing the reading, there is no certainty. There is no certainty that Rebecca is the one . . . That Maine Tirry is the one doing the reading, there is no certainty. There is no certainty that . . . That Teo Tirry, named after God, Teo Tirry who looks both ways before answering a question, is the one doing all the reading, there is no certainty . . . That all the reading was meant to be out loud, there is no . . . That I am, you are, he is, she is the person reading . . . Or being read to . . . There is no certainty. That we'll meet in Miami,

139324137